THE

CONTINGENCY
Plan

KELLY LORD

I'm dedicating this book to my amazing beta readers.
Ashlie, Rachel, Henri, Jael, and Riki.
Thank you for all your help and support. I appreciate you
sticking by me, listening to my ramblings, throwing ideas my
way, and helping me to bring my stories to life.

CHAPTER *One*

Bexley

"**B**ex? If you had to choose between giving up alcohol for a year, or sex for a month, what would you pick?" my childhood bestie, Caroline (Caz for short), slurred her words.

All I could smell was alcohol and stale perfume. My bra was saturated with wine because I missed my mouth twice; now it felt sticky and gross. The best thing about wearing a dress made from sequins was it could hide all the drink spillages. It was a glitzy practicality I learned through trial and error.

Caz's dark-brown fringe had stuck to her clammy forehead. Beads of moisture dotted across her upper lip like a sweaty moustache. It was three o'clock on a Sunday morning, and people were staggering out of all the bars like extras from a zombie film. Caz and I were exhausted from dancing for two hours straight, drunk on shots and vodka cokes. So drunk, we collapsed into the back of a taxi in a tangle of limbs.

Ugh! It was Sunday already!

I would have to sleep off my hangover before meeting my dad. We had a dinner reservation tonight. He had an important announcement to make, and the fact that he had chosen somewhere public to deliver the news meant I was nervous about what he was likely to say. I couldn't make a scene in a crowded restaurant. As straight-talking as I was, I could never show myself up, and Dad knew that. I was head-strong, just like he was. We either got along fine, or we clashed like a thunderstorm. It had always been the same since I was a little girl. I trusted my father, I really did. But Dad had been secretive about whom he had been sneaking off to meet with, and that bothered me. All he kept telling me was that this person was an old friend and I shouldn't worry because I had met him lots of times. So basically, he could be anybody. I had met all of Dad's friends. He always liked to show me off as his proudest achievement, which was cute . . . I suppose. But there was only so much hair-ruffling and cheek pinching that a grown woman can take.

Dad's friends were all cut from the same cloth as him. My father was an ex-serviceman, built like The Rock, and inked from the neck down. People at school used to joke that he left the Navy to become a professional hitman. As far as I know, that wasn't true. He set up a home security company that specialized in burglar alarms, window sensors, and multi-point locking systems. He made his money, and that's how we could progress to more advanced technology, such as surveillance systems. There wasn't a household to date that didn't use at least one of our products, but in the dog-eat-dog world of business, we were battling to maintain the spotlight. Our competitors had been biting at our heels every step of the way, and the competition was getting tougher each year. We needed to think of an idea to expand in a style that our rivals couldn't. I had a few ideas in the pipeline, but I had yet to pitch them to Dad.

I wondered who this old friend was, and why his idea had Dad so excited. Last night, when I asked about it, he replied, "it was about time that he and his friend discussed their plans for a merger". Nothing had been decided yet, but it would combine his friend's personal security company with our surveillance software. Dad was so vague with the details that my mind was whirling with a plethora of possibilities. Did this guy hire professional bodyguards to protect the rich and famous, or was he part of MI6 or something? The suspense was killing me. Dad arranged for us to meet at the Grosvenor at five o'clock in the afternoon because he would never dine past seven. He claimed that eating late gave him indigestion. The Grosvenor was one of the city's finest places to dine, so at least I knew that the food would be good. That was always a bonus. I tended to binge eat after a night out. Especially after an uneventful one. Most of my friends pulled a no-show and put it down to having childcare issues.

My friends had all settled down and had spawned young, leaving me way behind on the starting line. Now our group had whittled down to just Caz and me; the two of us slapping on the war paint, glamming it up on a Saturday night like a pair of sad spinsters. The truth was, I wanted what my friends had, despite telling everyone that I was happy, and that I didn't need a man to complete me.

Lies!

It was the lies I told myself to conceal the loneliness of a cold bed and a microwave meal for one. Maintaining relationships had always been difficult for me because I grew bored with them. I was the walking cliché of "It's not you, it's me" because it really was me. They did nothing wrong. It's just that I'm constantly looking for the next best thing and cannot appreciate what I already have. Maybe it was a sign I hadn't met the right man yet, who knows? All that I know is, I am married to my job. The company comes first above all else. That was my father's other baby, the older brother that had given us the life that we'd grown accustomed to. I had it good . . . I honestly did. But sometimes, it would be nice to share it with someone interesting enough to maintain my interest, if you know what I mean.

I rolled my head to the side so I could answer Caroline's question. Not that I had to think about it, because I knew the answer straight off.

"I'd rather give up sex," I replied, earning a shocked splutter from the cab driver, who was eavesdropping.

Caroline looked at me like I had grown a second head. Even the cab driver expected me to say I would renounce alcohol. It just went to show that his job wasn't as stressful as mine was. As the future CEO of Barker Security, I had to meet certain criteria before my father would hand over the reins to me. I had been shaped and moulded for this since the day I was born

No pressure or anything.

A glass of wine now and then always helped me to relax a little. A full-bodied Malbec was always there for me when no one else was. Caz scrunched her face with an incredulous grimace.

"Seriously? No sex for a month?" she returned, sounding gobsmacked

I don't know why, because she knew damn well that I hadn't got any "D" for a long while.

"It's not like I'm tripping over sexy guys everywhere I go," I retorted, side-eyeing the snickering driver through venomous slits.

As a natural redhead, I was known for my fiery temper. The cabbie couldn't have known that I dyed my hair brown. "Hey," I berated him. "If I were you, I would concentrate on the road or you'll miss our turning"

The back roads from Chester were scarcely lit. You had to slow right down to a crawl or else you would cruise straight past my driveway. The houses along this road were all detached six-bedroomed dwellings with swimming pools and huge landscaped gardens. Which was funny because in all the years I had lived here, I had never once taken a swim. My favourite haunt was the hot tub beneath the veranda on the patio.

"You ought to employ someone to hack away that bush," Caz commented as we approached the entrance to the property.

Sarcasm was the lowest form of wit, but not in this instance. The trees that loomed across my half-mile drive had practically merged, forming a gloomy tunnel all the way to the house. The bushes covered the intercom, so even the postman had trouble locating my whereabouts. It was just how I preferred it, hidden from view and secluded in my own little bubble. I had been this way ever since my mother's passing. It still hurts to think about her; especially on the anniversary of her death. Which was today — I meant yesterday. It was the reason for my current drunken state

The taxi came to a halt, and I shoved a tenner through the gap in the divider.

"You take care now," the cheeky cabbie muttered. "And make sure you trim that bush."

Caz spluttered with laughter as she scrambled out of the taxi. I sifted through the leaves as if I was on a jungle expedition, found the keypad, then punched in the four-digit code.

The metal gates rolled to the side, but we didn't wait for them to open all the way before we began staggering across the gravel like sailors on a swaying vessel.

After we clambered through the front door, kicking off our heels, we tossed our clutch bags on the side table then crawled upstairs to bed. Caz was living here since her ex-boyfriend had cheated on her and threw her out of their house. Her parents lived abroad, so she had nowhere else to go.

The sound of my phone vibrating beneath my pillow woke me up with a jolt. My mascara had left a lasting impression across my white pillowcase, reminding me I had fallen asleep without taking it off. I rolled onto my back as I answered the call. My stomach bubbled with nausea.

"Hello?" I greeted with a sleep-drunken slur.

"Bexley Barker!" Dad's sharp tone shook me awake

"Dad, what's the matter?" I winced, clutching my forehead

My bedroom danced in front of my eyes and my temples impersonated a slow clap. I mashed my lips together to resurrect my withered tongue, but it was no use, I needed water and a miracle. The sun pooled in through the vertical blinds, filtering a hazy yellow hue onto the whitewashed walls. My room was like my life, orderly, and devoid of any colour. It might seem drab to some, but at least nothing clashed.

"You better be getting ready for dinner?" he spoke in a warning growl.

I squinted to tell the time on my alarm clock. It was just past three in the afternoon. I had to blink to clear the blur from my eyes.

Did I just read the time right?

The digital display altered another minute, mocking me for being a lazy, hungover sloth.

No! How on earth have I slept in for so long?

"Yes," I lied, scrambling out of bed and catching my foot in the duvet.

My knee hit the laminate floor with a thump.

"Ow," I whined

Dad's heavy sigh rattled down the line, not believing me for a second.

"Oh, and Bexley . . . dress respectably," he added before ending the call.

I would've taken offence to that remark, but I was feeling a little worse for wear. The train-wreck staring back at me in the mirror only proved Dad right. I needed all the help I could get — a fairy godmother,

Gok Wan, and a pint full of Alka-Seltzer. If I wanted to be taken seriously, I had to radiate professionalism. Dad would never hand over the keys to his car to someone who didn't hold a valid driving licence. So, I needed to convince him I was more than capable of running the company

CHAPTER
Two

Bexley

I was back again so soon, right where my night out ended. Only this time, in the cold light of day, the Roman city of Chester was bustling with shoppers. Not drunkards. It was almost five o'clock on a Sunday afternoon, the boutiques were getting ready to close for the day but all the restaurants remained accessible. The buskers were all packing up their equipment, counting the loose change that had been tossed into the open guitar cases. Pigeons pecked around for crumbs outside the bakery stores. Shop assistants were dragging in A-frame boards as a subtle hint that they wanted to go home on time, and the shoppers who took notice were all heading for the bus shelters and car parks.

Clutching the strap of my Louis Vuitton handbag, I hurried towards the Grosvenor hotel. It was situated at the heart of the city centre, surrounded by shops, and set next to the iconic Eastgate clock. The multiplex shopping mall ran alongside it and was connected by a domed roof. It stood in stark contrast to the Grade 2 listed building with its elegant black and white timbered walls that boasted sixty-eight bedrooms, twelve suites, each one full of character and individual appeal. Dad was meeting me in one of the two restaurants — The Simon Radley, which had held a prestigious Michelin star since 1990. He dined here so often, they honoured him with his own table.

The doorman held the door for me to enter, and was dressed in a black top hat and tails suit. The interior was the epitome of sophisticated luxury, a mix of cream and golden colours with dark wooden furnishings. Dad rose from his seat upon my arrival. He took one look at my smart dress suit and breathed a sigh of relief

"Bexley, darling. How are you?" Dad embraced me and kissed my cheek.

"I'm fine, Dad. How are you?" I inquired, noticing the dark circles beneath his eyes.

Dad always had trouble sleeping this time of year. The pain of losing Mum tore his heart in two. She was the love of his life, and he was hers. Dad gave me her pendant on the day she died, saying I would know what to do with it when the time comes. Mum worked for the military as a codebreaker. It was how they met. Mum used to tell me stories of their time together, the missions they would share, and the problems they had to solve. She used to leave me clues in my school books or my lunch bag, and if I managed to solve them, I would get a treat at the weekend. Her pendant was nothing more than a small golden cylinder, made up of six rotary charms. To everyone else, the symbols that were etched into them looked like they could be ancient runes, but I knew what each one meant. She had spent years teaching them to me, and now I knew them by heart.

"I miss her, Bexley," he admitted, showing a slight flicker of vulnerability. "But we have to keep moving forward, don't we?"

I nodded in agreement. "We do. Mum wouldn't want us to waste our lives away."

A deep crease formed across Dad's brow. "I know." His gaze faltered and a shadow of sadness veiled his eyes.

The grief had aged him, sucking the vitality from his soul. He was giving up trying, and watching him slowly deteriorate was breaking my heart.

"Have you ordered already?" I asked, suspecting that he'd neglected to eat since goodness knows when

It was why I was reluctant to move out of the family home, but Dad insisted I needed my own space. He always encouraged me to be more independent throughout my teens, which was why I was the self-sufficient woman I was today.

Dad nodded. "Entrées and appetizers," he answered. "I know you like to pick whatever takes your fancy, so I left off the main course and dessert."

"Dessert? Now you're talking," I chuckled, lightening the mood

Dad blew out an amused huff. "I doubt they'll be generous with the portion sizes here." He chuckled. "I don't drink as much as I used to, and I've never smoked a day in my life. But offer me a jam roly-poly with custard, and I'll snatch your hand off for it."

Dinner progressed from idle chit-chat to the serious topic of business. I wondered if there was something else Dad had neglected to tell me. He seemed anxious as if something was worrying him.

"So, what's this all about a shake-up in the company?" I inquired, wondering what had gotten him so stressed lately

"I just want to make sure you're financially secure, that's all. And I need to know that the business can sustain itself if you ever decide to take time off to start a family," he explained, being meticulous with his words.

"Dad, I'm not even in a relationship with anyone, never mind taking time off to have kids. There's about as much chance of that happening as there is of you re-enlisting in the Navy."

Despite Dad's hearty chortle, I could tell that he was being serious. "But what if things were to take a drastic change? What if you decide to settle down and marry?" he asked. "It would give your old man some peace of mind, knowing you're safe and secure"

Safe and secure? What has brought all this on?

As much as I wanted a fairy tale ending, it felt as if I was fishing in a pond filled with frogs. I didn't want to have to kiss each one to find a prince.

Couldn't you catch warts from frogs? Or was it toads?

Some of my friends had found their life partners

when they weren't even looking. The harder you seek, the more you'd likely settle for second best. I didn't wish to have to settle in life, never mind in love.

I stopped eating to cast him a pointed look. "As I said, it's not even on the horizon yet, so don't worry about it. I thought I could pitch a few of my ideas to you and see what you think. When is the next meeting?"

Dad wiped his mouth with his napkin, letting it drop onto his empty plate. The fact that he was hesitant was making me nervous. Surely Dad wouldn't have made any plans without talking to me first.

"Look, Bexley . . .," Dad began.

"Oh God, you've sold part of the company, haven't you?" I thought of the worst-case scenario first.

I always did that because it softened the blow for lesser revelations.

Dad cleared his throat and flicked his gaze to me. It was hardly a denial, and I could see the trepidation in his eyes.

"Not so much as sold," he stated, making a cringe face. "More like agreeing to a merger with a very good friend of mine. If things were to ever take a turn for the worst, we would be prepared for it. This agreement has been in place since you were a baby. It will suit us all."

"Dad, what the fuck?" I let my cool demeanour slip

He had already made a deal.

My cutlery slipped through my fingers and clattered onto my plate. Some diners turned suddenly, the unexpected noise startling them from their quiet dinner. Dad's jaw pulsed as he waited for my outburst. I was angry that he went behind my back. Were we in some kind of trouble? Was this what all the secrecy was about? All this talk about wanting me to be financially secure seemed to make so much more sense.

"How bad is it?" I asked, cradling my head in my hands. "How far in the red are we?"

Go on, just give it to me straight. No matter how bad it is, I can figure something out.

Dad bristled. "Our rivals are undercutting us at every corner. It's not feasible to price-match and still make a profit. Our options are to cut the workforce down by half, or agree to a merger to save jobs."

I could see the predicament he was in. It would break Dad's heart to let go of staff. The majority of our employees had been with us from the start. Times were hard for everyone. Our economy was at an all-time low. There was no guarantee that these people would find alternative employment. People would lose their homes, their income, and would struggle to feed their families. We couldn't let that happen. Dad and I owed it to them to do all that we could to make this work

"So, as you said . . . you've already agreed to a merger? Would I be correct in guessing that it has something to do with your acquaintance from the personal security firm?" I inquired; my suspicions were aroused by this mystery friend of his.

"Yes, I believe working alongside his company is the smart way forward for all of us," Dad reinforced.

A merger would mean any decision-making would be put down to a vote. We wouldn't necessarily be in control despite owning fifty per cent of the business, but what other choice did we have? Borrowing money against the business would only put us further in the red. If things were as bad as Dad claimed, then we would never recoup the losses before the next tax year.

"You have to tell me who this friend of yours is," I stressed, needing to see all the facts and figures with my own eyes. "How can you be sure he's as trustworthy as you say he is?"

"We can trust him," Dad assured, sounding certain of it.

A waitress came to remove our empty plates. I waited for her to leave before I continued the conversation

"Can I at least look at the business proposal?" I asked hopefully.

Dad leaned forward, resting his arms on the table and let out an exasperated breath. He hated having to explain his decisions, but this was my business too. I could see that his intentions were good, but that didn't mean that his judgement remained intact. Dad always seemed highly-strung during this time of the year, and the last thing I wanted was for someone to take advantage at a time like this. He might be my father and protector, but the same fierce loyalty worked both ways.

"That won't be necessary," Dad dismissed. "Everything will be explained when we arrive in London tomorrow'

I blinked my eyes, shaking my head at all the cloak and daggery. There was something he wasn't telling me. He was protecting me from something else. Dad knew me too well; I would worry and overthink things until I learned all the facts. If he wasn't going to tell me until tomorrow, then so be it. It wouldn't kill me to wait for one day.

"Okay, so now we're travelling to London." I bounced my shoulders in a cooperative shrug. "So, I take it we're going to see Uncle Teddy then?" I assumed

"Not Uncle Teddy," Dad said, wincing his eyes.

I called all of Dad's old Navy friends "Uncle" as a term of endearment. They were not related to me in any way, but family doesn't always have to be blood, right? If Dad wasn't going into partnership with sweet Uncle Ted, the man who used to make pound coins appear behind my ears, then who could it be? Who else would Dad trust with his livelihood?

With his only daughter's future?

"You remember Uncle Zane from Dorset, don't you?" Dad mentioned, sending chills down my spine.

Uncle Zane? No . . . does he mean Zane Wolfe?

Uncle Zane was a scary-looking bastard. He was ninety per cent muscle and ten percent body hair. I used to joke that he was a werewolf and howled up at the moon. His tattoos were barely visible beneath the thick, wiry hairs on his arms and chest. And he had one of those big bushy beards that concealed half of his face. He reminded me of Popeye's love rival, Bluto, but a lot grouchier. Despite having the personality of a cactus, Uncle Zane wasn't the problem, it was his four sons. The Devil's spawn, as I used to call them. The Wolfe brothers — Asher, Braxton, Cruz, and Dominic. Two sets of identical twins that made my childhood a living nightmare. The last I heard, they had followed in their father's footsteps and enlisted into the Merchant Navy. I prayed to God they had been deployed somewhere far, far away, so I never had the displeasure of seeing them again

"Uh-huh," I murmured, wrinkling my nose as if I had just smelled a fart. "Why is he meeting us in London? I thought he lived in Sandbanks?"

I wondered if Uncle Zane still looked the same, and if the Omen Brothers were still as awful as I remembered. They would be grown men in their mid-twenties, probably married with lots of demonic offspring by now. Gosh, I shuddered at the thought. Dad could tell by the reserved look in my eyes that I was not looking forward to going to London.

"They all moved closer to the business premises, but they still own the beach house in Sandbanks," Dad replied, sparking further questions.

Sandbanks was a peninsula that crossed the mouth of Poole Harbour. With its Jurassic coastline, golden sandy beaches, cute little bistros, and water sports facilities, it was considered the English Riviera. The view from Uncle Zane's balcony terrace was spectacular. I loved to watch the sun sinking into the ocean horizon at the end of the day.

A part of me wanted to ask whether they were all still living together, but I resisted because that would imply that I cared . . . and I didn't.

I made a disgruntled huff. "Oh, how could I ever forget those treasured memories," I exaggerated, my words laced with bitter sarcasm.

Fine . . . some of the memories were beautiful, but the bad ones outweighed the good times. No thanks to those awful brothers.

"I hated when you and Mum used to drag me there every other weekend. It was bad enough that they hijacked our summer holidays." I shook my head with revulsion. "They were always pissing in the swimming pool and trying to blame it on me. Asher undid my bikini top as I went down that water slide. All right, I didn't have any boobs back then, but it was still humiliating for me. Then there was the time when Dominic squirted tomato sauce on my seat when I was wearing that gorgeous white dress. Everyone thought I had started my period. Honestly, Dad. You don't know what they put me through."

Dad waved his hand in front of his face in

dismissal. "I know you didn't always get along with the boys," he breathed airily. "They were always quite a handful."

"Which is the understatement of the century," I replied with a roll of my eyes. "The Wolfe brothers hated me. They were constantly picking on me, making fun of my name, and one time, they even set fire to my pigtails with my own birthday cake candles," I reminded him, crossing my arms in front of my chest.

My actions made me seem like a petulant child pouting for attention, but some old wounds never healed. Right now, all I wanted to do was bury my face into my hands and cry.

My worst nightmare is coming true.

"Boys tend to show off whenever they like someone," Dad cited his words of wisdom. "Zane always mentions that they ask about you all the time."

Did they really ask about me?

My natural response was to laugh at that. "Don't give me that crap! They are probably reminiscing about all the times they hid spiders in my bed, or sprinkled itching powder onto my knickers that year in Cannes."

Dad reached out and took hold of my hand. "Oh, Bexley, life is too short to hold on to silly grudges.

They never knew their mothers. Zane brought them up on tough love. They weren't used to being around girls. I think they saw you as some kind of novelty."

Trust Dad to lay on the guilt trip. Zane had used surrogates to bear his offspring, rather than settle down and marry someone like a regular guy would. The Wolfe Brothers were a business transaction. Zane paid two women to be artificially inseminated with his sperm; they were to carry his kids for nine months, then hand them over an hour after giving birth. In return, they each received fifty thousand pounds per child. I guess I feel sorry for them in that respect, but they weren't exactly born into poverty. Zane Wolfe was loaded. You had to be wealthy to live in a place like Sandbanks. The boys had always been spoiled, over-privileged pricks in my opinion.

"When Mum died, I didn't turn into the school bully," I preached, making an excellent point. "They were horrible to me. There's no excuse for that. Don't you remember the day I almost drowned in their pool?"

Dad frowned as he recalled the memory. "Yes, darling. But saying you almost drowned is a bit far-fetched. Braxton gave you a little nudge because you bragged you were the better swimmer. In his defence, you had challenged him to a swimming race, and were taking a lifetime to dive in. He didn't know you couldn't swim. If I recall correctly, it was Cruz who came to your rescue."

Trust dad to make Cruz the hero of the hour.

I rolled my eyes. That wasn't how I remembered it at all. In my version of events, they were the bad guys, and I was the innocent victim. It was so typical of Dad to make excuses for them just because they didn't have a mother figure. I remember how much they doted upon my mother, and I felt a slight twinge of guilt. Maybe they were jealous of me for having a mum. That thought always crossed my mind.

"I did not boast," I spoke in my defence. "I was just sick of hearing all about Braxton, the champion swimmer. He was getting on my nerves."

Maybe I boasted a little, but so what? They claimed to be experts at everything. Braxton could swim through the water like a torpedo. Dominic was a computer whizz. Asher was freakishly clever, and Cruz thought he was a Teenage Mutant Ninja Turtle. Okay, he took up martial arts at a young age and won every tournament he ever entered. I might sound bitter, but it wasn't easy living in the shadow of the Wolfe brothers. There was no way I could compete with the number of trophies they won. Their father had an entire room dedicated to their achievements, just to rub salt into the wounds of us mere mortals. It made the rosette I won for coming second in the egg and spoon race look like a cheap piece of tat. It was, but that's beside the point. I was eight, and had the steadiest hand at my primary school. There wasn't anything else I was particularly talented at. Not really. That's why I needed to succeed. I had nothing else going for me. Our money would soon run out if we were not careful with it.

"Please tell me they won't all be present at the meeting," I groaned, pleading with my eyes. "They don't all work for their father, do they?"

I could cope if it was just Uncle Zane, but the guilty expression on my father's face made my heart plummet into my stomach.

No . . . they were all going to be there.

We were merging our companies. That could only mean I would be seeing a lot more of the Wolfe brothers from now on, so I'd better get used to it. A lot of time had passed since I saw them last. Maybe they had matured

I won't hold my breath.

"Why do I let you do this to me?" I complained.

"Because you love me," Dad said with a grin. "Now, shall we order dessert to go? We have a lot of packing to do."

For an overnight stay?

"Why, Dad? How long are we planning on staying?" I asked, flaring my eyes with sarcasm.

And there was me thinking that men liked to travel light.

Dad met my gaze, his expression unreadable. "For however long it takes."

CHAPTER
Three

Asher Wolfe

"So, Bexley definitely agreed to a meeting?" I double-checked with Dad.

I had to raise my voice over the sound of the coffee grinder. The early morning sun pooled in through the floor to ceiling windows, providing a striking view of the Dorset coast. I skipped my usual run on the beach because I wanted to grill Dad about talking to Uncle Jaxx. He wasn't my real uncle; it was just a term of endearment we used for all of Dad's old Navy friends.

Dad didn't so much as lift his gaze from his paper as he responded with, "Uh-huh. That's what Jaxx said." He located his plate without looking and raised a triangle of buttered toast to his mouth.

I blew out an astonished breath, dragging my fingers through my dark-brown hair. "I can't believe she said yes. I assumed she would refuse."

Braxton and Cruz were both sitting opposite Dad at the kitchen table, both sported military-style crew cuts, but Braxton's dark hair was a contrast to Cruz's honey-blonde. Cruz took a sip of his orange juice while Braxton swirled the dregs of his tea around the bottom of the mug. Dominic was leaning against the kitchen island, flicking through his phone. He had been stalking Bexley's Instagram page like an obsessive maniac, blowing his floppy blond hair from his eyes. When he wasn't surfing the net, he spent the rest of his time catching the ocean waves.

This time Dad glanced up from the sports page. "Don't get your hopes up just yet. She agreed to meet us in London. She knows nothing about the contents of the contract, or that her life is in danger. Jaxx wants to keep it that way until we can come up with a plan"

That was my area of expertise, planning covert operations and tracking down the spies who had been sent to steal from our government. Dominic was our tech expert, Braxton specialised in artillery, and Cruz was our very own field agent, just like James Bond. Dad and Uncle Jaxx were recruited straight from the Navy to head the counter-terrorist division at MI6. They had been hunting a man known as the Chameleon for quite some time. Uncle Jaxx came close to taking him down, but he got to Bexley's mother, Aunt Safi, before he could stop him. She knew the Chameleon was coming for her, so she entrusted her pendant to Bexley. It was a good thing she did, or the Chameleon would have got vital information about our military defences. As soon as Dad told us our cover had been blown, and that Bexley's life was in danger, it took everything I had not to go after him myself. But our nemesis lived up to his reputation, and that is how he earned the name "Chameleon". He was impossible to catch. But when he does come for Bexley, we would be ready.

Cruz rolled his hazel eyes. "By contract, you mean our marriage proposal?" he muttered, sounding as sarcastic as ever.

"She can't legally marry all of us," Braxton grumbled. "What are we meant to do, play rock, paper, scissors at the altar?"

That was the issue we had. There were four of us and only one of Bexley. It meant she would have to choose between us if she wanted to exchange vows in a church. My brothers and I had shared everything — toys, our taste in music, and sometimes even women. There was only a week separating me and Braxton from Cruz and Dominic. Our mothers were surrogates who gave birth to twins. We never knew who they were, but Braxton and I inherited our blue eyes from our mother. Cruz and Dom got Dad's hazel eyes, but they must have inherited their mum's blond hair. Dad was reluctant to talk about our birth mothers. I bet they took off before the ink on their cheques had time to dry. Luckily for us, we still had each other . . . and Dad. Good ole' Dad. He had the emotional capacity of a silverback gorilla, and all the finesse of a thistle beneath a picnic blanket on a warm sunny day at the park. But he loved us. He wanted us. Even if it was only to train us to become his soldiers, he made sure we never went without.

But enough about that. Neither one of us wanted Bexley to be forced to choose between us, so Dad had his legal team draw up a civil contract that bound

Bexley to each of us at once. It was a legal loophole that allowed us to reap all the benefits of a matrimonial lifestyle without Bexley being arrested for bigamy. It mentioned future offspring, and our desire to keep the paternity anonymous. We would remain true to our marriage vows and raise our children in a stable family unit. It also specified that we were to keep Bexley safe at all costs. She held the clue to unlocking a treasury of classified government documents. Vital information that would have catastrophic consequences if it fell into the wrong hands. Her mother died keeping the same secret.

"Dad thinks he can control everything," Cruz added, his bored tone pissing Dad off as usual. "I bet there's a clause that determines how many grandchildren he'll get out of it. He's probably hoping for an entire battalion of little Wolfe sprogs."

Dad arched a brow, shooting Cruz a warning frown. "Don't push it. It's not too late to add abstinence into the contract."

Cruz's face flooded with alarm. "You wouldn't fucking dare"

Dad returned a deadpan look which suggested "try me".

"All I know is our arrangement isn't the most romantic," Braxton stated. "It feels like a business transaction, and I for one think Bexley will be insulted when she hears about it. She hates us. I doubt she'll be eager to jump on our dicks — chop them off more like ."

"Not romantic?" Dominic scrunched his face in an incredulous expression. "But we love her. It's always been her. I can't imagine us settling down individually. Going our separate ways. If we can't have Bexley, then we will have no one."

At least we were all in agreement with that statement.

I pointed my finger at Dominic. "And that's exactly what we'll tell her when we see her tomorrow. That we love her and we want her in our lives."

Braxton made a doubtful snort. "Yeah, tell her that and brace yourself for a slap."

Dominic ignored our brother's comment and went straight back into stalker-mode. "Look at the photos she posted on Saturday night." Heart emojis were practically popping out of his eyeballs. "I think I need a cold shower."

Our ears pricked up like the security dogs we trained. "Let me see," I said, looking at Dominic's phone screen. Braxton and Cruz rushed to see for themselves.

My heart skipped a beat as I viewed an image of

Bexley in her figure-hugging outfit. Even though she was an adult, she still held the exuberance of youth. Her eyes were just as blue as the ocean and sparkled with happiness; her skin was smooth and flawless, glowing with health. She had the body of a pin-up model, with curves in all the right places and legs that went on for miles. She had dyed her hair. That was the only obvious difference. Her brown hair flowed around her shoulders in soft waves, drawing my attention to her full breasts and killer cleavage. If we could convince her to be our wife, my world would be complete

"Okay, that's enough, boys," Dad berated us, finally discarding his newspaper. "If you want to win the heart of a girl like Bexley Barker, you have to woo her the old-fashioned way"

Cruz gave Dad a double-take. "Woo her? Dad, you do realize what century we're in? Next, you'll expect us to take chaperoned walks and court her individually"

"Hold on a minute, maybe Dad has a point," I mentioned

All eyes landed upon me. As the eldest by minutes, my brothers looked up to me as their leader.

"What if we leave out that part of the plan?" I

suggested, witnessing my father's brows raise with intrigue

Dominic and Cruz looked to be mulling that over, but Braxton appeared to have a problem with it.

"That's deceitful, Ash. A relationship needs to be built upon a solid foundation of truth and honesty. I don't think we should lure her into this under false pretences."

"How is it lying if we don't mention it?" I was grasping at straws, anything to ensure that this plan would succeed. "All I'm saying is maybe we could spend some quality time with her and let nature take its course. We're resourceful men, surely we can get her to fall head over heels in love with us in under six months."

Cruz was nodding as if he thought it could work.

Dominic was happy to go along with whatever we decided, and Braxton was being as pessimistic as ever.

"I won't hold my breath," Braxton muttered, always the voice of negativity.

If he wasn't my identical twin, I would punch him straight in the face. He had it bad for Bex the same as all of us, but he was scared shitless of rejection.

"If all else fails, just show her your dick," Dominic replied with a shrug. "We should thank our lucky stars to have been blessed down under. Few men can boast about owning a ten-inch penis. Women who say size isn't everything are only lying to themselves."

Dad scrubbed his hand over his face. "Keep it clean, please. You're twenty-five years old for crying out loud"

Braxton stalked to the sink and dumped his mug into the basin. The scowl on his face looked as if it had been permanently etched there.

"I don't care about what other girls would want or wouldn't want," he muttered, sparing an over the shoulder glance. "The only girl whose opinion counts is Bexley's. Just don't get your hopes up." And with that, he thundered from the kitchen and into the gym.

I knew better than to run after him. Braxton just needed to blow off steam by lifting weights, then he would be fine. Cruz was sitting hunched over the table, reading the front page of Dad's newspaper.

Dominic stalked towards the coffee machine to fill up his empty mug, and Dad rose to his feet with a sigh

"I want you all ready within the hour," Dad insisted. "The helicopter leaves at eleven hundred hours."

"What time is the meeting?" I asked, needing to prepare.

Dad checked his watch. "Jaxx sent a text to say he was on his way. So, depending on traffic, they will arrive around lunchtime," he explained. "We've scheduled the meeting to start at fourteen hundred hours.

That gave me plenty of time to talk to my brothers and figure out how we were going to win Bexley over. It just so happens . . . I had a few tricks of my own up my sleeve.

Braxton Wolfe

I stood beneath the shower faucet, letting the steamy water sluice down my body. In just a few hours, the woman of my dreams would be sitting within an arm's reach of me. I have been waiting for this moment, ever since Dad sat us down for "the talk" at the age of ten. They had kept Bexley in the dark her entire life. Shielded like some untouchable princess. Uncle Jaxx was a happily married man, and conceived Bexley out of love. But my brothers and I were test tube soldiers who had been bred for one purpose — to protect Bexley with our lives. Growing up with that knowledge wasn't easy. We said, and did, some cruel things to her that I wished I could take back. I know my brothers all felt the same

My workout was effective, ridding me of the tension that had been building this weekend. Out of the four of us, my brothers considered me to be the silent brooding type, maybe even the most sensitive of the litter. I use that phrase because that's what it felt like we were — a wolf pack. The Wolfe brothers, born to protect their Queen and country, and that title was so befitting of Bexley.

I towel-dried and dressed quickly, relishing the burning sensation in my overworked muscles. Dad wanted us to make a good impression, insisting we dress appropriately. He aimed his subtle hint at me, ensuring that I covered my tattoos. Everything was riding on this meeting; our dad's life's work, the safety of the codes, and the future they promised us with Bexley. I was the last to go to the helipad, sauntering across the manicured grounds with the wind in my face

"Better late than never," Asher commented, shouting over the noise. "Dad was about to release the hounds to come and drag you out of there."

Cruz and Dom hopped in the 'copter alongside

our father, fixing their harnesses and headsets into place

"After you," Asher said, always such a gentleman. "It's nice to see you dressed in a suit," he remarked.

We all met my father's standard of dress, opting for tailor-fitted black Armani suits. With the solemn expressions on our faces, anyone would think we were heading to a funeral, not to meet our potential wife. Out of all of us, I was the only one who saw this for the shit-show it was. There was no way that a woman like Bexley would swallow this crap.

"What are you looking so smug about?" I shot my twin a question as he pulled the sliding door shut.

I buckled my harness and Asher took a seat alongside Dad and secured his own, pulling the headset over his ears.

"While you were busy sulking in the gym, Dom, Cruz, and I had an insightful chat," Asher informed me

"You discussed things without me?" I accused them, eyeing my brothers with contempt.

Dad checked his watch and then muttered something to the pilot. We lifted off the ground, circling the coastline before heading off to London .

Cruz sneered, flicking his gaze out through the window. The guy was a fucking mystery. We never could tell what he was thinking. Dominic shoved his phone inside his jacket pocket, turning to us so he could partake in the conversation.

"Just listen to what he's got to say, Brax," Dom urged

Asher cleared his throat. He gestured by circling his pointed finger around at each of them. "We decided Bexley should come and stay at Sandbanks with us. Dad and Uncle Jaxx will stay at our London base to confuse the chameleon."

I huffed in aggravation. "And how are we going to get her to agree to that? Bash her over the skull with a mallet, or drug her coffee?"

Asher pressed his lips together and scowled. It was a sign that his patience was wearing thin.

"None of those things will be necessary because we're going to tell her the truth." He cocked his head to one side as he deliberated something. "Well, actually, you are. It'll sound believable coming from you"

My eyes almost bulged out of their sockets. "Why me?"

Cruz turned to us with a lazy grin plastered across his face. "I told you he would love that part of the plan"

All the moisture evaporated from my mouth and I had to swallow hard to revive it.

"I thought you were supposed to be a genius? That's the stupidest thing I've ever heard in my life," I roared, outraged.

Asher chortled. "Think about it. Bexley is a codebreaker like her mother. If we give her a task to do, she won't question spending time with us. She'll assume it's all part of the job and comply because she won't want us to take any of the credit. We can watch over her without her knowing what is going on, and Dad and Uncle Jaxx can take care of business in London." He seemed convinced this could work, and if I had to be brutally honest, I thought so too.

"Bexley will insist she's in charge. You know how bossy she can be," I reminded him. "She has to be in control of everything."

Ash made a face that suggested he had doubts about that. "Maybe when we were kids, but times change. I'm pretty sure that Bexley is desperate for an adventure. So, that's exactly what we give her. Excitement, adrenaline, and plenty of thrills along the way"

I bobbed my head in agreement. "Yeah . . . get her to fall for us without even realizing it."

"Precisely," Asher finished.

I glanced around and saw the same level of determination staring back at me. My brothers looked hopeful. If we were really going to do this, there could be no room for errors.

"Leave it to me. I'll make her an offer she can't refuse," I assured them.

CHAPTER
Four

Bexley

T he Wolfe pack was cutting it fine, strolling into the boardroom like they all swung the world's biggest dicks. Uncle Zane headed the procession. His beard wasn't as wild and unkempt as I remembered it to be. He cropped it short, which suited his angular jawline. Dad stood up to shake their hands, but I remained seated, casting them all a catty smile as they sauntered past. I used to call them A, B, C, and D.

Asher and Braxton were always the dark-haired devils, and Cruz and Dominic were the poisonous blonds. A and D were the brains behind their quartet, and B and C were the brawn. It was how I could tell them apart.

I stored their profiles in my memory bank — Asher was the evil villain, Braxton was the sporty one, Cruz had an aura of danger, and Dominic clung to his Game Boy like it was a vital organ. They were as thick as thieves. Where one would go, the rest would follow. I always felt like an outsider. Like I was never good enough to join their stupid club.

Was that the root of my hatred? Did I resent them for pushing me out, when all I ever wanted was for them to accept me? Probably. I guess time doesn't heal all wounds.

"It's nice to see you, Bexley. I hope life has been treating you well," Braxton inquired.

I swallowed thickly. "It has. It's good to see you too," I lied through my teeth, and it showed.

I still held a grudge over the swimming pool incident.

Dad cast me a steely glare, warning me to play nicely.

A permanent scowl creased my brow as I kept my guard up, waiting for them to show their true colours.

It would only be a matter of time before they did. After all, you couldn't polish a turd, but you could roll it in glitter. Maybe they had Dad fooled, but they certainly didn't fool me.

"You look amazing," Cruz mentioned, dragging his gaze all over my body. Dominic was doing the same. Asher and Braxton followed suit.

It was unlike Cruz to make complimentary remarks. I couldn't believe it. Were they checking me out? In front of my dad, too. How could they be so shameless?

"Thank you for agreeing to meet with us with such short notice," Dominic added. "We can appreciate just how busy you are. If there's anything else we can do to accommodate you or make your stay more pleasurable, then don't hesitate to contact us. We're available night and day to cater to your needs." His eyes bounced down to my exposed cleavage, and he caught his bottom lip between his teeth

"Dom, cut it out," Asher hissed, giving his brother an elbow nudge.

Oh my God. It was blatantly obvious what he wanted, and although I was flattered by that, my pride took the lead

I slapped a hand over my chest. "I'm perfectly

fine, thank you very much. My needs are none of your business." I glanced at Dad, but he was busy speaking to Zane.

He was talking in code; it was something he did whenever he met with Uncle Zane. He knew how much that pissed me off. The Wolfe Brothers were eyeing me up like an all-you-can-eat buffet. Some filthy part of me liked the way they were looking at me. Knowledge was power, and I intended to use it to my advantage. Maybe if I changed my attitude and flirted a little, I could have them eating out of the palm of my hand.

It was worth a try.

I stretched my leg out beneath the table and trailed my foot along what I thought was Dominic's shin. He didn't flinch, but Braxton did, sucking in a sharp intake of breath. His breathing stuttered and his nostrils flared.

Shit! Wrong brother.

We made eye contact, and I went with it, holding his gaze and casting a sultry smile.

"If I change my mind, I know where to find you," I added, twisting my pendant between my fingers to draw his line of sight to it.

Braxton's chest heaved beneath the suit. A look of dominance blazed behind his eyes. Did he realize I was playing them? I noted the challenging glint he cast back as if to say, "game on".

Damn it. This could backfire on me.

Asher's eyes twitched and formed suspicious slits. Nothing ever got past him. I was sure they could all mind-link, holding private conversations inside their heads.

"Pressing on with important matters . . ." Dad took the lead. "We ought to lay all our cards down on the table, starting with me."

His comment snatched my attention, and I flashed my father a startled glance.

"Dad, what are you doing?" I asked in a moment of alarm.

Rule number one when cutting a deal — never be upfront and honest. A boardroom table was no different from sitting at a poker game. You had to hold your cards close to your chest and bluff like you were gambling with your life.

Dad scrubbed a hand over his stressed-out face. "Bexley, I need to be straightforward with you. I should have told you years ago."

My posture froze, and my lungs failed to function. A split-second of fear locked my mind into the present.

"Dad, what are you talking about?" My palms

grew sweaty and moisture pooled from my pores like a wrung-out sponge.

"The businesses are just a smokescreen to hide what we're working on," he confessed, making no sense at all.

Had he gone mad and finally lost his marbles? What did he mean by a smokescreen? For what?

My gaze bounced from each pair of eyes in a game of "what the fuck is going on in here roulette".

"You better start talking," I warned, dreading his next words.

Dad reached out to take my hand, but I pulled away as our fingers touched. His eyes flinched with sorrow, but I didn't back down. He started this. He brought me here, and now he owed me a damn good explanation.

"We work for the Secret Intelligence Service, and so did your mum." He pointed to my necklace. "She designed the pendant herself. It acts as a key. When using the correct combination, it opens a file containing classified Military of Defence documents. Your mother died protecting those files. She entrusted you with her secrets," he revealed, shocking me into oblivion.

"Jesus, it's hot in here?" I breathed, feeling overwhelmed.

My cheeks were heating to combustion-level, my upper lip and brow beading with perspiration.

"Why isn't the air conditioning turned on?" I complained, fighting to remove my jacket. "I can't breathe"

"I'll check," Asher offered, dragging his chair back

The silky lining of my jacket clung to my arms as if it was afraid to let go. I couldn't bring myself to look at the Wolfe brothers, but I could feel their eyes boring into me. My sleeve became caught on my watch bracelet and pulled itself inside out.

"Here, let me help," Asher tugged on the offending garment, freeing my arm.

"Thanks, I've got it," I uttered, snatching it from his grasp and flinging it across the back of my chair.

Dominic hurried to the window and flung it open. A life-saving breeze swept in to rescue me, quenching the fire that was raging inside. The vertical blinds made a Mexican wave around the room, just to add insult to injury. I plucked at my neck scarf, pulling it free. Asher huffed a smile, his almond-shaped eyes creasing at the corners.

"Better?" he asked, eyeing me fondly.

"What do you care?" I replied briskly. "I just found out that my entire way of life has been a lie, and you're asking me if I feel better?" I pointed to my face. "Does it look as if I'm jumping for fucking joy?"

For the first time, I rendered Asher speechless.

"Bexley, that's enough," Dad scolded me.

"This is bullshit," I exclaimed, burying my face in my hands. "I'm going back home to salvage what's left of my life."

"Please, just hear us out," Dad begged me. "We need . . ."

"We need your help," Uncle Zane finished Dad's sentence

"Me?" I spluttered, looking around at them like a deer caught in the headlights. "What use could I be? I have a degree in business management. Not a licence to kill."

Cruz huffed a smirk. "That's my job."

"Oh my God, have you killed people?" I blurted out my words. "Actually, don't answer that. I don't want to know." I swatted my hand in dismissal.

Dad moved from his seat and crouched beside me. "I appreciate it's difficult news to swallow, but it's all true. Your mother was an agent, and we believe someone known as the Chameleon poisoned her. She didn't die of cancer, but the symptoms were the same. It was easier to let you think that. That's why she became ill so suddenly, and why she wasn't able to have treatment."

My throat swelled with emotion and tears distorted my vision. "And you couldn't tell me this before?" I grimaced with despair. "My mother was murdered, and the person responsible is still out there living their life. They need to be punished. They should face jail time for what they've done."

"And they will," Dad promised. "But first, we must destroy the one thing they're after — the classified files. It's only a matter of time before they strike again. If they succeed, then your mother died in vain. We can't risk the information being leaked to terrorist groups. It has to be destroyed."

The room was revolving, my mind was whirling like I was sitting on a carousel that kept spinning around and around relentlessly

"I know it's a lot to take in, but it's true," Braxton reinforced what my dad said. "You are the only one who can decrypt the codes. We need to unlock the files to destroy them. We can't risk them falling into the hands of the Chameleon."

I flicked my gaze to my father. "Is this some kind of wind-up?" I asked, wondering whether a film crew was going to come bursting into the room and announce that I was being Punked.

Braxton leaned forward in his chair and his eyes softened with warmth. "Of course not. We can verify it."

I didn't want them to prove it. I just wanted to wake up from this nightmare.

"Can I just take a moment to get my head around this?" I asked, pushing back on my chair.

Dad stood up and turned away, pinching the bridge of his nose. I needed to step out of the room and hyperventilate in private. Braxton's chair tipped backwards and toppled over as he leapt to catch me. Asher caught him by the arm and urged him to let me go. I ran down the corridor and bumped into an office junior, causing him to drop a stack of papers all over the floor. Tears were rolling down my face by this point. It embarrassed me to be seen like this, so I darted into the ladies' toilets and ugly cried.

CHAPTER
Five

Bexley

My fingers curled around the cold basin for support. I lifted my gaze to the mirror and saw pure fear etched across my face. What was I going to do with the information I had just been given? If what Dad says was true, then there wasn't a damn thing the police could do about it? Chameleons could camouflage themselves to blend in anywhere. If he — for some reason, I'm assuming the Chameleon is a man — could evade MI6, the police had no chance of catching him. The door opened, and I expected a woman to come strolling in to use the toilet. Instead, I was shocked to see Braxton wading in like a man on a mission.

"Are you okay?" he asked, coming to stand right behind me

I splashed water over my face, trying to rid the blotchy patches from forming across my cheeks.

"No," I replied, snapping back at him. "Get out and leave me alone."

He came closer, resting his hands against my shoulders. The warmth of his touch seeped through my cotton blouse, and I'd be lying if I said it didn't comfort me. Braxton pulled me against his broad chest, wrapping his inked arms around my waist.

"I'm scared," I admitted, curling my fingers around his forearms, my eyelids closing like shutters.

Braxton had been the one to poke fun at me when I cried. He used to pull the heads off my dolls, and let the air out of my bicycle tyres. Yet here he was, holding me in my moment of weakness, and whispering to me that everything was going to be fine

"Shh, it's all right," he promised.

How could I trust a word he said? As children, we

were mortal enemies, and as adults, we were nothing but strangers.

"No, it's not," I whimpered.

Braxton buried his nose into my hair, sucking in a deep intake. "I know it seems that way, but you have to believe me when I tell you it will be fine. We will not let anything happen to you. You have our word."

Our word? Did he mean all of them?

"Why are you being so nice to me? I thought you and your brothers hated me?" I asked, dragging up old wounds.

He jerked his head back with confusion. "Hate? No. Whatever gave you that idea?"

I rolled my eyes with a click of my tongue. "Oh, you know . . . all the infantile torture you and your brothers inflicted upon me over the years."

Braxton moved my hair to one side so his lips grazed against my ear. I dared to look in the mirror and saw us locked in a lover's embrace. My eyes flared wide with uncertainty. I didn't understand why he was here.

Why was he comforting me in my moment of weakness?

He trailed his fingers along my cheek. "You're so beautiful," he murmured. "You always were. I've thought about you a lot, just lately. I can't let you go without telling you how I feel. We were idiots. I'm sorry for everything I ever said and did to hurt you. Just know that I didn't mean any of it. None of us did"

My heart fluttered upon hearing that. "You're just saying that because you think it's what I want to hear."

"I know you're bored shitless. You're crying out for excitement. I can tell," he breathed, sending a shiver down my spine. "Take a risk for once in your life. Do something reckless."

"I'm happy. I like my boring life. It's safe," I replied, dismissing his claims. "The only risks I take are with the business, and I never lose."

"You want to kiss me," he said, sounding sure of it. "I know you do"

I shook my head. "No, I don't."

I did. Really, I did.

He pressed his groin against my backside, letting me feel the full extent of his arousal. "Liar," he teased. "You say one thing, but I can tell how turned on you are by how your nipples are punching holes through your bra."

His fingers traced the curvature of my body, over my clothing, circling my treacherous buds, calling me out on my bullshit excuse. My head rolled back to rest against his shoulder, his fiery breath caressing my cheek. I hated him a few hours ago, and now I was grinding against his dick like a thirsty slut, wondering what it would feel like to be impaled upon it. Braxton's lips curled into a lazy grin; his hands were busy pulling my blouse from where it was tucked into my trousers.

"We can't do this. Someone might come in," I told him, fearing that we'd get caught.

I should push him away, turn around and slap him hard across the face. We needed to stop this before it went too far. What would his brothers think if they could see us right now? What would my father say? It was thrilling, exciting, and scary as fuck in case someone burst in and saw us.

"So?" He challenged, pressing kisses to my throat, weakening my knees and quickening my breathing. "We'll give them a show. What do you want? Tell me, and you can have it."

I blinked, staring blankly at our reflection. What did I want? Until now, I had never felt so alive.

"Do you prefer to play it safe with my fingers? Would you prefer to lean back and spread your legs so I can eat your pussy? Or do you want me to fuck you fast and hard over the sink?"

Fucking hell! He just came straight out and said it without so much as a blush staining his cheeks.

"We can't do that in here," I cautioned, glancing to see if the door could lock from the inside.

Yes, I was giving it some thought. I was a red-blooded female who wanted some action like the next woman. Sue me. Braxton was drop-dead gorgeous, and I hadn't had an orgasm in years.

"Time's ticking," he reminded me. "People are going to look for us." He sucked on my sweet spot at the base of my throat. "It would be a shame to waste the opportunity. I want you, and I could tell by the way you were flirting with me that you like me too.

Shit! So, this was what it felt like to be bitch-slapped by Karma

"Brax?" I moaned, forgetting all my troubles, my mind emptying of all thoughts.

His touch was the perfect distraction. Just what I needed to release my frustration. He thought so too, plucking at the button of my trousers and tugging down the zip. His fingers bypassed the elastic of my panty line and delved into the wet heat he'd created.

"Uh, stop," I uttered, as he dragged his finger back and forth down my slit, dipping deeper and deeper each time. "Someone will see if we do it here. Take me into the cubicle."

"But where's the danger in that?" he teased.

"Brax?" I mewled his name.

"You want me to stop?" he asked as if he doubted it.

Ah, fuck it. I needed this. So what if someone walks in?

"Keep going," I urged, hearing his husky chuckle. "Just use your fingers."

"Okay, we'll play it safe, this time," he breathed, implying that there would be a next time.

My trousers slid around my hips and I stepped out of one leg. Braxton pulled at my underwear until he tore it free and stuffed the screwed-up lace inside my mouth. Using one knee, he pushed between my legs and spread my thighs apart. My slick wetness cooled in the air, providing him with a natural lubricant.

"Look at me," he commanded, urging me to stare at our reflection. "I want to watch as you cum."

This was devilishly sinful, bent over the sink with Braxton stroking me. I reached between us, running my nails across his crotch and feeling the iron rod thicken beneath his slacks. Fuck, he was big. The three H's — huge, handsome, and hung. I wanted him as much as I craved all of his brothers. I fantasized about them all. But I refused to admit it before. His fingers pushed deep inside my heat as his thumb found my clit. I spat the lace out as I gasped, my body arching as I rose on my toes. My fingers set to work unbuckling his belt, wriggling my hand inside his boxer briefs, and seizing his mighty organ. It felt like silk around steel, jerking him into a frenzy. Braxton moulded against me; his brows scrunched with desire. My knees shook, and I struggled to keep my eyes open. He nipped my earlobe, forcing me to obey. This was insane. We shouldn't be doing this. But we were, and it was magical.

"Are you ready to cum for me, baby?" he rasped against my ear. Using his free hand, he tugged my bra over my breasts so that he could fondle them, rolling a nipple between his finger and thumb. "You're gonna make me blow."

"Yes, oh god, yes," I panted, angling my face to his.

Our lips locked like two magnets drawn together and our tongues swirled in an erotic dance. The sound of my climax played out on Braxton's fingers like a filthy, wet symphony. My fingers curled around his length, milking him for all he was worth.

Our bodies tensed like coiled springs. Lights flickered behind my scrunched eyelids. Braxton sucked my tongue as my lips pulled back into a perfect "O".

"Uh," I cried, my hips undulating as I rode his fingers. "Fuck, God, don't stop"

"Oh, yeah," Braxton grunted as he splashed hot, sticky come down the crease of my arse.

A tidal wave of euphoria came crashing over me, soaking his fingers, and I slumped into his arms like a boneless mess.

"That was perfect," he cooed. "Next time, I'm gonna fuck you raw."

Yes! God, let there be a next time.

He withdrew his fingers and sucked off the juices. Shame washed over me, giving me a slap of reality. I clutched my ruined underwear and rushed into the cubicle to clean myself up. Braxton's seed was trickling down the back of my thighs, so I wrapped toilet paper around my hand to wipe it off. How could I face him after this? We kissed, and we fooled around. But it meant nothing. It was just a distraction

"Don't go back to Cheshire. Come back to Sandbanks with us. Help us, Bexley. We can't do any of this without you," Braxton spoke from the opposite side of the door.

Do the Wolfe Brothers need me?

"I'm not my mother," I expressed as I dressed quickly. "What if I can't crack the code?" I doubted myself at every angle, which was my worst trait.

Braxton tapped on the door. "Come out of there.

The Bexley Barker I remember would never hide in the toilets. She would show the world and its uncle just what she is made of"

He knew me better than I gave him credit for. I never backed down from a challenge.

I turned the latch and stepped out from the cubicle, tucking my hair behind my ears. Braxton was leaning with one arm against the panel beside me. He caught me around the waist, crashing my chest against his.

"Fine," I decided, pushing back and crossing my arms beneath my tits. "I will help you, but it'll be on my terms."

His eyes flared wide. "Anything you want; you name it, you got it," he assured.

"I want in on everything," I voiced, making myself clear. "All of it. If you leave me out of the loop, then I'm done. I return to Cheshire, and I stash the necklace where no one will find it."

His lips pulled down at the corners, and he nodded in agreement. "Fair enough, but there are hackers who can infiltrate our system. We need to destroy the files."

I tapped my palm against his solid pectorals. "And another thing . . . can we please keep what just happened here to ourselves? If we're going to be spending a considerable amount of time together, I don't want there to be any misunderstandings between us," I insisted, hoping that we could at least be friends.

Fine, I wanted to be more than that, but I wasn't entirely sure he did. Although, it would be good to have one ally among the Wolfe Pack.

Braxton's eyes flinched with hurt. "What?" he held me steady, keeping me there. "I can't just ignore what happened between us, Bexley. We will discuss this when we return to Sandbanks. Make no mistake about that."

A storm raged behind his blue eyes. He wanted me, and he wouldn't be denied.

"Why do you have to insist on complicating things? We had a few moments of fun. Let's not turn this into something it's not," I argued.

"Because you're looking for more than just fun, Bexley. You want to be chased," he returned, calling me out. "You crave excitement."

It was true. The thrill of the chase was always the best part, but so was a secret affair. Catching Braxton's jaw in my hand, I ran the pad of my thumb across his bottom lip.

"If you're serious about this, come to my bed

tonight. This stays strictly between you and me," I affirmed, making my intention clear.

This was all about sex. No strings. No feelings involved. That way, no one was bound to get hurt.

"You're the boss," he replied, sounding satisfied with our arrangement.

The door burst open, but this time it was Asher who walked in. He saw the way I was holding his brother and assumed we'd been arguing.

"Whoa!" he held up his palms. "Take it easy . . . what did he do?"

"Nothing," we both spoke at once.

Asher cocked his head in observance. "If you're finished doing nothing, you might want to start making your way to the rooftop. We're heading back to Sandbanks." He bounced his gaze to me. "Your room is all set up ready for your arrival."

I let go of Braxton's face and released an agitated huff. "You assumed I'd say yes?" I shot Asher a scathing look

He stuffed his hands inside his trouser pockets. "Actually, I knew that as soon as you heard the truth you wouldn't say no," he replied, turning my question into an accurate statement of fact.

The smug bastard was always one step ahead. It drove me wild just as much as it infuriated me.

CHAPTER
Six

Cruz

"You better take good care of my daughter, or else," Jaxx warned, staring us all down. He glimpsed over his shoulder. "Speaking of Bexley . . . where is she?"

I cleared my throat. "I'm sure Braxton and Asher are bringing her here as we speak," I replied hopefully

Either that, or they were busy spit-roasting her in the ladies' toilets.

Dad scowled, lifting his finger to point at me. "I need you to call me with regular updates. If you spot anything unusual, I want you to get Bexley out of there. Do you understand me?"

"Of course," I responded, scrunching my face with irritation. "We're not amateurs."

Uncle Jaxx's face lit up as he saw past Dominic and me

"There they are," he announced, giving a vigorous wave.

I turned to see Bexley hurrying across the rooftop, holding on to Braxton's hand. Asher lagged a few strides behind, carrying her handbag, jacket, and scarf

"Dad, what about my luggage?" Bexley mentioned as soon as she reached us. "I left it all at the hotel."

Jaxx pulled Bexley into a tight hug. "I'll take care of it," he promised.

Bexley's expression pinched with emotion. "I love you, Dad."

Jaxx stroked her hair and pressed a kiss to her cheek. "I love you too." He drew back and braced her shoulders. "Do as they tell you, and try not to be so stubborn. This isn't a game, sweetheart."

Bexley nodded, her brows dimpling in the middle. "Stay safe, Dad. I'll see you soon."

Jaxx managed a delicate smile. "You too."

He released Bexley and steered her into the chopper, flashing us all another warning look. "I'm counting on you, boys. Don't let me down."

"We won't," we all pledged.

"Take care, Uncle Jaxx," I answered, returning a curt nod out of respect.

Dad lifted his hand in a simple wave as Jaxx slid the door closed. Braxton assisted Bexley with her harness. Dominic offered her a stick of gum, but she politely declined. Asher flashed me a winning grin that I instantly recognized. His scheme had worked. Something had transpired between Braxton and Bexley, just like Asher had arranged.

I fucking love it when a plan comes together.

"What the hell am I going to do about clothes?" Bexley fretted half-way into our journey.

"Who said anything about wearing any clothes?" Dominic teased, wiggling his eyebrows suggestively.

Bexley blanched. "You better be joking."

"He is," I assured, beating Asher to it. "You will

find everything you could possibly need in your room."

I expected Dominic to retort with a witty comeback, but he held his tongue. It was a good thing too. We didn't want to piss her off, or worse . . . spook her by confessing the details of our fathers' pact. She might jump head-first into the Thames, and it was a long way down from this height. I didn't fancy giving her a sky-diving lesson, just yet.

Bexley narrowed her eyes. "You picked out clothes for me?"

This time, Asher jumped into the discussion. "Yes, you're a size ten, right? You wear a size six shoe, and a thirty-four C bra?"

Her face contorted with outrage. "How do you know? You must've . . . uh! How dare you invade my privacy!" she ranted, getting all incensed over nothing

If this was going to work between us, and I'm not just talking about our potential harem, I mean us working together to catch the Chameleon, then all this unnecessary drama had to stop.

"We're part of a team, and that includes you too," I interjected, adopting a no-nonsense approach. "We have planned this entire operation right down to the finest detail. It's our job to leave no stone unturned. I know everything there is to know about you; your weight, height, eating habits, everything down to your fucking menstrual cycle. Say, for shits and arguments sake, we have to evacuate to safety. You can rest assured we remembered to pack tampons."

Bexley swallowed that information, taking some time to let it digest. "That uh . . . that makes sense," she conceded, her fierce scowl disappearing from her face. "I appreciate you're treating me as an equal part of the team. So, thank you."

"No problem," I added, flashing a lazy grin. "You can thank Dominic for picking out your underwear . . . or lack thereof"

Bexley cast Dominic a sceptical frown, which he returned with a flirtatious wink. She rolled her eyes and huffed a defeated sigh. I spotted movement between Bexley and Braxton and saw their pinkie fingers interlock. They assumed I couldn't see them from this angle, but the reflection in the glass never lies. I was almost envious of him, but patience was a virtue. I would have my chance with her soon enough

We arrived home less than thirty minutes later and touched down on the helipad. Bexley gazed through the window, admiring the stunning view of the quartz sandy coast.

"I can't believe it's been so many years since I came here," she muttered, more so to herself. "Mum adored this place. She always talked about moving down here when she retired." Her eyes glazed like polished glass.

Braxton turned to her, giving her hand a gentle squeeze. "We all loved your mother, Bex."

She lay her head against his shoulder and closed her eyes for a moment. Seeing her take comfort from him didn't spike my jealousy like I thought it might. It felt just as natural as breathing.

"I remember the time she came to our nursery school's Christmas play," Dominic mentioned, capturing Bexley's attention. Her eyelids fluttered open, and she listened to him, a wistful smile tugging the corners of her lips. "You know . . . before our dad took us out of regular education."

"Some kids at school used to make fun of us for not having a mum, and they saw your mum waving at us from the audience. She was sitting between your dad and ours with a huge, beaming grin on her face like she was proud of us. You were there too, but you were pouting and complaining that it was boring. You were wearing a red coat and gold tinsel in your hair."

Bexley chuckled. "I think I remember that day."

"Well, one kid asked if your mum was ours, and I told him she was. I didn't even feel bad about lying." He held Bexley's gaze and a mutual understanding passed between them.

"Even though I pretended, I felt proud to call her our mother," he continued. "She was the kind of parent you wished you had. I just wanted you to know that it's okay to miss her and remember her at the same time. I feel her sometimes . . . especially when I'm out surfing or sitting on the beach, waxing my board. I turn to look at the balcony, and I know in my heart she's there."

Bexley's tears quivered on the rim of her eyelids. "Thank you, Dom. That means a lot to me."

He pressed his lips together in a narrow smile, then glanced through the window to conceal his grief. We all took a moment to reflect on the people we had lost and counted our blessings for all the things we were lucky enough to have, or likely to receive. Time was short. I had never taken a day of it for granted, and nor will I ever. We had just days to train and prepare Bexley for the greatest adventure of her life. I don't know where that will take us, but if she falls in love with us along the way, then great. If she wanted me to quit this life, I would. I would resign from the agency and live a normal life. The next endeavour for me would be to slow down, and lay down some roots.

I had given so much of myself to this country, but now it was time for me to devote myself to another queen

---

Dominic

My emotions crept up on me when I least expected them to, kicking me right in the balls. I could count on one hand all the times I had broken down over the years. Not counting the early stages of childhood when I was a baby, or when I dropped my ice-cream onto the sand, or stepped on a Lego, or when the bank of Dad said no. I had cried over trivial things as all children did, but that was irrelevant. I was talking about the post fifteen "shit-happens" kind of grief, like making the heart-breaking decision to have my beloved Retriever, Pixel, put down. Her liver was failing, and she was going blind in both eyes. She was old, and had lived a glorious life, but it still killed me to say goodbye to her. Another occasion was when I crashed my first-ever car, writing it off on the motorway — almost killing myself in the process. Then there was the time I bawled like a baby during the ending of The Fast and the Furious 7 — which was emotional as fuck. There wasn't a dry eye in the cinema, except from Cruz, whose expression remained ice-cold as always. But we all cried when Dad told us that Bexley's mother, Aunt Safi, had passed away, and he named the person responsible. The Chameleon. It was a cruel, callous attack on a woman who didn't deserve it. That only left one of my fingers unchecked, but I didn't plan on shedding any more tears.

Not if I can help it.

There was no point in dwelling on the past because it wouldn't change anything. I didn't own a time-travelling DeLorean that could take me back to stop the Chameleon, but I concentrated on inventing gadgets to catch him — or her. That way, we could focus on living the rest of our lives without constantly looking over our shoulders.

Bexley relaxed as soon as we touched down on the helipad. As we reached the house, I tapped the six-digit code into the control panel beside the door, then pressed my thumb against the touchscreen. The green laser light scanned my print, and the lock clicked open. Bexley's heels clacked against the marble floor tiles, echoing in the vast open space.

Light flooded in through the domed skylight, the golden fleck glittering across the floor.

"I forgot how jealous I am of your home," Bexley commented. "It's so clean, bright, and luxurious. Just look at that," she said, gesturing towards the bifold doors in the kitchen. "How beautiful is that? You get to eat breakfast with a panoramic view of the ocean."

"Make yourself at home," Cruz insisted. "What's ours is yours."

Bexley cast him a quizzical look, but he was quick to add, "partner," to the end of his statement.

Our residence was now hers, subject to contract. Any other time I would have thrown that into the conversation, but I didn't want to jinx it. We still had to convince her to stay here and marry us. Well, technically, sign a civil contract that would bind her to each of us. I wasn't worried. We could be pretty persuasive when we wanted to be.

"Would you like something to drink, Bex?" Asher offered. "Tea, coffee, perhaps something stronger?"

She took a seat at the breakfast bar, her elbows resting against the cream marble countertop.

"I'll have whatever you're having," she answered, not seeming fussy

"Is beer okay?" Asher asked

Bexley scrunched her nose and shook her head.

"No, on second thoughts . . . I'll have a glass of your dad's best Chardonnay. I know he has a cellar full of the good stuff. That's the only reason I agreed to come." The underlying humour in her tone implied she was only joking.

Nope, she is still as fussy as ever.

Asher huffed a smirk and chortled to himself. I could tell he was thinking the same as me — she was going to be quite a handful. Lucky for her, he had the patience of a saint. We were same in that respect. Cruz and Braxton were the dominant ones who wouldn't stand for any crap. Here's believing Braxton will pull through on Asher's ice-breaker challenge and fuck her ready for the rest of us.

Asher dragged a condensation-glazed bottle from the chiller. "Hand me the bottle-opener, please," he asked Braxton because he was standing right next to the drawer.

Our brother obliged, disturbing the utensils as he searched for it. "Here, don't cork it like last time," Braxton muttered, poking fun at his twin.

Under a minute later, Asher filled a glass and handed it to Bexley. Her fingers coiled around the stem, and she brought the rim to her lips.

"Mm," she made a grateful noise as she savoured the taste. "Better than sex."

"Then you've been having shit sex," I voiced, confounded by that.

Bexley bounced her shoulders in a disinterested shrug. "It's been too long to recall."

I saw the audacious look upon Braxton's face and smirked to myself, knowing he was about to knock the cobwebs off her formally redundant pussy. With that amount of muscle powering a ten-inch cock, he would be sure to have her howling the house down.

Cruz loosened the knot of his tie and pulled it free. "Who's up for a cookout tonight? I feel like we should celebrate."

I raised my eyebrows with intrigue. One mention of the waterfront and I was game. "Count me in."

Asher, Braxton, and Bexley liked the sound of that too

"So, what happens after tonight?" Bexley aimed her question at Cruz.

He leaned back against the kitchen counter as he removed both his cuff-links.

"We will need to prepare," he said, looking her dead in the eye. "You'll be spending time with each of us. I will show you some basic self-defence techniques. Asher will train you how to think and react under pressure. Braxton will teach you how to handle a gun, and Dominic will kit you out with some exceptional spy gadgets."

Bexley snapped her gaze to me, her eyes wide with awe. "I get to play with spy gadgets?" The excitement in her voice was too cute, even for a techie like me

"I've been saving the best for a queen like yourself," I told her, stroking her ego. "But it's a surprise that I'm keeping for another day."

Bexley was mesmerized. I guess Asher was right — she was crying out for some action and was craving an adrenaline rush.

"I still can't believe you all work for MI6 — my dad, too. Right under my nose for all this time. I should have known something was off. I bet this house is like Tracy Island with fucking rocket ships that pop out of the swimming pool, and secret doors that lead to an underground lair. It wouldn't surprise me. I've seen every James Bond film that ever was, I know how things work."

Cruz barked with laughter. "Oh, no. You might need to lower your expectations a little. You're talking about the British Secret Service. They're a bunch of tight-arse twats when it comes to spending money. We do have an underground shooting range, and a huge storage bunker." He jerked his head towards me.

"And this one has a workshop where all the magic takes place."

I rolled my eyes at that comment. "It doesn't just happen down there," I added. "Most of that goes on in the bedroom too."

Bexley flicked her eyes up and down as if she expected my lewd comeback.

"You don't believe me, eh?" I muttered, fully intending to prove my point.

"I believe you," she chuckled. "But thousands wouldn't."

"You haven't changed one bit," I asserted, flinging the truth out there. "You're just as snarky as ever." I slapped a hand over my heart, pretending to be wounded

"Me?" Bexley snorted. "I think you'll find it was the other way around, she circled her finger to gesture what she meant. "You were the nasty ones. Not me"

Asher scrunched his lips as he thought. "Maybe we should erase the past and start on a clean slate."

He raised his beer bottle, and we all did the same. Bexley rolled her eyes and wiggled her almost empty glass in front of her.

"To new beginnings!" Asher toasted.

We all drank to that. All except for Bexley, who

stared up at Asher with a sarcastic expression stamped on her face.

"Oh? I was holding out my glass for a top-up," she muttered, giving the glass another wiggle.

She was asking for trouble. The little minx was hell-bent on pushing our buttons, just like old times. My brothers and I were going to take great delight in seducing her into submission. I was going to show her just how magical a night with me could be. Did she honestly think I spent all of my time in my workshop inventing spy-gadgets? I had an arsenal of sex-toys that could get her wetter than springtime in England.

Bexley Barker . . . you're in so deep, and you don't even know it yet.

CHAPTER
Seven

Bexley

T he house was exactly how I remembered it —
a spacious, contemporary glass palace with
cream and golden tones. The bi-folding glass doors
framed the oceanic scenery, complimenting the
maritime-themed kitchen.

*You could take Uncle Zane out of the Navy, but you
couldn't take the Navy out of Uncle Zane.*

"Can I have a look at my room?" I asked as the

brothers moseyed around, pouring more drinks and taking snacks from the cupboards. The alcohol had weaved its magic, making me feel all tipsy.

Cruz looked up from the opposite side of the island countertop. "You don't have to ask, Bexley."

I gave Braxton a slight head-jerk. He took the bait and cast a subtle glance around. "I'm going to change out of this suit," he mentioned. "Get me another beer, please, Asher."

Asher pulled another bottle of beer from the drinks chiller and removed the metal cap.

"I'll bring it into the den," he suggested, following Cruz and Dominic into their man-cave at the far side of the estate. "Come join us whenever you're ready, Bex," he offered.

"Okay, I will," I accepted, feeling honoured to be invited into their domain.

Braxton was hot on my heels, slapping my backside as I rushed upstairs. As we arrived at the top in fits of laughter, we veered to the right and paused outside the room between his, and Asher's.

"Would you like to share a shower to save water?" Braxton asked, sounding unabashed by his blatant comment. "I can think of ways in which we can get dirty and clean all at the same time?"

I held my bottom lip between my teeth as I pondered his offer.

So can I.

"You're determined for us to get caught, aren't you?" I accused, running my nails across his chest. I got a rush of butterflies feeling solid muscle beneath his shirt, like some love-sick teenager with a crush.

Braxton's eyes blazed with hunger, and he pressed me against the door, his fingers holding my throat in an act of dominance. I liked the lack of control. He towered over me, making me feel small in comparison, but not in an intimidating manner, more like a safe, treasured, and desired sort of way. It was exhilarating

"So, what if they see? It's not like they wouldn't all love a slice of the action," he mentioned, his lips hovering over mine. I could practically taste the beer on his breath.

My heart skipped a little faster, wishing he would kiss me. "Yeah, right?" I rolled my eyes, not believing that for a second.

Dominic — maybe. But Asher and Cruz? Nah. They were not interested in me.

Braxton arched his brow. "I beg to differ. My brothers would jump into bed with you in a heartbeat."

Really?

I thought about that, liking it more than I should. "Why are you telling me this? I assumed you wanted me for yourself?"

Braxton covered my mouth with his, dominating me with a salacious kiss. His coarse stubble grazed my lips, leaving them feeling bruised and swollen. It filled my head with a sex-hazed fog, unable to think straight.

Braxton's fiery breath gusted against my ear as he whispered, "I do. But it's more fun to share."

Holy shit! Did he just give me the green light to fool around with his brothers?

"They would never go along with this . . . no way." I was certain of it. "And even if they were game, what makes you think I would offer myself around so loosely? I'm up for a bit of harmless flirting, but I'm not an easy lay."

Braxton let out a huff of amusement, then pulled me into my old room. It was a little different from what I remembered. They had repainted the My Little Pony décor with a neutral beige to tie in with the rest of the house. Thank fuck, because that would have been a passion-killer.

Braxton began peeling away his clothing and tossing it aside. "If we're going to get along, you ought to relax," he suggested, hooking his thumbs beneath the elastic of his boxer briefs.

My eyes bulged wide as I saw his giant cock for the second time today. It was so thick and long, he could bludgeon someone to death with it.

"Come on," he encouraged as he stepped out of his clothes. "Get naked for me."

I remained there, slack-jawed, awed by his godly physique, his muscles inked and toned. He peeled off his socks last. His cock swung between his thighs, drawing my eyes to it. "Go ahead." He permitted. "Feel it."

My tongue darted out to dampen my parched lips. Liquid heat flowed from my core, soaking into my suit pants. I craved to touch it — I really did. My clit swelled with the assurance of a good, vigorous fuck. I was commando thanks to him, and dripping with desire. Mirroring his striptease, I unbuttoned my blouse, exposing my heaving breasts, and his cock gave me a standing ovation. Discarding my bra and my trousers, I stepped forward and curled my fingers around his iron-hard rod, rewarding him with soft, dexterous strokes.

"You're so big," I told him, admiring his impressive length. "Biggest I've ever seen."

Braxton shuddered with need, hissing through his clenched teeth; pre-cum beaded at the tip of his cock then dribbled down the head. My ex-partners had been average, if that. A few were even smaller. I had never had an orgasm through penetrative sex before. At least I wouldn't have to fake it with Braxton. The guy had sent me to Heaven and back with his fingers. I couldn't wait to see what his cock could do.

"We're all pretty big, babe," he stated, steering me backwards onto the bed. "Just wait until we take you all together."

The back of my thighs hit the bed and I toppled onto it with a bounce. Braxton grabbed my ankles, yanking me towards him. He dropped to his knees, tossing my legs over both his shoulders.

"All at once?" I breathed; my mind was reeling with the thought.

Did he really mean it?

"It's what we want," he explained, trailing gentle kisses down the insides of my thighs. "One woman to share forever. We don't want to split up and lead separate lives."

I let out a moan as his breath gusted against my mound. My clit pulsed with anticipation.

"Would you go for that? The four of us taking

you to bed each night, worshipping you like a Goddess?" he murmured before his tongue speared between my folds.

"Oh, oh, yes," I moaned, as he varied between dragging lazy circles and soft flicks around my clit.

At this moment, I would have agreed to anything.

Braxton growled as he feasted, lapping me like a professional porn-star. The guy had won medals for every sport under the sun, and right now he had just scored gold at cunnilingus.

"Fuck, yes!" I wailed, dragging a pillow over my face to bite down on.

Braxton Wolfe was eating me better than any man had ever attempted before. This was the best sex of my life, and he hadn't even used his dick yet. I came with a shriek of pleasure, gripping the pillow for support.

"So, was that a "yes" to fucking us all, or a "yes" because you just came apart on my tongue?" he asked, shooting me an accomplished grin.

"Uh!" I groaned, unable to see straight. He blew my mind through the stratosphere, and I was floating back down to earth. "Remind me . . . what was the question?"

"Flip over and turn around," he ordered,

delivering a stinging slap to my thigh. "I'm gonna give you something to think about." He paused for a moment. "Are you on the pill?"

"Yes. You can check my bag if you like," I replied, offering proof

"I believe you," he answered, getting up to his feet.

I did as I was told, rolling over onto my hands and knees. This was just what I needed. I had been dreaming of this moment for so long. Whether it be with Braxton or another of his brothers . . . maybe even all of them, I wasn't too picky. They were all fit as fuck, and the prospect of being intimate with all of them was my deepest, darkest fantasy.

"How do you want it? Fast or slow?" he rasped.

My pussy walls quivered with anticipation.

"Hard, just fuck me fast and hard, so I cum again," I said, needing another body-shaking climax.

His blunt heat pressed against my entrance, then he burst through my cunt as if he was driving my walls apart. Fuck me, Braxton exceeded all my expectations, making my eyes bulge wide. My kitty purred with exultation, welcoming her guest with a fresh gush of cream. He slapped my arse, creating a fiery handprint against my skin. Dragging his length through my inner muscles, he found a steady, pounding rhythm.

"Uh!" I grunted, biting down hard on a pillow.

His ruthless momentum caused the bed to shake. I became more vocal as I reached the crest of my orgasm with Braxton following closely behind. His balls slapped against my labia, the head of his cock hammering against my cervix like it was trying to break through.

"Just like that . . . uh . . . I'm cumming," I cried.

"Oh, fuck," Braxton let out a ragged groan.

His hips jolted with each ejaculation, then he sagged against me, wrapping his arms around my limp body. We lay on the bed together, both wrung out in a post-orgasmic haze.

"I'm so glad you agreed to come here, sweetheart," he cooed, pressing kisses to my throat. "I've waited years for this."

Why didn't he ever reach out to me then? I would have jumped at the opportunity of a relationship with him.

I exhaled with a smile. "You still want to share me with your brothers?" I inquired, doubting if he felt the same as he did before.

Braxton stilled, resting his chin on my shoulder. "Did I convince you to give them a chance?" he swung the question around on me. "You would be getting it four times over."

Why was he pushing this? Didn't he know how wrong that would be?

"I asked you first," I stammered.

Braxton chortled. "Yes, I want that. We all do."

I shuffled around to face him. "Wouldn't that make me a slut?"

Yes, I had fooled around with Braxton within an hour of us being reacquainted, but I could be forgiven for giving into my wanton desires. We were both consenting adults who clearly liked each other. It wasn't as if this was likely to be a one-night stand because he made it clear to me that he wanted more. But sleeping with all of the Wolfe brothers would be crossing some sort of invisible line. One that would change everything

I don't want people to think badly of me?

Braxton flinched as if I just said something scandalous. "Plenty of people share one lover between them. It's called a harem, and there's nothing sinful or degrading about it."

"Is that so? I doubt anyone would see it that way. Men receive a pat on the back for sleeping around, whereas women get branded with a shitty label," I argued

I had spent years building a credible reputation for myself. It would only take one scandal to bring it all crashing to the ground.

"Fuck what anybody else thinks; life is too short to spend worrying about what people might say," Braxton muttered, getting to his feet and ambling into the bathroom.

Shit. I think I just hurt his feelings.

I pushed myself off the bed and staggered after him to use the toilet. My pussy was sore, and that made it uncomfortable to pee. If this was what the aftermath of fucking Braxton felt like, then I could only imagine what it would feel like to sleep with them all. He switched on the shower, waiting a few seconds before stepping into the cubicle. As he closed the panel, his muscular body distorted behind a cloud of steam. Could I really go along with this? The thought of taking them all at once caused my heart to flutter with excitement.

The old Bexley would have seized the opportunity to flush the toilet while Braxton was in the shower, then laugh as he screamed out in pain, but that was then. We're lovers now. The new Bexley slid alongside him and peppered soft kisses against his chest, then reached up onto her tiptoes so she could kiss him.

"My answer is yes," I decided, wanting to explore a relationship with each of them.

Braxton grinned, picking me up in a powerful bear hug. "You won't regret this, Bexley." He put me down, then grabbed the shower gel and a sponge.

We washed and changed into casual clothes. I sent a quick text to my dad, informing him we got here okay, and then to Caz, telling her not to worry and that I would call her as soon as I could. Braxton waited around for me like the perfect gentleman, proving that arseholes could change. I knew I felt something stronger than lust; I was just too afraid to admit it.

The walk to the den seemed to take forever. My heart thumped inside my chest like a slow clap. I was nervous to face the others. Too scared that this was all a joke. We rounded the hallway, turning toward their man-cave. Dance music boomed from inside the room and the heavenly scent of steak and burgers wafted along the hall. I stepped through the door and my jaw fell open with shock.

"Bexley?" Asher eyed me with amusement. "We were about to send out a search party for you." The blue swim shorts he was wearing were just hanging below his V-line. I could make out the dark thatch of hair at the top of his groin. He was the carbon copy of his twin, but with less ink. A nautical themed tattoo covered his left arm in a full sleeve.

It wasn't just the smell of the food that was making me salivate. Cruz was out on the decking, supervising the barbecue with nothing but an apron covering his modesty. The sun was melting into the ocean behind him and the orange hue outlined his firm arse like it was a second layer of skin. Dominic was in the hot tub, submerged to the shoulders in frothing water. He was wearing a pair of aviator shades, which meant I couldn't tell if he was looking at me or not.

Asher walked towards me and held out another generous glass of wine. "Here you go, beautiful."

I took it gratefully, needing a little liquid courage

"Bexley has something she wants to say to you all," Braxton announced, flinging his arm around my shoulders.

Suddenly, my tongue was as dry as the Sahara Desert, and I gulped my wine like I was dying of thirst.

Braxton flashed me an expectant look. "Well, go on then. Don't keep them all in suspense."

"What are you doing?" I whispered from the corner of my mouth.

All eyes settled on me and I wished that the ground would open up and swallow me whole.

"It'll be okay," Braxton prompted.

I turned to them all, blushing furiously. "If this is some kind of joke, I'm going to kill you all," I muttered with humiliation.

"Is it a joke that we want you?" Asher spoke up, confirming everything his twin had said. "I can assure you, it's no joke."

Dominic lifted his shades, letting them rest above his forehead. "We want you to be our girl," he reinforced

"That's a yes from me!" Cruz yelled from the terrace. "So, that's four yeses," he chirped a second later.

"Honestly? You're not just winding me up?" I still waited for the punchline.

I would die if this was just another one of their pranks.

The heat in their eyes conveyed more than words could ever say.

"Sod it; let's go for it," I answered, not one to look a gift horse in the mouth.

Asher produced a bottle of champagne. "This calls for a celebration," he announced, popping the cork

This has got to be a dream. All these years, I

thought the Wolfe brothers hated me. And all this time, they wanted me just as much as I wanted them. For once, I was going to throw caution to the wind and grab the bull by the horns. Braxton was right. Life was too short. Especially with this Chameleon guy lurking around. Who knows what was likely to happen tomorrow?

CHAPTER
Eight

Bexley

I was still coming to terms with the prospect of being shared by the Wolfe brothers. The more champagne I consumed, the looser my tongue became. I lost all my inhibitions whenever I was drunk. It was an awful trait, and I wasn't proud of the way I behaved. When we were young, I always tried to better the boys, but I never came out on top. Collectively they were better, stronger, smarter than me, and I could never compete with that. Time had changed them, maturing them into better men, whereas I was still running to play catch up. Still the same old Bexley. Always two steps behind. Tonight marked the beginning of a new era. I had agreed to take two reckless risks. One that could kill me, and one that could ultimately break my heart.

"So, this is what you boys like to do for fun?" I said, gesturing around and sloshing alcohol onto the decking

Asher's eyes flicked down to the tiny puddle on the floor and amusement flared his eyes.

"Maybe you should slow down, Bex?" he recommended, implying that I'd had enough to drink

I guarded my half-filled flute with my life, preparing to fight him for it. Maybe they were all trained killing machines, but a drunken Bexley wasn't a force to be reckoned with.

"Just you dare try to take this glass from my hand and I will punch you so hard in the dick, it'll become a vagina," I warned.

Dominic and Braxton chortled. I recited how that sounded in my head, failing to understand why they were snickering.

"How about a trade for this burger?" Cruz suggested, wafting the last one in front of my face.

I had devoured three already and wasn't sure if I could stomach another. They were huge, not that I could expect anything less from these guys. Everything they owned was on the large side.

"No, thanks," I declined, scrunching my nose. "I feel so full."

He shrugged as if to say "suit yourself" and ate it himself. It was his eighth one.

Greedy pig

How did he maintain those abs?

Asher wasn't taking no for an answer. He wanted me to step away from the booze and eye-signalled the others a silent plea. I didn't notice them creeping up on me from behind; Braxton curled his fingers around the stem of the flute as Dominic held me around the waist and started kissing my neck. It was a shameless tactic, but together they attained their goal.

It didn't surprise me that they ganged-up on me. They always did perform well as a pack. It was an unfair advantage, but being an only child, I envied the bond they shared.

"Do you want to take a walk on the beach?" Dominic suggested distracting me. "It's a warm night."

Perhaps an evening stroll was just what I needed to clear my head. "Sure, why not?" I replied. "Just as long as the mosquitoes don't bite me to death. They seem to love my blood type. Annoying little bastards," I complained.

Despite the insects, Sandbanks was a beautiful place to grow up, and I could understand why my mother adored it so much. I hadn't been here long, and already my memories were coming back to me in fractured snippets. I thought I remembered something about the pendant, and recalled my mother mentioning how each piece represented me and the Wolfe brothers, but I couldn't be certain if it was a dream or reality. Maybe she designed it to bring us together again. Who knows? That was a question that only my mum could answer, and when she died, she took the truth with her. My insecurities were telling me to tread with caution because I could end up getting my heart broken. The Wolfe brothers had always been out of my league, and for all I knew, our arrangement could have an expiry date.

What if they want to end things once the mission is complete? What then? Are we just supposed to go back to being friends? I'm not sure I can do that.

Dominic took me by the hand. I liked the intimacy even though it seemed strange. A short while ago, I was upstairs having sex with Braxton and now I was accompanying his brother on a romantic stroll on the beach. It was so exhilarating.

Braxton hung back to help Cruz clear away the dishes, which left Asher free to join us. He jogged across the sand until he caught up to us, his feet sinking through the soft grains until he reached the water's edge. He arrived at my side, entwining his fingers with mine. Now I was wedged between them, allowing them to swing my arms back and forth like this was the most casual thing in the world. Dare I say it . . . I felt happy; even with the looming uncertainty of what tomorrow might bring, this moment of unity touched my heart and breathed life into my soul.

I couldn't let myself fall for them. I mustn't.

It would be fun while it lasted, and then we would go back to our old lives as if nothing had happened. They'd soon forget about me, whereas I would carry the shame forever. This had to be kept secret between us five. My father could never find out about this. No one could. They wouldn't understand.

"How come you're not ready to settle down?" I asked, fishing for information.

The thought of them being with anyone other than me caused my innards to squirm with jealousy. I wanted them all for myself. I didn't care if that meant I was greedy. It was just how I felt.

"Who says we're not?" Asher answered as if he had decided. "But this business with the Chameleon throws a spanner in the works. We can't afford to let our guard down. Our happily ever after will have to wait until we complete the mission."

It was just as I thought, this was just a bit of fun to pass the time.

"Yeah, I suppose so. But what about after?" I mentioned, disguising the hurt in my voice.

I want you all to choose me.

"That's the spirit, Bexley," Dominic praised, sounding upbeat. "I knew we could count on you to think positively in a moment of a crisis. You're already talking about what happens afterwards." He brought our entwined hands up to his lips and pressed another kiss to my skin. "That, babe, is up to you"

Wait! What?

"Up to me?" I bounced my gaze between them.

I wish I hadn't drunk so much. My head was spinning. The mixture of alcohol and the sea air was making me giddy. But he just said it was up to me, and his words sobered me up like an ice-cold wave had crashed over me.

Dominic pressed a kiss to my temple and my heart melted. "We don't want to rush things with you; we're in this for the long haul."

"Really? Do you mean it?" I asked, unable to grasp reality. "Do you really see this going somewhere?"

"Yes," Dominic answered, side-eyeing me.

"Of course, we want this to work," Asher reinforced. "We wanted to wait until we are all together, so we can explain how we feel."

I was floating on air. "All right, we can talk about it later," I agreed.

"Before I forget. You have your first lesson tomorrow at 06:00. Cruz will train you in the gym," Asher mentioned as an afterthought.

"The gym at six?" I half-choked on thin air. "Bloody hell, that's early. I thought he was going to teach me how to fight?"

And there was me thinking it was going to be at a reasonable time during the afternoon. Not at the bum-crack of dawn.

"You can't just jump straight into hand-to-hand combat practice without a little preparation first. You have to build muscle mass and work on your inner core. We need you to be fighting fit in under six weeks. That includes sticking to a strict dietary program," Asher explained, reminding me how much of a know-it-all he was, and how it used to irk me.

At least he didn't follow me around, pointing out random facts like he used to.

"So, no more booze and burgers?" I muttered with sarcasm.

Asher huffed a smile. "Tonight was a free pass to celebrate. We will be eating clean from now on."

It seems we had conflicting ideas on how we could work on my inner core. From the moment they mentioned sharing me, I had dragged my mind through the gutter. As the sky transitioned from light to dark, we made our way back home.

Braxton and Cruz were relaxing in the hot tub when we returned. The decking was wet where they had scrubbed the barbecue clean and rinsed it off. Asher wasted no time in hopping in the frothy water, followed by Dominic.

"Leave room for Bexley," Cruz berated them, making sure there was a space for me.

My stomach fluttered with nerves. I watched their casual interaction through hungry eyes, ran my tongue over my lips as droplets of water skated through the contours of their muscles, and clenched my thighs together as they cupped water in their hands to splash over their faces. Asher and Dominic raked their hair into slicked-back styles, and Cruz and Braxton scrubbed their palms over their buzz cuts, all clearing the water from their eyes. Their damp skin glistened beneath the soft hue of the patio lights. These four mouth-watering Adonises were mine, and now they were looking at me with questioning frowns, wondering why I hadn't stripped down to my underwear to join them.

"Come in, Bexley," Braxton urged, beckoning me over. "There's plenty of room."

"Yeah, we promise not to bite," Cruz rasped, followed by a dark chuckle.

CHAPTER
Nine

Bexley

The look on their faces suggested they would eat me alive if I wasn't careful. My cheeks blazed with heat. I turned away, so I could undress with a little confidence. Not that it worked because I could feel their eyes roaming all over my body. The black lacy undergarments were enough to cover my modesty but left nothing to the imagination. They had picked it out purposefully, along with the rest of my wardrobe. Everything hung, clung, and hugged my curves, emphasizing all my best assets. The awestruck expressions on their faces told me it was all money well spent.

Their arms reached out for me as I stepped into the warm water, hands caressed me as I settled down between them, their lips and stubble delivering a contrast of rough versus smooth against my shoulders. I couldn't tell who was who as I closed my eyes, but I didn't care. They moved like a single entity, warming me up and making me feel good. This was the welcome back I envisaged in my dreams, and the reality exceeded all of my expectations. Their fingers trailed across my skin, evoking a plethora of sensations. I wanted them all, but I was too afraid to say that out loud.

"This is what it means to belong to us," Braxton murmured against my ear, "the four of us pleasing you. You're ours to love; ours to protect, and we hope that you learn to love us given time."

Asher turned my chin so I was facing him; his eyes flicked down to my lips and back again as if seeking permission. My heart was beating so fast, I thought I was going to pass out. I leaned in, and he met me half-way, stealing my breath with an earth-shattering kiss. The euphoric buzz fogged my head as they passed me around, taking it in turns to kiss me. Braxton was second, Dominic third, then Cruz made his turn count, lifting me by my arse and seating me onto his lap. My pussy rocked against his solid cock before noticing he was bare. He swallowed my gasp of surprise, meeting my gaze with a lewd grin.

"So, this is serious?" I had to check. "You're not just going to dump me the second I crack this code?"

Hurt flickered through their eyes, but it was a sign I wanted to see. It meant they cared about me in the same way that I felt about them.

Cruz held my waist, giving me a gentle squeeze. "Never," he replied without a moment's hesitation. "You're here where you belong"

I leaned in to kiss him again, this time curling my fingers around his impressive length, shocked that he was as big as Braxton.

"Fuck, Bexley," Cruz hissed under his breath.

He reached up and unclasped my bra with a flick of his wrist and I shucked it from my body like I was glad to be rid of it. The man was a mystery, but I knew exactly what he wanted at this moment, and that was me. Cruz dragged me against him; the heat from his breathing gusted over my bare breasts before he sucked a nipple into his mouth.

The Wolfe pack surrounded me like I was theirs to devour. I gave in to temptation, feeling their exploratory touch encompassing me, and not knowing whose hands wandered where. Cruz ripped my thong to one side and his cock presented against my parted slit. I was still tender from where Braxton had taken me earlier, but my pussy offered little resistance as it welcomed the intrusion. Cruz applied an upward thrust that filled me, taking my breath away. He snarled with lust as he tore my thong to pieces, then tossed the ruined lace onto the decking. Dominic swallowed my moans in a sensual kiss, and Asher and Braxton toyed with my nipples as Cruz stroked me into oblivion. The water frothed around us, spilling over the sides as we fucked like savages.

"You like that, Bexley?" Cruz grunted; his face scrunched with pleasure. "Do you think you could take us all?"

"Yes," I mewled.

I threw my head back as I rocked my hips, succumbing to the pressure that claimed my body. Heat, suction, the force of Cruz's cock as it pummelled my abused pussy. Then his thumb hit the detonator of my sex, rubbing my clit and blowing my brains all over the decking.

"That's it . . . cum for us," Cruz encouraged; his words strained with need.

"Uh, oh god," I cried, letting myself go.

Lights flashed behind my eyelids, my body tensed, Cruz's cock jerked as my walls constricted around it, holding it there in a death grip.

He came with a grunt, his fingertips digging into my flesh as he rode out his climax. My god, Cruz Wolfe looked as sexy as hell when pleasure consumed him.

My lovers drew back, giving me a minute to breathe. Cruz eased me up to slide his cock out of me; the temperature of the water helped to ease the after-burn, but after a night with the Wolf pack, they made sure to ruin it for any other man. Maybe that was the point. I would never want anyone else after I had a taste of them.

Asher peeled off his swim shorts and tossed them over the side of the tub. They landed on the decking with a splat. I took it as a sign he wished to go next, so I slid onto his lap to kiss him. He turned so I'd miss. At first, it confused me, but as he started trailing kisses along my throat, breasts, jaw, and up to my lips again, I knew that he wanted to savour his turn. His controlled movements left me shaking with desire. He knew exactly how to excite me, swirling his tongue against mine like he was making love to my mouth.

Cruz, Braxton, and Dominic relaxed back to watch the show, their hands clasped behind their heads in the lounge position. Two more pairs of shorts landed with a splat, letting me know there was more fun to come. As Asher pushed into me, he groaned with satisfaction, his breathing quivering as he exhaled. Unlike Cruz and Braxton, his pace was slow and controlled. Each roll of his hips felt like a nudge against the apex of my sex, eliciting breathy moans from my lips.

"We want you to stay with us forever," he murmured; his eyes looked deep within mine as if he was searching my soul for the answer. "What do you say?"

His sensuous whispers and his reverent touch fanned the embers of my desire, setting my body alight.

"I want that," I replied, matching his pace with every hip-roll, our lips touching. "Oh, god, I want that so much."

My abdominals tightened as another orgasmic wave engulfed me, drowning me in an ocean of bliss.

"Then you're ours. We're yours. We belong

together," he breathed; he had reached the pinnacle of his climax, I could see the tension in his eyes.

All it took for me to push us over the precipice was to say the magic words, "I'm yours."

Our bodies locked in a lover's embrace, feeling the exchange of heat flowing between us. His kisses remained gentle, his eyes glimmering with affection. We were wrung out and spent; I sagged against him, needing something sturdy to anchor on to. The moon shone above us like a spotlight; the stars glittered like a canopy of twinkling lights, reflecting on the ocean like scattered diamonds.

"This is amazing," I confessed, unable to accept that this was real. "I can't believe how cool you are about this."

"It's always been you, Bexley," Asher declared. "This was how it was always meant to be."

He had a way with words that could make a woman swoon, and this was a perfect example. It didn't matter why or how he came to that conclusion. All that mattered was here and now.

Asher shifted beneath me, allowing Braxton and Dominic to claim their prize. They had waited long enough. Asher took a seat beside Cruz, admiring my swollen breasts and how my flushed skin glowed blue under the moonlight.

"Isn't she stunning?" Asher said to Cruz.

Cruz's eyes were glazed with lust. "The most perfect woman I have ever seen," he agreed with Asher.

Braxton stroked the wet hair back from my face, gazing down upon me with pure devotion. "And she's ours. She accepted us."

"I did," I assured them all, "I told you already. I don't want this to end."

And I didn't. Whatever the cost, my heart was invested. I was trusting them not to break it.

"It won't," Dominic murmured, circling his finger around my areola before suckling the puckered bud into his hot mouth. Braxton did the same on the other side; their foreplay progressed into a tag team where Braxton leaned me back as Dominic draped my legs over his shoulders. My sore pussy cooled in the evening breeze, still pulsing from all the friction.

"Keep her still," Dominic coached, his mouth covering my mound as his tense muscle speared between my folds.

"Oh, uh," I moaned, writhing in Braxton's arms.

Dominic's tongue slithered around my clit like a serpent, fluctuating between smooth glides and ruthless flicks. He inserted one finger into my fleshy cavern, then another, stretching me with a scissor motion. Just when I thought I couldn't cum again, I did. This time, it was with such ferocity, my pleasure splashed straight into Dominic's open mouth.

He chuckled his approval. "Oh, you are a filthy bitch," he remarked as he lapped it all up, feasting upon me like he couldn't get enough. "You're gonna get fucked so hard, you'll struggle to walk tomorrow."

My body spasmed with sensitivity, my eyeballs rolling to the back of my skull. I had never had so much cock in one year, let alone in one day. They were in complete control of my body, and I was loving every minute.

Dominic lounged back as I sank on his dick, then pulled me down for a kiss. I could taste myself on his lips, and that only made this seem dirtier.

"Just try to relax," he cooed as Braxton caressed me from behind.

"What are you going to do?" I asked, tensing as the pad of his finger pressed against the tight knot of my arsehole.

Braxton chuckled, then leaned over me, pressing his chest against my back. "I'm not going to take you there tonight . . . but soon," he promised, making me shudder with desire.

"Are you climbing aboard with us?" Dominic

offered; he made it sound as casual as hopping on to the back of his surfboard to catch some waves.

"What do you think, Bex? Is there room inside for one more?" Braxton rasped, presenting his massive erection against my arse.

"Both won't fit inside there," I panicked, afraid they would split me in two.

"They will," Asher assured from across the tub. "A vaginal muscle is elastic; it can achieve double penetration as long as you take things slowly and breathe through it."

I had done nothing like this before and wasn't sure what to expect.

"You can try, but the moment it hurts, I want you to stop," I told them, entrusting them to take good care of me.

At first, it felt impossible. I was already filled with Dominic's cock, but Braxton kept pushing a little at a time. It burned at the second intrusion, and I wasn't convinced my pussy could take it. Braxton's persistence paid off, and I could feel myself opening up to accommodate him.

"Uh, oh god," I chanted my mantra as the stretch and burn delivered another wave of pleasure and pain

"Fuck, Bexley," Dominic groaned beneath me as Braxton continued to work his cock inside.

This was a whole new level of sinful; two brothers fucking me in unison, their cocks sliding together inside me, their hunky bodies sandwiching me with all their godly gorgeousness.

"Look how great we are together?" Braxton grunted into my ear.

Dominic placed his hands behind his head as he lay back and enjoyed the ride. All I could do was hang on to his sculpted shoulders for dear life. My body thrummed with each hard thrust as Braxton took charge of the helm, steering us to our climactic destination. A tsunami of pleasure hit me, rocking me to the core. Dominic was the first to roar his release, and I came a close second, Braxton increased his momentum as he chased his finish, barking out a harsh cry. Their cocks swelled and at first, it was too much, and I let out a shriek of discomfort. The pressure subsided within moments, enabling us to relax and slump together in a boneless, panting mess.

"Marry us," Dominic uttered breathlessly.

Shocked gasps came from the other three, like Dom had spoiled some kind of surprise.

"What?" I spluttered, astounded by those two words.

My men came at me from all sides, stroking, kissing, touching, taking good care of what was theirs.

"We wanted to wait a while to do this, but Dominic is right, why wait? Bexley Barker, will you do us the great honour of becoming our wife?" Braxton asked

My jaw hung agape as I struggled to process what just happened.

CHAPTER
Ten

Bexley

"I just froze like an idiot," I admitted, pacing the room with my phone against my ear. "So, now you know everything"

Caz growled with irritation. "Ugh, Bexley!"

I cringed, shoving images from last night's events to one side. "I know," I groaned. "You should have seen their faces; they were crushed."

"Tell me what you said, you heartless bitch?" she

teased. "I'm still amazed you bagged yourself four blokes, you lucky cow." I could hear the envy in her voice

The sound of footsteps approached my room and my stomach sank with caution. I wasn't supposed to be making calls, but I needed to tell my best friend.

"I said that I had to think about it. I have to go, someone is coming," I explained, rushing my words before hanging up.

I hid my phone beneath my pillow and scooted away from the bed. A gentle knock alerted me to the door, and I faked composure.

"Come in," I called out.

Cruz emerged wearing a grey muscle top and loose-fitted shorts; his brown eyes flitted around my room with suspicion. "Did I just hear you talking to yourself?" he asked, sounding puzzled.

I swallowed thickly. "Yeah, I often mutter to myself when I'm looking for something," I lied.

He cast me a dubious look. "That's the early symptom of lunacy, you know?"

"Yeah, well," I returned, curling my arms across my exposed midsection. "Things have been a little crazy lately. I might as well hop aboard the loony train"

His stoic expression gave nothing away, making

me wonder what he was thinking about. Last night was special for all of us, and I wrecked it by behaving like a coward.

"I see you're dressed and ready for training," he commented, checking out my gym attire with approval.

The pink crop top and black lycra shorts clung to my body like a second layer of skin. I might as well be nude for all the good it did.

I assumed he was going to bring up what happened last night, but he didn't. "Have you eaten any breakfast?" he asked, making sure.

I nodded. "I snuck downstairs while you all went for a run," I admitted, feeling sheepish.

He huffed through his nose, shaking his head as he turned to leave. That was my cue to follow. I wanted to make it up to them but didn't know how.

"Wait, Cruz," I called him back, rushing to catch up with him at the top of the stairs.

He slowed his pace but didn't spare me a side-glance. I could feel the tension rolling off him in waves.

"I'm sorry about last night," I blurted out, meaning it. "But you sprung it on me."

And was it too much to ask to get a massive shiny

diamond? They were wealthy enough to afford a huge platinum dazzler.

As we arrived at the bottom step, he turned to me. "I know, we shouldn't have bombarded you." He gripped the bridge of his nose and released a heavy sigh. "I hope you haven't changed your mind about giving this a go."

He wasn't upset with me; it concerned him they might have spoiled things.

"Of course not," I reassured. "And I never said no. I said I needed space to consider it. Marriage is an enormous step, and I have to make sure that my father will support this."

I caught the flinch in his eyes and wondered what that might mean. Had he realised the ramifications of our relationship might have and all the trouble that might cause? We may be on board with living a harem lifestyle, but our parents might not be. I didn't want this to drive a wedge between my father and me. If he wouldn't support my decision, then this couldn't proceed. It just couldn't.

Cruz nodded. "Don't think about that now. We ought to concentrate on training you."

"But we can still have fun, right?" I asked, hoping that this wouldn't change the things we started.

"Fun?" He chuckled, flashing a kilowatt smile. "I think we had more than fun, Bexley."

He was right, it was incredible. It was the most erotic, and most exhilarating feeling I had ever experienced

Cruz began the morning session by teaching me some stretches. They were like Yoga positions and my mind strayed to the gutter when he eased me into the Downward Facing Dog position. He explained how this would strengthen my inner core. My arm muscles strained with the torture of maintaining the plank position for thirty seconds; I was so out of shape, red-faced, and groaning. By the time the stopwatch beeped, I collapsed to the floor in a breathless mess.

"Now we're going to do some HIIT exercises," Cruz announced like he was Mr Fucking Motivator. "Let's start with some climbing ladder circuits, aiming for the highest level within twenty minutes: ten burpees, fifteen dynamic planks, ten diamond push-ups, fifteen squat jumps, and twenty-five jumping jacks."

He lost me at the first one. "What the fuck is a burpee?" I asked, not understanding what it was.

It wasn't like I was a gym virgin; I had been to the gym with Caz many times, but we went to the Clubbercise classes. That was the highlight of my week. Every Tuesday at half-past-eleven in the morning, we got to jump around the sports hall to Clubland classics, waving orange and pink glow sticks around. I thought dynamic planks and circuit ladders were items in a hardware store.

"Allow me to demonstrate," Cruz voiced before performing the four-step action, then showing me how each one should be done. He completed a full circuit without breaking so much as a sweat.

"Now you try," he insisted, holding his stopwatch.

The torture lasted for two-and-a-half hours before I tapped out, demanding we take a break.

Cruz towered over me as I lay with my back against the floor, staring up at his handsome face. Any woman would be ecstatic to marry one of the Wolfe men, not to mention all four.

"Help me up," I whined, holding out my hand.

Cruz grinned, then grasped my clammy fingers, yanking me up from the floor. My muscles wept with dismay. The fucking evidence had seeped out through my pores and had formed a Bexley-shaped puddle on the mat. And if Cruz kept looking at me the way he was doing with such heated intensity, I would need to find a wet floor sign for another slippery issue. I was gross, sweaty, and destroyed from last night and this morning's antics, but I could still happily spread my legs for this fine specimen of a man.

"Shower?" he suggested, now that I was standing

"I better had," I mentioned, hoping I didn't stink too badly.

The label on my deodorant tin claimed I would be floral-fresh for twenty-four hours, but that was before I turned into Sweaty Betty. I didn't want to take any chances. Cruz's warm, salty essence smelled of raw masculinity. It was arousing, not unpleasant. Beads of perspiration covered his brow, and his muscle top darkened in places where the moisture had absorbed.

For a lingering moment, it looked as if he might kiss me. I licked my lips to moisten them.

"What?" I asked, wondering why he was hesitating

Whatever he was thinking about, it was there on the tip of his tongue, but he refused to spit it out. That frustrated me. I wanted to hear him say it.

"Last night," he mentioned, dallying around the subject as if it were a fragile topic. "It was the best night of my life."

My heart melted into a puddle, gushing straight through my pussy and into my knickers.

"Mine too," I told him, pulling his sticky shirt at the front.

Cruz took the hint and leaned down for a kiss. His lips were warm, my tongue exploring every inch of his wholesome, clean mouth. He smiled against me, breaking the kiss and leaning his clammy head against mine.

"How about we shower together?" he offered; his voice was thick with lust.

He didn't need to ask me twice. Cruz scooped me into his arms and carried me to the bathroom. Who could have guessed that this strong, dominant man could show such reverence? The man was immense in every possible aspect. He turned on the shower, toed off his trainers, and peeled off his clothes.

When he placed me down and stripped away my clothes, he raked his eyes over my body and said, "Up against the tiles or on the floor?"

"Surprise me," I returned, grabbing his cock by the root.

"My kind of girl," he rasped, flashing a lascivious grin

He was already hard and pulsing in my hand, his balls swelling with the urge to fuck.

Climbing him like a tree, I held on to his shoulders and wrapped my legs around his waist.

Cruz carried me into the shower; the heat of the water jets and the cold wall tiles contrasting against my skin as he nudged against my entrance. Steam filled the room with a white mist.

"Permission to come aboard, miss," he rasped, his voice drenched with need.

I shoved against him, pressing my heels against his arse. "Granted . . . now just fucking do it already."

His thrust impaled me, slamming me into the wall. "Fuck," I moaned, loving the stretch and burn he gave as his thick, meaty cock speared through my pussy walls, again and again.

Cruz groaned his enjoyment, ravishing me like a beast, his lips sucking my neck in a claim-staking hickey. The pressure was building and I could no longer fight it; he was hitting all the right notes to make my body dance to his tune. We came simultaneously in the throes of ecstasy, matching his thrusts until we mashed together in a tense spasm.

"Christ, Bexley," Cruz panted. "You feel amazing"

His seed oozed out of me as he withdrew, our chests heaving as we caught our breath.

"Mm," I hummed with contentment, wrapping my arms around him like he was a hunky teddy bear. He made me feel safe, just like the day he swam to my rescue in the pool. "I always wanted a big strong daddy like you," I confessed a secret desire, one that I used to fantasize about.

"All I've ever wanted was a princess to spoil, so good things do come to those who wait, wouldn't you say?"

I never would have imagined a stern man like Cruz would admit to that and show his soft side. My heart chimed with delight.

Cruz reached for the shower gel and a scrubbing poof and washed me, then cleaned himself. He did the same when washing my hair, and I let him, cherishing the precious moment between us. This was a *"for my eyes only"* side of Cruz that he was reluctant to share with anyone else, not even his brothers. My very own James Bond replica, but much more attentive

---

Asher

"You just had to propose," I huffed, glaring at the back of Dominic's head. "Even an idiot knows you should never propose to a woman while you're fucking her."

He had been ignoring me all morning, tapping away on his computer screen like his fingers were possessed

"Don't blame him, he was following his heart," Braxton defended him, scowling through the window at the tide going out. "Your heart isn't the only one on the line. We all love Bexley."

My twin was right. Now that we'd had a taste of her, we were terrified of losing her. I could tell by Dominic's brooding that he was shouldering the guilt. We agreed that we would ease her into things before we presented her with a marriage proposal. I just hope we didn't scare her off.

"Well, it could have been worse," I conceded, looking on the bright side. "At least she didn't say no."

Dominic stopped typing, his fingers hovering over the keyboard. He sucked in a breath and released a weary sigh. "Yeah, but you didn't see the look in her eyes. I couldn't miss it because she was sitting on my dick at the time," he muttered, sounding crestfallen.

I placed my hand against his shoulder and felt him sag. "But it wasn't a no," I reiterated. "She said she needed time to think about it, so that's exactly what we'll give her."

Braxton pushed off the countertop and turned to

face the hall. "Bexley?" he acknowledged, the tone of his voice brightening

"Hi, guys," Bexley greeted as she slumped into the kitchen and collapsed onto a stool beside the breakfast bar. Her hair was wet from showering. "Cruz is a nightmare," she complained. "I'm wrung out."

You look like it, too. Don't think that love bite hasn't gone unnoticed

"It's nothing that an hour in the hot tub won't solve," I suggested, forgetting myself for a moment.

Bexley flicked her gaze to me with an arched brow. "Don't even think about it. I'm aching all over."

I wasn't insinuating we have sex, just pointing out that we have a perfectly good form of relaxation sitting out there on the veranda, that's all. My brothers and I exchanged a puzzled look between us, shocked that she wasn't recoiling at the idea, just stating that she wasn't in the mood. Cruz entered the room with a towel slung over his shoulder. He had showered and changed into a pair of military shorts and a clean T-shirt. He tossed his towel and a bundle of dirty laundry into the basket beside the washing machine

"She did good," he told us, motioning to Bexley. "She kept up with me"

Braxton's brows lifted with surprise. "Did she?"

It was obvious they had sex in the shower. They both radiated an after-sex glow. No wonder she walked into the kitchen as if she was saddle sore. I bet she hadn't recovered from last night.

Cruz nodded, staring back at Bexley with pride in his eyes. "We can start with the weights tomorrow morning. You can join us if you like?" he suggested, glancing at Braxton.

Bexley flicked her gaze to me and flashed a shy smile. Braxton and Cruz began talking about ways they could combine their training regime. Dominic resumed working; his lips pressed into a tight, thin line as he frowned at the monitor. Bexley glanced at him; her lips parted as if she wanted to say something but decided against it.

"How about some lunch?" I asked her. "I bet you're famished."

She nodded, gingerly. "I am; that would be great, thank you."

I rustled up some chicken salad and made a simple lemon dressing from scratch. My brothers liked to tease me for my culinary skills, but at least I knew how to please a woman in more ways than one. Bexley loved food, and from what we learned about her last night was that her sexual taste varied as much as her appetite.

The house phone rang and Dominic snatched the handset to answer it. "Hello?" he spoke, holding the phone between his shoulder and jaw as he carried on working. Fuck, the man could multitask.

He flicked his gaze to me. "It's Dad. He wants to talk to you," he notified, passing the phone to me

I took it and walked out onto the patio. Bexley watched through the window as she nibbled her lunch

"He's on the move," Dad warned, and I sensed the anxiety in his tone. "One of our agents tipped off Intel, informing them that the Chameleon left Moscow this morning. He disappeared quickly after carrying out a hit. His target was a Russian diplomat named Mikhail Volkov."

What? This doesn't sound good.

The moisture evaporated in my mouth. "Where is he now? Is there a location marker on him?"

Dad's breath rattled down the line. "No, he eluded capture yet again. He could be anywhere, posing as anyone."

Shit. That's not what I wanted to hear.

"What was his motive for killing the diplomat?" I probed further.

"We can rule out any speculation of a hired strike because he was part of the Russian Mafia. They assume it was a rival family, and are out for blood," Dad reported. "This was just a means of distracting our agents so he could make his escape."

Nah, there had to be more to it than that.

"What did you say his name was again?" I asked, struggling to connect the dots.

"Volkov," Dad repeated.

My gaze drifted out to sea as I thought, then it struck me like a comet. "It's a message."

"How so?" Dad queried, "I don't quite follow."

"The name Volkov derives from the word volk, meaning wolf. He's sending us a message. He's coming for us," I mentioned.

The hairs on the back of my neck bristled in the ocean breeze.

He's after Bexley's pendant.

"You know what to do," Dad instructed. "Lie low until you receive the signal. In the event of a security breach, relocate to Alpha One."

"Where are you?" I asked, noticing the line was crackling. "The line is terrible."

"Do you remember that decommissioned vessel Jaxx and I salvaged from the Navy? The HMS

Triumph. She's docked in Portsmouth. I'm speaking to you from the helm."

"Don't go planning any last crusades," I warned, dissuading my father from another reckless quest. "The last one ended disastrously."

"Where's Bexley?" Dad asked, changing the subject.

I glanced over my shoulder, witnessing Bexley averting her eyes. "Eating her lunch. She's been training with Cruz all morning."

"Step it up a notch," Dad insisted. "Your brother has been working tirelessly to decipher the clues that Safi left. He needs Bexley to fill in the missing pieces of the puzzle"

I locked eyes with Bexley, and this time she didn't look away.

"We're running out of time," Dad said with an exhausted sigh. "We're all counting on you kids. Millions of lives are at stake."

"No pressure then," I muttered, just as Bexley stepped out on the veranda.

I hung up and tapped the phone against my palm.

"What is it?" she asked, sensing that something was wrong.

I couldn't lie, but I couldn't terrify her either. This called for a tactful distraction.

"That was my dad. He has only gone and salvaged a boat," I announced, rolling my eyes.

Bexley raised her brows in acknowledgement. "Oh. Well, I'm sure there is a reason for that. It might come in useful."

Yes, to take you to the other side of the earth and out of the Chameleon's reach.

I ushered her back inside and closed the doors, not leaving anything to chance. Dominic glanced up from his computer monitor and frowned.

"What did he want?" he muttered inquisitively.

I gestured to a chair. "Sit down, Bex."

Dominic bristled, still reeling with the wounds of rejection

"I'm afraid this can't wait," I told them. "We need to work on solving the clues."

"Right now?" he replied in a clipped tone. "I'm sure Bexley feels exhausted after her workout session with Cruz."

Bexley took a seat beside Dominic and pressed a kiss to his cheek. Her hand slid along his leg and settled in his groin. His eyes danced between hers with an air of uncertainty.

"Who says I'm tired? I'll make it worth your while," Bexley cooed.

I turned to leave, intending to give them some privacy

"Where do you think you're going?" Bexley called after me

I spared a backward glance and saw the heat in her eyes. Her fingers set to work releasing Dominic's belt, then wriggled beneath his khakis to seize his cock. I watched his head roll back with pleasure.

"Fuck, Bexley," he hissed as she began to stroke him.

"Stay," she urged, tapping the seat beside her. "I want to make it up to you both for last night."

Only an idiot would have refused, and I wasn't considered one

CHAPTER
Eleven

Bexley

I t was a race to see who would finish first. Both Dominic and Asher's faces scrunched with pleasure, their cocks thick and hard, like silk and steel beneath my fingers.

"Bex—" Dominic sounded breathy.

Lust swirled like a storm in their eyes. Asher's groans were getting desperate. It was only a matter of time before ecstasy engulfed them, reaching the height of their climaxes. My arm muscles burned with the effort, but it was worth it to see the end result. They were putty in my hands, their hips jerking in their seats as hot strands of cum erupted from the tips of their cocks and splashed onto their stomachs, some seeping over my hands.

"Uh," Asher groaned, slumping back in his chair. "Fuck, Bexley. Your touch is like magic."

"I thought we needed to clear the air after last night," I mentioned. "It wasn't a no — it was a "let me speak to my father first"," I reinforced.

"So, it would be a "yes" if your dad approves?" Dominic asked, panting for air.

The elated smile on his face aroused my suspicions. It wasn't going to be as simple as getting his blessing. Maybe one of them could achieve it, but not all four. My dad would have a stroke if he knew I had slept with them all. Mum helped to change their nappies for fuck's sake. He considered them his nephews.

"Do you know something that I don't?" I challenged, darting my eyes between them.

"Save it," Asher interrupted. "There isn't time for this. I just got off the phone with Dad. We need to work out how we're going to unlock the files because the Chameleon has fled Moscow. He could be headed to the United Kingdom for all we know."

Dominic and Asher left to clean up while I washed my hands in the sink. When they returned wearing lounge shorts and casual T-shirts, we settled around the computer monitor and watched as Dominic worked

I glanced at my pendant, noticing the six different markings matched the symbols on the screen. There were many more. To anyone who didn't know better, they looked like ancient runes, but I knew differently. It was a language my mother developed long before I was born. I studied the screen, realizing that she had arranged them into sentences, just like the ones she used to give me to solve.

"I know this," I mentioned, pointing at the screen. "My mother came up with those symbols as a way of talking in code. Those are messages. Each one means something unique. It's not so much an alphabet, but the ones with dots and dashes represent numbers. This one represents "home"." I pointed to a triangular marking, then explained a few more that represented "night" and "day". I held up my pendant. "It is the same with the symbols on my necklace," I told them. "The first four sections represent the four elements, earth, air, fire, and water.

Mum said she chose those particular symbols to represent you."

Braxton had to be the water element. Cruz was definitely fire. Dominic was best suited to air, leaving Asher as earth. There were two more, but I wasn't sure which one of them applied to me. The universe and life. My mother told me that one day, I would figure it out.

Asher peered at the screen with intrigue. "They have to mean something. Maybe she left a trail of clues to follow." He handed me a pad of paper and a pen. "Try to remember what each symbol means and write them down in that same sequence. We might just be on to something here."

I did as he instructed, jotting down all that I could think of. At first, it didn't make sense, but then Asher spotted something that I didn't.

"What is this? These are all numerals, star constellations, and a load of old waffle. What was my mother thinking when she came up with this?" I complained, feeling like I had wasted the afternoon going around in circles.

"I think that was her point. Only someone who knew what they were looking for would figure it out," Asher explained. "I think it's a genius idea. Even if the enemy tortured you for this information, they wouldn't know what to do with it. These are codes inside codes, and I have a hunch that they represent coordinates. It's as I thought; she left us a trail of clues to follow"

"So, why are we trying to break it if it's so well protected?" I questioned. "We could leave it be and the Chameleon will never get his hands on it."

Asher sighed. "It isn't as simple as that. Some powerful people will stop at nothing to get their hands on them. Thanks to the Chameleon, they knew your mother was the key to obtaining the files. When she died, she entrusted her secrets to you. As long as those files exist, Bexley, your life is in danger."

The severity hit home, leaving me no other choice than to end this once and for all. The alternative would be to do nothing and die. That didn't sound very heroic to me.

"If we follow the clues, mum will lead us to the location of the real code," I realised, astounded at all the thought my mother had put into all of this.

"Bravo, Miss Barker," Dominic praised her memory. "Your mum was a phenomenal woman."

"You're telling me," I agreed. "Home-maker by day, and code-breaker by night. I hope you're not measuring me by her standard or you'll be sorely disappointed"

"I think we should share this information with Braxton and Cruz," Asher suggested, not wanting to waste any time. "This is huge. We are one step closer to destroying the files, then we can put this nightmare behind us."

Dominic winced. "Actually . . . there are six steps before we can put an end to this." He tapped his finger against the pad of paper. "We have five locations to visit before we obtain the last clue," he reminded us, pointing out that we still had a long way to go until we reach our goal.

We shared the frustration, mirroring the same pained expression. This would be the perfect opportunity for me to open a bottle of wine and finish it within the hour, but thanks to Asher's clean-living rule, alcohol was out of the question. I would kill for a large glass of Malbec and a slice of chocolate fudge cake right about now. Maybe the boys would bend the rules if I took a jar of Nutella into the bedroom and offered to use their cocks as spoons. A girl could dream.

"Will you excuse me for a moment?" I said, getting up and stretching my arms with a yawn. "I need to go to the loo."

"We'll be in the den if you need us," Asher

mentioned, getting up to take a bottle of water from the fridge

I used the downstairs toilet, then crept back into the kitchen in search of a chocolate biscuit. What could I say? I was weak-willed. I savoured every lip-smacking morsel of that Kit-Kat. It was so good, I dived back into the cupboard for another one, then hid the evidence beneath a discarded newspaper in the rubbish bin. The only clean-eating I could think of was checking the corners of my lips for crumbs. There was no way I could live on salads for the next few weeks. I wasn't a rabbit, although I had been behaving like one recently

As I approached the den, I heard them mentioning my name. Pausing to listen, I strained to hear what they were all squabbling about.

They weren't still upset about last night, were they?

"She's going to go off her tits when she finds out about this," Cruz expressed, keeping the volume of his voice to a minimum. "Why can't we just tell her the truth?"

My heart jumped in my chest, wondering what they were keeping from me this time. It was typical of me to assume the worst. I could hardly breathe as I waited, my fingers trembling against my lips.

"She's one of us now," Braxton spoke up, easing

my worries. "She loves us, and we love her. What is there to worry about?"

How sweet?

Someone exhaled a sigh, then I recognized Asher's voice next. "I know, but what if it ruins things?"

"What if it doesn't?" Dominic stated his point. "You heard what she said." He must have been expected to elaborate because he began to explain, "The only reason she turned down our proposal was that she was afraid of what her dad might say."

"Yeah, she told me the same thing," Cruz mentioned

"But it's nuts. Our parents planned for this to happen. It was all part of their master plan," Dominic continued, rendering me dumbstruck. "It was the reason we were born."

What the hell did he just say?

I pushed the door open and stumbled into the room. The dazed look on my face told them I had heard everything

"Bexley?" Asher's eyes flared wide with shock.

I held out my hand, signalling him to keep his distance. This was a lot of information to take in. I just needed a moment to process this. Fuck the rules. I needed hard liquor in my system because this news was a hard pill to swallow. None of them stopped me as I stalked to the bar and helped myself to a large brandy. I gulped it down, grimacing as it burned my throat.

"Start from the beginning," I urged, topping up my glass. "I'm all fucking ears."

Their Adam's apples bobbed in their throats like a game of ping-pong. Why was it that a riled female could instil the fear of God in a man, just by demanding information?

Braxton scowled at his feet with his fingers stuffed into the pockets of his jeans. Cruz slouched against the pool table, folding his arms across his chest. Dominic winced his eyes, giving me the injured puppy look. Asher took another step toward me, his eyes planted on me the entire time.

"Do you want the short version or the long version?" he offered, taking a seat on the barstool.

"Just give it to me straight and leave out the bullshit," I remarked, preferring nothing but the truth or so help me God, they were going to get it.

"Before we start, I just want you to know that your parents loved you very much. Your situation was nothing like ours. You were born out of love."

I frowned at that. "What do you mean "I was

born out of love"? Your dad wanted kids but just never met the right woman."

Braxton chuckled, but the bitterness in his tone suggested he disagreed with that.

"Our father did love someone once. Long before we were born. She was killed in active service, just like your mother was," Asher explained.

His brothers were happy to let him take the lead, taking charge like he always does.

"They wanted a team of elites, and who better than to raise their soldiers from infancy? Our biological mother harvested her eggs so that in the event of her death, Dad could still carry out their plan. He used surrogates and paid them off as soon as we were born. They didn't mind leaving behind children they had no biological ties to. Dad got what he wanted. His soldiers were born."

"But where do I fit into all of this?" I asked, urging him to get to the point.

"Regardless of whether you were male or female, we were all going to form part of a team. The arrangements would have been different, but when your parents found out they were having a girl, our fathers came up with a contingency plan. It was their way of ensuring your safety. You would be the key to all of your mother's secrets, and we would fight to the bitter end to protect you," he held my gaze as he delivered the final part of his speech, showing me that he meant every word

"So, you're saying they wanted us to be together?" I asked, getting my head around that concept. "My father, who hated every man I ever dated, wanted me to shack-up with four blokes?"

Asher winced at my indelicate comment. "We're not shacking-up, it's a marriage contract," he corrected me.

Was this why they resented me so much when we were kids? It was because of me they had to be the best at everything. They were unable to go to school like regular children, confined here in this house like lab rats. No wonder they envied me for having a stable family unit. Each time they saw me it must have been a huge slap in the face. So, what changed to make them feel differently about me? I behaved like a brat, so why would they want to go along with this contingency plan when they could go off and lead separate lives? Marry one woman each, and defy their father's wishes.

"Why would you want me when you could have any other woman?" I directed that question at each of them.

Asher huffed a smirk. "Because, we could have

any other woman, but she wouldn't be you, Bexley. Even if there was no plan, we would still want you to be our wife. You're the glue that binds us together. You are our universe."

Their universe? Just like the symbol on my mother's pendant. Is that how they saw me?

I blushed, managing a shy smile. My heart swelled with so much love, it was fit to burst.

"When can I sign this contract?" I expressed, keen to get things rolling.

It was Braxton who answered, "We need to sign it in the presence of a solicitor because it's a cohabitation contract. It's the only legal way you can marry all four of us without having to choose."

"Like I could ever choose," I spoke fondly. "Come here," I dragged them all into a group hug, kissing them each in turn. "Of course, I will marry you. You're stuck with me forever."

"We can live with that," they muttered in response

CHAPTER
Twelve

Asher

There was nothing more fulfilling than sipping coffee while watching the sunrise. The floor-to-ceiling windows framed the picturesque coastline. It was a stunning view. Braxton and Cruz had to fly to London to meet with Dad and Uncle Jaxx. Dominic was out there surfing the waves, making the most of the calm before the storm. The house was peaceful and homely because Bexley was back here where she belonged

"Good morning," Bexley spoke as she entered the living room wearing a floaty lemon maxi dress and wedge sandals.

She caught me off-guard, startling me with her sudden announcement.

"Morning," I returned, drinking in the vista of her appearance. "Are you ready to begin the lesson?"

She cringed, baring her teeth. "Ready as I'll ever be." She didn't sound too convinced about that.

I set my half-empty mug onto the white marble coffee table and took a seat on the cream leather sofa. Bexley straightened her skirt before sitting down. Sunlight kissed everywhere it touched, outlining us in a warm yellow hue. Dust particles danced in the air all around us like tiny flecks of gold. It was magical.

"Have you ever played Poker before, Bexley?" I asked

"No," she answered, wringing her hands in her lap. "I'm not very good at card games."

"It doesn't matter," I reassured. "I can teach you."

Bexley sat up straight, paying close attention.

"To be a good spy, you must train your mind to absorb information, remembering important details without writing it down. You may have no choice but to react within a fraction of a second, like answering a question without breaking a sweat, shooting a target, or defusing a bomb with only moments to spare. Your practised game-face comes in useful for bluffing. Remember your lies because your opponent will not forget them. Your ruse is your cover; it's the only thing stopping the enemy from putting a bullet in your skull." I stopped to check if she had taken that in.

"Okay," Bexley answered, hanging on every word

I recalled the time she used to roll her eyes and accuse me of being a know-it-all. Our nanny used to say that women were attracted to intelligent men and that a stimulating conversation was just as important as physical attraction. I wasn't as buff as my twin, but what I lacked in brawn I sure made up for in the brain department.

"One of the tricks I learned to master was the art of manipulation. Convincing the enemy that I possessed information that could potentially ruin them. That is the ultimate bluff, tricking them into revealing their plans because they assume the game is up. Getting them to crack won't be easy, but the longer you wear them down, they will let things slip. The key is getting them to think that you know everything there is to know in the hope that it'll trigger a reaction."

"What happens if the enemy captures me?" she asked, bunching her brows with worry.

"It's our job to prevent that from happening," I reassured her. "But in the unlikely event that it happens, I want you to outsmart them with that quick-thinking attitude I love so much. They won't kill you as long as you can be of use to them. Even if things seem hopeless, I want you to shine with confidence. Let them believe that they would be making a huge mistake if they were to kill you. Lie if you have to. Lead them on a wild goose chase around the world. The Chameleon wants that information, and he will stop at nothing until he gets it."

Bexley nodded, giving me an indication that she understood

I reached across to the coffee table and retrieved a deck of playing cards from the drawer. Bexley watched with keen intrigue as I slid the cards from the box and began to shuffle them.

"Lesson number one," I schooled, dealing out the cards. "We're going to work on your Poker face."

Bexley took her hand and arranged each card so that it was fanned out in front of her.

"Are we playing for any particular reason other

than working on my game face?" Bexley asked with cheeky intent.

"How about we play for control?" I suggested. "The loser has to do anything the winner wants."

"You're on," she agreed

The wry smile on her face and the wicked gleam in her eyes implied she would be the winner either way

I dealt the cards, then explained the rules of the game. Bexley assured me she understood. She had always been a fast learner, so I gave her the benefit of the doubt.

As the game progressed, Bexley made a few novice mistakes. She studied her hand, her lips pulling to the side in a thoughtful twist as she decided her next move.

Just as I thought, she knew more than she was letting on. She lost some, then she won some, giving me nothing but doe eyes and cute smiles. She was a natural.

I got chills watching her act. The little minx knew how to play all along, thrashing me by the fifth round.

"How am I doing?" she asked, looking pleased with herself

"You're quite the little fibber, aren't you?" I mocked playfully.

She flashed a Mona Lisa smile and I wasn't sure how I was supposed to interpret that.

"Dad taught me how to play when I was six." She sucked back her laughter. "Sorry, but bluffing is my speciality. It's how I get my way in the boardroom."

"Good. You'll need to use it to your advantage," I coached. "Remember what I said about hesitating. Your body language can give you away with a simple twitch of the eyes, or a lick of the lips. Keep your mind sharp and your emotions poised. Never give them a reason to doubt you," I told her, feeling proud of the woman she'd become.

Bexley edged closer to me, then straddled my lap, her hands pressing my shoulders onto the backrest.

"I beat you fair and square," she uttered, her lips hovering over mine. "Now it's time to claim my reward."

"Name your price," I bargained, willing to give her anything she wanted.

"Complete control," she replied, looking me dead in the eyes without flinching. "I know that's going to be hard for a man like you, Asher. But trust me to take the lead and you won't regret it."

Dominic

H*oly fuckery!*
What the hell have I stumbled in on?

Bexley was straddling Asher, grinding herself on his lap like she was riding him fully-clothed. My cock kicked inside my jeans, swelling like it was trying to break free. I watched as her fingers worked to open the buttons of his shirt, and sucked in a breath as she raked her nails across his chest, tracing circles over his lean abs. I shouldn't be here. This was a private moment between them, but I couldn't seem to help myself. I couldn't take my eyes away from the erotic scene that was playing out before me.

"Put your hands behind your head," Bexley ordered

Asher obeyed; his hungry eyes trained upon hers like he was lost in submission. Bexley flicked her hair over one shoulder, then slowly unzipped the back of her sundress, letting it pool around her waist. She was braless. Asher's chest heaved with shallow pants. His greedy eyes landed on the pert nipples that only he could see. Bexley shimmied out of her clothes, toeing off her footwear, and knelt onto the floor between my brother's parted knees.

Her thong was a thin scrap of lace, neither here

nor there. The thickest part plunged between the globes of her derrière; no doubt soaked with the essence of her arousal. My cock ached to be stroked, pulsing to be handled, and my balls filled with the need to release. But this wasn't my turn to muscle in on the action. This was Asher's. He had earned this small slice of heaven. Who was I to take this moment from him? We have our entire lives to build memories with Bexley. I would get my one-on-one with her, but that didn't mean I couldn't watch my brothers take theirs. My loins stirred with the urge to watch. So, instead of turning to walk away, my feet rooted to the spot.

"I'm going to make you feel so good," Bexley cooed as she loosened Asher's belt.

Asher held his bottom lip between his teeth as Bexley tore through the buttons of his slacks, pulling the zip down painfully slow like she wanted to drag out the torture for as long as she possibly could. She tugged on the fabric, yanking it over his hips with a little help from him.

"You're so big," she told him, stroking the tent in his boxers. "All this belongs to me and only me."

"Yes . . . only for you," he agreed, his voice breathy and restless.

I couldn't stand it a moment longer, pulling open

the buttons on my jeans and delving a hand inside my boxers. My cock jerked in my hand, cold moisture dragging across the back of my knuckles where pre-cum had oozed from the tip. I worked my jeans midway down my hips, just enough to free the goods, giving myself enough room to work with.

"Good," Bexley replied, sounding satisfied with his response

She did something to make him hiss through his teeth, then he released a strangled groan. I worked myself in a steady rhythm, hardly breathing through the fear of getting caught. Bexley leaned forward on him and started bobbing her head. Asher's grunts of pleasure made my balls boil with excitement. I closed my eyes, imagining it was my cock she was sucking. I was so close to my bursting point, my toes curled inside my Converse; my stomach clenched as I reached the pinnacle of my release. Where was my stamina? I couldn't allow myself to cum just yet. This show was too good to miss. I slowed my momentum, preventing the spark of my desire from reaching a climactic explosion.

"Fuck, Bexley!" Asher moaned, rearing his head back on the sofa. "This feels incredible."

Bexley came up for air, getting to her feet. She tugged the lace over her hips and let the thong drop to the floor. Asher scooted down the sofa cushion, allowing her plenty of room to climb aboard. I expected her to straddle his lap and start riding his cock, her tits bouncing in his face as they fucked.

"Uh, oh god," I mouthed the words but nothing but air came out.

The imagery inside my head made my balls swell and fizz like a shaken bottle of pop, the tingling sensation boiling over the point of no return and firing through the end of my cock in thick, long, spurts. I caught it in my palm and smeared it against the side of my leg

"Oh fuck," I yelped a strangled whisper.

I lifted my gaze to find Bexley had straddled my brother, but not with her back to me. She was sitting on him in reverse, watching me as I came. Her heels resting on the edge of the sofa, legs parted, giving me an amazing view of her pussy. I saw everything. Her swollen lips, reddening with arousal, her puckered nub just begging to be licked, the way her entrance pulsed around Asher's cock having sucked him down to the root.

"Well, don't just stand there with your meat in your hand. Get over here and taste me," she demanded, reaching down to caress Asher's balls.

I stood there like a deer caught in the headlights,

having been caught red-handed. The voyeuristic haze drained from my mind the second she rumbled me.

"I . . ." I swallowed away the dryness. "I didn't mean to. I just couldn't resist," I provided a feeble excuse, not wanting to encroach any more than I already had.

"Our woman gave you an order," Asher spoke with authority. "Are you really going to deny her wishes?"

Not likely.

Leaving my jeans open, I yanked them up and staggered forward to comply. As I sank to my knees, I could see Bexley's pussy pulsing, stuffed full of my brother's cock. Her cream trickled from within her and rolled down his ball sack. Fuck. The heat she was throwing off was enough to make me dive right in and feast upon her like a starving man.

Asher's hands clasped her sides, helping to ease her up and down as I teased her pussy. Her body quivered into a frenzy, desperate to cum. She looked down at me through hooded eyes, her crescent lashes fluttering as she lost herself to a maelstrom of emotions. Asher's upward thrusting made her moan. My fingers stroked her labia, sliding around her clit, dragging out the teasing until she begged me for more

"Please," she mewled, needing that final boost to catapult her brains through the stratosphere.

Asher's face scrunched with pleasure, needing the constricting clench of Bexley's pussy to tip him over the edge

I leaned down to taste her, fluctuating between dragging my tongue around in lazy circles and taut flicks. Her cream was sweet and I couldn't get enough of it. The feel of my tensed tongue, soft lips, and rough stubble delivered a plethora of sensations, and she flew apart within seconds.

"Fuck." Her voice was strained, her back arched as Asher kept her moving through her orgasm.

Her moans became whimpers, and she sagged like a wrung-out rag doll. Asher barked out a harsh cry as he came, his cock rooted deep inside her, holding her there as he filled her. A strong scent of sex clung heavily to the air, sweet versus protein. It was so fucking sinful, I leaned down for one more lick, loving how she shuddered with sensitivity. Asher lifted her off his cock and tugged her body against his. His chest heaved against her back, sweaty and spent. I glanced between her parted legs to see his seed oozing from her shrinking muscle like a flower in full bloom.

"Could you please go and run our fiancée a bath?" Asher delegated the task to me.

I got to my feet, not bothering to fasten my jeans. "We could all use a bath after that," I said, gesturing at all the dark stains in the denim.

When our parents designed this house, it was done so with a large family in mind. It was why our father was giving it to us as a wedding gift. The bath could accommodate us all at once.

CHAPTER
Thirteen

Braxton

Dominic and Asher strolled into the den with smiles like the Cheshire Cat. They relayed the day's findings, which was an impressive turn of events. It meant we were one step closer to getting the codes. I felt lousy about being the bearer of bad news. From what we could decipher from the press report, the country was in chaos. Cruz turned his attention to the television; his brows had set in a perturbed frown and his jaw pulsed with anger.

"We think the Chameleon has reached London," I told them, slapping the glee from their faces. "There's been a security violation in MI6; Dad is going through the CCTV footage as we speak."

"What?" Asher blurted, wide-eyed with shock.

Dominic staggered, then toppled into the recliner. "How the fuck?" he sighed exasperatedly.

Cruz batted the air, signalling us to be quiet. We paused, shifting our attention to the television to watch the news report.

The clip showed Malcolm Lewis, the Home Secretary, giving a press conference outside the Houses of Parliament. Then someone photobombed the shot with a homemade billboard, claiming that our government is keeping secrets from us. He cried out, "The elections are rigged! We're ruled by a dictatorship!" before being removed by the police.

My phone vibrated in my pocket, but I ignored the call. This was a disaster. We couldn't peel our eyes from the T.V screen.

Shaken by the outburst, Malcolm resumed his speech, but instead of appeasing the irate mob around him, he fuelled the fire by playing the whole thing down

"I repeat . . . we will not play into the hands of terrorists, and we refute the claims that have been made against us. As I understand, this was a social media hoax, meant to disrupt our fine society. Do not be hoodwinked. There was no breach of data, no conspiracy to monitor you via your household appliances." He shook his head as if he found the idea ludicrous. "The rumours are false, and we urge you all to remain vigilant when receiving bogus messages and emails. Don't click on any links if you're unsure of their source. Scammers will use any means to collect your passwords. This is old news . . . and sadly, it will not be the end of it. I assure you our security remains intact. There is no cause for alarm. The perpetrator will be found and brought to justice"

Cruz huffed a cynical chuckle. "And if you believe that, you deserve to be shot at point-blank range"

"What exactly do those files contain?" Dominic muttered. "Does Dad know"

"Good question," I replied. "Let's ask him."

Asher paced the room, looking anxious. I could tell my brothers were all thinking the same ominous thoughts. Could we trust our government? Were we defending a lesser evil, stuck between a rock and a hard place?

I swiped my phone screen to unlock it, then saw the missed call was from my father. My heart hammered in my chest as I pressed to dial, and lifted the handset to my ear.

"Brax," Dad answered in a rushed breath. "It's a hot day in Cairo. Pack light, travel fast and don't forget to pack your factor fifty. You'll need it."

My blood pressure must have dropped because I became light-headed. I had to brace myself on the counter of the bar until my vision stopped dancing.

"Got it," I replied, letting Dad know I understood the message. "We'll be in touch when we land."

The phones were hot. We were being watched. It was no longer safe to remain here at Sandbanks.

I ended the call, dismantled the phone, so I could rip out the SIM and destroy it. My brothers saw what I was doing and did the same with theirs. We had to be prepared to go dark and disappear from the grid, but we didn't think we had to hide from our agency. This was bad, and anything that rattled Dad's bones, sure as hell sent shivers down my spine. We didn't just replace the SIMs, we fired-up four brand-new phones. Our anxiety was at an all-time high as I called the emergency number that Dad saved to the device

"We're clean," I assured, hearing him sigh with relief.

"Good . . . now listen closely," Dad cautioned. I placed him on loudspeaker so my brothers could partake in the conversation. "Jaxx and I are heading to the Maldives to . . ."

Dominic cut him off bluntly, "Now is not the time to fuck off and soak up the sun, old man. We need you here."

Asher would usually step in at this point and defuse the situation, but he seemed to agree with Dom.

"Dad?" Asher looked dismayed. "Start talking. All hell is breaking loose here."

"We set up a base on a private island and named it Alpha Two," Dad explained, "Jaxx and I are going to create a diversion to cover your tracks. We're going to scramble their signals and buy you some time."

"Who is coming after us?" I pressed. "What's going on?"

"The agency has screwed us over, that's what," Dad replied. The stress in his voice was clear "They don't trust us. Those files contain world secrets. If they became public knowledge, democracy as we know it would cease to exist."

"What are you saying?" Asher frowned.

"We're being framed by our own organization. And to make matters worse, we think the Chameleon has a guy on the inside. We can't pinpoint who, but we think that's who keeps tipping him off and why he's always one step ahead. Jaxx and I don't even know who we can trust anymore. Our government is looking for a scapegoat, and guess whose name came out on top?"

"Who?" I asked, swallowing a gulp.

"Bexley," Dad replied, leaving a long pause for us to process that. "They're accusing her of treason, insinuating that she is working with the Chameleon. The papers have already gone to press with a damning story, claiming that Barker Security was behind the entire scandal. They have it all figured out."

"That's bullshit!" Cruz roared. "They just want to locate her so they can force her to break the codes."

"Exactly," Uncle Jaxx spoke this time. "We're counting on you boys to keep her and the codes safe."

"Like you even need to ask," Asher affirmed. "We'll protect her with our lives."

"I know . . ." Jaxx breathed a sigh of relief. "But it's a parent's job to worry. This has been brewing for a long time."

It was almost dusk. We didn't have much time. By

nightfall, the waterfront would be crawling with soldiers.

"We'll touch base as soon as we reach Alpha One," I vowed before cutting off the call.

"Where's Bexley?" I inquired, my hands shaking with adrenaline.

"She said she needed to lie down, so I presume she's sleeping," Asher answered, scrubbing a hand over his stressed face. "We better wake her."

"I'll get her," I asserted. "We don't want to scare her to death."

Cruz had already switched to spy-mode. "Grab what you can. Be ready to fly within the hour." He turned to Dom. "Load the Chinook with as much artillery you can get your hands on."

Dominic nodded. "Got it," he returned before dashing out of the den.

Asher's face pinched with concern. "So, we're fugitives now? We're the bad guys? That's just perfect."

Cruz bounced his shoulders in a shrug. "It seems that way, doesn't it? After everything we've done for this country . . ." He turned away with disgust.

"Nothing has changed," I told them. "We are still going to follow the clues to crack the codes, and when we're done . . . we decide what we're going to do with them. Our mother . . . Bexley's mum died protecting the secret. There has to be more to this than meets the eye. The truth rests in our hands. Maybe destroying it isn't the answer. What if their plan was to unveil it?"

"What if the Chameleon was hired to make sure they didn't, and was double-crossed by the agency? I mean, it's plausible. It could be the reason why he's resurfaced after all these years. After today, I'm inclined to believe anything is possible," Asher muttered; his nostrils flared with a swift intake of breath. His gaze trailed off into the distance. "We take out two birds with one stone," he muttered. "We expose government corruption and eliminate the Chameleon once and for all. It's either that or we rot in jail."

Cruz seemed a little uneasy as he paced. "Yeah, but this could be huge. It could change everything. We can only speculate our findings. It'll be like opening Pandora's box."

"Which is why they're all coming after Bexley." I locked eyes with Cruz and saw the vulnerability within them. "We can't let them get to her. We don't know who the informer is. If they take Bexley into custody, it's only a matter of time before the

Chameleon gets his hands on her. The guy is a ghost. He could be anyone."

"Who says the Chameleon is a man?" Asher rightly pointed out. "It could just as easily be a woman. No one knows for sure. Their true identity has never been revealed"

"That's all the more reason to get the fuck out of here and go to Alpha One. Our location has been compromised. It's no longer safe to be here," I stressed

Dominic came rushing by, bumping my shoulder as we met in the doorway. "Our security system is picking up a strange signal. Someone is trying to hack us," he rushed his words. "I can't track the I.P address. It keeps changing"

"I'll load the ammo; you block the signal," Cruz suggested

My brothers' voices penetrated the hall as I made my way upstairs. The one thing I liked best about this house was that we could see who was coming at all angles. As the sun sank into the ocean horizon, the floodlights lit up the grounds. The tinted glass provided all the privacy we desired and cloaked us from prying eyes. Something was out there on the water, sliding across the skyline like a solid black mass.

I recognized it as a Navy vessel and knew we were in trouble

As I reached Bexley's room, I raised my fist to knock. The mellow tone of her voice chimed from the opposite side of the door. Wasting no time at all, I burst in and startled her. There, in her hand, was the source of our problem. Whoever it was, has been tracking her phone calls.

"Bexley!" I yelled, incensed at what I saw. "Hang up the phone, now

CHAPTER
Fourteen

Bexley

B raxton blocked my doorway with a scandalized frown. Anyone would think he had just caught me cheating, standing in the middle of my room in my underwear, doing something that I shouldn't. I tossed my phone between my hands like it was a hot potato

"Jesus, Braxton! Don't you ever knock?" I rounded on him with an angry snarl.

"I did, but you didn't hear because you were too busy on your phone," he berated me, then pointed at my mobile. "Is it switched off?"

I double-checked and saw the illuminated home screen. "Caz will wonder what the fuck is going on," I complained. "She's worried sick, all alone at my house with no one around for miles."

Braxton muscled into my room and snatched the phone from my hand.

"Hey! What do you think you're doing? Give that back!" I protested.

He used a tiny pin to poke the SIM holder free, then I watched with horror as he held it between his teeth to snap it. The tiny little thing proved to be quite a task. Then discarded it, flicking the broken pieces from his tongue.

"All of my contacts were on that SIM," I whined. "I have no way of getting them back."

"How many times did you contact your friend? Who else have you called since you've been here?" he roared with a contemptuous glare.

I didn't need an interrogation. Today's events had worn me out, and all I wanted to do was chill in my room until dinner was ready. What was so wrong with me checking up on a friend? Caz had been living with me for a while; she had no income and no support from her family. The way he was breathing smoke through his nostrils, you would think I had committed a crime.

"I needed to make sure that Caz was okay. My life doesn't come to a standstill just because of the Chameleon. I still have responsibilities I need to take care of, and she is one of them," I explained, hoping to make my point. "She has to eat, Braxton. I transferred money into her bank account so she could buy food. Not everyone was born with a silver spoon rammed in their mouth. It's been hard for her to find work. So, I said she could live with me in the meantime . . . just until she can sort herself out. I can hardly leave her destitute, can I?"

Braxton blanched. "What exactly did you tell her?"

I flapped my arms in a shrug. "Just that I had to go away on a business trip, and that my dad set me up with four guys. It's not a complete lie, but it avoids the bare truth of what we're really doing."

He seemed satisfied with that, but his eyes winced with unease. "You can't trust anyone, Bexley," he asserted. "Someone has tracked us here. Grab your things and prepare to leave, immediately."

"What?" I gasped. "But what about my training? I'm not ready," I stammered; fear splintered through my veins, scratching the underside of my skin with an icy chill. "You promised to teach me how to shoot."

Braxton stepped forward and pulled me into a warm hug. He rested his chin upon my head and exhaled a long sigh. His body heat seeped into my skin and I sucked in a lungful of masculine spice. It didn't calm me like it usually did because I could sense that he was scared too.

"We're heading to a secret location where we can lay low for a while. You can finish your training there," he mentioned

I hugged him tighter, and he pressed a kiss to my head. "Just because I love you, it doesn't mean that I'll let you off the hook. You can wrap Dominic and Asher around your little finger, but Cruz and I will punish you for breaking the rules."

Pushing back on his chest, I glared up at him. "What do you mean, punish me? I don't think so." I scowled. "Who do you think you're talking to? I'm a grown woman, not a child."

Braxton huffed a smirk that suggested he would have his way. "You're not getting away with this scot-free, Bexley. It is our job to keep you safe, and what you did has put you in mortal danger. Someone has been tracking your phone calls and has pinpointed you here. We will have to set some boundaries in place to help you follow instructions. If you break the rules, there will be consequences. Severe ones."

I swallowed a gulp, ignoring his threat. "They were tracking me? But we're protected by the British Secret Service, aren't we?" I shook my head as the disclosure left an unsavoury taste on my tongue. "Can't they intercept the signal and find out who it is?"

Braxton lifted my chin, forcing me to meet his gaze. "Like I said . . . we can't trust anyone. We're going rogue."

"Rogue . . . as in, we're on our own?" My stomach rolled with nausea. "I feel sick."

I staggered back as the news knocked the wind from my sails. This can't be happening. My mother was right. I was being circled by sharks, and they were bloodthirsty predators, all wanting their pound of flesh. With the lines between good versus evil growing blurry by the second, how was I supposed to determine what was right or what was wrong?

Braxton's wristwatch began bleeping. A red dot flashed, illuminating the face.

"Shit," he hissed. "We need to move."

I didn't wait for an explanation, rushing around to throw on some clothes and shove my feet into a pair of boots. Braxton snatched up my handbag and stuffed the notepad into it, leaving nothing behind for the enemy to find. The Chameleon, the agency, our government . . . fuck knows how many more people wanted to get their hands on those files.

"Hurry," he urged, coiling his fingers around my wrist.

We dashed downstairs to where two of my men were anxiously waiting. Cruz tossed Braxton a handgun, and he caught it with ease.

"Where's Dom?" I asked, searching for him with frantic eyes.

The glass shattered all around us as the windows imploded. Braxton lunged for me, dragging me to the floor and covered me like a human shield. The sound of rapid gunfire swallowed my screams.

Asher and Cruz crouched low, taking shelter behind the furniture

"Go! Get her out of here!" Cruz yelled to Braxton. "We'll cover you."

"We can't leave without Dom," I wailed, fighting against Braxton's grasp as he pulled me along with him.

The night breeze hit me smack in the face with a strong odour of gunpowder. All I could hear was a caterwaul of yelling, shooting, and the whooshing sound of helicopter blades slicing through the air.

Dom waved from the cockpit of the helicopter, urging us to hurry. Bullets flew past us like fiery wasps with deadly stings. My hair whipped around like wild vines, stinging my face with brutal lashes. Fuelled by adrenaline, I ran as fast as my legs could carry me. Braxton heaved me inside and I dove into the seat, fumbling with the harness, then he crashed beside me, followed by Asher. Cruz wasn't behind us like I assumed he was. My heart jolted with alarm, but then I saw something phenomenal emerging from the green. It was like a scene from a Thunderbirds episode — a real-life Tracy Island. The lawn split apart, revealing an underground chamber. A Boeing Chinook emerged from the ground, its twin blades spinning like samurai swords. The mansion resembled a disturbed ant's nest, overrun with soldiers dressed in black. Navy vessels lined the ocean, and military Jeeps littered the beachfront in a hostile invasion

"Hang on to something," Dominic communicated; his voice filtered through the speakers.

We veered around in the opposite direction and huge spotlights followed us. I squinted through the window, desperate to find out whether Cruz was okay. He hovered high above the house and then caught up to us moments later. I relaxed in my seat, resting my head against Braxton's shoulder and felt him bristle with pain. He grunted, and I lifted my head and saw a dark stain spreading through the light material of his T-shirt.

"You've been shot!" I panicked; my face grimaced with tears.

"It's okay, I'll live," he responded, downplaying it for my benefit.

He wasn't okay at all. He was trembling; his skin was pale and sweaty. Asher dragged a first aid kit from under the seat and set to work, digging out the bullet. Braxton's cries of pain rocked me to the core. I didn't know whether to puke or bawl my eyes out.

CHAPTER Fifteen

Bexley

Asher gave Braxton something to anaesthetize the pain, and his breathing steadied. His hand found mine and our fingers entwined.

"Are you all right?" he asked, still concerned about me, even though he was the one who got shot.

"Yes, are you?" I returned, my eyes landing on the bloodstained gauze on his shoulder.

"I've had worse," he mentioned. "It's just another scar to add to the collection."

Asher grunted with amusement. "One of these days, our luck is going to run out."

"Don't say that," I snapped. The thought of one of them dying felt like a stab to the heart.

If tonight had taught me anything, it was how much they meant to me. Trust Asher to mention the unthinkable. Now it was all I could think about.

"Is my dad and Uncle Zane okay?" I inquired, fretting about everything.

Asher turned to answer, "They're fine. The last we heard they were heading to the Maldives."

Well, that was a relief. At least they were safe — for now

Maybe it was the shock, but I fell asleep listening to the chuffing sound of the rotary-wing. A firm shake was enough to wake me and I snatched a breath, not knowing where the hell I was.

"Wake up, gorgeous," Dominic said as he loomed over me in the darkness. "You'll need to put on a coat, it's freezing outside." He provided me with a thermal jacket with a drawstring hood.

Asher yanked the door back and an arctic blast greeted us square in the face, sending a snow flurry into the cabin. I thrust my arms through the sleeves, my teeth chattering and my limbs tensing in the arctic air.

"Fucking hell! Where are we, the North Pole?" I griped, dragging the zip to my chin.

I couldn't identify where the earth ended, and the sky began. It was a haunting shade of glacial blue with minty streaks above us. As I scanned my surroundings, I could make out the twinkling stars and saw the gleaming moon appearing from behind a hazy cloud. Snow stretched across the uneven terrain like a glittering blanket, unblemished by footprints or tyre tracks. There would be no way to see this place from up above. The base poked out of the snow like it was raising its head from its bed sheets, ninety-nine per cent camouflaged and only distinguishable from the ground

"No," Asher replied. "This is Svalbard. Dad worked out here for a while after our biological mother died. It's illegal to die here and has been since the 1950s," he made a light-hearted joke to lift the mood. "Corpses cannot decompose. It causes many problems," he explained with a shrug, "People speak Norwegian here — not that we're likely to run into any of the locals. It's more probable we'll see a polar bear or an arctic fox."

"Do we have alcohol?" I shot him a pleading

look, one that would make even the meanest person feel sorry for me. "Please, tell me we have some Brandy?"

"No . . . but we have enough tea to sink a battleship," Asher answered. "We need to keep our wits about us, not get blind drunk."

Tea?

I crossed my arms across my chest, shivering. "So, there's no alcohol; we have to endure sub-zero conditions, we are fugitives on the run from our government, and all we have to knock the edge off is fucking tea?"

"Pretty much," Dominic replied in a breezy tone. "It sounds awful when you say it like that."

I was too overwhelmed to dwell on that now. All I wanted to do was get inside and out of the blizzard.

Cruz and Asher helped Braxton walk to the base. He was weak and was drifting in and out of consciousness. The arduous task of trekking through the snowstorm was zapping up the last of his energy. He needed plenty of rest, clean water to keep hydrated, and antibiotics to avoid the risk of infection. The snow reached my knees, numbing my lower limbs and stinging my toes raw. My thin socks weren't sufficient to stop the chill from seeping through. Dominic was the first to reach the base, clearing the frozen obstruction from the keypad on the door. Once inside, we stamped our boots and I let the boys lead the way. It was as bitter inside as it was outside; ice crystals clung to the interior windows like frosted glass. My breath billowed from my lips in a stream of white vapour. Asher and Dominic left to find the generator so they could fire up the heating system and turn on the lights.

"Dad hasn't been here for years," Cruz mentioned as he searched a storage cupboard for blankets. "It's stocked with medical supplies and survival packs. Do you remember those ration packs you used to make fun of whenever we went hiking?"

I rolled my eyes. "You mean, *you* went hiking. I travelled home after a day," I recalled. "I didn't know you could get an all-day breakfast out of a little foil packet. I would rather devour a steaming pile of shit than one of those."

Cruz chortled as I shuddered with revulsion.

"You'll eat anything if it keeps you alive. We may need to hunt if we run out of food," he mentioned.

What was worse? Eating a polar bear or one of those rancid ration packs?

"Where's Braxton?" I asked, changing the subject.

We had missed supper and my stomach was growling

"He's resting." Cruz jerked his head in the direction for me to follow. "I'll take you to him."

I accompanied him into the military-style dormitory where Braxton was sprawled out on a bed. The neutral room comprised six metal beds, each with basic mattresses and thin pillows that had been vacuum-packed to keep out the moisture. They had placed tall grey lockers at the side of each bed, and each had a small bedside table with a single drawer. I opened one of the vacuum-packs for myself. The generic blankets were scratchy and smelled of plastic. Uncle Zane wasn't thinking of comfort when he kitted-out this place. This was just a base to lay low for a while.

"Put these on," Cruz advised, tossing me a pair of insulated mittens. "You need to maintain warmth."

I slid my stiff fingers inside the soft faux fur and felt the feeling creep back to them again. It was painful to bear, like holding my hands over a naked flame. I had to move around to keep the blood flowing through my limbs. My toes were numb inside my boots. Cruz connected two single sleeping bags, turning them into a double.

"It's for you and Brax," he mentioned. "It's gonna take a while to reheat the place, so the next best thing is to share body warmth."

Dominic strolled into the chamber with a hand-held thermostat. "The heating is on," he announced. "We have power in the control room. Asher is talking to Dad, letting him know what happened."

The thought of my dad panicking sent my heart racing. "I need to talk to my dad," I told him, desperate to hear his voice.

Braxton toed off his boots and allowed Cruz to help him climb inside the sleeping bag. "Take her to the control room," he insisted. "I'll be fine. I just need to rest my eyes for a bit."

Cruz returned with a medical kit and perched on Braxton's bed. "Go ahead. I'll stay here with him and I'll check his wound."

"Will he be all right?" I asked, stroking the hair from Braxton's eyes.

Cruz huffed a smirk. "He'll be back on his feet by the morning, you'll see. We're used to this way of life, Bexley. It'll take more than a bullet to keep us down."

"I'll hold you to that," I returned, keeping my gaze on Braxton.

Dominic nudged my side. "Come on . . . let's give them some space."

I felt better knowing that he was going to be all right. Dominic walked at my side, escorting me through the industrial corridors that were lit by caged lighting

"It's impossible to get lost inside here," he mentioned. "There are floor maps at the end of every corridor. Dad hid our Christmas presents here once. We didn't know it as Alpha One back then. We thought this was Santa's workshop."

I laughed out loud, remembering what they were all like as children. "Dad stashed mine in the loft, knowing that I could never get up there."

Dominic exhaled a soft chuckle. "Just think of the fun we could have with our kids." He threw me a side-glance to check my reaction. "Sorry . . . was that presumptuous of me?"

I linked arms with him as we walked. "Not at all," I replied, welcoming his positive outlook on life.

Dominic brought me to the control panel and let me talk to my father. I felt better after hearing his voice. I followed the signs back to the dormitory and climbed into bed with Braxton. Cruz wanted to train me bright and early, which meant I needed to get some rest.

CHAPTER
Sixteen

Bexley

I t didn't seem like five minutes since my head touched the pillow. I forced myself to get up. Cruz was waiting for me in the gym, so I scarfed down the ration pack breakfast and hurried to meet him. An hour into my workout session and I was sweating profusely. Cruz counted the number of reps as I completed a set of deadlifts. My biceps were still burning from the bench lifts and hand curls I had done. We concentrated on my upper body. He had my workout programme stored in his memory bank. Sweat poured from my skin like I was a slimy swamp creature. In my determination, I shoved my mind elsewhere, so I could focus on endurance.

"Just fifteen more, and we can stop for lunch," Cruz coached, counting me down from fifteen to one.

I grunted through the torture, letting out an exhausted exhalation as I reached my target.

"I need water," I panted, snatching my towel from the floor so I could mop my brow.

I drank the contents of my bottle in a series of gulps.

"You killed it today," Cruz praised, planting a kiss on my clammy cheek.

I nodded once as a way of saying "thanks" with my mouth full, then swallowed the last gulp, so I could breathe.

"Do you want to join me in the shower?" Cruz asked, arching a brow.

My shoulders bounced as I chuckled. "Stop distracting me with sex. I have to train harder than ever if we're going to find those clues. Dominic and Asher wanted to meet me down in the control room."

Cruz flicked his gaze over my shoulder. "Uh, I think someone else would love to greet you first."

I turned to see who he meant and saw Braxton ambling across the gym. He seemed like he was back to his old self, dressed in dark grey combats and a black baseline shirt. His heavy boots were leaving footprints on the training mats, so he wasn't here for a workout. What was he here for? And why was he out of bed?

"I'll take things from here, Cruz," he insisted, relieving his brother from his duties. "Bexley is late for our shooting lesson."

The excitement fizzed inside my belly. "Really? Are you sure you're feeling up to it?"

Braxton cocked his head in a quizzical pose. "You're not getting out of it that easily."

"Who said I wanted to?" I glanced between him and Cruz like a kid who had just won a year's free pass to Disneyland. "Are you teaching me now?"

They exchanged a wry smirk and Cruz shook his head as he made to leave. "I'll rub one off in the shower," he joked. Or was he? The thought of him touching his thick, meaty cock turned me on.

"Preserve your stamina," Braxton encouraged. "I think Bexley could use a little group therapy tonight."

My heart jumped in my chest. "Yeah, save it for later," I added, keen to have the Wolfe brothers all at once like I did in the hot tub. "It feels like forever since the last time we all . . . you know?"

Cruz flashed a megawatt smile that could have melted the polar ice caps. "As the lady wishes," he said, grabbing his crotch through his shorts. "I'll keep it fully loaded for you."

I rolled my eyes and slung my towel across my shoulder. "Where are we going? Please don't say "outside"." I turned to Braxton, pleadingly.

He pointed, flicking his finger to the left side of the building. "The shooting range is next to the mess hall. It isn't as modern as the one we have back home, but it serves a purpose."

I followed Braxton down the corridor and across to the opposite part of the base. We passed the kitchen and entered another concrete stairwell, just like the one that led to the control room. Every door needed a four-digit code to open it. The combination being 1066. When I inquired why that was, Braxton mentioned The Battle of Hastings, said that made it easier to remember.

"How come Uncle Zane uses battle dates as security codes?" I asked, curious why that was.

Braxton chortled, then punched the digits into the electronic keypad beside the door. The little light switched from red to green, then slid to the side, granting us entry.

"It was a way of teaching us a lesson when we were kids," he answered, his voice softening with childhood nostalgia. "Dad said we should always choose our battles wisely. Fight for what is right and let the rest go"

"I never knew Uncle Zane could be so insightful," I muttered. "I always thought of him as a sullen old grouch"

Braxton choked on thin air as he spluttered with laughter. "He was, ninety-nine per cent of the time."

I couldn't see anything as I followed him into the pitch-black room, holding the back of his T-shirt with my finger and thumb. The second we tripped the motion sensor, the fluorescent bulbs along the ceiling flickered to life, illuminating the vast open space. Cream walls encompassed us and strong lighting banished the shadows. Black panels separated each lane. The target zone looked different beneath the bluish hue of the lights. It wasn't darker, it just appeared that way because of the black sides and hanging targets. They had pitted some with bullet holes. I wondered if Uncle Zane had left it like that or if the boys had come down here to blow off some steam. They were doing a superb job of shielding their emotions from me. But they had to know, I wasn't some fragile princess they had to protect. I wanted to look out for them too. Tonight's rendezvous seemed like the right opportunity to show them that.

Braxton stalked toward the gun cabinet and came back with a pistol. I hope he wasn't expecting me to know what it was called. That was his expertise. I was here to learn all of that. His mouth was moving, rhyming off the make and model and showing me how to use it. He showed me how to reload and then handed it to me. I shook my head, needing him to repeat all he just said at least three or four times. What can I say? His charismatic charm mesmerized me. It took everything I had not to jump his bones.

"Check the rounds," Braxton insisted. "You have to know how many you have."

"But you just loaded it." I frowned with confusion

He released a nasal exhale. "You should always check"

Taking his advice, I pulled the slide back to investigate. He stood behind me, covering my hands with his rough, calloused fingers and raised our arms together. Resting his chin against my shoulder, he angled with his lips, his breath grazing my ear. The warm caress was slightly off-putting, stirring my arousal.

"Only raise your weapon when you're preparing to shoot, do you understand?" he murmured, the deep husk of his voice sending vibrations through my body, straight to my core.

I nodded my head up and down. It satisfied him to see me holding it correctly and his fingers left mine, trailing a soft tickle as he stroked along my arms before grasping my hips.

"Keep it steady, then aim," he coached. His calm and level tone relaxed me. "Spread your feet a little," he advised, standing so close to me that the heat of his body seeped through my sticky gym attire.

The column of his cock nestled between the cleft of my arse cheeks, letting me know how much he wanted me. My blood pounded in my ears, snatching my attention to what was happening between us. A slow throbbing ache swelled my clit and his fingertips gravitated towards it, stopping within striking distance. I moaned softly, and Braxton's laboured breathing billowed fiercely against my ear.

"Steady," he murmured in a gentle wisp. "Stay focused"

His fingers crept at a snail's pace until they reached my crotch, sliding over my lycra-covered mound

I struggled to concentrate, and he knew it. He nipped my ear before reminding me, "The safety's on," then he chuckled salaciously.

Desire welled up from within me and I undulated on his cock like the greedy girl I was. I smirked, feeling the kick in his boxers.

"Two can play that game, Brax," I purred in response

He held me in place, breathing haphazardly.

"How about I up the stakes," he suggested, turning the heat up a notch

His finger didn't dip beneath my clothing like I wanted him to. He traced slow, lazy circles, driving me mad with desire until I reached the point of climax

"Now pull the trigger," he whispered as I shuddered through it.

My eyes closed for a fraction of a second, just enough for me to squeeze the gun. The deafening shot echoed through my ears, but my mind needed a few seconds longer to catch up. My intense orgasm was just as explosive as the adrenaline rush. I was trembling from head to toe.

Braxton pressed a loving kiss against the curve of my throat and murmured, "Well done."

I opened my eyes to see a gaping hole, straight through the bullseye.

CHAPTER
Seventeen

Bexley

I took my time to shower, scrubbing the dirt and sweat from my skin until it tingled. The soap smelled of forest pine, and the shampoo left my hair feeling as coarse as straw, but there was nothing I could do about that. The boys didn't pack a luxury hamper. They packed emergency essentials. It wouldn't matter if my locks were silky smooth if I ended up dead in the gutter somewhere. All that mattered was we were safe . . . for now at least. I knew we had to act soon. We couldn't stay hidden in Svalbard forever. Dad would be sailing to the Maldives by now on the SMS Triumph. I knew in my heart that I would see him again.

The bathroom was freezing, and that prompted me to dress quickly. I dried my hair with the small hairdryer I found in the bathroom. It was the size of a water pistol, and I giggled as I noticed it had two settings — cool, and barely warm. I couldn't dry my pubes with it, so I rubbed the towel through my mane until it was damp to the touch, then finished with the dryer. It was better than drip-drying.

The boys were waiting for me in the mess hall, gathered around the centre table. They had heated a ration pack for me and poured a fresh cup of tea from the kettle. It wasn't as cold in here than it was in the rest of the bunker. I supposed being so close to the kitchen helped. The hot-water pipes groaned through the walls each time the boiler flared up. I didn't need to wear my fleece here, so I took it off and tied the arms around my waist.

"Grub's up," Cruz mentioned, tapping his fork against my metal dish. "You better eat it before it gets cold"

He was right about that. The packet shepherd's

pie tasted inedible as it cooled. I had to dab a sachet of brown sauce over it to improve the taste.

"Now that Bexley is here, we can discuss our findings," Dominic expressed anxiously.

He peeked at Asher to seek his support, then proceeded with his blessing.

"I — uh — we," he stammered after Asher coughed. "We figured out the positions of the coordinates and charted them on the ordnance survey map. Your mother chose specific locations to plant each clue, and right now, I have no idea why. She must have had her reasons. We're guessing it's significant to solving the mystery."

"My mother and your father were more alike than I thought because she taught life-lessons through her actions too," I replied, paying attention to their discovery.

Cruz was the first to finish his food and set his fork down on his plate. "They're going to expect us to travel together, you know. I think we ought to split up and cover a broader scale. I know that's not what we agreed on, but we're up against the clock here," he raised his point, one that made more sense than it did before.

Asher was wearing his glasses today. He bunched them up so he could pinch the bridge of his nose and clear his vision. "Ugh," he groaned. "I don't like this one bit, but I think you're right. Maybe not the *splitting up* part, but about us travelling together."

"Cruz, Dominic and I will all travel separately. You should go with Bexley, posing as newlyweds or something," Braxton suggested.

Dominic reached inside his jacket pocket and flung five passports onto the table.

"I already covered that problem. We have money and secret identities," he notified us, watching us dive for the small burgundy booklets like a game of snap.

We passed them around as we searched for our own, perusing the images and descriptions on the photo pages.

"Mrs Margaret Stanley?" I wrinkled my nose. "I look like a virgin librarian," I complained, eyeing the digitally altered image with scrutiny.

"Now there's my ultimate fantasy," Asher responded with a sinful chuckle. "I love those thick-rimmed glasses, and that ponytail. Those lenses really make your eyes pop."

"I've shown you mine, now you show me yours," I demanded, curling my fingers back and forth.

Asher let me glance at his passport and I roared with laughter. "Look at you, Mr Derrick Stanley. That moustache is just." I kissed my fingertips like a

French chef. "There's the reason I married you, for that fluffy caterpillar above your lip. It stops all the nonsense from gushing through your mouth."

Asher smirked. His lips curled over his teeth in amusement. He always hated being mocked as a child, but since adulthood he had learned to loosen up

"I'll shave off my stubble and keep the moustache." He ran his finger up against the grain. "I will have to add to it, but I can think of a substantial reason to keep it," he declared, wiggling his eyebrows, suggestively. "Bexley likes a bit of friction downstairs." He bounced his gaze, gesturing towards my pussy.

The photo made him look like a Swedish porn star. Braxton looked like an old man of around fifty. In his photo, he was bald, wrinkled, with age spots under his eyes. Cruz was the only one of us who looked good as well as different. He had a full head of dark hair, combed back into a sophisticated style. It made him seem like a regular guy who was travelling for business. Dominic disguised himself as a female named Dominique. I could hardly recognize him beneath the blonde wig and makeup. The sound of their rumbustious laughter amidst my brash cackling filled the mess hall with mirth. We soaked up the moment, making the best of our bad situation.

Dominic fanned his hand out in front of him, skimming the surrounding air. "Move over, Chameleon. Asher is the master of disguise around here. He will organize the prosthetics, helping us to blend in. No one will recognize us. Just try not to blow your cover on the first day. I only have three new identities for each of us."

"What else do you have?" I asked, wondering what other tricks they had up their sleeves.

Dominic jerked his head. "Finish your dinner, and I'll show you," he offered, earning a chorus of "Oh" from his brothers. He cast them a scolding look as if to indicate he was being serious for once. I forced down the tasty meal (cue the sarcasm). It was shit. And then I washed it down with some hot, sweet tea, which was not so shit.

"Are you coming?" I glanced around, noticing that Asher, Cruz, and Braxton showed no sign of moving

"We've seen it," Braxton answered, then plunged straight back into their conversation, leaving me free to follow Dominic.

He led me below ground to a chamber behind the control room. It reminded me of a superhero's lair. My eyes drank in all the gadgets, the vehicles, and goodness knows what else that made up the exhibition of spy-wear.

"Whoa! You really are like Q from the Bond films," I expressed, awed by the advanced technology

"It took us a while to unpack," he told me, rocking back and forth on his heels like an excited kid who was revealing a science project to his parents. "We were awake half the night, cataloguing everything"

"Did you design and build all of this yourself?" I was impressed, and it raised a cute blush to his cheeks.

Dominic bunched his shoulders in a shy shrug. "Yeah, but just the gadgets. I can't take credit for the Jeep. I modified it . . . oh, and the snowmobile."

I picked up a watch that looked a lot like Braxton's and Dominic acted fast to remove it from my hands. "Steady there . . . that's a bomb," he warned, making me blanch.

"Show me something else," I requested, glancing around the room. "Have you got anything that can fit inside my handbag?"

Dominic led me by the hand and took me to another bench that was filled with dressing table items. He held up a pair of jewelled earrings and pressed the central gem. Sharp blades popped out of it, making it look like a deadly frisbee.

"These are throwing stars. They're detachable . . . look." He showed me how to remove them from the hooks and then flung one across the room. It flew through the air and lodged into the opposite wall.

"What does this do?" I asked, picking up a pocket mirror. "It has to serve another purpose if you designed it. It can't just be to check around corners."

Dominic opened it to reveal a compact mirror and pressed powder. It looked like an ordinary handbag item, but he urged me not to sniff the product or get it on my skin. "There's enough powdered chloroform to knock out an elephant. Don't inhale any of that," he advised, placing it back down onto the table. "You are to use the puff and blow the powder onto your victim's face."

He held up what I assumed was a lipstick. "This is real lipstick, but don't put it on and lick your lips. I call it the kiss of death."

My eyes bulged. "Does it really kill?"

Dominic winced. "Yeah, it works as well as any cyanide capsule, killing you as well as your captor. So, you're not getting your hands on that one."

His expression brightened, and he picked up a perfume bottle. "Watch what this one does," he commented, then sprayed it onto a stool leg. I observed with astonishment as the liquid fizzed as it corroded the metal. Seconds later, the area dissolved and the stool clattered to the floor.

"What do you think?" he muttered, analysing my reaction

"You made spy gadgets for me." I was so turned on by all his nerdiness, I was ready to fuck him there and then

I saw his brown eyes flare as I pounced on him and attacked him with kisses.

"I'll make more if it means I get paid in kind," he quipped, adjusting the front of his combats.

"I want you and your brothers, naked and in bed in precisely five minutes," I ordered, setting a deadline of my own.

CHAPTER
Eighteen

Bexley

"You're going to love what we've done in the dormitory. Just wait until you see it," Dominic mentioned as we walked hand-in-hand.

As Dominic smiled at me, I felt a little warmer. My heart thumped and my cheeks flushed with heat.

"I said five minutes, but it's been twenty," I commented, swinging our hands back and forth.

"Good things come to those who wait," Braxton

called out from our sleeping quarters, hearing what I said. "We're not ready"

I could hardly contain my excitement. Dominic dropped my hand and rushed inside

"Wait there for another minute," he insisted, closing the door, not allowing me to pass. "You wanted us all nude and I'm still fully clothed."

I heard chattering and boisterous banter, which was usual for them. I could tell they were ready because the bedsprings creaked. The noise settled to a minimum and I waited for them to call me inside.

"Bexley . . . we're ready," Dominic beckoned me, and I hurried inside to find all four Wolfe brothers lying bare on one huge, pushed-together bed.

I noticed a rope and chains dangling from the corners and saw that they improvised by tying the bed frames together.

"How resourceful," I praised them, loving how they all functioned collectively. "That better be sturdy enough to withstand a pounding."

"Get your sexy ass over here and we'll prove it," Asher muttered, laughing. "We need to work up a sweat if we want to stay warm."

My pussy clenched at the thought. I sauntered to the bed, slipped off my shoes, and crawled to the centre. Asher and Braxton moved to the left and

Dominic and Cruz moved over to the right, allowing me enough room to roll onto my back and spread my arms like a starfish. Braxton was the first to touch me, lifting my hand and bringing it to his lips.

"Do you think you can handle having us all at once, again?" he asked. "We exhausted you last time."

"That was then," I replied. "And this is now . . . so you better hope that you can keep up."

He rolled closer, placing his lips on mine, sliding his hand over the bare skin of my belly, and up under my jersey. I closed my eyes to focus on his touch, but then there was movement on my right, and another hand followed a similar path. More hands peeled away my socks and unbuttoned my trousers. I couldn't tell who was who, but I didn't care. I trusted my men to put me first, to treat me with respect and handle me with the gentlest touch. Fingers lifted my shirt and peeled it away. They removed my bra and pulled my knickers off like they were unwrapping a present. Hands softly squeezed my breasts and fingers rolled my nipples. Lips kissed every inch of my body and then teased the inside of my thighs. I was so hot between my legs, so desperate and needy that my hips wriggled, seeking more contact. I knew what I wanted, and that was their tongues on my clit, followed by their long, thick cocks in my snatch.

"She's ready," Cruz said as he dipped a finger inside me, pumping it in and out.

"I can hear the squelch of your juices on Cruz's fingers," Braxton whispered against my ear and I whimpered

"She'll get wetter with a tongue inside her pussy," Asher mentioned, his voice is gruffer than I've ever heard it.

"Fuck, see how swollen her clit is." There was a chorus of appreciation as they all feasted their eyes on my wide-open cunt.

I could imagine what it looked like, soft and pink and dripping wet with arousal. I glanced down and saw Cruz kneeling between my legs. Our eyes met, and it was the hottest thing ever. I gazed around me and found Dominic, Asher, and Braxton, all reaching out to stroke me in places, pressing open-mouthed kisses against my skin.

Their tan muscles, sexy ink, and scattering of body hair, made my stomach flutter. My two sets of identical twins, so beautifully unique, gorgeous to behold. I could come from just lying here, looking at them and appreciating their magnificence.

"Lick her," Braxton ordered. Cruz didn't need

telling twice. He grinned as he settled between my legs, inhaled deeply and nudged my clit with his nose. "If there's one thing I love, it's the sweet scent of pussy," he added.

"Me too," Braxton said, nipping at my earlobe.

Cruz's furious breath sent my pulse racing as his tongue flicked over my swollen clit then lapped at my entrance

There was a murmur of appreciation as I moaned my approval, arching my back off the mattress. I moved my hand to hold Cruz's head, but Braxton snatched it and pinned it to the pillow. "Ah-ah," he admonished me. "Lie back and take it."

It was hot as hell. Dominic's lips latched onto my nipple. Hands stroked my thighs as Cruz licked me with a ruthless technique. Asher's lips found mine, and he kissed me as though he was pretending that his tongue was his cock; long languid strokes match his brother's rhythm over my clit, and I undulated my hips. I couldn't take the overwhelming feeling of so many hands, so many fingers, so many tongues. It was like I had died and gone to Heaven.

"She's getting close," Dominic murmured, pinching my nipple between his fingers. "Her thighs are quaking."

"Her pussy's pulsing, too," Cruz commented. "I can taste her cream."

"Look how sexy she looks as she cums," Asher breathed

Fingers pressed against my hips, holding me tight against Cruz's face, preventing me from wriggling free

"That's it," Dominic urged. "Don't hold it back, Bexley. Let it go."

"Uh, uh, uh," I moaned; my eyes rolled into the back of my skull and my stomach coiled as I came.

"That's it, you dirty girl. Come on his face," Asher commanded.

Oh, God. His words set me off, blowing my brains to smithereens. A warm gush flowed through me like a tsunami, then I floated in an ocean of bliss.

"So beautiful," Dominic murmured, stroking me gently

His brothers followed suit as Cruz pulled away, letting me ride the waves of pleasure.

The bed shifted between my legs, then knees nudged them wider apart. "Cruz is going to fuck you now," Braxton whispered. I nodded, letting him know it was okay, even though I couldn't speak. I remembered how amazing Cruz would feel. Hard, thick, and huge, with all that power behind his thrusts.

His cock nudged at my opening; my slickness eased the passage, feeling every veiny ridge rippling against my walls.

"Fuck," Cruz muttered as he pushed inside. My back arched and warm lips found my breasts again, sucking my nipples into stiff peaks.

Asher shifted away, and I assumed someone was going to take his place, but that wasn't what happened. He knelt next to my head with his dick in his hand, stroking his foreskin back and forth.

"Suck it, babe," Asher insisted.

He moved closer, and I parted my lips to take the engorged crown, tasting the salty sweetness of his pre-cum, a sign of how excited he was. He was so big, and the angle was uncomfortable, but he seemed to know just how deep to push inside me without making me gag.

"That's it, suck him off," Braxton encouraged.

He was enjoying the show, watching the action at both ends. I looked up at Asher and saw the pained-pleasure on his face as he fucked my mouth. Cruz was fucking me with slow languorous strokes, grinding his hips in sensuous circles, his expression pinched with rapture. I didn't think I would be able to cum again so soon. I'm way too sensitive. But the way things were going, I just might. Asher was close, though. I tasted his excitement, felt the swell of his cock, and observed how his balls were tensed. He tried to pull away, but I grabbed him, wanting him to ejaculate in my mouth.

"Bexley . . . Bex," Asher panted; his face contorted with pleasure as he blew his load. He came so much, I almost choked.

Cruz's hands gripped my hips so hard, I worried I would bruise. His slow, languid pace sped as he got near to his finish. A guttural moan built in his throat — a sign he was going to come. The impetus of his thrusts felt incredible. My pussy was so wet, my juices soaked into the bedding

"Uhh," Cruz roared his release, then slumped against me to catch his breath.

"My turn," Braxton insisted, tapping his brother's shoulder to get him to move.

Asher and Cruz moved away to make room for Dominic and Braxton. They rolled on their sides and watched us through hooded eyes.

"Get up on your knees," Braxton suggested. "I want you on top of me," he asserted. I nodded, not wanting him to overexert himself, then rolled onto my knees to straddle him.

Braxton's cock stood big, thick, and proud. His veins looked like snakes beneath his skin. All I had to do was take hold of it and impale myself onto it. Their cocks were all similar, but the stretch and burn of each of them still made me gasp as I tried to accommodate them.

"Do you think you can take us both?" Dominic asked. I remembered what it felt like to have two of them at once, but I was afraid that it would hurt. "Go gently," I told him. "We're not in the hot tub this time." I hoped that I was wet enough to take them both

He shifted closer, aligning himself, then pushed. The stretch was incredible. I leaned forward, braced over Braxton. Hands stroked my back and my rear. Cruz and Asher were there at my side, murmuring words of encouragement. Braxton raised himself to kiss me. I relaxed, and that was when Dominic pressed a little harder. The pressure was immediate, and Braxton thumbed my clit to get me wetter. They watched my expression as I grimaced with the intensity of it all.

"That's it, babe," Braxton soothed. "Just relax."

"Easy," Asher warned Dominic. "Go slowly."

He moved with unhurried shallow thrusts and Braxton closed his eyes, placing his hands behind his head. They had taped a clean patch of gauze to his shoulder, and I noticed the lack of blood. It means he was healing, and that made me feel so much better. Braxton seemed unaffected by the wound, enjoying how good my pussy felt. I could imagine how amazing it was for him. The tightness of my muscle and the taboo of fucking the same hole at the same time as his brother.

"That's our girl," Asher said. "Our wife . . . the mother of our kids."

"Beautiful," Cruz agreed. "Daddy likes . . . Daddy likes it a lot."

My legs were trembling, my clit grinding against Braxton from the weight of Dominic behind me. I knew I was going to cum soon. My orgasm was rising fast, and I saw stars. I was hoping and praying my men would catch me if I sagged.

"She's close," Dominic stated, moving with equal vigour.

"So am I," Braxton hissed through gritted teeth.

"Oh god, I'm there," Dominic announced breathlessly

He seized hold of my hair and wrapped it around his fist, pulling me into him. I loved his roughness. This pushed Braxton over the edge; his face screwed up like he was in pain.

"Fuck," he gasped.

"Uhh," Dominic groaned a guttural noise that vibrated through my back.

All I could feel was intense pressure. My pussy was bursting with two expanding cocks. I couldn't move and I sure as shit couldn't breathe. Braxton tensed and Dominic strained, holding onto my hip for anchorage. I felt their cocks jerking with ropey jets of cum, spasming until they finished. My palm slipped on Braxton's sweat-slickened chest and I shuddered and shook in-between them.

Asher's eyes were wild as he watched, stroking his dick back to life.

"Stay on your knees," he ordered, wanting to go for round two.

Dominic moved from behind me and I slid off Braxton's cock, it flopped onto his stomach with a wet slap. Asher took Dominic's place behind me and mounted me hard, making me jolt with a gasp. His thumb circled my arsehole and he applied a little pressure. Not enough for him to pop it inside, but it was enough to make me shiver. His heavy balls slapped against my labia with the momentum of his thrusts. My breasts bounced with the force of his strokes, and my teeth rattled in my mouth. It was fast; he speared into me without an ounce of mercy. His fingers dug into the flesh of my hips as he increased his, almost brutal velocity.

Slap, slap, slap.

My mouth formed a perfect "O" as my hot nerd fucked me into oblivion.

"Uh!" I wailed, loud enough to rattle the window frames. Asher was right there with me, chasing his release. And when he came, the world and his uncle knew it.

"Fuck," he groaned; we rolled onto our sides in a breathless heap.

Nobody said anything for a while. We just cuddled, basking in the afterglow of our lovemaking and enjoyed the contentment that encompassed us.

CHAPTER
Nineteen

Bexley

L ast night was just what we needed to boost our morale and embark on this mission with a positive mindset. I was ready. My men and I gathered around the mess room table, drawing up a plan of action

"Here are the coordinates," Asher explained, pointing to the red crosses on the map. He had placed mugs at either corner to prevent the sides from rolling up. "The five locations are, Norway, Sweden, Austria, Spain, and Ukraine."

Braxton scrunched his eyebrows as he viewed the markings, his eyes flitting to each position. Cruz peered over Dominic's shoulder as he typed the figures into his laptop. I wondered why my mother had chosen these particular places; I was sure she had a reason, being the queen of secret messages. But before I could throw in any suggestions, I needed to know where each clue was hidden. They could be anything, numbers, letters, or words that made up a password. Until we found one of them, we would be stumbling around in the dark.

"I think we have our locations, guys," Dominic announced, tapping away on the keyboard. "The Sofia Church in Stockholm, Sweden; Sofiyivka Park in Ukraine; the Reina Sofia National Art Museum in Madrid, Spain; Laxenburg Castles in Vienna, Austria; and The Seven Sisters waterfall in Norway."

Asher and I locked eyes as we made the same connection. "Did you say Sofia?" We spoke at once

My mother's first name was Sofia, but everyone called her Safi.

"Uh-huh," Dominic confirmed.

"It can't be a coincidence," Asher responded, seeming hopeful that we were on to something.

"All apart from the waterfall," I added. "I wonder what significance that location holds."

Asher nodded. "Yeah . . . me too. But knowing your mother, there would be another meaning behind it."

I massaged my temples as I thought, wracking my brains to remember something crucial.

"It's called the Seven Sisters because there are seven waterfalls," Cruz muttered, sounding downbeat. "Where the hell would we start? It will be like trying to find a needle in a haystack."

Braxton groaned. "He's right. The waterfall is located along the Geirangerfjorden in Stranda Municipality, Møre og Romsdal county. It is 410 metres tall with seven separate streams, the tallest has a free fall that measures 250 metres. I know because Dad dumped me there as part of my training. There's nothing but river and mountain terrain for miles. If we are travelling there, we will need to be prepared. It's a long walk back to civilization if things go wrong. I don't fancy being stranded out there for days on end."

I thought for a moment, remembering all the stories my mum used to tell me about the star constellations. One in particular stood out — the Seven Sisters. Pleione was their mother; she was supposedly beautiful and had flowing red hair. She was known as the protector of sailors. Seamen would often get tattoos of her as a tribute. Dad had one on his chest with my mother's name beneath it.

The memory hit me like a lightning bolt and I gasped with excitement. "They were known as the Pleiades, the seven daughters of the titan Atlas and the sea-nymph Pleione, born on Mount Cyllene. They were the sisters of Calypso, Hyas, the Hyades, and the Hesperides. Collectively with the seven Hyades, they were seen as the Atlantides and were teachers to the infant Dionysus. They were thought to have been tossed into the night's sky as a cluster of stars and were associated with rain." My men listened to me without interrupting. "Mum mentioned one in particular — Electra, the wife of Corythus, to whom she bore Lasion. Zeus seduced her, and she gave birth to his son, Dardanus. According to legend, she was the lost Pleiad, disappearing in grief after the demise of Troy. It always felt as if she was referring to someone she knew, but I never questioned her about it. Now I wish I had."

Dominic scrunched his brows into a compassionate frown. "Don't beat yourself up about it, babe. How were you supposed to know what it meant? For all we know, it might have been nothing, not a metaphor for a cheating wife."

Asher side-eyed Dominic. "One who was seduced into having another man's child," he raised a good point. "This might give us an idea where Aunt Safi hid the clue, but I'm hoping that's all there is to it."

"We must decide who's going where," Cruz commented, eager to complete the plan.

All eyes fell to the map, studying each location. Splitting up meant travelling to different countries. We wouldn't be able to run to each other's aid if things went south. The anxiety was genuine, and my stomach churned with dread. What if this was the last time that we could all be together? We were standing upon the cliff edge, getting ready to take the plunge. The only thing that was keeping me going was the Wolfe brothers, and the life they had promised me when all this was done.

Dominic's laptop beeped with an incoming message, and we all glanced to see it.

"Alpha Two is secure. The coastguard found the wreckage, and they reported it as a tragic accident. They are searching for Bexley's remains, but we all know it's the pendant they want. Think of it as a head start, so don't waste the opportunity. When they don't find our bodies, they will assume we're still alive." We viewed the note from Uncle Zane and my dad, relieved their plan had worked out. "We'll keep you posted if we hear anything else. As long as you remain under the radar, the British Secret Service will be blindsided. However, the Chameleon will not be so easily fooled. He will see it's a ruse to throw the agency off your scent. Remain vigilant, and stay safe"

Dom was quick to reply, "You too." Then clicked the cross in the top right-hand corner of the message to shut down the chat.

I felt better knowing that Dad and Zane were out there, watching over us from afar. Alpha Two seemed like the perfect location to relax and unwind after all this was done. I imagined them strolling around on a hot, sunny beach, sitting beneath a palm tree in their swimming trunks, drinking from a coconut cup. You know . . . one of those exotic cocktails that has curly straws and paper umbrellas. Dad would be soaking up the warm rays, muttering about, *"this being the good life"*, and Uncle Zane would be perving through his Ray Bans at all the women who would be splashing around in their bikinis. Maybe they'd be topless, and Dad would be looking too

I've been here in the cold for far too long. If there was an

ice bar, it wouldn't be as bad, but there's nothing for miles and miles.

I need something stronger than tea.

"Right, so —" Cruz said as he scrubbed a hand over his face, looking agitated. I pretended I hadn't been carried away with my thoughts. "Who's flying where?" he asked with a huff.

"I'll go to Austria," Dominic volunteered.

Asher looked at me, giving me a choice of where I wanted to visit. "We'll take Spain," I answered, craving a warmer climate. "I appreciate it's not a holiday, but I just need some fucking sun." I left out the part where I was craving a cocktail.

"I'll fly to Ukraine," Cruz insisted. "I've been there plenty of times, I know exactly where to lay low if things turn ugly."

Braxton shrugged. "Sweden it is then," he uttered as if it made no difference to him where he went.

"That just leaves Norway — the Seven Sisters Waterfall," Asher pointed out. "It's the closest. What do you guys think? Do we head there first, or save that one for last? Bexley spoke of Electra. She's named as the second sister, so that narrows down the territory. I'm guessing we need to search around the second waterfall." He turned to Braxton. "What do you suggest? You're familiar with the terrain."

Braxton exhaled a weary sigh. "It could take forever for one of us to search around the area. Five pairs of eyes are better than one, especially when we don't even know what we're searching for."

"So, we save Norway until last, when we know what we're looking for," I decided on behalf of everyone. "At least then, if anyone comes looking for us, we can retreat to Alpha One." I never wanted to step foot onto Svalbard again, but if it meant that we would all be safe, then it would be worth the sacrifice.

Asher made a move to stand, then we all followed suit.

"It'll be wise to travel during the daylight hours." He exhaled a tremulous breath. "Your prosthetics and hairpieces are ready." He turned to me, wincing his eyes. "Sorry, Bexley, I'm going to have to make you look like a sexy librarian," he said with a chuckle. He didn't seem sorry at all.

Oh my god, this was happening. I couldn't stop myself from shaking as we made our way down to Dominic's bunker. Braxton placed his palm against the small of my back as he guided me through the door. Cruz noticed I was looking worried and took hold of my hand to kiss it. Dominic and Asher were there in a heartbeat, encapsulating me in a Wolfe clan group hug

The moment had come for me to fulfil my mother's legacy. It was going to be dangerous. We may not survive. I feared losing the most important men in my life — my dad included. Only time would tell if guardian angels existed or not, and if what my father said was true, my mother really was looking down on me from heaven. I closed my eyes in silent prayer, hoping she would take care of us. That she would bring my loved ones back to me, safe and sound

CHAPTER
Twenty

Asher

After putting my exceptional prosthetic skills to good use, my brothers were unrecognizable. Bexley was the embodiment of my teenage wet dreams, standing before the mirror as she struggled to secure her wig in place. Dominic helped, having successfully fitted his own. Hundreds of bobby pins later and the transformation was complete

"How do I look?" she asked, slipping on a thick-rimmed pair of glasses.

I sucked the drool from the corner of my lips. "Like the mother of my future children," I muttered, causing my brothers to splutter with laughter. "No, seriously, you look convincing. No one would ever believe it's you under there."

"And this turns you on?" she retorted, casting a critical eye over her nerdy attire. "Sensible shoes, a floral ankle-length frock, and a chunky knitted cardigan?"

I flicked my eyes up and down, dramatically. "It's what's underneath them that counts."

Bexley's eyes bulged and her nostrils flared.

"Whatever floats your boat," she muttered

Dominic handed out gadgets to Braxton and Cruz, leaving us for last.

"Bexley, Ash, come take your pick," he encouraged. "You're going to Spain, so how about heat-censored sunglasses and a hand-held fan that can double as a rotary blade? Pick up as many items as you need. They'll fly through the security checks without a hitch. I travel with them all the time."

Bexley put on the custom-made jewellery and knocked the cyanide compact, kiss of death lipstick, and a bottle of perfume into her hand-luggage. She did it discreetly, but I was onto her stealthy movements.

"Be careful with those, they are not toys," I warned, frowning.

She maintained a look of innocence. "I know, I'll be careful." Then she picked up a ladies watch, snaking it around her wrist. "Could you help me with this, please?"

I fixed the clasp into place, then held on to her wrist. "Don't tamper with it," I advised. "Not even to set the hour hand forward. It'll automatically adjust to suit the time zone. To detonate the bomb, take off the bracelet, push the side button, then throw it at your target. It'll act like a grenade. The back is magnetic. It will stick to any metal surface. The same rule applies; press it, then run for cover."

"Got it," she answered, absorbing the information

We were ready to leave. Dominic piled his belongings onto the snowmobile, then changed into his snow gear. Braxton loaded his Jeep, Cruz prepared a private plane, and we planned to hop on board with him to catch a ride to the airfield. Bexley almost broke down in tears as we all hugged goodbye.

"When we reach our designated safe zones, we have to report to Alpha Two. Dad and Uncle Jaxx are on standby; they will update us when we've all checked in," I reiterated the plan, going over what we agreed with Dad.

"Be careful," Bexley said, kissing Dominic and Braxton one last time. "I love you so much."

She fought back tears as they left, unable to look away until they had disappeared out of sight.

"Babe," Cruz beckoned, draping his arm across her shoulders in a protective gesture. "It's time to go."

Bexley nodded, letting him escort her into the jet. As he warmed up the engines, I completed the shutdown procedure, eliminating the data from the computer system. If our enemies ever found this place, they would presume it was an abandoned military outpost and not our secret hideout.

We were up in the air within minutes, peering out through the windows at the arctic landscape. Bexley was determined to spot a polar bear as we reached the coastline. But after no such luck, she slumped back with disappointment. It didn't take long for us to arrive at Svalbard regional airport at Longyearbyen. They granted Cruz permission to land, thanks to the false identification Dominic provided. Then Bexley and I said our farewells to him. We boarded a flight to Norway, and from there we caught a direct trip to Madrid. Bexley seemed on edge throughout the entire flight, scared to death that the authorities would be there waiting for us.

"Relax," I whispered, leaning closely as the flight attendant passed. I glanced back with annoyance. "Excuse me," I spoke, much to Bexley's dismay.

The flight attendant flicked her gaze to me and flashed a megawatt smile. "Yes, sir. How can I help?" she asked, shuffling backwards with the trolley.

"Can I have two bottles of bubbly for me and the wife?" I inquired. "We're celebrating our honeymoon."

Her face lit up with glee. "Oh, congratulations!" she exclaimed. Then she handed over two plastic glasses and two miniature bottles of champagne. "Have a drink on us," she offered kindly.

It was the first time I had seen a champagne bottle with a screw cap. I met Bexley's death glare as the attendant bustled away. Then I busied myself, pouring the drinks.

"Let's make a toast to the start of our new adventure," I suggested, not realizing that we had attracted everyone's attention. They were all fawning over our news, joining in with the toast.

"To the happy couple!" a passenger commented.

Bexley snorted her mouthful of champagne, looking every inch the awkward geek that she was supposed to be. "Thank you," she replied, shying her eyes away.

A round of applause erupted around the cabin.

"See," I murmured, keeping my voice low. "Just act naturally and everything will go as planned."

I practically had to eat my words as we arrived in Madrid. My suitcase was nowhere to be seen and I was just about to lose my shit. Everyone was leaving, and we were among the last few remaining passengers who were waiting. My heart was beating so fast, I almost went into cardiac arrest. That wasn't like me at all. I was usually so composed.

"Darling, stop stressing. You're acting like a typical Brit," Bexley teased, fighting the urge to giggle. "Look there it is." She pointed at the luggage conveyor.

The couple we met on the plane had already collected their cases and loaded them onto a trolley. The guy turned to me with a sympathetic grimace. "It would be a different story if it was her case, wouldn't it?" he said, injecting a little light-hearted humour into the situation

I grinned. "I know. I would never hear the end of it," I agreed.

Bexley dragged my case from the conveyor and I hauled it onto the trolley.

"Where to now, Derrick?" she asked, using my fake name.

I waited until we were safely outside to resume our conversation.

"We have a reservation at the Mandarin Oriental Hotel Ritz," I told her, noticing her startled expression

"That's lavish, isn't it?" Bexley panicked. "Shouldn't we stay somewhere discreet?"

"It's perfectly reasonable for a young couple to stay at the Ritz on their honeymoon. Derrick Stanley is no cheapskate, Margaret — or should I call you Marge?" I retorted.

Bexley shot me a side glance. "Don't you dare."

"We have to look the part. You wouldn't want to stay in a dingy bed-and-breakfast on your honeymoon, would you?" I explained. "We can search for one if you'd prefer."

"No, the Ritz is fine," Bexley was quick to answer. "We'll just have to maintain a low profile."

"Newly-weds spend most of their time in the bedroom," I commented, hinting at my smutty thoughts. "But since we're here to locate clues, I included attractions on the package. Tomorrow we'll visit the Reina Sofia National Art Museum and see what we can discover."

We arrived at the prestigious hotel, famished and fatigued. As Bexley showered, I checked in with Dad, then called room service to order a late dinner.

Dad text back within moments, notifying me I was the last to reach out. That meant my brothers had made contact. We set the wheels in motion and initiated phase one of the plan.

"Is everything all right, babe?" Bexley asked, emerging from the bathroom in just a towel.

She raked her hand through her wet hair, casting me sultry eyes like a sex kitten. My cock thickened beneath the thin material of my boxers. I had stripped down to my underwear to cool off, but Bexley sent the temperature soaring.

"It is now," I rasped. "Come here, I'm starving."

I patted the bed, then lay down flat against the mattress. As Bexley crawled over me, I grasped her hips, hoisting her to my face. With her knees at my ears, I pulled the towel from her body, baring her gorgeous physique. Her feminine heat greeted me as I kissed my way up her thighs, finding the slick cleft of her pussy too good to resist.

"Ash," Bexley groaned. "Dinner will be here in a minute"

"They don't work that fast, babe, and neither do I," I rasped, going in for the kill.

Bexley arched her back as my tongue speared her clit and began to stroke.

"God," she gasped, curling her fingers around the bedpost.

Her bud swelled against my lips, the sweet juices rolling down my tongue, licking, lapping, tasting, until her legs shook with the rapture of her climax.

"Fuck this, I'm taking what's mine," she murmured, freeing my iron appendage from my boxer briefs.

Bexley angled it where she needed it and enveloped her mouth around the crown. My balls shrunk to the size of walnuts as she bobbed her head, swallowing me down to the root. The position was perfect, a sweet orchestration of oral pleasures. Her ravenous sucks and my greedy feasting soon had us flying apart. My balls tingled at the same moment her thighs clung to my head, our frantic momentum increasing as we chased our release. I drank her delicious nectar and she swallowed my musky cream; our bodies writhing on the crisp white sheets as we worked up a sweat. My dream woman.

CHAPTER
Twenty-One

Braxton

There was no direct ferry to and from Svalbard. The only way I could travel by boat was to hitch a ride with one of the excursion ships. I bargained my way onto the Ocean Atlantic, a robust Arctic ship that was large enough to navigate through Greenland's ice-choked waters, and docked at Tromsø, Norway. I then had a nineteen-hour drive to Stockholm, Sweden. Lucky for me, I passed no tolls on route to Slussen. My eyes stung with fatigue from driving such a long distance. I needed to rest, so I checked into the Hilton and grabbed some much-needed shut-eye.

After a revitalizing sleep, I resumed the persona of a wrinkly old bastard who was here on a soul-searching mission. That was the thing about old people, the crankier they were, the more people tended to give them a wide berth. I had an abundance of crankiness. My brothers could vouch for that. Right now, I was hungry, and a food-deprived Braxton was worse than any bad-tempered geriatric you were ever likely to meet.

The room service was dismal, barely enough to feed a pigeon. If I wasn't undercover, I would have complained, but I chose not to because I didn't want to draw any unnecessary attention to myself. I checked my phone app to scout out the local eateries, needing something substantial to fill my stomach. We still didn't know what we were looking for; the clues could be tangible items or scratchings on a wall, they could be anything. It would be impossible for me to gain entry to the church at night without permission. The priest would never agree to that. I had to get in and out of there without people noticing what I was up to, but that was easier said than done.

I had to remember that I was supposed to be an elderly man, not an able-bodied soldier as I ambled through the streets taking laboured steps. Just to add a little authenticity to the act, I stopped every few yards to catch my breath, using the opportunity to assess my surroundings. The weather was mild, the wind rustled the leaves on the trees, people were passing me by on the pavement, and cars drove past at a leisurely pace. I used the nearest crossing and headed to the small café on the corner of the street. In a typical Swedish style, the pristine modern establishment was warm and welcoming, the coffee and pastry infused air hit my tastebuds with a bang. I chose a table beside the restrooms as most elderly people did, and perused the rectangular menu as if I was ordering my last supper. My stomach roared like a mountain lion awaiting a fresh kill. People looked around to see what was making the noise. It could be worse, like a bad case of flatulence. I ordered meatballs and a refillable coffee, opting for decaf because of my gastro-inflammatory problems. I don't really suffer from that but it prevented the waitress from asking any further questions.

To my delight, I was served quickly. And like a dog with a bone, I was likely to bite the hand of anyone who dared to disturb me.

"Excuse me, dear?" a voice called out from yonder.

I continued to feast away in blissful ignorance.

"You're not from around here, are you?" the same voice spoke, and I placed the voice to her face as she took the seat opposite me.

Frowning, I replied, "I'm on holiday." My abrupt tone didn't put her off, she just smiled, reminding me of Helen Mirren, a silver vixen from the Bond films. Cruz would have taken a selfie with her lookalike, but I was just irked about being disturbed.

Can't she see I'm eating? My food is getting cold.

"What a coincidence. I'm here on holiday too," she replied. "Would you like to do a spot of sight-seeing together?"

I shifted uncomfortably on my seat, thinking of a polite way to decline. This lady was old enough to be my grandmother. I didn't want to come across as rude

Remember what Asher would say . . . "Be subtle, Braxton"

"I'm acting on my late wife's last wishes, God rest her soul," I answered, hoping that she would take it as a hint and leave of her own accord. "She wanted me to scatter her ashes in the memorial garden. It wouldn't feel right for me to enjoy the company of another woman so soon after her passing."

The mortification etched across her face. "Oh, I'm so sorry. I didn't mean to . . . ugh, I'm so embarrassed," she rushed her words, hiding her face with her hands.

"Don't be," I returned, softening my tone. "I'm rather flattered you asked," I played along to ease the moment. "I don't get approached by beautiful women often, as you can probably tell."

She chuckled, dabbing the wrinkly skin beneath her eyes. "You have to grab the bull by the horns at our age," she joked, then reached out to grasp my hand. The prosthetic liver-spotted skin felt natural to touch. She gazed deep into my eyes, her ice blue irises sparking with a hint of mischief. "If you ever change your mind and decide you'd like some company . . ." I got the feeling she was after more than a late-night chat the way her thumb circled my skin, suggestively. "I'll be staying at the Hilton. I noticed you are too. Maybe we could keep each other occupied if you know what I mean." She winked.

If that wasn't enough motivation for me to find the clue and get the fuck out of Sweden, then I didn't know what was.

"I'll bear that in mind," I replied. "I'm George by the way."

"Rose." She stood up to leave and grabbed her coat and handbag. "I'll see you later."

I waited until she left the café before choking into my paper napkin, having suddenly lost my appetite. My meatballs belonged to Bexley, not to be fondled by a saucy gran named Rose. There was no way that I would ever tell this to my brothers, or Bexley. They would never let me live it down. I paid for the half-eaten lunch and hailed a taxi at the side of the road. I made a mental note of the road signs: Renstiernas Gata, Borgmästargatan, Skånegatan, Stora Mejtens Gränd

Oh, fuck, what was the first one again?

The road circled the Sofia church and the manicured lawns surrounding it. Tourists and locals were lounging lazily across the green. The ostentatious architecture stood proudly from the earth like it was offended by it, boasting magnificent stained-glass windows and a blue slate roof and steeple

Like a devil in disguise, I felt judged from the moment I crossed the threshold, ambling across the medium oak floorboards and into the heart of the building. The cream walls surrounded me, caging me in like a claustrophobic sinner. I brushed my fingertips against the oak wood pews as I marvelled at the painted mural wall at the head of the altar and the tall organ pipes that climbed the highest pinnacle.

Where in God's name would our aunt choose to hide the fucking clue?

I searched everywhere. My eyes scanned the room, looking for the slightest scratch, disturbed artifact, or anything remotely suspicious. It was getting dark, and the church was almost empty except for the caretakers who came in to clean it. I leaned against the font at the foot of the altar and let out an exhausted sigh.

My feet almost gave way beneath me as the stone moved an inch. Alarmed that I had damaged it, I attempted to drag it back into place. But then a small gap in the floorboards drew my eyes to the darkness within it, and I realised that there was a hidden compartment beneath the heavy object. Sparing a glance to check that the coast was clear, I moved the font to one side, almost bursting a vein in my forehead. I was on my knees in a heartbeat, reaching between the boards until my fingers coiled around something small and solid. Footsteps alerted me that someone was coming, so I quickly dragged the font back into place and shoved what looked like a flash drive inside my jacket pocket. That had to be it. I had found a hidden clue, or some dirty priest's sordid little secrets, who knows? I had searched the place from top to bottom and found nothing else.

A caretaker yelled at me in Swedish, urging me to get out or else she would lock me inside. I made my apologies and ventured back to the hotel, narrowly avoiding my admirer. Rose popped her head out of her doorway and I could see she was dressed in a black satin negligee and robe.

There was only one thing she was after, and it wasn't a tube of denture adhesive.

I shuddered, hoping that I could contact Dad and make a sharp exit. After gathering my things, unplugging my phone from the charging cable and tossing the remainder of my belongings into a backpack, I dialled my father.

Dad picked up on the third ring, answering with a gruff, 'Hello?"

"One down," I announced. "Where's the rendezvous point?" I asked

"Paris," Dad answered gruffly. "Father Fournier is expecting you all to arrive at Notre Dame in two days. We have another mission for you to complete before you head to the waterfall."

My shoulders sagged. "Another church?" The sarcasm was real.

"Yes and no," Dad replied vaguely. "You'll be attending the Versailles masked ball. I will brief you when you arrive. From there, you will seek shelter in Father Fournier's chateaux until the coast is clear."

"Who is the target?" I inquired, out of interest.

"The real traitor to our country." Dad paused, causing my innards to twist with anxiety.

"Who?" I felt my heart pulse with adrenaline.

"We're counting on you to find out," he replied.

A knock on the door startled me temporarily, and I ended the call, shoving my phone into my pocket.

"George, are you okay in there?" Rose murmured

Shoving my arms through my backpack, I crawled through the window and pulled the hook from my utility belt, making sure it was secure before abseiling onto the pavement. I cut the wire with a pocket knife and jogged around to the car park. After conducting a quick scan of my Jeep, I was good to go. The digital display screen lit up blue, determining the fastest route out of Stockholm.

CHAPTER Twenty-Two

Dominic

Since arriving in Austria, I had to undergo two outfit changes. It wasn't easy. I discarded my snow gear and snowmobile back in Svalbard and changed into a grey Juicy Couture tracksuit, pink Sketchers, and a black Khloé Kardashian headband. If I earned a pound each time that I caught some bloke giving me the eye, I could end world poverty. Men are pigs, always thinking with their dicks. I should know. I could have given them a glimpse of my fake bodysuit, or let my balls hang out, but I didn't want to blow my cover. My dick had to behave and stay strapped against my thigh. All thoughts about Bexley had to be boxed away in my brain, only to be brought out when I'm alone in my hotel room. As soon as I reached Finland, I purchased a trip to Austria, then slept during the entire journey.

My hotel was within a mile of the castle. After a bum-numbing flight, I checked-in, grabbed a bite to eat, then freshened up, ready to plan my attack. Dominique was a flamboyant character, so I turned her into a star wedding planner? I could try charming my way inside, pretending to be scouting locations for a top-secret celebrity wedding. The castle played host to corporate events and other official conference meetings; they would snap up the opportunity to make a fat wad of cash. Celebs were known for splashing the cash around, doing magazine deals, and doing crazy shit to get tons of publicity. Getting in there would be a doddle.

Dressed in a chic Oscar de la Renta black-and-white striped dress with pointed shoulder pads, and black Christian Louboutin heels, I strutted my stuff as I flounced in from the lakeside grounds and into the entrance hall, my matching handbag dangling from the crease of my elbow on a golden chain.

I flicked my bouncy blonde curls over my shoulder. "Excuse me, darling?" I announced my presence to an official-looking chap who was dressed in formal attire.

My brothers always said I could pull off a feminine French accent, and once suggested I could run a phone sex chat line and that men would never know the difference

The guy glanced up from behind the reception desk and his blue eyes bulged as they landed on me, ping-ponging from my tits to my face.

"Hallo," he replied, flashing me a welcome smile. "French or English?" he asked, unsure which I preferred

"Ooh, I love a bilingual man, but English if you don't mind. My client thinks I could use the practice," I excused with a humoured shrug.

The square-jawed blond swatted the air. "Nonsense, your English sounds perfect to me."

I covered my mouth as I giggled, then fluttered my fake eyelashes.

His female colleague shot him a side-glance, but he was more interested in me. "My name is Lukas. How may I be of service?"

I pulled my tablet out from my bag and tapped the blank screen. "Bonjour, Lukas. I'm Dominique Moulin." I stole the name from The Moulin Rouge. "I realize I should have called in advance, but the thing is, my client wants to make an enormous gesture to the love of his life. Football players and their popstar women; they expect us to work miracles. I'm not a magician or a fairy godmother, but I can throw a spectacular event at short notice. That's why they all hire me. It's what I do." I preened my hair and let out an accomplished sigh.

This maintained his interest. "Are you saying he wants to hire the venue for a wedding?" He sounded excited about that.

I nodded. "Uh-huh, and he sends me thousands of miles away to search for a fairy tale castle." I splayed my hand, setting a dramatic scene. "And I thought, why not Laxenburg Castle in all its splendour? The magnifique gardens, charmant interior," I added extra ambience, using a mixture of French and English words. "I said to him . . . I said, Becks . . . Posh will be over the moon to renew your wedding vows there."

His female colleague was sold on the mention of the A-listers, leaning her elbow against the desk in a dreamy stupor.

"Do you mean who I think you mean?" the enthralled male spoke.

"Oui," I confirmed. "Sir Golden Balls himself."

I'm such a convincing bull-shitter.

"Some parts of the grounds are off-limits to tourists, but I suppose we could make an exception for such a sporting legend," he added, with a rapid lick of the lips. "Would you mind if I gave you a guided tour?"

Ugh, no. How was I going to search the castle with an eighties version of Schwarzenegger tagging along beside me?

That wasn't part of the plan. I would have to lose him and pray that he doesn't come back. Like his famous catchphrase, he was harder to shake than the common cold.

"Okay," I replied feebly. "I'll be mostly taking pictures." I held up the tablet. "Snippety snap."

Lukas escorted me around the majestic castle, guiding me through each opulent room. I scanned my tablet to no avail, finding every embellished surface true to its nature. My heart sank with each passing hour. Lukas gave me a thorough history lesson about the arch-duchess Sophie of Austria, born on the fifth of March 1855, and died on the twenty-ninth of May 1857, age two. He was meticulous and fluent with the details, as if this place was his life. The name Sophie was vital to discovering the clue. I had to convince my rambling tour guide to show me something of great importance. An heirloom, a portrait, or a statue perhaps.

"Oh, that poor little bébé," I fake whimpered. "You know, I love children. I just haven't met the perfect man to impregnate me in all the right places . . . by that I mean the womb," I spoke in a low, sultry husk, almost giving away my manliness.

Lukas didn't seem to notice. He seemed aroused.

"Do you believe in fate, Dominique?" he replied, his voice sounding a little laboured and breathless.

I brushed my palm across the lapels of his jacket, ridding him of non-existent dust. "You know something, Lukas, I think I do."

He leaned closer, moistening his lips as if he was about to pucker them up for a kiss. My heart jump-started in my chest and I veered around to admire the wall of portraits.

"This is beautiful . . . they are going to love it . . . all of it," I mentioned. "It's perfect."

As I turned to face Lukas, I saw him composing himself. "Uh, yes, that's wonderful news."

"You've got me wanting babies, Lukas," I told him, giving him a playful tap on the shoulder.

His lips curled into a side smirk. "How so?" his

tone suggested sex, and he glanced around as if he was checking to see if we were alone.

"You naughty, sexy man," I chuckled. "I know what you want, but I'm not that easy, you know. If you want a date with me, at least buy me dinner first."

I held the tablet up as if I was taking his picture, seeing his full skeletal system on the screen. Another tap displayed a heat-censored image, displaying his white-hot crotch. I had to take an actual picture just in case he wanted to see it for himself. The time was running out. We had trawled from room to room and I had found nothing of any interest yet.

"Would you like me to show you the doll that Elisabeth of Bavaria had made in the memory of her beloved Sophie?" he asked, wanting to impress me. "It is called "Sophie" after the late duchess."

A doll?

The excitement on my face must have shown.

"There's a doll? I love dolls," I lied, recalling the time Braxton had forced me to watch Annabelle.

Chucky, Annabelle, Dolly Dearest, and Toy Soldiers, they were all as freaky as fuck.

Lukas led me into an ornate nursery with a hand-crafted crib and a threadbare rocking horse. Brass railings created a walkway between the furniture, and they placed signs in Austrian warning people not to touch anything. He unbolted a railing and ushered me through a door disguised as a bookshelf, guiding me through the darkness.

Lights flickered on all around us, and my eyes danced around the plain cream walls, landing on the glass cabinet in the centre of the room. The doll was a nightmarish depiction of horror with a pale porcelain face, awful hair, and a frock that Vivian Westwood could have designed when she was drunk. I sucked in a sharp intake through flared nostrils, hoping Lukas didn't catch the grimace on my face.

"Just one second," I excused as my phone rang inside my bag

I called myself from the tablet purposefully; it was an excuse to retrieve my tranquilizer pen. A single click sent a dart the size of a needle flying through the air and it stuck into Lukas's neck. I acted fast, catching him before he hit the floor, then placed him on the ground to sleep it off

"If I was a woman, I would, mate," I said to him while he was out cold.

The cabinet wasn't locked, but even if it was, I could have easily picked the lock. The doll's body wasn't soft and full of stuffing, it was hard and something rattled inside it.

"Shit, please don't fucking haunt me," I muttered as I pulled off the head .

I tipped the body upside down and a memory stick fell into my hand.

"Bingo," I celebrated, dropping it into my handbag

I stuffed the doll's head back into place as best as I could. It wasn't perfect. Then I placed it back inside the cabinet and closed the door.

With my chaperone out like a light, I had to remember the way back by myself. The woman at the reception desk was on the phone, too busy complaining about Lukas's flirting. She didn't notice me leaving. Kicking off my killer shoes enabled me to run as fast as I could back to the hire car and away from Castle Freak Show.

Once I was back inside the safety of my hotel room, I checked in with Dad to update him of my findings.

"Well done, Dom. That's two down, three to go," he informed me. "Braxton got lucky too."

Yeah, but I bet he didn't get hit on by the Terminator.

"What's the plan from here?" I asked, slumping down on the queen-size bed.

I was missing Bexley and hoped that Dad's next instructions would lead me back to her.

Dad's breathing rattled down the line. "I'm sending you an address in Paris. Travel safely and be careful," he advised. "Braxton is on his way. We're just waiting on Cruz, Asher, and Bexley to find the remaining clues."

Paris? The city of love? Maybe I believe in fate after all.

CHAPTER
Twenty-Three

Cruz

Thanks to Asher, I looked every inch a jet-setting entrepreneur as I strolled through Kyiv International Airport, having stashed the plane in a private bunker. The fake I.D enabled me to hire a car with no issues, and from there I endured a three-hour drive to Sofiyivka Park, stopping once to refuel.

I checked into the Lomo Hotel Uman, close to

where I needed to be. My phone battery was almost dead, so I plugged it in and arranged my spy gear on the bed. Dominic had given me a pair of x-ray sunglasses, a sonar watch that could detect objects that are hidden underwater, a small oxygen tank and mouthpiece for searching the surrounding lake, and a Glock handgun with a silencer. I wasn't sure if I could cover the entire area during one visit, so I used an I.P address scrambler, so I could pull up an aerial view of the land. This enabled me to narrow down the search into several zones.

Dad wanted me to check-in with him, so I dropped a text to say that I had arrived. He replied, informing me he had sent Uncle Ulrich to collect me from the hotel. He was always my contact whenever I came to Ukraine. Dad told me the agency had failed to recover the bodies from the wreckage, and until they found us, we were all presumed missing as opposed to dead. I ate the rest of the food I purchased from the petrol station, then set my alarm for 6 am. Bexley's face swam into my mind's eye as I drifted off to sleep, and I imagined her lying here beside me. I hoped to God that wherever she was, Asher was keeping her safe.

I left the hotel bright and early before anyone else.

Dressed like a typical European tourist, I wore my backpack upon both shoulders, my packed lunch hiding all the spy equipment beneath a hidden panel. So, if they check my bag, or run it through a machine, all it would show is the hotel-provided ration pack. The warm weather encouraged people to step outdoors, and soon enough the park was bustling with families and individuals who loved to walk among nature. I searched from zone to zone, inside every building, conservatory, and ornate gazebo, among every flower bed, and used the watch to search every body of water. Count Stainislaw Potocki founded the gardens in 1796. He was a Polish noble who rebuilt Uman after a peasant uprising. He named the garden after his Greek wife, Sofia, and gifted it to her on her birthday. There had to be a monument, a focal point, or an object of significance. My aunt wouldn't hide something of such great value in any old place.

"Hey, mister." I glanced up from the flowerbed and saw I'd attracted an audience of four small children. "What are you doing?" a girl with blonde pigtails asked in Ukrainian.

It was lucky I could understand their native tongue

"Are you looking for fairies?" a girl with red curls

inquired

"Boys don't search for fairies, they look for elves," a boy with dark spiky hair grumbled, crossing his arms with a scowl on his face.

"Have you noticed any?" I inquired, pretending to look around the flower garden. "They were here a moment ago, lots of little elves and fairies."

The children gasped with amazement.

"Really? You've met them?" the boy asked.

I nodded. "Hundreds of them, everywhere," I fibbed

The children exchanged awestruck glances, then they flicked their eyes to me

"I knew it," a little girl with a short brown bob muttered

"Have you ever met the fairy queen?" a girl with pigtails inquired.

I sank to one knee so I could speak to the kids at eye-level.

"Yes," I replied, thinking of Bexley. She was the light in my life. "She's my favourite."

"Grown-ups aren't supposed to see them," the girl with red curls stated. "You must be special."

"Well, I can see them perfectly well," I assured her. "And if you capture one, they have to grant you three wishes," I added, sounding as convincing as possible. "But you mustn't wander away from your parents. Fairies are playful, but they can be mischievous too. They like to get you into trouble, so stay alert, and don't let them trick you."

The children whispered among themselves and decided on something.

"Okay, we'll be careful," they chimed in response. "Thanks, Mister Fairy King."

I winced at that comment, thanking the heavens that my brothers were not here to witness this.

As they scattered away, giggling, I resumed my search for the clue. I followed the path around a small algae-dotted pool that was half-concealed with a mass of lily pads. The surrounding foliage provided a shroud of mystery, and as I peered over the footbridge, I noticed a cave with a white marble sculpture inside. Using the x-ray sunglasses, I could see beneath the bridge and rock and discovered a pocket of air through an underwater tunnel. Not wanting to get covered in pond filth, I climbed over the edge and dangled above the water, swinging back and forth to vault onto the slimy surface. I collided with the feminine figure and clung to her naked frame, my feet sliding through the slick green moss. I must have dislodged debris from the ancient water feature because brown sludge oozed from the lip of the stone and plopped into the pool, then water cascaded from a filter above me like a waterfall, churning the murky pond. Acting quickly, I removed the oxygen tank from my backpack and shoved the mouthpiece between my lips. People could walk by at any moment and question what I was doing down here. Thinking on my feet, I secured my bag around the statue's shoulders to keep it dry, then dived beneath the surface, searching around for a slight cavity in the stone. My watch illuminated the way, guiding me to the correct spot. I swam through the tunnel, found the hidden chamber, and came up for air, finding that the thirty-centimetre gap was filling fast. There, on a narrow ledge, was a metal tin, no bigger than a box of cooking matches. I grabbed it, and swam back through the tunnel. As I returned, a young couple were peering over the bridge. It startled them as I broke through the surface to snatch my bag from the statue. They watched with alarm as I scrambled onto the embankment.

The woman screamed, and the man embraced his frightened lover. I raised my thumb in a friendly gesture and spat out the mouthpiece.

"Sorry about that. I'm the maintenance guy, checking the water pumps to see if they are working correctly," I said, noticing them sag with relief. "Carry on; don't mind me."

I peeled the wax seal from around the tin box and retrieved a memory stick from within it. My clothes were soaked. People assumed I had taken an unfortunate step and tumbled into the lake. I took no notice as they chuckled, my shoes squelching as I strode down the path, shoving the oxygen tank into my backpack. I hadn't packed a change of clothes, but thanks to the evening sun and my lightweight attire, I was soon dry in no time.

The children from earlier waved to me as they enjoyed a picnic on the green. "Look, there's the Fairy King," they chimed. I gave a polite wave, ignoring the amused snorts from their mothers.

Finally, I had got what I came for. Now I could return to the hotel and wait for Uncle Ulrich to arrive

The roads were empty, the streets were calm. The receptionist greeted me with a disinterested grunt as I retired to my room, using the stairs instead of the temperamental lift. I was glad to be back, keen to scrub myself in the shower. Food wasn't my top priority. The pond slime in my underwear was. I swiped my key card, but it refused to cooperate. It opened with the second attempt and the scent of food greeted me square in the face. Something was amiss. I whipped out my pistol and crept inside. A dark figure moved in my peripheral and I whirled around and aimed my gun at the intruder's head.

"Easy, Cruz. It's me," Uncle Ulrich blurted, raising his palms. "Zane told me you'd be here, so I let myself in." He held up a code-cracking device as evidence. A present from Dominic

Ulrich sported the same military buzz cut, although it was turning grey with age. The scar that sliced through his left eye made him appear scarier than he was. I remembered his teachings and always loved him as if he was my real uncle, not just a friend of my father.

I sagged with relief and lowered my weapon. "Jesus, you scared the shit out of me."

Ulrich met me halfway and yanked me into a fatherly hug

"Speak for yourself; you look like shit," he retorted. "And you smell like a sewage drain." He drew back, wrinkling his nose.

I shoved my gun into the waistband of my combat gear and flashed a humoured smile.

"Yeah, well, I smell food," I commented, savouring the mouth-watering aroma from the paper bag on the counter.

Ulrich crossed the room and rummaged inside, retrieving foil containers and two forks.

"Go shower first. You stink," he remarked, flicking his finger as if to shoo me away. "I'll fix dinner. Then we can talk."

After a much-needed shower, I returned to the room to dig out some fresh clothes from my luggage. Ulrich was half-way through his meal as I dressed. Then I took a seat at the vanity table to eat my dinner.

"I take it you found what you were searching for?" he asked, then shoved another forkful of pierogi into his mouth

"I did," I answered, flicking my gaze back to Ulrich

"Well then, call your father and let him know you have it," Ulrich barked, raising his voice as if I was eight years old and back in his training academy. He rolled his eyes and muttered swear words in Ukrainian

I did as he said and balanced the phone between my neck and shoulder as I ate.

"Cruz, I'm surprised to hear from you so soon," Dad commented, sounding hopeful.

"Mission accomplished," I confirmed. "Where do I go from here?"

Ulrich resumed eating, stabbing his fork into the savoury-filled dumplings.

"Paris. Mention to Ulrich about a hidden vineyard. He'll know what I'm talking about," Dad assured, his lewd chortle hinted at something crude.

I bounced my gaze to Ulrich. "Hey, we need to travel to Paris. Something about a vineyard. Dad said you'd remember."

Ulrich let out a dramatic groan. "Why?" he complained, shoving his food container to one side. "That place is filled with the devil's juice, not the church wine they led me to believe," he muttered to himself. "It was fun though. Especially the threesome with those French nuns."

I choked on my pierogi. "What about the others? Have they made contact yet?" I asked, changing the subject.

"Braxton and Dominic have. We're just waiting on Asher and Bexley," Dad informed me. "Don't use chartered flights. It's time to go dark. That's where Ulrich comes in; he has a Russian stealth jet on standby."

"We'll be there," I replied, ending the call.

I glanced up at Ulrich, seeing him in a whole new light. "Ménage à trois with nuns, huh?" I commented, arching my brow in a quizzical pose.

Ulrich was always quick to retort, countering me with logic. "Says the man who shares a woman with his brothers."

"Touché." I grinned. "Get us to Paris, and I'll introduce you to her."

CHAPTER
Twenty-Four

Bexley

S tretching out on the lounger, I reached for the tall glass of mimosa. The sun's rays caressed my skin with fiery kisses, and now and then a subtle breeze would drift by to soothe me. A Latin pop song filtered from the pool speakers, an evocative upbeat rhythm that made me want to get up and dance. I took a generous sip of the zesty orange beverage to quench my thirst, noticing Asher lurking in the background

"Darling, have you forgotten why we're here?" he mentioned, stepping out onto the balcony to admonish me. "To find the clue, remember?"

I flopped back onto the padded lounger and groaned. "Just five more minutes," I pleaded. "This might be the last time I'll ever get to enjoy the sunshine"

He rolled his eyes, huffing a lopsided smirk. "I'm just going to put on some shoes and grab our tickets, so start getting ready."

I opted to wear denim shorts, flat jewelled sandals, and a purple strappy top. Asher assured me he was packing the relevant spy gear into his backpack, and not to waste mine. We would need it for Paris. Dad was sending us on another mission, but I wasn't sure what it was. I would have all my men under one roof again. It had only been twenty-four hours since we parted ways, but I mourned their absence as if they had gone to war.

"Are you ready, Mrs Stanley?" Asher asked, standing at the door waiting for me.

I crossed the cream floor tiles and planted a kiss on his lips. "I would rather be called Mrs Wolfe, but yes, I'm ready as I'll ever be."

Something glimmered behind Asher's eyes, as if he was holding out on me. It aroused my suspicions. But as much as I begged him to reveal what he was hiding from me, he kept dodging the subject. I continued to peck for crumbs as we made our way down to the lobby.

"I know there's something you're not telling me, George, I can tell by the expression on your face," I accused, not letting it drop.

Asher chortled as we vacated the lift and stepped out into the busy lobby

"I don't know what you're talking about," he replied, half laughing.

"You're a terrible liar," I told him. "I saw that look in your eye."

He held my hand as we ventured through the glass doors and into the blistering sunlight.

"Maybe we have a surprise arranged. Have you thought about that?" he retorted, shutting me up.

Have they planned something romantic for me?

"Really? In Paris?" I fawned, wondering what wonderful treat lay in store for me in the city of love.

"Yes, we were thinking we could kill two birds with one stone," he muttered, not giving anything else away

Asher looked from left to right, waiting for the

stoplight to change from green to red, then led me across the street. We arrived at the bus stop and stood a short distance away from the other tourists.

"Killing birds is not romantic," I uttered impatiently.

Asher chuckled, drawing me in for a hug. "You'll see when you get there. I'm not spoiling anything. All I can say is, you shall go to the ball."

I knew what he meant, and I snatched an excited gasp. "The Versailles Masquerade Ball?" I whispered, pulling back in a lover's embrace.

Asher nodded, and I grinned, gleefully. I always wanted to go because my mother and father went there for their first date. It held a special place in my heart. I had a good feeling about Paris. Our coach arrived and took us on a sightseeing tour of the area. They dropped us off outside the Reina Sofia National Art Museum, and we fell into line at the back of the queue. Asher handled our tickets, taking back the stubs as a souvenir. I linked arms with him as we perused the spacious exhibit, looking for something eye-catching and relevant to my mother's past teachings.

The serious frown on Asher's face showed me he meant business. We passed comments on the art, trying to see if we could make sense of it all.

"Braxton said he discovered his item beneath a font. That could mean a test of faith or something unorthodox. Dominic found a flash drive inside an antique doll, so that represents a deceased infant, or a child who was presumed dead. I still don't know if Aunt Safi was casting light on the illegitimate baby theory. Cruz claimed she hid his clue beneath a cave. And I know from my research that Zofia Potocka acted as an agent in the Russian secret service. So, we have an agent, an illegitimate child, and a fall from grace. Let's hope this clue gives us something more to work with. Where would your mother choose to hide a memory stick in an art gallery?" he muttered, trying to rationalize things.

We kept moving, analysing each painting to see if we could solve the puzzle with logic. There was the "Guernica" by Pablo Picasso; one of the most iconic pieces produced by the Spanish painter that represented the Spanish Civil War. We studied it for a long while, but nothing seemed to fit. Juan Gris's "La table du Musician" didn't fit either. I wasn't sure about Salvador Dalí's "Grand Masturbator" I hoped Mum wouldn't be so crude.

"Babe, come look at this?" Asher alerted me to Braque's painting of "Cards and Dice".

I hurried over to admire the artwork.

"Braque painted this before the First World War," Asher explained. "He and Picasso were artistically comparable at that time, but both artists progressed differently. This piece illustrates a civilization revolving around games of chance." He narrowed his eyes on something, then pressed his forefinger against one dot on the dice.

I glanced around to make sure no one was looking. As if activated by a spring, a memory stick emerged from the canvas. Asher was quick to retrieve it and push the clear compartment back into place. No one would ever guess someone had tampered with it.

"Come on, let's get out of here," Asher urged, shoving the memory stick into his pocket and making sure he secured the zip

The sound of heavy footsteps echoed around the gallery, then we spotted armed guards, dressed all in black, heading straight for us.

"Run!" Asher yelled, taking me by the hand so we could escape.

We pushed past the jostling crowd, fighting to get outside, the sight of the guns caused people to react with terror. Their screams rattled through my ears as we darted across the busy courtyard. My heart exploded with trepidation, scared shitless of getting caught.

A taxi slowed down for a guy who was waiting at the edge of the road, but Asher nudged past him and stuffed one-hundred euros into his fist.

"Hey!" he yelled in protest.

The guards filtered through the doors, parting the crowd of tourists like the Red Sea.

"Thanks, but we need to leave quickly," Asher rushed the words, desperate for us to make a getaway. The guy glanced over his shoulder, then ran away.

"I'll give you one-thousand euros if you can get us to The Ritz in one piece," he bargained with the taxi driver.

"Get in," he offered.

The guards opened fire, narrowly avoiding the speeding taxi as it ushered us to safety. Asher and I collapsed back against the seat, panting for air.

"We grab our things, and we get the fuck out of Madrid," Asher advised.

"Who were they?" I asked, realizing they were not like any Spanish police I had ever seen before.

The pinched expression on his face told me this was bad.

"Agents from The Spanish Secret Service," he replied, scrubbing a hand over his jaw. "The ministry is on to us. They know we're alive and now they will know that we're onto something"

"Shit," I hissed. "How did they recognize it was us?"

Asher exhaled heavily. "It has to be someone close to your mother. In her messages, it's as if she's trying to warn us about someone."

"But who?" I huffed the words in frustration

"That's what I'm struggling to figure out," he muttered sombrely. He leaned forward to speak to the cab driver through the gap in the headrests. "I will give you fifty-thousand euros for your car, and another fifty-thousand for your silence. Do we have a deal?"

The flustered Spaniard shrugged. "Sure, I could use the extra cash."

We parked a short distance from the hotel, just to play it safe.

"Good, wait here. I'll be right back," Asher promised

Asher made me remain inside the taxi as he scaled the hotel walls like a spider monkey, climbing and leaping from balcony to balcony until he reached our room. I could see him from the backseat window, my stomach twisting into knots in case he fell. He wasn't gone for long. I noticed him using a zip wire to lower our luggage down to the poolside. My paranoia was on high alert, scared stiff of getting caught. Just as I was about to get out to help, Asher hurried back, then shoved our cases into the boot of the car. He paid the cabbie his money, then drove us away from the city. Blue and red flashing lights appeared in the side mirrors, detonating my last nerve.

"We're being followed," I panicked, checking behind us.

Asher accelerated, manoeuvring past the traffic in a blare of honking horns. I screamed as I jostled from side-to-side, seeing the landscape whizzing by in a streaky blur.

Asher maintained our velocity, not even breaking a sweat. "Bexley, take the wheel," he ordered, rolling down the window.

I grabbed it with shaking hands, terrified of crashing into another vehicle. The rear window shattered, and a vortex of cool air rushed inside. Asher took out a pistol and started shooting back in retaliation

"We're gonna die. We're gonna die," I whimpered.

The high-speed chase lasted moments, but it felt like an hour. I swallowed my heart several times as our car swerved from left to right to avoid slow-moving traffic. Asher fired shot after shot, then dove back into his seat as the police cars collided and rolled onto the dusty roadside. And just like in every action film Dad had ever forced me to watch, flames engulfed the scene behind us. My face contorted with horror.

"Asher, what are we going to do?" I asked, unable to stop myself from shaking. "We're in so much trouble."

He placed his hand on my knee, circling his thumb in a gentle caress.

"Don't worry. We did what we had to do for our queen and country. Don't fall apart on me now, Bexley. We must stick to the plan. I have other ways to get us to Paris," he assured. "There's a bloke called Emilio who owes me a favour, now it's time for me to collect the debt."

"Can we trust him?" I asked, doubting everything.

Asher flashed me a reassuring smile. "I should hope so, he's like a cousin to us."

"So, he's another Navy brat," I assumed, trying to recall which one of our father's friends had spawned offspring. I only ever met the Wolfe brothers.

"Good old Uncle Ted sowed his wild oats back in his heyday," Asher told me. "You remember Teddy, don't you?"

Of course, I did, he was my favourite. A huge smile spread across my face. As soon as he mentioned Uncle Ted, I knew we were safe, although it would take more than making a pound coin appear from behind my ear to pull us out of this mess. He would have to work a miracle.

"Emilio is his son. Uncle Ted retired to cultivate a lemon orchard in Torrelodones two years ago. He trained his son to fight for the cause the same as ours did for us," he explained, putting my mind at ease.

Asher called ahead, planning to obtain us a plane, a chopper, anything to take us off the ground. He took me to Uncle Teddy's villa, which was a rundown shack in the middle of nowhere. The rickety door burst open before we got the chance to park, and Ted ambled out to greet us, followed by a dark-haired Spaniard

"Asher, Bexley," Uncle Teddy exclaimed. "It's been a long time since I saw you, kids. You were this tall," he said, lifting his hand to measure how big we must have been back then.

The tall Adonis loped forward and shook Asher's hand. He turned to me and flashed a welcoming smile

"You must be Bexley. I've heard so much about you," he mentioned in a deep Spanish husk.

Asher draped his arm across my shoulders, protectively. "Easy, Emilio. She's taken."

I saw his eyes bulge wide and realised he knew what that meant; that I was claimed by the entire Wolfe pack, not just Asher.

"Come inside and have something to eat before we leave," Uncle Ted offered. "I'll need an hour to get the old girl up and running."

I hoped to God he was talking about his aircraft and not Emilio's mother.

CHAPTER
Twenty-Five

Bexley

U ncle Teddy's place was devoid of a woman's touch, which left me wondering about the whereabouts of Emilio's mother. I felt it was rude to pry, so I didn't ask. We ate paella and drank iced tea. I helped Emilio to wash the dinner dishes as Asher and Teddy hid the shot-up taxi and dragged an old propeller plane from the barn.

"I still can't believe I'm standing here beside Safi

Barker's daughter," Emilio mentioned as if awed by her memory.

As a child, I always looked up to my parents as if they were my heroes. I knew my father acted heroically in the Navy, but during the last few weeks, I realised just how courageous my mother had been. There was no way I could live up to a woman of her calibre, but it still encouraged me to try.

"Is it weird that I'm only just figuring out who my mother truly was?" I asked, exhaling a wistful sigh. "It seems like everyone knew her better than I did. I miss her so much."

"I miss mine too," Emilio confessed, taking the time to dry a cup he was holding. "Mine died when I was ten. My aunt tracked down my father, and he flew out to meet me. He was a total stranger, but he's been my rock ever since."

I flashed an empathic smile. "I love Uncle Ted. He's such a good man."

"Speaking of men," he muttered, casting a quizzical eye over me. "How does it work having four of them?"

Any other day, I would have blushed profusely at that comment. But not now. I wasn't ashamed to be involved with four brothers at once, even if society frowned upon it. Emilio was curious, as many people would be. It won't be the first time someone inquired, and I'm sure it won't be the last.

"Well, for starters, I'll never get bored," I replied, flashing a salacious grin.

Emilio chortled. "Do you all . . . you know? All at once," he asked, enthralled by our sexual dynamic

I shrugged, tipping the dirty dishwater down the sink. "Yes, they take turns fucking me. There's no jealousy. No favouritism. We spend time alone, or more than one will take part, or I will have them all at once. There's nothing gross about it. They don't pay attention to each other, just me."

Emilio placed the dry cup onto the table and turned to pick up a plate from the rack. He didn't seem shocked, more like relieved.

"What if they were not brothers, but lovers? Would it bother you if they took an interest in each other as well as yourself?" Something in the way he asked made me wonder if there was more to this than plain old curiosity.

"Well, no," I answered as honestly as I could. "As long as there are rules in place to protect everyone, then no one should get hurt. If my men were lovers, not brothers, and they wanted alone time together, then I would adhere to that, just as they would respect me having alone time with each of them. Relationships are all about give and take."

I narrowed my eyes, homing in on the rising blush spreading from his neck to his cheeks. "Emilio, are you okay?" I asked

He swallowed thickly. "Yes, it's nothing," he dismissed, even though there was clearly something he wasn't telling me.

"Whatever it is, maybe I can help?" I offered to lend a sympathetic ear.

His broad shoulders sagged as he sighed.

"There's a couple I've been seeing for almost a year now," he began, hesitating with the details as if he didn't quite know how to explain it. "My girlfriend, Tania, and I met at a bar four months before I was introduced to Carlos, her husband. Things were going great, then one day she confessed that she was married. I was mad at first, but then she said they had arranged this, that they chose me to be a part of a threesome. I've always been into women, not guys. So, when Tania mentioned her husband wished to meet me, I planned to tell him thanks, but no thanks. We met at the same bar, and to my surprise, we got along well. We met up a few more times, and I couldn't deny the growing attraction between us. The next thing I know, we were checking into a hotel. Things heated quickly. We kissed, we started touching, then we had sex. It was incredible. I wanted it as much as he did. When we told Tania, it thrilled her. She wanted to watch us. Carlos and I share her, and we enjoy one another as she watches. The point is, I'm in love with them, but I'm afraid of getting hurt. They're married. I'm just the extra piece on the side."

"Is that how they make you feel?" I asked, trying my best to help.

Emilio shook his head. "No, they say they love me too. And I want to believe it. It's just . . ."

"It's just hard to trust they'll never abandon you," I answered, appreciating how that felt. "It's difficult being the outsider; not knowing whether they'll wake up one day and decide you're no longer needed"

"Yeah, that's just it," he replied, his brows furrowing into a pained frown. "We don't use birth control, so if Tania gets pregnant, I'm scared of being pushed out of my kid's life. I wouldn't survive that."

"They came looking for you because something was missing in their relationship," I counselled. "You're the glue that holds them together, like a missing piece of a puzzle. They need you just as much as you need them. I don't think you have anything to worry about. And if you have kids, there will be an abundance of love to go around. It doesn't have to be complicated. You have the chance to become a part of a stable family, so just embrace it."

"Thanks, Bexley," Emilio said, his grin brightening his handsome face. "I needed to hear that."

"You're welcome," I returned a friendly smile.

Asher waved his arms to capture our attention through the warped glass. We glanced through the window as he mouthed, "We're ready to go!" Then pointed to the plane.

Emilio tossed the dish towel to me, so I could dry my hands. I grabbed my bag from the kitchen table and ambled outside. Emilio locked up behind us, intending to tag along for the ride. Uncle Teddy grinned from the cockpit as the propeller whizzed around, creating ripples through the sun-parched grass. Asher helped me climb inside the four-seater plane, then took a seat beside me. Emilio shuffled in alongside Uncle Ted, assisting him to fly the damn thing

"Will it get us there in one piece?" I murmured, worried that the nuts and bolts might fall out while we were hundreds of feet up in the air.

Asher's eyes creased at the corners as he laughed. "Don't jinx it," he warned.

We started moving along the dirt track, gathering speed. My stomach lurched as my back pressed against the seat, then the ground drifted further away as we ascended the sky. Emilio began chanting in Spanish, signing the cross against his body.

"What's he doing?" I muttered curiously.

"Praying," Asher replied, chuckling.

For fuck's sake. How many more near-death experiences am I going to have in one day?

I buried my face into the crook of Asher's neck, squeezing my eyes closed as the plane juddered and strained. The moment the plane levelled out, I felt my posture relax and I could breathe again. Asher threaded his fingers with mine and kissed the back of my knuckles.

"How are you feeling, love?" he inquired. I could tell he was referring to the aftermath of the car chase. People were dead. The authorities were not just going to allow us to walk away from this. We couldn't fail the mission. It had to be worth the sacrifice.

"I don't know," I replied earnestly. "But I'll feel better when we're all back together again."

He circled the back of my hand with his thumb.

"I know a way to take your mind off things," he hinted. "How about we play a game?"

I scrunched my face in an incredulous grimace. "What? Like I Spy?"

Was he really trying to distract me with such an infantile tactic? When we were children, he would always cheat. He would choose the most minute, amoebic particle like a speck of dust or a pollen spore, or a germ that could lurk in the atmosphere. Asher Wolfe disliked losing at anything. He was such a sore loser. I didn't want to throttle him to death as we headed to Paris.

Asher rolled his eyes with a click of his tongue. "No, not that game. How about we play "What's Your Favourite?" he suggested. "I'll go first. What's your favourite flower?"

The corners of my eyes twitched as I pondered that for a moment. "Pink roses. But it makes no difference if they're pale or vibrant. They're all pretty."

Asher pursed his lips as he considered his next question. "What's your favourite type of gold?"

"Ash, where are you going with this?" I narrowed my eyes with suspicion.

He huffed with impatience. "Bexley, just play along."

"White gold because yellow looks tacky on me," I answered, humouring him. "Platinum, if I'm allowed to be greedy."

A subtle movement drew my eyes to his side, and I noticed he was typing a secret text. He caught me peeking and hid the screen from view.

"What's your favourite cake flavour?" he questioned, piquing my curiosity further.

"Red Velvet because I'm a saucy minx. Is there anything else?" I countered, arching a brow.

Asher finished typing, then a notification tone signalled that the message had been sent and received

"Nope," he replied, sounding satisfied. "I've got everything we need"

He refused to elaborate further, insisting I will love what they have planned. The cogs inside my brain continued to turn, mulling over every plausible scenario. All that thinking wore me out and I dozed off during the flight, only to wake at the bumpy landing. As the sun melted into the horizon, it cast majestic rays across the landscape, its golden fingers stretching through the withered grapevines. We were here. I sat up straight and swiped the drool from the corner of my mouth. The light shone in my line of sight, obscuring my view of the winding pathway ahead of us. Uncle Teddy cut the engine, and the propeller slowed to a stop.

Asher helped me to climb down onto the dusty ground, the gentle breeze lifting my hair from my shoulders, raising the hairs on my skin. Three dark silhouettes approached from the nearby chateau; their determined steps breaking into a steady run. Uncle Ted and Emilio hung back, not wanting to intrude on our reunion. As they came into view, Dominic, Cruz, and Braxton looked like their old selves again. I hurried to greet them. Their kisses were full of love and devotion as they swaddled me in their arms. Our family unit was back together again.

CHAPTER
Twenty-Six

Bexley

"Thank God you're okay," I exclaimed, kissing them. "I never want to be apart from you ever again."

They held me for what felt like an eternity, enjoying the moment as if they were branding a memory.

"Why don't I show Bexley to her room, so she can freshen up?" Braxton offered.

"Good idea," Asher replied. "I'll take a shower and change into some fresh clothes. I trust everything is in order?"

Dominic scoffed. "Oh please, you're looking at an event planning guru. It took me no time at all to achieve"

Cruz shot him a pointed look. "Excuse me, we all chipped in. Don't steal all the credit."

I chuckled. "I'm confident, whatever it is, will be perfect. I'll see you all shortly."

Asher and Braxton dragged our luggage back to the Château. The cream clad walls were half-hidden with climbing ivy, the gardens astir with colourful flowers and terracotta pots. Paint peeled from the weathered window shutters, adding to its true rustic beauty

"Is Father Fournier around?" I asked as Braxton ushered me inside

Braxton and Asher shared a subtle exchange before he answered with, "He's busy at the moment. He wanted you to make yourself at home. We're staying here until after the Masquerade Ball."

The uneven walls remind me of warm porridge. A coat stand peeked out from behind the front door, laden with all-weather jackets. The boot rack overflowed with assorted footwear, and a tall pot had been crammed with umbrellas. It was homely. I assumed many people passed through here whenever they needed a quiet getaway. Cinnamon wafted from the kitchen to tantalize my taste buds, sending my neurons into a feeding frenzy. As we ascended the stairs, each footfall emitted a creaky groan from the pitted steps. Braxton directed Asher to the master bathroom and steered me to an en-suite shower cubicle in a large bedroom suite. I peeled away my clothing and let it slip to the floor. No sooner had I worked out how to operate the shower taps, finding a pleasant temperature, a naked Braxton muscled in to envelop me in a kiss.

"Scoot up, I'm coming in," he murmured against my lips.

"There's barely any room," I pointed out, bracing myself against the chilly tiles.

The intense look in his eyes told me we would improvise. His shoulders practically touched the sides of the cubicle, the flimsy curtain clinging to his colossal body like it wanted to cop a feel of that arse. Braxton voiced his discomfort, yelping that it was too cold. We laughed, coiled in each other's arms. God, I missed him so much.

"How's your wound?" I asked, running my fingertips around the gnarled flesh.

"Much better," he replied, kissing the side of my neck and letting his hands wander around the meaty globes of my backside.

"Braxton, I'm filthy. Let me wash," I chortled.

There was only one thing on his mind, and that required us getting down and dirty in the shower.

"Yes, you are . . . such a filthy girl," he rasped, taking my hand to rub it against his engorged appendage. "Look at what you do to me. You've given me a raging hard-on."

The steam from the water filled the air, warming my blood. The sight of his body sent all that molten heat rushing to my core in a swell of liquid desire. Braxton grabbed the soap, slathering it between his hands, then caressed my skin with attentive strokes. After the day I had, his calloused fingers felt heavenly. This wasn't all about sex, it was about taking care of me. I just stood there under the spray of water as Braxton cleaned me, scrubbing my body from head to toe. He handed me the soap, so I could return the favour. My explorative touch tracing the contours of his muscles, leaving nothing out. The intense look of want and need on his face made it hard for me to concentrate. It stole my breath away. My breasts were heavy, my nipples tightening with arousal. As the spray sluiced over us, it did nothing to quell the ache inside. I wanted to feel every inch of him. So, instead of letting him direct the sex, I took charge, lifting my leg to rock my pussy against his cock. He was raring to go, his swollen crown pulsing with pressure. Braxton held me steady, dipping his knees, so he could nudge his way to victory.

"Brax," I moaned. My legs shook, my core pulsating

His thick fingers squeezed my hips, the soapy residue causing them to glide against my skin. The anticipation was killing me. A moment passed, and then he was there, spearing through my folds, driving his mighty meat inside me.

"You feel so good, babe," he murmured, kissing me. He pushed forward, squashing me against the wall.

I couldn't answer, too busy feeling the full extent of Braxton's cock as he thrust like an animal. He was a beast of need, possessively claiming me, the pressure building in my stomach like a coiled spring.

"Cum for me," he rasped, finding that punishing momentum to tip me over the edge.

Waves of blissful pleasure rocked through my body, drowning me in ecstasy. Braxton roared a fearsome sound, lifting me off my toes as he pumped his seed inside me. Stars burst in my vision, then I was floating, panting, sagging against him as I rode out my climax.

"I love you," he told me, stroking my hair back, his eyes bearing into mine as if he was searching my soul. "Marry us, Bexley."

"I said I would," I answered, pulling him down for another kiss. "I love you all too. There's no way I could live without you all now."

His smile reached his eyes and glimmered with joy. "You're going to love your surprise then."

Braxton and I rinsed off for a second time then I turned off the taps. The cool air soothed my skin as I towel dried. Braxton secured his towel around his waist, and I wrapped mine around my body, leaving my hair damp.

"We better get dressed before the others wonder where we are," Braxton commented dryly.

He led me back into the bedroom and I noticed the boy's luggage had been stacked up in the corner.

"Are we all sleeping in here?" I asked, surprised by that.

Braxton glanced around the room with amusement. "Yeah, where else do you expect us to sleep?"

I was quick to add, "Nowhere, I just wondered . .

. with this being a priest's Château, and us not being married?'

He pulled away his towel, revealing his now flaccid cock. "We just fucked in the shower, and you're worried about us all sharing the same bed?"

He had a point. "No, it's fine. If I'm going to Hell, I might as well enjoy life while it lasts," I mumbled sarcastically.

Braxton blew out a forced breath. "I'm so fucking nervous. I need to get ready." He pulled on his underwear and dragged a suit bag and dress shoes from the bed

"Hang on then, let me look for something nice to wear," I replied, reaching for my suitcase. "I want to look my best if you're all dressing up."

Braxton grabbed my hand and took me to the rustic wardrobe. "Your dad thought ahead and shipped this over before he left for London. There is a note with it," he uttered with reverence. "I'll give you some privacy. But if you need a hand to dress, Martha will help," he mentioned, slipping out of the room.

He talked to someone in the hallway and then an elderly lady entered the suite wearing a pale blue smock, white canvass slacks, and a nun's headdress.

"Bonjour," she cheerfully announced herself. "Je m'appelle Martha."

"Parlez-vous Anglais?" I inquired, asking if she spoke English

"Oui, a little," Martha answered, holding her thumb and forefinger an inch apart.

I admired the ornate grapevine pattern that had been etched into the oak wardrobe doors. The brass handles resembled bunches of grapes. All the furniture in the room matched, even the four-poster bed with a cream lace canopy. I opened the doors, only to find my mother's wedding dress inside, and a small white envelope that had discoloured over time.

With tremulous fingers, I ripped the seal and pulled out the note, unable to breathe as my eyes scanned the familiar handwriting. The last wishes of the mother who loved me, immortalized in the blotted ink.

"Bexley, if you're reading this, it means I'm no longer with you. Just know that I'll be smiling down on you today with a whole heart, a proud mother whose daughter is where she is destined to be. Give my love to the boys. Love them fiercely. You're exactly what's been missing in their lives. Live a long and happy life together, full of adventures, and most of all, no regrets. You are my greatest achievement. All my love, Mum"

A tear slipped from my chin, landed onto the parchment, and distorted the ink.

"Mademoiselle?" Martha asked, her voice filled with concern.

I brushed the moisture from my cheeks, swiping my hands against the terry towelling. My mother's wise words reinforced what I was already feeling. The time had come for me to get out there and claim my men

"Could you help me with the dress, please?" I requested, needing some assistance.

Martha was happy to oblige. She helped me to style my hair, and I applied tasteful makeup, feeling every inch a blushing bride. The gown clung to my body like a second skin, lace over silk, hugging my curves. The sweetheart neckline boosted my natural assets, and the crystals captured the light with a dazzling sparkle. I felt like a princess. The soft material gathered around my calves in a fishtail finish. There wasn't a doubt in my mind as I stepped into the fading sunlight, following the trail of pink rose petals they scattered around the Château, leading me into the hazy garden. My mum was right, I was exactly where I needed to be. My men waited anxiously beneath a delicate floral arch, dressed in identical black tuxedos. I breathed in the intoxicating scent that carried on the breeze, the mixture of floral notes and their spicy cologne. A priest stood at the head of the altar, I'm assuming he was Dad's friend, Father Fournier. Uncle Teddy and Emilio were standing across from the Wolfe brothers, smiling as they saw me approach. They had arranged a picnic party with finger foods, a three-tier white-frosted cake with pink roses between the layers, and Champagne bottles poked out from silver buckets filled with ice. Butterflies fluttered across the backdrop of the vineyard, and bees buzzed from flower to flower. The scene was magical. It was like something from out of a dream. Martha muttered words of reassurance as I gathered my nerves, then handed me a bouquet of long-stemmed roses she had tied together with white lace. My pulse was pounding so fast, I swear they could hear it hammering like a drum. Asher, Braxton, Cruz, and Dominic turned to see me, their expressions melting with awe. Emilio loped over, carrying Braxton's phone. My father's tearful face was staring back at me from the screen; he couldn't be here to walk me down the aisle, so he face-timed me instead. Martha handed Emilio an acoustic guitar, and he took a seat to the side of us, strumming a beautiful Spanish melody that struck a chord in my heart.

"Bexley," my men breathed, sounding mesmerized. The look in their eyes needed no further words — I captivated them.

I took my place alongside them, pledging my heart and soul before God, my father, and my mother who was here with me in spirit. The blessing was beautiful. Fairy lights lit up the garden as the sky transitioned from peach to purple, with blue seeping in from the edge of the horizon. We each said, "I do," exchanging platinum rings and kissing as we sealed our bond. It wasn't like a conventional wedding. I couldn't legally marry all four of them, but Farther Fournier blessed us all the same. It felt real to us, that's all that mattered. The contract was our fathers' contingency plan, and we signed our names on the dotted line, making our relationship permanent. I was theirs, and they were mine

My hands were shaking as I signed my married name for the first time.

Bexley Wolfe.

CHAPTER
Twenty-Seven

Bexley

I was deliriously happy, taking turns to slow dance with my husbands before the sunset backdrop. We were married, bound by a contract where only death could separate us. It was good enough for me. The Wolfe Brothers were finally mine

"How did you pull this off in the middle of a mission?" I asked, impressed.

Asher huffed a smile. "I can't take any of the credit. It was all Braxton, Dominic, and Cruz."

"The game *'what's your favourite?'* was a ploy to get information from me, wasn't it?" I figured that out for myself

I admired the platinum ring, wondering where they had the time to find this at such short notice. It was a perfect fit.

"How did you know my ring size?" I inquired.

"It is easy to measure your finger when you sleep like the dead," he quipped.

I swatted his chest, delivering a playful tap.

"We have our sources," he replied, giving nothing away. "You have Martha to thank for picking up the ring." Asher toyed with my fingers, tilting my hand so the diamond-encrusted platinum sparkled in the light.

There was still so much we had to discuss, but it could wait. This was our night. As our friends retired to their beds, my husbands led me by the hand for another surprise

"Where are you taking me?" I asked as we meandered through the vineyard,

I was so tempted to reach out and pull a grape from a vine. The red berries looked juicy and ripe for the picking. The champagne had gone straight to my head. I was glad to have four sober chaperones to guide me through the maze of fruit. My men had taken care of me, keeping me on my toes all night. Now they brought me to a fairy-lit gazebo, laden with plush cushions for us to lie upon. I pulled off my shoes and carried them in one hand, tossing them alongside the wooden structure. We had a magnificent view of the vineyard from here. The roof of the slumbering château poked out from behind the vines, and a dilapidated windmill that had lasted throughout the ages, creaked in the gentle breeze. I could see for miles, following the patchwork blanket of fields that led down to a small body of water. In the fading light, my eyes expanded in the beauty of this moment and a genuine sense of peace touched my soul.

"It's not much of a honeymoon, but you get the idea," Cruz mentioned, hinting that we'd be consummating our vows beneath the stars.

The châteaux walls were not as thick as we'd like them to be, so this would have to suffice. Cementing our vows was one thing, but our friends wouldn't appreciate being kept up for hours with bouncy bedsprings.

"It's perfect," I told them. "This is such a wonderful surprise"

"The night isn't over yet," Asher assured. "Turn around and let us get you out of this gown."

"Be careful with it. This belonged to my mother," I reminded them. "If we have a girl, I want to hand it down to her."

Maybe that was presumptuous of me, both assuming we would have a daughter and that she would want to wear a dress from the eighties, as timeless as it was. It had always been my dream to wear it on my wedding day. I couldn't ask for anything more

"Hold still," Asher urged as he plucked at the laces, then unhooked the bodice.

The delicate tulle floated down to the ground. I stepped out of it. Asher gathered the mass and folded it neatly, placing it somewhere safe. My men marvelled at the sight of me like I was an angel sent down from Heaven.

"I still can't believe she said yes to us all," Cruz admitted his thoughts out loud.

Braxton held me around the neck and waist as he tipped me backwards, his lips hovering over mine.

"I can." He looked at me as if I was the centre of his universe. "If there's one thing Bexley loves more than anything in this world, it's cock," he muttered. A lewd chuckle tickled my lips as he kissed me.

The next thing I knew, I was lying on my back with my men writhing above me, feasting upon my bare flesh like creatures of the night. They peeled away their clothes, so that we were all completely naked. One minute, I could touch and feel my way around them, and the next, they bound my hands with a long piece of silk. Helpless and at their mercy, all I could do was lay there and accept the pleasures they granted me, their furious breath teasing me, kissing, sucking, biting, creating a plethora of sensations that would drive a saint to sin.

Another silk tie covered my eyes, stealing my sight to heighten my other senses. Silky rosebuds traced the contour of my face, my neck, and body, circling the puckered buds upon my breasts. My pulse soared, my skin flushing with molten heat as they took turns kissing me, changing places as they pleased me, licking between my thighs. My clit bounced as they devoured me, building pressure in my stomach. The vast countryside swallowed my gasps of rapture, the moon and stars bearing witness like celestial voyeurs. I couldn't tell who was who as they made love to me slowly, rolling me onto my back, my front, dragging me to my knees and mounting me from behind. I lost count of how many times I came and how many times they filled me. Electricity raced around my body with every passionate stroke, and whispered "I love you." My loins ached with fulfilment, slumping against the cushions in a breathless mess.

We lay together, boneless, wrung out, and spent, staring up at the glittering stars, wondering what the future held for us. It wasn't easy to block out the fear, not wanting to ruin such a beautiful night. But we avoided the subject and talked about where we saw ourselves a year from now.

"I always wanted to learn how to paint," Asher mentioned, gazing heavenward as if he was making a wish. "Maybe I'll give it a go someday. If you think Lowry's stickmen are good, just wait until you see mine"

We lay side by side, Asher and Dominic on one side of me and Braxton and Cruz on the other. Moonlight bathed our bodies in a pale silver hue. The crickets chirping among the twisted vines. This was what it felt like to be happy

"I've seen your stick figures, and all I can suggest to you is, keep reading your psychology books. I was going to say, don't give up your day job, but look how well that's working out for all of us." Dominic realised his mistake and was quick to change the topic. "On a brighter note, I'm going to teach Bexley how to surf," he promised.

Braxton gave a low whistle. "That I'd love to see," he agreed. "But first, I want to teach her how to skydive"

"You will not," I flat-out refused. "I prefer to keep my feet on the ground, thank you very much. Why can't you take up safe hobbies, like knitting? Or bird-watching?"

That would happen when pigs learned to fly

Cruz chuckled. "There's only one bird we're interested in watching, and that's you." He trailed his fingers along my thigh, causing me to shiver. "But that reminds me, I've been thinking . . ."

"Uh-oh," Dominic dragged out the ominous words. "Wait for it . . ."

Cruz turned to lean upon his elbow. "Hold on, give me a chance to say my piece."

His brothers paused, allowing him to continue. "I think it's time we put a little thought into what we're going to do when all this is . . . you know." He didn't dredge up the current situation, just hinted at it. "We all agreed that after we marry Bexley, we would resign from the agency and merge our security companies into one elite organization"

"We did," Asher agreed. "I know our present circumstances are not great, but I'm confident we can resolve things. We just have to remain positive. As for branching out alone, well . . . I think we ought to discuss this with Bexley."

I gazed up at the stars. "Will our merger entail us travelling the globe, solving mysteries, and saving the world from dangerous criminals?"

"Maybe," Braxton replied, dragging out the word. "Has Asher let it slip already?"

"No," I defended. "But I appreciate you can't retire from this life without keeping one foot in and one foot out. If I know you as well as I think I do, you're planning to form your own Secret Service."

They didn't deny it. This confirmed what I thought.

"What if I choose to be involved?" I put the question out there for them to mull it over.

"Where do I fit into your plans or do you intend to keep me barefoot and pregnant? I read the contingency plan from cover to cover before I signed it. You all want children. I'm not saying that I don't desire the same things as you do, but what I don't want is for my husbands to be half-way across the world doing God knows what while I'm stuck home at Sandbanks, or wherever we decide to live"

Please don't say Svalbard or I'll throw myself off the Eiffel Tower.

"We plan to hand-pick from the S.A.S and train

them to become like us. It may take a few years, but we're aiming to have Alpha Elite up and running by the time you feel ready to conceive our first child. After all, our kids will have two retired grandfathers to play nanny to them, won't they?" Cruz reinforced, nominating my dad and Uncle Zane for babysitting duties.

It was just as I hoped. We were in this together.

CHAPTER
Twenty-Eight

Bexley

I woke up alone in a warm bed, then hastily washed and dressed to search for my husbands. There they were around the huge kitchen table, sitting with Emilio, Uncle Ted, and a man I hadn't seen in ages, Uncle Ulrich. The battle-scarred grump glanced up at me and nodded once in acknowledgement, his mouth too full to speak. The smell of eggs and bacon caused my stomach to rumble, letting me know just how hungry I was.

"Good morning, Mrs Wolfe," Cruz greeted me, leaning up for a kiss.

Asher, Dominic, and Braxton all craved the same intimacy, passing me around like a cuddly toy.

Ulrich rolled his eyes and flicked his gaze to Teddy

"Let the woman eat," Uncle Teddy said, motioning for me to sit. "We have a lot of planning to do"

I filled my plate with toasted bread, bacon, sausages, and scrambled eggs, then set to work on devouring it. Asher poured some fresh coffee into a mug and placed it beside me. Cruz returned to the newspaper he and Braxton were reading, scanning his eyes across the headlines. Braxton scowled at the article, his face reddening with outrage.

"Congratulations, guys, we just made the top of the most wanted terrorists list," he fumed.

Suddenly, I didn't feel so hungry. My throat refused to swallow the mouthful I was chewing, so I nudged the scrambled egg with my fork, pushing it around my plate.

How were we ever going to get out of this mess?

"We knew they would pull this shit. There's

corruption in the chain of command, and they know we're capable of bringing them down. We have them backed into a corner and this is their desperate reaction. I'm not losing any sleep over it and neither should you. How about we do something useful and go over tomorrow's plan?" Asher asserted. "It mentions in the paper that Malcolm will be present at the ball. Dad wants us to plant a bug on him, so he and Uncle Zane can hear what he says. For all we know, he could be the Chameleon's informant."

Ulrich produced three tickets from an envelope and handed them to Dominic. "I've been out scoring you these," he mentioned. "They weren't cheap. I paid a small fortune."

Asher glanced at them and continued, "So, here's the plan. Bexley will accompany Emilio to the ball."

Emilio seemed surprised about that.

"You'll both be wearing masks, so no one will recognise you. It's too much of a risk for you to be seen with us," Asher explained. "They'll be expecting that. Braxton will pose as a masked waiter. Cruz will dress as a member of their security team, and will be on standby in case we need a diversion. I'm taking the place of Count Graff, who is currently indisposed thanks to Dad and his questionable connections in the Maldives. We don't have to worry about him ratting us out because he's not leaving the island anytime soon. Don't worry, Bexley," he assured, noticing my concerned frown. "They won't recognize us thanks to the art of prosthetics."

"And where will Dominic be?" I probed further.

Dominic's eyes sparkled with mischievous intent. "I'll be controlling everything from the nerve centre with Ulrich, making sure it all runs smoothly. Uncle Teddy is your chauffeur."

I massaged my temples to mitigate the pounding pressure in my head. This was dangerous, but what other choice did we have?

"How are we going to plant the bug? We'd need to get close to Malcolm, and that's such a huge risk. What if he recognises us?" I questioned, voicing my fears aloud. "I'm not comfortable with dragging Emilio into this. I'll compromise his safety, and I'm not okay with that."

Emilio grinned as he forced down a mouthful of coffee. "I appreciate your concern, hermosa, but I'm a big boy. This isn't my first rodeo, you know."

His admission made my husbands and Uncle Teddy chortle. Here was me being all noble and protective, yet they somehow managed to swing it around so that I was the one who needed protecting. I guess I'll just need to prove my worth to them, then they would see just how wrong they all were.

"Don't send a man to do a woman's job," I spoke out, realising what needed to be done. "If you think I'm attending the ball as a piece of arm candy, you're gravely mistaken. I'll plant the bug on Malcolm." I shrugged

Asher's eyes twitched with intrigue. "How will you manage that?"

"It's a Masquerade Ball," I uttered with sarcasm, lowering the pitch of my voice. "People drink, dance, and mingle, do they not? It's amazing what a little drunken flirting can do; not that I'll be intoxicated because I'll need to keep a clear head. But hands can roam . . . especially into pockets . . . providing his costume has one. If all else fails, I'll improvise. I'll find some way to distract him, pickpocket his phone, then attach the bug, and sneak it back to him before he notices."

My men released nervous exhales all around.

"Are you sure?" Asher checked

I couldn't afford to doubt myself. We had one chance to find out what we were up against, who the traitor was, and their connection to the Chameleon. Too much was at stake.

"Yes," I replied. "I'm ready to do this."

"Good," Braxton responded, scrubbing a hand over his face. His stubble was starting to poke through his skin, casting a dark shadow across his jawline.

I listened as the boys relayed their recent experiences, trying hard not to laugh at Dominic who went into great detail, or Braxton who shuddered at his encounter with a much older woman. These were stories that I couldn't wait to tell my grandchildren, and it was that positive mindset that made it seem worthwhile. Bugging Malcolm was just a pitstop in our plans, but it would enable us to stay one step ahead of the authorities. If the European leaders had been coerced into believing a web of lies, we can only assume they'd hired mercenaries to hunt us down.

After breakfast, the boys gave me the space and freedom to roam the vineyard alone. With my bare feet on the warm, yellowing grass, it enabled me to find anchorage among all the instability. The gentle breeze rustled the leaves, lifting my hair around my shoulders. I sucked in a lungful of nature and exhaled the fears from my thoughts. It was like standing on a cliff edge, preparing to jump, but not knowing what to expect as I reached the bottom.

"Hey . . . is everything all right? You've been out here for hours," Asher alerted me to his presence after I'd lost track of time.

My mind snapped back to the present, and the daydream faded

"I've been going over all the clues over and over in my head, trying to piece them all together," I told him, turning my gaze back to the open fields.

Dominic loped over the parched lawn, followed by Cruz and Braxton. I began a slow stroll down to the stream, allowing them the chance to catch up to us.

"Me too," Asher confided. "I have no doubt that Aunt Safi was trying to send us a message, maybe even a warning."

The others caught up to us at this point, keeping in step with us.

"What's up?" Braxton asked

"We're just discussing the clues and trying to make sense of them," I informed them all, keeping them up to speed. "It's no coincidence that Mum chose places with the name Sofia in them. She was referring to herself. Asher and I discussed something when we were searching the art museum. We think the church symbolised a desecration of faith, trust, or a betrayal of something sacred. The doll represented a child, maybe the illegitimate child theory, or a deceased infant. We're still on the fence about that. The garden represented a female spy. The art symbolized a game of chance, and its about two similar artists who diverged onto separate paths. I'm inclined to think that Mum was betrayed by someone she considered a friend, or a close personal ally. Maybe they had the same goals, but went their separate ways. Mum wanted to protect the information, and the other wanted to use it for other purposes."

We stopped several feet from the lazy stream and took a moment to absorb that theory.

"What if, whoever it is, knows how to crack the code, but never knew where Safi hid the flash drives?" Dominic commented

Asher exhaled a shaky breath, his face draining of colour. "The Chameleon killed Aunt Safi. That must be the ally-turned-traitor. But who could they be? Our fathers have been trying to track him or her down for years. They devoted their lives to hunting that person down. If it's someone they know, they would have told us."

"Unless they didn't know," I added, thinking outside of the box. "What if they assumed that person was dead? A chameleon can blend in as well as a ghost."

The fragmented pieces of what I thought to be an impossible jigsaw slotted together in my mind. I had tried everything, lost countless nights' sleep going over it. But the answer had been staring us in the face the entire time

"Spain," I checked each country off on my fingers. "Ukraine . . . Sweden . . . Austria . . . Norway. My mother did reveal the identity of her killer."

I watched through teary eyes as the horrific news contorted their faces with horror.

CHAPTER
Twenty-Nine

Bexley

"S.U.S.A.N," I rhymed off the letters that spelled out my mother's killer, letting that revelation sink in

Cruz glared distantly across the stream. Dominic slumped to his knees, burying his face in his hands. Asher looked as if he might be sick. Braxton swore under his breath and scrubbed a hand over his face.

"Our biological mother is dead, Bexley. Dad saw her body. He buried her. He still visits her graveside for fuck's sake," Asher snapped with vehemence. "He would know . . . he would . . ." his voice trailed into a defeated whimper.

"He saw *a* body, not necessarily hers," Cruz said as he pulled out his phone, dialled a number, then held the phone to his ear.

I crouched down to comfort Dominic who had been hit hardest by the news. He always longed for a mother, and often talked about what she may have been like as they were growing up.

"I want to be wrong," I told him, feeling like utter shit for dropping the bombshell. "But I've racked my brain trying to come up with another explanation, and there isn't one. Susan was her best friend. They developed the coding method together. I'm not sure what happened between them, but if your mother is alive, and she's acting under the alias of the Chameleon, then she faked her death and killed my mother to get her hands on the files. Mum must have known something was amiss because she hid the flash drives well. I'm sorry, Dom. I know it's not what you want to hear, but what if I'm right?"

"Then it changes nothing," Braxton gruffed, his

voice full of contempt. "We may have her genes, but she's not our mother. Dad picked out surrogates. He still grieves for Susan to this day. He never remarried or met anyone else." His face twisted with anguish.

Cruz turned to us, shoving his phone back inside his pocket. He had spoken to Uncle Zane, and by the grim look on his face, it didn't go well.

"Dad is just as shell shocked as we are," Cruz revealed. "Uncle Jaxx is keeping an eye on him to make sure he doesn't do anything stupid. All I heard was Dad raging and smashing things up before I cut off the call."

"I'm speechless," Asher muttered, rubbing the base of his throat as if it burned with emotion. "For once, I have nothing . . . absolutely nothing constructive to say."

"So . . . what do we do now?" I searched their distraught faces for answers.

Their mother was alive. Mine was dead. A slow-pounding ache filled my heart with the rhythm of a death march. I always wanted to come face-to-face with my mother's killer, but I never once thought I would get the chance. Nothing could have prepared me for this. *Their mother.* Did this compromise our mission? I knew how Braxton felt by the displeasure on his face, but did Cruz, Asher, and Dominic feel the same? I had to know. I needed to be sure we were all singing from the same hymn sheet before we set off for Norway.

"Are we still in this together?" I asked, holding out hope

Their outraged gazes snapped to me, giving me the reassurance that I needed

"Of course, we are," Cruz answered, scowling back at me. "We're a team."

He didn't have to seek assurance from Braxton because he responded with a fast, "Too right."

Asher nodded in confirmation. "Always."

Dominic held up his hand, and Asher dragged him up from the ground.

"One for all and all for one, right?" Dominic mumbled, dusting the dry grass from his palms. "Just like the Musketeers."

"I prefer the Wolfe Pack," I interjected. "It sounds sexier."

They turned to me, scrunching their faces with questioning grimaces. The penny dropped, leaving them glancing among themselves as if considering who should be Alpha. I gave a subtle cough, then pointed at my chest.

"As I'm the only female, I'm nominating myself as the leader," I asserted. "That way, there's no squabbling"

I flicked my hair over my shoulder as I flounced back to the chateaux. We needed to inform Teddy, Ulrich, and Emilio of our findings. They were bound to be as shocked as we were. My forlorn men trudged behind me in silence. I still didn't have solid proof that Susan was the Chameleon, but I trusted my mother's message. She wanted to keep everyone safe — me, the Wolfe brothers, Dad, Uncle Zane. I owed it to her to lure Susan out of hiding and bring her to justice

Father Fournier joined us for lunch then left for afternoon mass, and Ulrich and Teddy went to fetch our outfits for the Ball. I was excited to see my gown, but Braxton wouldn't allow it. He wanted it to be a surprise and got Cruz to bribe me with some chocolate doughnuts from a patisserie in Paris. Time dragged by at a leisurely pace, giving me too much time to think. I worried about everything, especially Caz, and whether she believed all the rumours about me being a terrorist. The last thing I wanted was for her to get caught up in all of this. If the Chameleon went to my house and hurt her, I don't know how I would live with myself. I couldn't call the police and ask them to guard her without giving away my whereabouts. An anonymous phone call from a remote chateau in France would flag up to the authorities. I might as well place a huge neon arrow over the vineyard and announce my presence to the world. As much as it pained me, I couldn't risk reaching out to anyone

As the night crept across the vineyard, my husbands' moods turned grim. Sadness had turned to anger, and with it came the resentment.

"She was never our mother," Asher said as they chatted on the patio terrace. He took a swig of beer, sucking the froth that gathered at the top of the bottle. "Harvesting eggs doesn't make her a part of this family. Don't let her get inside your head," he counselled Dominic, who cradled an empty bottle between his hands.

"I know . . . and I won't," he assured his brothers. "I'm just sickened by all that she's done. All this time . . . and she never let us know she was alive. She only cared about getting hold of the files. We didn't matter to her at all."

Asher pressed his lips together in a tight thin line. I didn't know what to say to make this better, so I just placed my hand on Dominic's thigh to reassure him I was here.

"Dad wanted us," Braxton slurred, after knocking back another shot of whiskey. I lost count how many drinks he had, but after the beers had little effect on him, he'd drained half a bottle of Black Label in under an hour. His eyelids drooped with fatigue, and the fact he was drunk didn't help. He swayed in his seat as he poured another shot, spilling the amber liquid onto the metal bistro table. Then he sucked the liquor from his fingers and held up his tumbler, sticking his forefinger out to point with. "She fucked off, so he made his own family. We didn't need her. Selfish bitch." He snorted, then went to take a drink and missed his mouth. The whiskey rolled down his chin and soaked into the collar of his T-shirt.

"She faked her death," Cruz reminded him, removing the bottle from Braxton's reach as a sign that he'd had enough. "There was nothing stopping her from walking back into our lives when we were born. Dad would have bought any cock and bull story, as long as she came back. She chose her path in life. It was the opposite to Aunt Safi. When the time comes, I won't hesitate to pull the trigger."

His words filtered into the night, allowing the bitter truth to settle among us. We sipped our drinks in silence, having said all there is to say. Braxton's head bowed forward and the glass tumbled from his slackened fingertips, shattering onto the patio. The noise didn't startle him as it did to us; he had passed out in a drunken coma.

Cruz and Asher hoisted him up by his underarms and carried him into the Chateaux, leaving Dominic and I alone on the terrace.

"Are you okay?" I asked what I thought was a stupid question given the circumstances. Of course, he wasn't fine. Who would be?

He curled his arm around my shoulders and pulled me against him. His warmth seeped into my skin, a welcoming contrast to the cool night breeze.

"Yeah," he answered. His tone held a hint of sadness that suggested otherwise. "I'm just disappointed, that's all."

He buried his nose into my hair and inhaled, then released a breathy sigh.

"Dad painted a picture of her in my head, making her out to be a paragon of virtue. A fearless soldier who died for her country. Dad spent his entire life, sacrificed our childhood, to hunt the Chameleon down, not knowing it was her all along. She played us all."

"I want to be wrong, but I don't think I am," I replied, cuddling him, feeling the heavy beat of his heart against my cheek. "I'm sorry, Dom."

He lifted my chin to kiss me and I tasted the beer on his lips. His fragile smile creased his eyes with sadness, and I could see the torment behind them.

"She took away your mother," he murmured, "it's her who will be sorry."

CHAPTER
Thirty

Braxton

L ight burst into the room, waking me from a warped dream of a half-lizard, half-human version of our mother, who I had only ever seen pictures of. Whoever yanked the curtains open so aggressively didn't care that I had the world's biggest headache, and stomped around as if they had a point to prove

"It's past ten. You need to get up because we have

to prepare for tonight," Cruz lectured me, standing over the bed.

"Fuck off," I croaked. "I'll get up when I feel like it."

Cruz didn't respond to that, he taught me a lesson by pulling away the sheets and drenching me with water.

"Get up, get showered, and come downstairs. There's something wrong with Bexley," he informed me, grabbing my attention. His revelation prevented me from punching him in the face.

I scrubbed a hand over my jaw, then pinched the sleep from my eyes to clear my vision. "What's the matter with her?" I asked, my mood switching from furious to concerned in a millisecond.

"She's worried about you, so you better come down and fix it," he replied.

Cruz stalked from the room and his boots thundered down the wooden stairs. I staggered into the bathroom to do my business, aiming straight into the basin like a water hose. My head throbbed like a bastard, and the shower jets sounded like pebbles were hitting the base tray. I washed away my night of regret, and resurrected my brittle tongue with my toothbrush and some minty toothpaste. My recollection of last night's antics a little hazy. I might have said and done things to upset Bexley, and that made me feel even worse. Resting my forehead against the cold wall tiles, I wallowed in my misery.

Of all the people in this world, why did the Chameleon have to be her? I know it's her. There's no smoke without fire.

Her traitorous blood ran through our veins, making me feel dirty and corrupt. I wished that Dad had chosen better, and that he hadn't just picked those women to be surrogates. It wouldn't have mattered if we weren't full brothers — at least not to me

I found them all gathered around the kitchen table, sipping their tea in silence. Bexley was sitting on Cruz's lap, her head nestled into the crook of his neck. It was a submissive position that my brother and I both preferred. We loved it when she felt safe in our arms. I dragged my gaze to the left of them and Emilio flashed me a sympathetic smile as he leaned awkwardly against the counter. Ulrich and Asher scanned the newspapers, looking for further articles about us. Dominic tapped away on his laptop with Uncle Ted leaning in to look at the screen. Martha washed the breakfast dishes in the sink, humming to herself like her mind was someplace else.

"Do we have any pain killers?" I asked, wincing sheepishly

It felt like a woodpecker was attacking my skull.

"In the top right-hand cupboard, next to the stove," Asher muttered, without looking up from the paper.

I rummaged around and found a box of Aspirin, then popped two pills out of the blister pack. Then I swallowed them down with a mouthful of water. After twenty minutes of massaging my temples, listening to Asher huffing and swearing under his breath, the pain began to subside and I felt somewhat human again.

"Would you like some coffee?" Martha offered.

"Thanks," I replied, accepting an espresso-sized cup and eyeing it with scrutiny. "You better leave the pot," I suggested. "I'm used to drinking from a bigger mug than this."

"More like a plant pot," Bexley remarked, chortling. It was good to hear her laugh. It lessened my guilt for acting like a drunken neanderthal last night.

"Braxton can't function without his morning coffee," she told Martha.

I caught the cheeky glint in her eyes that suggested it fuelled something else.

I huffed a smirk, glad that she hadn't lost her wicked sense of humour.

"So . . . have we made today's papers?" I asked, in

a disinterested tone. I couldn't give a fuck whether we had or we hadn't.

"No," Asher replied, bunching his brows as he scanned through the centrefold, finding nothing of significance. "It's all quiet on the western front. But I'm sad to report that Chelsea beat West Ham by two nil. I'd offer my condolences, but I couldn't give two shits."

"You're fucking joking," I swore under my breath. "That's three strokes of bad luck I've had up to now." I started to count on my fingers. "I've been shot. We found out that Mum is a fucking lunatic. And my team played like a bag of shite. I give up. This year can go and fuck off. I've had enough of it."

That put me in a grim mood for the rest of the afternoon. It wasn't until Bexley emerged hours later, dressed like an ethereal goddess in a glittering white and cream toga, golden sandals, and white mask with glittery golden feathers, that I cheered up. This year's theme was deities of Mount Olympus, and Bexley wowed us all. My mouth ran dry as I watched her descend the staircase, the sides of her gown flowing around her long, tanned legs. The material hugged her curves perfectly, accentuating every delectable feature. I wanted to whisk her away to the master bedroom and barricade us in for the night. And by the heated look of desire in my brothers' eyes, they all felt the same way

Seeing Bexley in her dress was distracting enough, but witnessing her tucking a gun into a lace garter was like a dream come true. She was wearing the throw-blade earrings that Dominic had invented. I think I can speak on behalf of all of us when I say it scared me to see the bomb watch coiled around her wrist.

"Please tell me you're not wearing the kiss of death lipstick," Asher uttered ominously.

Bexley smirked. "No, but I have it in my bag, along with the toxic perfume you let me keep."

"Please be careful with them. Those are not toys, Bexley," Cruz warned her.

Our wife rolled her eyes and huffed with irritation. "I'm not stupid; I know what they are. I just feel safer knowing I could use them if I need to."

"I'm just sorry I won't get to dance with you in that dress," I cut in, changing the subject.

Bexley stroked her finger across the underside of my chin. "Oh well, maybe you'll be lucky enough to take it off"

"Maybe I will," I agreed, grinning.

Bexley rearranged her boobs in her dress and checked her appearance in the hall mirror.

"Right . . . let's do this, shall we?" she said, rallying us all together.

My brothers and I had to leave individually, taking separate methods of transport. Emilio and Bexley would be driven to the palace by Uncle Teddy, who looked unrecognizable thanks to Asher. He worked his prosthetic magic on us all, apart from Bexley who said she wouldn't need it. Her cream and gold mask would suffice. It is enough to conceal her identity from prying eyes as long as she doesn't take it off. I made her promise not to remove it under any circumstances. She agreed, but her eyes sparkled with a hint of mischief

I was the first to arrive, followed minutes later by Cruz. He fell into line with the other security staff after an hours' briefing. It was the same with the kitchen and serving staff. We were given the grand tour of the palace and told what we should and shouldn't do. Under no circumstances should we fraternize with the guests. Our job is to keep them fed and merry, not to canoodle in the halls or the gardens. Eyes would be watching us I got the impression that this was a reoccurring issue. I caught the staff casting amused smirks amongst their colleagues. I was new, so our manager put me in charge of serving shrimp canapés and caviar. Then some patronizing twat named François, accused me of being a "clumsy oaf" when I dropped a tray onto the floor. I'm sure I caught him checking out my ass as I crouched down to retrieve it. Something clattered outside the door, and he scurried away to see what it was. I was still busy scooping up the mess with my fingers when Cruz sauntered past; he smirked at me and tapped his watch, prompting me to check mine. It was almost time for the guests to arrive. The others would be here any minute. I pressed the side button to determine their whereabouts. The digital display indicated that Asher was close by. I couldn't tell how far away Bexley and Emilio were because they weren't wearing synchronized watches like ours. Dominic's signal pinpointed him somewhere in the vicinity. That reassured me. There was no way we would throw Bexley to the lions without the protection from the pack. We would fight to the death for our woman.

I caught a glimpse of my reflection in one of the huge ornate mirrors, and admired the elaborate décor surrounding me. The palace was truly a sight to behold. The ostentatious display of wealth in all its Baroque grandeur was characterized by multifaceted designs and extravagant embellishments. It would be a shame if we destroyed it in a shootout. This time, we'd be liable for any damage. I doubt the agency would pick up the bill, even after we expose the traitors for who they were. Speaking of weapons, Cruz planned to stash my gun in a vase. I would never have passed the security check if I had kept it on me. He sent me the coordinates, but there was no way I could search for it while the palace was empty. Suspicious eyes followed me wherever I went, watching me in case I tried to steal something of value. It was common for the staff to take mementos and then try to sell them on eBay. I had to wait for the hordes of guests to arrive so I could avoid being detected by the CCTV, and security staff. Glancing around, I shoved my hand into the jewel-encrusted pottery and found my handgun. I felt safer with it stuffed into the waistband of my pants.

"Cough once if you can hear me, Brax," Dominic spoke into my earpiece.

I did as he instructed, curling my fist against my lips. It allowed the microphone inside my watch to pass the signal back to Dom.

"Good," Dominic replied, sounding satisfied. "We're all in position. I've tapped into the CCTV to get a bird's eye view of the area. Look up to your left and smile at the camera," he urged in a humoured tone. I glanced up to where he meant and saw a dome-shaped camera. I knew he could see me, so I looked into the lens and huffed

"There's still no sign of Malcolm, but I'll let you know of his whereabouts as soon as we locate him. Asher is here and is schmoozing with the upper-class elites. They've bought into the whole "Count Graff" guise, so bravo to his acting skills. Bexley and Emilio are walking in as we speak." Dominic made an ominous "hmm" sound. "I recognize those agents in the orangery. Wherever the Home Secretary goes, those guys are never far behind. Go check it out, then report back to base?" Dom's voice vanished from inside my ear, letting the music flow through.

Armed with my trusty Glock, and a silver tray of fish eggs, I weaved through the crowd, searching for any sign of our target, and who he may be meeting. An uneasy ugliness lined the pit of my stomach, and it wasn't down to the fishy smell because that was rather pleasant. It was the sickening thought of coming face to face with my mother, and how it would feel to be near her.

CHAPTER
Thirty-One

Bexley

I felt as if we had stepped into a magical time portal that transported us inside a fairy tale realm. It had always been my dream to come here, but I never seemed to find the time. Work always came first; I rarely had the time to play. My mother used to relish all the details to me when I was little, telling me that each year in June, around the summer solstice, the Palace of Versailles hosts a Baroque

Masquerade Ball. They call it Le Grand Bal Masqué de Versailles. It was just like in the old days, when the royals partied, leaving the peasants to starve. It was a disgusting display of wealth and glamour. But these parties went on until the early hours of daylight until the very last guest decided to leave.

The music thumped through the walls, filtering out into the gardens. Hundreds of people had dressed up to the nines, concealing their identities behind each elaborate mask. I felt like a fictional character who was living a fantasy life. The free-flowing champagne and canapés were too tempting to resist, but I needed to focus and not let the ambiance of the evening seduce me of my senses. We had a job to do. I curled my fingers around Emilio's arm as he led me through the crowd.

I touched my earlobe as a signal to Dominic, hoping he could see me. Emilio brought his fist up to his mouth and cleared his throat. The inside of my ear tickled as Dominic's voice rumbled through the earpiece

"We have located the target in the orangery," he informed us. "There's no sign of the Chameleon . . . I mean Susan. It was a long shot, expecting her to show herself in public. Cruz is searching among the guests, just in case she does put in an appearance. In just a few minutes, everyone will head to the gardens to watch the firework display. Follow them, and act like a regular guest. You'll notice Asher, but don't acknowledge him. He won't make eye-contact with you. If they're expecting us to crash the party, they'll be looking for any unusual interactions."

"Got it," I replied.

Right at that moment, Braxton approached us carrying a silver platter of canapés.

"Take one, and thank him," Dominic prompted. "To you, he is a regular server who is just doing his job"

Treating Braxton like a regular joe felt unnatural to me. I put my acting skills to great use, thanking him then turning away as if he was a complete stranger. Emilio scrunched his nose at the caviar canapé. He sniffed it, then stuck his tongue out to lick it. He looked as if he regretted not choosing the salmon. I watched the way he grimaced as he chewed, then tried not to laugh at him as he swallowed it most reluctantly. He reached out to grab a flute of champagne as another server passed us, and chugged it down in four large gulps. I took one for myself as Emilio swapped his empty glass for another filled with the sweet effervescent liquid.

"How do you eat that stuff?" he complained, then

used his tongue to probe the remnants of canape from between his teeth.

I bounced my shoulders in a shrug. "I'm used to it. I don't particularly like it. It's like eating oysters. They feel and look gross, but I still eat them because . . . well, just because."

"Oysters are good," Emilio replied. "Caviar is so salty, and the aftertaste is like swallowing a mouthful of spunk. I don't know how anyone can enjoy it."

He chugged more champagne, and I bounced my gaze to his flute and then back at him.

"Says the bloke who is part of a ménage," I retorted. "I bet you've swallowed your fair share of sperm." Emilio didn't deny it. "And speaking of enjoyment. Don't enjoy yourself too much, will you? I don't want to have to carry you back to the car tonight," I mentioned, in a humoured tone.

Emilio snorted with amusement. "We'll see who's carrying whom by the end of tonight." His gaze dropped to my heeled sandals and his eyes winced with sympathy.

"Come on, Zorro. Let's go and watch the fireworks," I suggested, in a mocking tone as I dragged him through the bustling halls and out into the cool evening air.

They decorated the vast gardens with

multicoloured lights. The fountains illuminated with fluctuations of neon pink, majestic purple, golden yellow, and icy blue. I couldn't spot Asher among the V.I.P area, but I didn't take the time to look for him, too engrossed by the captivating display. A magnitude of colours glittered through the sky, entrancing us all with a clever display of pyrotechnics. It was over before I knew it, and then the crowd dispersed. People ambled through the grounds to see what else the night had in store

Emilio tapped my arm. "Look over there," he urged, flicking his gaze to our right.

I looked and saw a tall male in a black and gold tuxedo. He was wearing one of those Venetian long nose masks in black with a golden trim around the edge. As he lifted it to sip his champagne, it looked like a huge dick was growing from his forehead. It was our target, our very own Home Secretary, Malcolm Lewis. And what a prick he was. I wasn't just saying that because he was an Eton graduate. I've known plenty of men to have gone to Eton who were as humble as could be. This guy climbed his way up the politics ladder and had charmed his way into power. People fall for his silver tongue without realising what a slimeball he truly is. He was busy checking out each female bottom that he passed. I turned to Emilio, and he was scowling at the exact same thing that I saw.

"Is that our guy?" Emilio asked; the shock in his voice suggested he hoped that this was a joke.

I nodded with an apologetic grimace. "I know . . . he's a massive twat, and I've got to get him to dance with me"

His eyes flashed with uncertainty. "Can't we just cause a distraction and let Braxton or Cruz knock him out?"

That made me chuckle. "Not if we want to get home in one piece." I placed my hand on his shoulder. "Trust me . . . I've got this."

"You better hope so, because he's heading inside," Dominic spoke through the earpiece.

We followed him down the dark garden path. The light was fading and gunpowder curled in soft whisps through the air. The footpath glittered like someone sprinkled it with magic dust, and people's laughter echoed around the grounds. Soft pink and purple lights twinkled around the orangery; just like Mount Olympus, it was astir with Gods and Goddesses. Warmth greeted us as we stepped into the hall. The ballroom enticed us in with its golden grandeur, elaborate chandeliers, and orchestral music. The air buzzed with excitement. People swayed to the music in their extravagant outfits, giant wigs, their faces hidden behind their masks. There was still no sign of Susan, so I dared to approach Malcolm in the hope that I would capture his lecherous eyes.

Emilio remained at a safe distance, watching and waiting as he sipped on his champagne. From the corner of my eye, I saw Cruz placing a hand on his gun, and then Braxton stopped to loiter nearby. And as I moved closer to Malcolm, Asher stepped from behind a pillar and made his presence known to me. It made me feel safe. Then Dominic whispered encouraging words into my ear, boosting me with confidence

"Don't approach him directly. His bodyguards won't let you get within an inch of him. He has to invite you into his circle. You must capture his attention," he advised me through the earpiece.

My heart hammered inside my chest, and all the moisture evaporated from my mouth. It was one thing to plan things, but it was another to actually carry them out. I made sure my pendant remained snugly between my breasts, then continued to move past Malcolm, pretending I had lost my dancing partner. I rose on my tiptoes as if I was searching for someone, then sighed with disappointment. It seemed to work. Malcolm stopped mid-conversation and leered my way.

"Hold that thought," he uttered to one of his guards. "I haven't had an ounce of fun since I arrived here, and I'm hoping that something better just came up"

CHAPTER Thirty-Two

Bexley

I hoped he was talking about the prospect of dancing with me, and not the contents of his underpants. The thought made me internally dry-heave

Malcolm advanced on me as I maintained an act of innocence

"Excuse me, mademoiselle. You seem to have misplaced your dancing partner," he joked flirtatiously. He didn't even attempt to hide behind his mask. "Would you care to join me, instead?"

I played coy, shying my eyes away in a bashful response. "Oh . . . thank you. I think my date ditched me for one of the waitresses."

"Well, then he's an idiot. Someone who is clearly unworthy of a gorgeous woman such as yourself. I bet you're a sight to behold underneath that mask." He handed his champagne flute to one of his bodyguards and shooed them both away.

Then he turned to me, holding out his hand. "May I have this dance?" he asked, trailing his eyes all over my body like he was imagining me naked. I couldn't stop picturing a giant penis on his head instead of a big nosed mask. It took all my effort not to burst out laughing. Maybe it was just nerves.

"Of course," I answered

"That was easy. Okay then . . . what if I told you that you have a nice body, would you hold it against me?" he told a lewd joke.

Swallowing down the bile in my throat, I forced a smile to mask my revulsion. "Maybe, if you play your cards right," I replied.

Malcolm snaked one arm around my waist and used his free hand to lace with mine. His cologne swamped my airways, and it wasn't awful at all. I recognised the Armani aftershave because my husbands wore the same fragrance, or something close to it. The pleasant scent calmed me, making it easier to carry out my task. Malcolm's fingertips migrated south to graze against my backside, and as I rested my chin upon his shoulder, I could see just how murderous my husbands' expressions were. Dominic's breath rattled through the earpiece, merging with the music. I knew I was treading on dangerous grounds the second I pressed my lips against Malcom's throat. His breathing stuttered, and something firm manifested against my groin. This time, he palmed the left side of my arse and I faked a delighted moan.

"I doubt it's just a dance you're after?" I hinted.

"You guessed correctly," he answered. "Why don't we slip away for a little privacy?" He leaned back to gaze into my eyes. "Sex with a masked stranger has always been a fantasy of mine."

Who even says that after five minutes of meeting someone?

And to think . . . his constituents voted him into Parliament.

I walked my fingers along his chest and drew circles around his collar bone. This was escalating as I intended, and now my fingers were free to roam wherever I chose because he'd assume I was flirting.

Asher looked on anxiously. I could see the

trepidation in his eyes. Malcolm leaned in to kiss me, and I let his lips linger on mine. Now I regret not wearing the kiss of death lipstick. He pressed his tongue inside my mouth and I heard Dominic growl inside my ear. Braxton looked as if he wanted to throw the silver platter at him, and I could see Cruz's jaw pulsing from where I was standing. The colour drained from Asher's face as if he wanted to be sick. Goodness knows what Emilio was thinking. He just stood there looking awkward as fuck.

My hands explored every inch of Malcolm like they were seeking out hidden treasure. He was too far gone in the kiss to notice I'd invaded his jacket pocket. My fingers coiled around the cool thin rectangle and removed it from his possession. Asher reacted almost instantly, walking past and taking the phone from my grasp. His fingers worked fluidly, competing against the speed of time as if they mocked it. Before I knew it, he thrust it back into my hand and I slipped it back inside Malcolm's pocket as if nothing had happened

"My cock is as hard as a rock," he murmured against my lips. "I think you should take care of it."

I curled my fingers around his hand and let him weave us through the crowd. My husbands tailed us every step of the way. One way or another, even if the Chameleon pulled a no-show, we would get her one way or another. She was bound to make contact with Malcolm at some point.

"Oh wait," I said, pulling back as soon as we broke free from the crowd and stepped out onto the garden terrace. "I think you ruined my lipstick."

I rummaged around in my purse, and Malcolm huffed with frustration.

"Don't bother trying to fix it. I'll only smudge it again," he commented.

I found the item I'd been searching for, and flashed Malcolm a dazzling smile.

"Yeah, but I want to look my best. After all, I want you to remember me in a good way." I pouted

If he knew who I really was, he'd be yelling for security

"If you want to try something a little risqué, we could fuck inside that pergola," he suggested.

Only one of us was about to be fucked right now, and I would be doing the fucking. Malcolm didn't raise an eyebrow as I took out my powder compact from my bag. It looked like a regular cosmetic item as I checked my reflection in the circular mirror; it enabled me to see my men approach us from all angles.

"Get a move on then," Malcolm spoke forcefully this time. "Or are you just a little cock tease?"

He made a move to grab me, but I managed to disturb enough of the powder to blow a dust cloud in his face. I held my breath, not wanting to inhale any of the particles.

Cruz and Braxton were there to grab him before he hit the ground

"It's time we got out of here," Asher asserted, steering me away from the scene of the crime.

Emilio took his place at my side, and we made our way back to the entrance hall. Something was wrong. The security guards pushed through the crowds as if they were searching for someone.

"Uh . . . guys," Dominic said through the earpiece. "We've got a problem."

"What problem?" Braxton rasped into his watch.

"Ulrich noticed several agents bursting through the main gates like they were the fucking S.W.A.T team. They are heading your way," he informed us.

"Copy that," Cruz replied. "I can see them approaching"

"We need a diversion," Asher advised.

"I'm thinking," Dominic responded, and I heard him tapping away on his computer keyboard.

"There's no time," I cut in, having had an idea, albeit a wild and crazy one.

I removed the watch from around my wrist and yelled, "Bomb!" at the top of my lungs.

People dove out of the way, covering their heads with their hands. The sound of shrieking and wailing filled the room. The agents ran into view and caught us like we were a bunch of rabbits who were trapped in the headlights. We looked as guilty as fuck — a mismatched band of miscreants who had no business being together. A servant, a security officer, an aristocrat, a Spaniard, and a frightened young woman

"It's them . . . they're here!" an agent announced, pulling a gun on us.

I acted fast without stopping to hesitate, clicking the side button on the watch and tossing it at the agents. A bright red flash dazzled my eyes as the ticking time bomb detonated. The ground shook beneath us as Cruz threw himself on top of me. My ears rang with aftershock bells, drowning out everything that Dominic was yelling. Smoke billowed before my eyes, masking the devastation surrounding us. I just hoped that no one got hurt, but I couldn't guarantee that they didn't. As much as I keep telling myself it was all for the greater good, it was a hard pill to swallow.

"Move . . . come on . . . get up," Cruz grunted, yanking me to my feet.

We scrambled through the debris and out into the crisp night air. Shots were fired from both sides of the driveway. My men fired back; Emilio included. Uncle Teddy came screeching around to shield us with the stretch limousine, and we all dove inside. He spun around the fountain in a tight semi-circle, then floored it before they got the chance to close the gates. It was a miracle we got out of there alive. I clung to Cruz as the car jerked from right to left, weaving through the traffic. Yet again, we'd had a brush with death and escaped within an inch of our lives.

"Mission accomplished," Asher leaned back, grinning

"Now all we have to do is wait," Cruz advised. "If Mr Lewis is working with Susan, we'll know when she makes contact."

I remained silent, and feeling slightly unsettled from hearing her name spoken among us instead of her alias. Calling her by her name seemed to humanize her. The Chameleon suited her best. This wasn't a woman who was capable of showing remorse no more than she displayed a maternal instinct. She murdered my mother for knowledge and power. Through my eyes, she was nothing more than a reptile.

"I'm hacking his phone records now," Dominic shared, and I could hear the keypad clicking away.

Moments passed before we heard a euphoric gasp through our earpieces.

"Well, fuck me sideways . . . I think I've found her," he exclaimed.

CHAPTER Thirty-Three

Bexley

"We located the phone signal a mile away from Charles de Gaulle airport," Dominic continued to explain his findings. "It wasn't too hard to figure it out. Malcolm stored a suspicious number as "C" in his contact list."

Asher narrowed his eyes as he thought. "Don't be too hasty. We still don't know if the number belongs to Susan. "C" could mean anyone, not necessarily the

Chameleon. He could have a secret mistress or an escort he uses. You need to be thorough. Pull up the phone records and go through each conversation. There has to be something more concrete for us to go on"

Cruz handed me a glass of brandy to calm my nerves. I took it and sipped a small amount. The burning sensation seeped into my tongue and licked a fiery trail down my throat. After several sips, I began to feel the smoky liquid taking effect.

"I think we've found something," Dominic replied a few minutes later. "We'll fill you all in as soon as we get back"

The boys seemed optimistic and that eased the knotted tension I was feeling inside. At least tonight wasn't a total waste of our time. We bugged Malcolm's phone and that gave us a vantage point. At least we could tap into his conversations and weed out all the corrupted ministers before stepping foot into Britain. There had to be someone who we could trust with this information. The leader of the opposition maybe. I had to think positively or else I would crumble under the pressure. Even after we prove our innocence, I would be surprised if my men went back to work for the agency. It had been a huge part of their lives for such a long time, but they turned on us when we needed them most. If they can't see what is happening under their noses, they don't deserve to have soldiers as good as the Wolfe brothers on their team. They don't deserve my father, or Uncle Zane. It will be a sad loss for Britain the day they turn in their ID cards and guns. They should mourn the loss of six great servicemen because they are an asset to our country. My husbands want to move on to new and brighter pastures, and I can't say that I blame them. They didn't fail our queen and country. The agency had

"Bexley we're here," Cruz announced, nudging me

I set down the glass tumbler and got out of the limo. Dominic and Ulrich had arrived a minute or two before we did, and were waiting for us at the front of the chateaux. It was half past midnight and shadows stood motionless across the vineyard. The moonlight shone down upon us, outlining us in its silvery hue. We had to be careful not to wake the sleeping priest and his maid. It was good of them to let us stay here, but we couldn't outstay our welcome. We would take the fond memories of our wedding day and leave at first light. The last thing any of us wanted was to put our allies in jeopardy and have the authorities accuse them of aiding and abetting wanted fugitives. I hoped to return here with our children someday, and show them where we recited our sacred vows. Not a business arrangement. It was so much more than that now.

"Let's go into the kitchen," Uncle Teddy suggested, lowering the volume of his voice.

Braxton led the way, removing his prosthetics. Asher and Cruz did the same. I was getting so used to them wearing disguises, it didn't faze me as they tugged the fake skin from their faces like a scene from a gory horror film. Asher had missed a piece beneath his ear and it started to bug me as we gathered around the table. I yanked it away like I was tearing off a plaster, making him flinch with discomfort. He rubbed the side of his face, glaring at me as if I'd just waxed off half of his beard. Everyone settled down around the table, sitting shoulder to shoulder. Dominic set up his laptop and turned the screen for us to see.

"Take a look at this," he mentioned, scrolling through the phone records. "Do you remember the Russian diplomat with the name Volk, meaning wolf? They tried to cover it up as a Bratva hit, but we all know it was a message from the Chameleon. Well, Malcolm received a call from "C" a week before the assassination. Then another five-minute conversation took place on the morning of the killing. And again, an hour before the agency raided our house."

"Are you saying that you can place "C" at the scene of the murder?" Asher asked, needing Dominic to confirm that.

Dominic's eyes flinched with regret. "No . . . not in Moscow when the shooting took place."

"Wait . . . what?" Braxton's expression morphed into a bemused grimace. "Of course, she was there. She murdered an undercover agent and assumed their identity. That's how she was able to travel to the U.K. She murdered Volk, and then she killed Agent Black. Jesus, Dom . . . I thought you said you'd found her?"

"I thought I had," Dominic retaliated.

Asher waved his hand in dismissal. "Can you pinpoint where the call took place?"

Cruz said nothing as he listened to the news. I couldn't read the impassive expression on his face. There wasn't a flicker of anger or surprise. The guy was a walking enigma. Emilio poured us all another drink and set down the glasses in front of us. Ulrich guzzled his down in one large chug and held his glass out for a top up. Uncle Teddy wore the same grim expression since we arrived back.

"Not exactly," Dominic answered, sighing

exasperatedly. "It's coming from somewhere in the North West of England. Whoever "C" is, they have a signal scrambler programmed into their device. I can't decrypt it unless they make another call. We can't risk calling them in case it backfires on us. So, as you can guess, we're in an awkward predicament."

"So . . ." Cruz finally spoke after finishing his drink. "Not only do we have the Chameleon to contend with, it appears as if we are dealing with an accomplice. Someone who is calling the shots from inside the UK. We know that the Chameleon was in Moscow on the day of the killing, but the caller was not."

The revelation startled me and I bounced my gaze around, witnessing the same level of understanding start to resonate between them.

"Of course . . . that's how she's able to be in two places at once, always blending in like a ghost. She's working with someone else," Asher said, piecing it together. "But then that begs another question as to who "C" is? If Malcolm believes he is dealing with the Chameleon, and no one else, then he's being fooled too. Susan is using him like a puppet to get what she wants."

"One of us needs to tell Dad about this,"

Dominic mentioned. "We need to keep him and Uncle Jaxx in the loop."

"Then you better explain it to him because my head is fucking scrambled with all this fucked-up nonsense," Braxton huffed.   "My brain shuts down past the stroke of midnight. If I can't shoot at it, punch it, or smash it to smithereens, then count me the fuck out. I'm going to bed," he grumbled.

Cruz flashed him a megawatt grin. "Goodnight, mate."

Asher scrubbed a hand over his stressed face and exhaled a weary sigh. "Night, Brax."

Dominic just raised his hand in acknowledgement, too busy scrolling through his phone. Teddy, Ulrich, and Emilio all mumbled "Good night" sounding equally as exhausted.

"Good night, babe," I murmured, following suit with everyone else.

Braxton stopped and turned in the doorway, eyeing me with amusement.

"In case you couldn't tell, that was a hint-drop for you to come upstairs, so I can rip off that dress and fuck your brains out," he rasped in his deep gravelly voice.   He jabbed his finger in an upward motion, signalling for me to get up from my seat.

His brazen comment made me blush from head

to toe, too embarrassed to look around at all the grinning faces around the table. Braxton was the type to pick me up like a caveman and throw me over his shoulder. He wouldn't think twice about lifting my dress and spanking my exposed backside for good measure. It wouldn't matter that we had company. Ulrich, Teddy, and Emilio would see more than they bargained for if I chose not to comply. He would take whatever he wanted, not caring that we had an audience. I didn't want him to prove his point in front of my so-called uncles, and our mutual cousin. It wouldn't be right.

Braxton waited expectantly for me to push back on my chair and follow him upstairs. Cruz, Asher, and Dominic would give us a moment and then they'd be up to join us. There would be no sleep for us until they had all satisfied their cravings. Kissing Malcolm would have its consequences as I was about to find out.

CHAPTER
Thirty-Four

Bexley

A s I stepped into the dark bedroom, Braxton was waiting in the shadows like a predator waiting to strike, naked and ready. He snatched me by the wrist and twirled me around, the action knocking the air from my lungs as I crashed against his chest, my palms sliding across his muscles as I struggled to find anchorage. His thumb smeared what was left of my lipstick across my cheek before his mouth covered my lips in a rough kiss. Our tongues duelled, dancing together like eels in a mating ritual, his fingers searching for the back of my dress, fumbling blindly. A harsh sound of ripped fabric tore through the air then the tattered gown slid down my body and pooled around my feet.

I snatched ragged breaths between kisses, but Braxton sought to eliminate any last trace of Malcolm, reminding me whom I belonged to, and barely giving me enough time to breathe. The stairs creaked with footsteps, letting me know we had company

"Did you enjoy making us jealous?" Braxton rasped, sounding every inch the Alpha male.

"No," I answered honestly, even though it thrilled me to wind them up. "Why? Were you jealous?"

Braxton kissed my neck in the most savage manner, ridding me of every last stitch of clothing. I knew he would leave suction marks. My fingers coiled around his hardness, feeling just how determined he was. Even in the dark, I could feel the intensity of Braxton's gaze bearing down on me. My man was possessive. He had no problem with sharing me with his brothers, but not with anyone else

"You're ours," he asserted, walking me back

towards the bed. My thighs touched the mattress, leaving nowhere left to run. Not that I would

Another figure moved within the shadows and started to strip, then another, and another. The rustling of clothing made up the background noise. I knew they were watching. I could hear them breathing and moving around, but they stuck to the edges of the room like voyeuristic creatures of the night, waiting their turn as their brother lowered me onto the bed and crawled over me. Braxton smelled of raw masculinity. His cologne almost worn away by his body heat. My pussy throbbed with the urge to fuck, eager to be filled. Braxton's ravenous kisses left a trail of goosebumps in their wake; my nipples puckered ready for the taking.

"You enjoyed teasing us, Bexley?" Braxton uttered in a dark and foreboding rasp.

"You shouldn't be so easy to tease," I retorted. "I did my job . . . sue me if it dented your ego."

Someone in the room chuckled and it sounded like Dominic. I wasn't ready for what came next. So, when Braxton pinned my hands above my head and someone held them in place, it took me by surprise. He had help, but I didn't know who. Something smooth curled around my ankles and I found I couldn't move. Then, in a whirl of blindness, they flipped me onto my stomach. My knees were unable to meet because of the obstruction between my ankles, but my arms were free. In the following instant, Braxton filled my mouth with something hard and round, buckling the clasp at the back of my head. This was supposed to be hallowed ground, not a sex den. My pussy creamed for some action, wondering what devilish things they were going to do to me.

"Bexley, Bexley," Braxton taunted, stroking the cleft of my arse with his finger. "How should we punish you?"

I knew what to expect before I felt an almighty slap, followed by a not-so-subtle intrusion. The stretch and burn in my anus as Braxton shoved his lubricated finger inside me brought tears to my eyes.

Motherfucker!

"Hmph," I bit down on the ball gag that muffled my cries. As much as I thrived off being a strong independent woman, there was nothing quite like being overpowered by a dominant Alpha male, especially knowing that there were three more waiting in the wings to step in when required.

"This belongs to me." Braxton made that clear as he finger-fucked my back passage. "You're going to remember that when you try to sit tomorrow."

Cruz muscled in and wriggled into the space

beneath me, grabbing my hips and positioning his cock at the mouth of my pussy, then sucked my nipples between his lips. He held me steady as Braxton squeezed something cold and sticky onto the tip of his cock and slathered it all over us. I knew what they were planning and I braced myself ready.

"This belongs to us," Cruz asserted in a controlled upward thrust that took my breath away. The push seemed to take forever until he bottomed out, burying his cock to the root.

"Uhhh," I squealed, my jaw aching around the solid ball.

Fingers stroked my chin, lifting my gaze to two waiting cocks that were eager to be handled. My hands coiled around Dominic and Asher's cocks, and stroked

"Permission to come aboard, baby," Braxton rasped, nudging his swollen crown at my rear.

I groaned with trepidation, not wanting to regret this later. This was going to be eye-popping uncomfortable, despite the lube easing his passage.

"Humph," I murmured, trying to tell him to go easy on me.

And I knew they would. Every touch, movement, caress, made me feel like a cherished queen. I relaxed against Cruz and breathed through my nose, his hands stroking my spine in a soothing manner. He knew just how to calm me with the gentlest touch; such a big tough beast, but with a heart as soft as caramel. Braxton's breath skipped in his throat as he pushed through my resistance, breaking through the ring of muscle until I was seeing stars. The feeling of having Cruz and Braxton filling me to the brink of breaking point almost felt too much. My swollen clit pressed against Cruz like he was holding it hostage, grazing against the thatch of curls on his groin for friction. Then Braxton started to move, stimulating both me and Cruz as he worked his cock like a piston, his undulated movements were like a well-oiled machine, forcing me to take my pleasure out on Asher and Dom as I stroked them senseless. Cruz hissed at each ministration, no doubt experiencing the slide of Braxton's cock through the thin layer of flesh. The room filled with erotic sex noises, grunting, groaning, and the sinful squelching sound of my pussy getting wetter, and my arse being fucked. The heady scent of dick and pussy filled the air with musk.

Before the Wolfe brothers, sex had always been mediocre in comparison. I never knew it could feel this good. Never did I think I would be lying in this position, taking four big dicks at once. I could have sucked one off if it wasn't for the restriction between my teeth, then I could have alternated working on them. But that wasn't their plan. They wanted me to feel everything they were giving to me. My nerve endings crackled with a frisson of excitement. I felt the tug on my stomach as my orgasm neared. My groans turned to desperate whimpers as my body became their instrument of sexual pleasure. I loved being theirs to share, theirs to love, to adore. If this was our last night on earth, I wanted to spend it being as close to my men as humanly possible. Asher and Dominic's cocks swelled in my hand; their hips started jerking as if they were chasing their release

"Bex . . .," Asher groaned, then didn't finish his sentence as thick, ropey cum sprayed me in the face.

Dominic came a close second, fisting my hair as he streaked my chest with the essence of his pleasure. It went all over Cruz too, but he was too far gone to care

My body trembled on top of Cruz, quaking as my climax rocked through me. And boy, did it just. I think they heard me from across the vineyard in the neighbouring farm. My men grunted as they humped me, their cocks swelling to enormous proportions to the point I thought I might pass out with the intensity

"Uhh," Braxton roared.

Cruz barked out a harsh cry beneath me, his fingers digging into my thighs just as Braxton's clung to my hips. Our skin was sweaty, hot, aiding our ministrations as we slid together on the bed.

Then liquid warmth filled my insides as their hips jerked against me, but I was too far gone, floating on a cloud of bliss. Right now, I didn't give a shit if I went straight to hell. The rush was worth it.

"Fuck," Braxton huffed as he slumped over me.

Cruz couldn't speak; all he could do was flare his eyes as he caught his breath, his muscular chest rising and falling with each ragged respiration. Asher left to fetch a washcloth, and Cruz freed me from my bindings. I was sticky all over and my jaw ached. They washed away their seed as best as they could, cleansing my face and body with warm wet washcloths.

"Was that to your satisfaction, Mrs Wolfe?" Braxton asked, adding a husky chuckle at the end.

"You know it was," I replied, stretching with contentment.

Dominic returned to the bedroom with a bottle of chilled champagne and five tall flutes.

"I want to celebrate the small victory we had tonight," he said, as he poured us all a large measure of the pale effervescent liquid. "We're about to face the final hurdle"

Braxton and Cruz were kneeling on the bed beside me, and Asher and Dom were sitting on the edge of the mattress, facing us.

Dominic continued as we paused with our glasses held out in front of us, "It's not going to be easy, but at least we all have each other." He raised his glass to make a toast. "Here's to family," he finished.

"To family," we chorused, then took a sip of champagne

When I think about how far we've come together, I know we can overcome any hurdles that life throws at us.

CHAPTER

Thirty-Five

Bexley

I woke with a jolt, my eyes snapping open with panic. It took a few seconds to realise that Cruz was standing over me with a mug of coffee in his hand

"Good morning, princess; it's almost time to leave," he announced

"Where is everyone?" I asked, sitting up to take the mug from him.

I felt tender all over; especially in certain orifices. Cruz chewed on the inside of his cheek as I winced.

"Are you sore, love? I hope we weren't too rough with you last night," he said in a contrite tone.

The sex was a bit more rampant than usual, but it was nothing that a salt bath won't soothe. Although, there wouldn't be time for one of those.

"I'll survive . . . unlike my outfit," I commented, pointing out the ruined garment on the floor.

Cruz crouched to retrieve it and shoved it into a refuse sack. "We're burning everything we don't need. It's better to be safe and destroy the trail of breadcrumbs."

That was true. Father Fournier had granted us refuge and put himself and his housekeeper, Martha, at risk. I would be eternally grateful for their warm hospitality. It felt like a holiday rather than a safe house. I finished my coffee in between gathering my belongings. Then I showered quickly, dressed, then joined my men downstairs in the kitchen

"Here she is," Asher chirped brightly. "Good morning, sweetheart." He stood up to kiss me.

Dominic held out his arms and greeted me with a cuddle. "Are you ready to go, love?"

My stomach flipped over. Was I ready? I would

never be ready for what's out there, but I didn't have much of a choice.

"Ready as I'll ever be," I replied.

Emilio, Teddy, and Ulrich talked among themselves. Martha busied herself with the breakfast dishes, and Father Fournier spoke privately with Asher and Braxton.

"What's going on?" I asked Dominic

His hold on me slackened and I was able to grab a croissant from the table. Not that I was particularly hungry, but I knew it would be foolish to leave on an empty stomach.

"Teddy and Emilio are flying to the Maldives to join Dad and Uncle Jaxx," he informed me. "They want to help, and they think they know how?

Cruz sauntered across the room and leaned against the countertop beside us. "Ulrich is taking us to Norway. His jet can pass through the airspace undetected. He's the best chance we've got," he told us. "There's no way we can risk passing through checkpoints. They'll shoot us on sight, and take Bexley into custody."

Martha packed us a hamper full of food and bottled water. She included a bottle of Father Fournier's finest wine, then winked at me as if she knew I would appreciate it. Father Fournier blessed us all as we made our departure, wishing us Godspeed, and may the Lord grant us a safe journey. He urged me to take care, and said that he hoped we would return to visit again soon. I hoped so too.

Outside in the gardens, we said goodbye to Teddy and Emilio. They were reluctant to leave us, but there was really nothing more they could do. Dad and Zane needed all the help they could get, and we would need them to pull through for us when we returned from our mission. Everything was balancing on a knife's edge. One wrong move, and all our effort would be for nothing. We would rot in jail for treason, and would be branded as terrorists. That couldn't happen, not when we were about to discover the truth. Maybe the only way to ensure our freedom would be to show the world what the files contained. If it was out in the open, then the information would be useless. We could stop running and we could all go home

Braxton checked my harness, then took the seat on my right. Cruz was sitting to the left of me, with Asher sitting in the adjacent seat. Dominic was sitting in the cockpit with Ulrich, assisting him with the coordinates. Mum had spoken of the Seven Sisters waterfall in Geiranger, but had never taken me to visit. I had only ever seen images from the internet.

It's lucky that Braxton was familiar with the place because I was in way over my head. At least he would know how to get us out of there when we found what we were looking for.

If this was a commercial flight, it would have taken us hours to get there, but Ulrich's jet got us there at a mind-blowing speed. Before I had the time to drink in my surroundings, we had reached the fairy tale landscape with its majestic snow-covered mountaintops, and lush green vegetation that spread as far as the eye could see. The fast-flowing waterfalls cascaded down the rock faces, churning the lake with frothy white plunge pools. Mist hovered above the surface, mimicking clouds. The deep, blue fjord ran proudly between the mountainsides, snaking across the land. As we flew overhead, looking for a decent landing spot, I could see the abandoned farms that nature claimed as its own. Some remained intact, and some had crumbled into a state of disrepair.

Braxton leaned over me to point through the small oval window. "If you look over there, you will see a waterfall called Friaren."

"Is that its name?" I replied, squinting to look. "Mum always referred to it as The Suitor because the sisters never stayed settled for long. Some married, but they never lasted."

This caught the attention of Asher and Cruz who seemed interested in the legend of the Seven Sisters. They only knew what I had told them previously, but I wasn't sure how much of it they remembered.

"Any information you have on Electra will be useful to our mission," Asher urged.

"There are many different accounts with reference to the Pleiades," I told them. "They were the daughters of Atlas and Pleione. The most common tale is that they were tossed into the sky as doves and turned into stars by Zeus so they could flee from the giant, Orion. Atlas was forced to hold up the sky for all eternity, so he was unable to protect his daughters when Orion pursued them. The faintest star of the Pleiades was thought to be either Merope, who was ashamed of loving a mortal, or Electra, after grieving the destruction of Troy, the city of Dardanus, who was named after her son with Zeus. Her name also has a connection to the organic gemstone "Amber". Mum told me Electra was known as the sun Pleiad. She claimed that Electra's waterfall shimmers golden beneath the sunlight. So, whatever is hidden can only be found during daylight hours, on a clear bright day, and not when it is raining. The falls are harder to determine during heavy rainfall. We need to find whatever it is, then get the hell out of there before sundown," I advised.

The cockpit door slid to one side and Dominic emerged into the cabin.

"Suit up, guys. It's time for us to fly," he announced

My eyes flared with horror as my husbands began reaching for identical backpacks and thrusted their arms through the straps.

"What's going on?" I asked, darting my eyes around as they secured the harnesses around their bodies.

"We can't land the plane on an uneven surface, Bexley. We have to jump from here," Braxton informed me, much to my distress.

I shook my head frantically. "No, I'm not jumping from the plane," I whined

I was shit scared of heights despite having flown around the world on numerous occasions. Being a passenger on board an aircraft was one thing, but free falling was out of the question. Fuck that. No way. I would rather land the plane and take my chances.

Braxton placed his arm around my shoulders and pulled me close. "Babe, I promised you a skydiving experience, and I aim to deliver."

That did nothing to alleviate my fear, making me hyperventilate even harder.

"I can't," I told him, and I was trembling by this point.

My heart was bouncing between my arsehole and my throat. One way or another, something was bound to come flying out, but from which end, I didn't know

"Yes, you can," Braxton reassured me. "You're going to be strapped to me. We're going to do a tandem jump together. I'll be with you the whole time"

I choked down the bile that threatened to creep up my throat. Then Cruz opened the door and a strong vortex of air came rushing into the cabin. He pulled his goggles over his eyes and held onto the top of the door frame as he peered down at the long drop. The landscape looked tiny from up here. My legs turned to jelly. I couldn't breathe. Cruz winked at me and then jumped before I could blink

"Argh!" I screamed, covering my mouth.

Asher went next, followed closely by Dominic. Braxton fixed the harness around me and edged us slowly towards the open door. My feet didn't want to move, they just shuffled an inch at a time. The wind ripped through the cabin, whirling my hair around my face.

"Put on these," Braxton said, helping me to put on some goggles. He pulled on a pair of his own and eased us closer to the edge. "It's going to be fine. Just relax and let me take care of things."

My teeth chattered inside my mouth like a pair of wind-up joke dentures. I have never been so terrified of anything in my life.

"On the count of three," Braxton forewarned. "One," he counted, then paused. "Two," he continued

But before I got the chance to hear him count to three, he lunged forward and sent us hurtling through the clouds at speed.

"Argh!" I screamed, but stopped because I swallowed too much air, I almost choked on it. It was nearly impossible to make a sound at this altitude. The G-force pulled at my face, manipulating my skin

We were soaring through the sky like a boulder. It went on for several moments. All I could see was the ground getting larger. Braxton checked his wristwatch, then pulled on the string to deploy the parachute. One harsh tug on my midriff and we lurched upward on a wind pocket. The fall was over, and now we were gliding down to earth above an incredible view.

"Oh my god," I uttered, still trembling with adrenaline

"It's beautiful, isn't it?" Braxton rasped against my ear.

It sure was. The exhilarating feeling rushed through me, overwhelming me and bringing tears to my eyes. This was living, and I felt more alive than ever.

CHAPTER Thirty-Six

Braxton

The Paracommander parachute was designed to give us a straight-down descent opposed to a swooping glide to the ground. It was a soft landing, considering this was Bexley's first time. That was good because she may be more inclined to try this again sometime.

"What a rush!" she exclaimed, pumped so full of

adrenaline, I could practically feel her energy buzzing

I removed the harness from around us and jogged to where my brothers were waiting

"I'm so proud of you," Cruz told our wife, then hugged her.

Bexley beamed up at him, basking under the glow of his praise.

I checked my watch. "We better hurry if we want to search the area before sundown. It may take us a while to find what we are looking for."

My brothers and I carried the climbing gear in our backpacks, leaving Bexley to walk unhindered. It was an arduous trek across the uneven terrain, and she was likely to tire before we reached the falls. We had to remember that we had been trained for this, but Bexley hadn't. She held her own and kept up with us. It no longer felt like a competition between us. She was part of the team, and it showed.

Asher lumbered two steps behind us to check something that beeped on his watch. We all received the same vibration, notifying us that our dad had sent us a message.

"Teddy and Emilio have arrived at Alpha Two," he informed us.

Bexley exhaled with relief. "Oh, good. At least we know they're safe."

Dominic took hold of her hand as they walked. "You should be more concerned about whether we'll make it back in one piece," he mentioned. "That water will be ice-cold. I don't want to die by freezing my nuts off."

Bexley chuckled. "I forgot my bathing suit. I might have to sit this one out," she joked.

Cruz flashed me a grin, and I knew he would be up for skinny-dipping if we had time. Maybe even a shag-fest near the falls. There was no way to make that happen without the risk of us developing hypothermia. As Dominic mentioned, I would rather leave here with metaphorical blue balls than the real deal.

"Well, luckily for us, we packed wetsuits," I pointed out. "Trust me, you'll be thankful when you feel the temperature of the water. It will suck the breath from your lungs."

Asher grunted. "I can't say I'm looking forward to it. The only consolation is that we're flying to the Maldives after this."

As we approached the cliff edge, the sound of fast-flowing water got louder. A dense mist of water particles hovered above the drop-zone and dampened the air all around us.

My brothers and I rummaged through the backpacks to retrieve the wetsuits. I carried an extra one for Bexley, along with our climbing gear.

"Put this on," I said, handing her the neoprene suit.

It was stretchy, durable, and absorbed little water. The suits were designed to retain body heat, which would be welcomed by us all. This was not going to be a pleasant experience. They only had to endure this for a matter of hours, whereas I had to stick this shit out for four days. I did not want to be back here again, but I had no choice than to find the missing clue. It could be anywhere among the falls. And as Cruz peered over the cliff edge, he glanced at me with an ominous look on his face as if to say "shit".

My thoughts exactly.

I helped Bexley to put on her climbing gear and waited for my brothers to put on theirs.

"I'll go first, since I know this land like the back of my hand," I volunteered. "There's a technique to climbing down. Just mimic the route that I take, and you will be fine."

Cruz volunteered to go next, but insisted he would shadow Bexley in case she got into any difficulty. That just left Asher and Dominic. Both decided to search the opposite side of Electra to cover all possible angles. That seemed like a strong plan. I took the first plunge and used the rope to lower myself. Just as I remembered, the rockface was slippery with moss and vegetation. Some of those plants were edible, and the mushrooms that grew there were considered a delicacy to the locals. Water hit me in the face, making me glad to be wearing goggles. The saturated rope kept slipping through my fingers and I knew I would have blisters after this.

"Hey . . . I think I found something," Dominic bellowed over the rushing water noise. He cleared the water from the lower half of his face to speak. "There are amber stones set into the rocks."

Without seeing the pattern for myself, it was difficult to determine what it meant. Bexley was better at recognising her mother's secret language than any of us would be. We only knew what she had told us. Only she would know what they meant.

"I knew it," Bexley announced not long after Dominic had mentioned finding them. "I can see the amber gemstones just like the ones my mum told me about."

This was Bexley's turn to decipher the clues. Our

input was useless. All we could do was to wait and assist her if she needed us to

"South, south west," she called out, then lowered the rope to search for another clue. "What did the pattern look like, Dom. I need to know."

Dom scanned his eyes around the area. "Uh . . . it looks like two dots, a line of four, and a pyramid of three dots below them," he answered

Bexley understood what he said and took a deep breath before reaching two steps to the right. The water crashed onto her shoulders and almost knocked her off course, but she managed to maintain her footing. Something else caught her eyes and she muttered something I couldn't hear. She used her rope to drop down three feet and then braced herself on a ledge. It took us hours to search the falls, climbing all over the rock face to look for the clues. Bexley figured it was a map with several decoys thrown in to waste time. She figured out that there were deliberate mistakes that only she would notice. Once she established that, she was able to move through them quickly

"Guys, get over here," Bexley yelled, having found something else. "I've found it. I need your help to move this rock"

We abseiled to where she was busy clearing moss away from an area of rock.

"Look." Bexley pointed. "It looks like this could be it. This area has been cut out and replaced. You can see the marks right here."

Dominic removed the axe hammer from his utility belt, and my brothers and I did the same.

"Stand back," Asher urged our wife to move to a safer distance as we set to work, obliterating the rock.

The laborious task took until the light faded and cloud-cover melted into the night sky. Our headtorches illuminated the places where the moon couldn't reach, and just as our effort began to waver, we smashed through to a cavity in the stone. We sagged breathlessly, our limbs trembling with exhaustion. Cruz cleared the debris out of the way using his pickaxe and allowed Bexley to retrieve the galvanised box that her mother had stashed inside.

"We did it," she choked with emotion. "We found the final clue."

But as she tried to peel off the lid with her fingernails, she found that it wouldn't budge

"I can't open it," she panicked.

"Let me see that," Asher insisted, taking the box from her to inspect it. "There's a hole that's meant for a key. We need the key," he mentioned despondently

I think the rest of us blanched with dread at that point. It was dark. Finding a key would be like trying to find a needle in a haystack.

"Wait!" Bexley gasped with realization.

She fumbled around her neck for her necklace and held the long, cylindrical pendant between her fingertips. "I think this might fit."

Asher held the box steady as Bexley slid the charm inside. The lid sprang open as if it was spring-activated, revealing a sealed plastic bag that contained a flash drive, and a wrinkled piece of paper inside. Bexley opened it and gave the flash drive to Dominic for safekeeping. He stashed it inside his backpack along with the others.

"What does the note say, Bexley?" he asked curiously.

Bexley unfolded it to read it. Her eyes creased with concentration.

"It's not a note; it's a haematology report belonging to Susan Wolfe . . . your mother." Bexley glanced at each of us before continuing. "It confirms that she was pregnant."

My brothers and I exchanged sombre glances among us. "So, it's true about the illegitimate child theory then?" I spat out my words with contempt.

"She cheated on Dad, and Aunt Safi found out the truth before Susan killed her."

"It would appear so," Asher spoke gravely. "We have no reason to believe that she went through with the pregnancy. If she did, then we have a sibling out there somewhere. Maybe he or she is our mother's accomplice. We can't rule that out."

Neither one of us had anything to say to that. We just nodded to show that we understood

The alarm on our watches began to beep, letting us know that Ulrich had returned and was waiting for us. He sent us the coordinates to a farm several miles from the falls. So, we would have to break it to Bexley that we would be walking well into the night. That was unlikely to go down well with her.

"We ought to make tracks. Ulrich has sent me the location of an abandoned farm outside Geiranger. It's going to take us a while to get there."

Bexley made a face as if to say "fuck" and whimpered her displeasure. She wasn't alone. We were all pretty fatigued at that point.

It took three hours to reach the farm, and we were all about ready to drop. Bexley slumped to her knees and rolled onto her back, groaning that she had blisters on her feet the size of marbles. I set my backpack down beside the jet then went to find

Ulrich. The gruff veteran emerged from inside the building with a tin of canned peaches in his hand.

"This is all the shit I could find," he said, discarding the dented can across the field. "I only have energy bars and bottled water on the jet. It will have to do until we reach Alpha Two."

Bexley groaned. "I don't care. At this point, I'll eat anything."

If we weren't all so exhausted, I would have held her to that.

CHAPTER Thirty-Seven

Bexley

Dad rushed out to greet me as we arrived at Alpha Two. I ran into his arms and hugged him tightly

"I've missed you so much, sweetheart," he expressed, burying his face in my hair. "Have they been looking after you? Are you hurt?" he asked, pulling back to scan his eyes over me for any sign of an injury. "I've been so worried about you."

"Dad, I'm fine," I promised, "but I could eat my way through your pantry; I'm starving."

Dad chuckled. "Let's get my princess something to eat," he said, putting his arm around me.

"And us," Dominic piped up behind us. "Don't forget us, Uncle Jaxx. I'm sure those energy bars Ulrich gave to us were out of date. They took ages to chew"

Dad and Uncle Zane escorted us inside their secret base. Their ship, the Triumph, bobbed lazily on the ocean, two miles away from land. Its purpose was to detect any vessels approaching the island. Dad and Zane used jet skis to travel back and forth, spending most of their time out on the water. The beachside base looked like a paradise retreat, surrounded by palm trees with hammocks, sun loungers, individual sleeping pods that were splayed out on jetties, and a main building with a round roof that resembled a shabby straw hat. Either they bought it straight from a holiday company or they purposefully designed it that way to blend in with the other resorts. I couldn't wait to enjoy a piña colada as I soaked up the sun. Emilio had wasted no time in acquainting himself with the beach; his skin had a sun kissed glow as if he had been sitting out in it all day. I took a seat at the rustic dining table and gazed out through the panoramic ceiling-to-floor glass doors at the moonlit view. My men slumped down onto the chairs beside me. We were all exhausted after our ordeal. This mission had zapped all our energy. All we wanted was to eat, then find somewhere to crash out.

Unlike Alpha One, this place had one resident member of staff, a housekeeper called Mae. She was shorter than me, and wore her dark hair up in a tight bun. It was difficult to determine her age because she looked amazing. Dad told me she was 43, unmarried, with no children. Those were the requirements to stay here and work for them. Mae didn't speak fluent English, but she understood the basics. Dad asked her to bring us some food, and she obliged. I caught the strange way Uncle Zane and my father were looking at her as she bustled past us, and the meaningful smiles she threw back at them. It made me wonder if there was more to their arrangement than just "keeping house" and if it was more like "playing house". That made me shudder. I did not want that imagery floating around inside my head. Mae set the table with bread, meats, cheeses, and fruit, then left to fetch some drinks. Uncle Zane accompanied her and offered to carry a tray. My eyes almost bugged out of my head as I noticed his hand slide to her ass as they were leaving the room.

"What is it?" Asher asked me, smirking.

"Nothing," I dismissed.

He chewed the inside of his cheek as if he found my reaction amusing.

Had he seen them? Did he know something that I didn't?

I glanced around the room at all the oceanic artifacts that had been collected over the years, wondering whether my mother had touched any of those items or if they had been accumulated beyond her time. Mum loved to scuba dive. It would be just like her to form a collection of large shells and remnants of a shipwreck.

God, I miss her.

Mae and Zane came back as we were all eating. He stayed, but she retired to her bedroom. Ulrich and Teddy followed her with their eyes as she left, then swung their gaze around to Dad and Uncle Zane. They shared a knowing look that I had seen before in the Wolfe brothers, and I wasn't sure what to make of it.

"Would you like to take a walk with me, Bexley?" Dominic asked, having changed into a pair of shorts and a vest top.

Despite being tired, my mind was racing a mile a minute. A peaceful moonlight stroll with Dom was exactly what I needed.

"Okay, just let me change first," I replied.

I left the table and went into the guest room to swap my outfit for a stretchy beach dress and flip flops. Dominic met me outside on the beachfront with a backpack on his shoulder and a rolled-up towel under his arm

"Where are we going?" I asked, hoping he wasn't expecting me to go skinny dipping at night. Not when I knew what lurked beneath the water. Barracudas, tiger sharks, jaws.

He took my hand as we walked. "To one of the overwater bungalows," he said, answering my question. "I want you all to myself tonight. The others agreed. They've all had you one on one except for me"

Moonlight illuminated the onyx ocean with tiny flecks of silver. We walked along the wooden platform, leaving the soft pale sand behind. The bungalow wasn't really floating; it was supported by wooden stilts. The ocean lapped at them, rippling all around us with the momentum of the tide. They were heavy-handed with the pesticide here, so you seldom saw or heard insects on the resorts. Not that I was complaining. I hated mosquitoes, but they loved me. It was so hot here, even at night. The geckos came out to scurry around on the sand, and the occasional fruit bat fluttered from the branches looking for a secluded place to feast. Dominic brought me inside and lit some candles; the orange flames danced on the wicks like tiny fire nymphs. I took off my flip flops and settled onto the huge round bed that faced the ocean. It was so peaceful out here. All my cares just melted away.

"Take off your dress and roll onto your stomach for me," Dominic instructed.

"Why? What are you going to do?" I eyed the rucksack dubiously.

Dominic let out a soft chuckle as if he thought of something wicked. "You'll see. Just trust me."

He took out a bottle of wine from the bag and fetched two glasses from inside the bungalow. I watched as he set them down on the outside table next to one of the flickering candles. He then took out a small bottle of massage oil and put it on the towel. I did as he asked, stripping down to roll on my front. Dominic removed his clothes too, then straddled me from behind, warming the massage oil between his hands. He started from the middle of my back, working outwards, gliding his warm soft palms across my skin.

"Does that feel good?" he asked, as he worked out the knots, his dexterous touch making my pussy clench. His hard-on pressed into me as he rubbed my shoulders, proving we were both getting a kick out of this.

"Mm," I answered dreamily, my body in a blissful state of serenity as he worked his magic.

"Do you think you could take more?" he asked, pausing for my reply.

"What do you have in mind?" I wondered whether it involved me rolling over so he could massage my front. Knowing Dominic, he would suggest such a thing, anything to get his hands on my breasts.

Dominic chuckled, then wiped his hands on the towel. "Roll over," he insisted.

I thought he would prove me right, but I was surprised to see him taking more strange objects from the bag. He held the first one up between his forefinger and thumb.

"This is a clit clamp that works in sync with this," he said, placing it down so he could show me the other object.

It was a circular rubber ring with nodules on one

side of it. I didn't need to see the instruction manual to figure out what it was for.

"This is the cock ring I designed to be used with the clit clamp," he said as if it was his greatest invention to date. "Each time the sensors touch, it should send a jolt of pleasure rushing straight through our sex organs," he explained, sounding pretty pleased with himself. "I've been saving this for our special alone time to try it out."

In one sense, I was glad he hadn't used this with another woman. But this meant it hadn't been tried and tested, therefore I was his guinea pig.

"If this goes wrong, you're a dead man," I warned him, eyeing the devices nervously.

"I only aim to please," he replied suggestively.

My eyes were glued to his massive erection, unable to peel my eyes away. Acting purely on instinct, I reached out to touch it, leaning forward, then flicked my tongue against the head. Dominic hissed; his cock jerked in my grasp. His warm, salty musk cascaded through my airways as I sucked him down to the root. Dom drove his fingers through my hair and thrust his length down my throat, his abdominals flexing and rolling with each rapid movement. My pussy and mouth were in competition to see which was the wetter, the steady trickle of juices matched the globs of saliva that rolled down my chin. I gagged as his cock hit the back of my throat, snatching sharp intakes of air through my nose, slurping him down until his musk tastes stronger, a tell-tale sign that he was getting close.

Dom pulled out and left me panting for air. "Get on your back and spread your legs for me," he insisted, his eyes blown, his voice strained with need.

His thick cock jutted proudly from his body and a long strand of pre-cum leaked from the bulbous head. Dom rolled the cock ring down the veiny shaft, facing the nodules upward. I heard the gentle lapping of the ocean around us, the breeze rustling the leaves on the palm trees, and the flames crackling as they devoured the candle wicks.

I crawled into position and rolled onto my back, trusting him implicitly as I parted my thighs. Dom took the clit clamp and positioned it around my delicate bud. It pinched — not painfully — just enough to make me gasp as it applied gentle pressure.

"Relax," he murmured as he took my hands and pinned my wrists above my head.

Dom nestled between my legs and anchored my arms to the pillow, exerting dominance. His hair tickled the sides of my face as we kissed, long, deep, and sensuously, his cock poised at my entrance, edging inside me one torturous inch at a time. I caught the smile in his eyes, a flicker of excitement, and I knew he would deliver. Dom always did. And as he filled me, my body responded to the plunge, widening to accommodate him. The clamp and the cock ring touched, sending pleasurable sparks shooting through my body.

"Oh," I moaned as the buzz vibrated through my bundle of nerves like cracking static.

The feeling didn't let up as Dom grinded his hips, triggering the vibrations with each upward thrust.

"God, Dom," I groaned his name, my eyes scrunched tightly as he rocked against me.

Even he began to lose his resolve, giving in to the pleasure that consumed him, kissing the crease of my throat, and sucking my soft flesh between his lips. The suction was strong enough to leave a mark, but I didn't care at this instant. I was too busy being fucked into oblivion. My thighs shook as I reached the pinnacle of ecstasy. It didn't take long for Dom to hit that climactic spot inside me, and my stomach muscles pulled so tight, I thought I might burst apart at the seams.

"Uh," Dom let out a ragged cry; the sudden loss of control tipped me over the edge, and my pussy contracted around his cock in a death grip.

Bump, bump, bump. The bed rattled on its legs beneath us. Our orgasmic moans carried away on the warm ocean breeze. I was his, he was mine, and he claimed me so possessively. Stars burst in my vision, making the astral backdrop seem like it was popping out in 3D. Every muscle in my body seized; my pussy fluttered with a rush of liquid that squelched as Dom pounded for the finish. His expression flooded with rapture as he came with a shout.

"Uhhh," he cried, matching my moans.

It took several long moments for the sex fog to dissipate, and we caught our breath as we held each other.

"How was that, Mrs. Wolfe?" Dom asked, a cheeky tone to his voice. "Does it get your seal of approval?"

It was difficult to answer with the toys still touching. I squirmed beneath him until he withdrew his cock and rolled onto his side.

"Yes," I managed a breathy reply, then carefully removed the clit clamp before flopping back down on the bed. "But now I'm too boneless to move." I let out a contented groan.

"So, don't," Dom suggested, removing the cock ring from his softening member. "Let's just stay here and hold each other for a while. The world can wait for five more minutes."

He threw the towel over us and curled his arms around me. I snuggled at his side, resting my head on his chest. If it was down to me, we would stay like this forever. The world might wait a few minutes more, but outside of our bubble it was an ugly place to be.

CHAPTER
Thirty-Eight

Bexley

"We should go back soon," I mentioned, still coiled in Dom's embrace. "We ought to get some rest."

Dom stroked my hair, pressing a kiss against my head as we gazed across at the glittering ocean. "Do you remember what your mother used to say to you when you were little? In an ocean filled with sharks, it's better to be a siren."

I huffed a fond nostalgic smile at the memory. "Yeah, I used to think she wanted me to become a mermaid."

Dom's chuckle vibrated through his chest. "Sirens were beautiful creatures who could lure sailors to their deaths. It didn't matter how strong or courageous they were, they were not able to resist a siren's song. They still fell for their charm and their heavenly music. She knew you'd make a difference. It's why she wanted you to be your own person. You don't have to match Susan to beat her. Just be you. You're more than enough."

I reached up to cup his jaw and angled his face to kiss him. Dom was the most insightful man I had ever met. He was as deep as the ocean, calm when it mattered, but perilous when angered.

His cashmere lips plucked gentle kisses from me, keeping me to himself for a little while longer. We had been out here longer than we anticipated. With great reluctance, I ended the kiss with one final press against his lips, and rolled into a sitting position, placing my feet flat against the cool decking.

"We better go now, or else your brothers will send out a search party," I told him, reaching for my dress and pulling it over my head.

Dom put on his shorts, then went around the

bungalow, blowing out the candles. We tidied up after ourselves, then took a slow walk back to the base.

Cruz and Asher grinned at us as we returned from our moonlight stroll. The fact he hadn't bothered to put his shirt back on, and the huge hickey appearing on my neck, left little to the imagination. Everyone knew what we'd been up to. Dad's voice rasped through the intercom, insisting we come to the control room. Emilio and Teddy were there, as was Ulrich, and Zane. Dad asked us to hand over the flash drives, and Dominic gave them to him. We were all eager to get started, intrigued to know what information they contained. Just like in Svalbard, the control room had a wall of computer monitors that curved halfway around the room, and a complex-looking panel with thousands of buttons and knobs.

"Is everyone ready?" Dominic asked, looking around at us all.

"Let's do it," Asher prompted, then exhaled a shaky breath

This was the moment of truth, and it was as if no one dared to breathe. One by one, Dominic plugged in the USBs and we saw the search bars pulsing across the monitors as the computer began decrypting each one. But just as it scanned the final flash drive, another pop-up box appeared, asking us for the key

"Shit!" Dominic hissed, then huffed into his hands. "Now what do we do? We can't take wild guesses or it will lock us out."

Asher flicked his gaze to me. "Bexley . . . what do we do?"

All eyes landed on me, and the pressure was tremendous. I took a deep breath to steady my nerves and thought about it logically.

"The only key I have is this," I said, taking hold of the pendant.

I removed the chain from around my neck and looked at the charm more closely. There were indentations at the bottom of the column as if it fit inside something else. I already knew it was the key to open the box, but what if it didn't just unlock the box, what if it was the key to unlocking the files too?

My eyes landed on the final flash drive and I noticed the circular hole in the middle. It was just a hunch, but as I began to insert the pendant into the hole, I found that it fit. The red triangle on the screen with an exclamation mark in the middle was replaced by a green tick, then the computer continued the download. Once it reached one hundred per cent, we were then asked to type in a four-letter password to access the files.

Asher removed his glasses and scrubbed a hand over his stressed-out face. Dad couldn't sit still and paced the room anxiously. Braxton was looking fed up to hell, and Dom looked as if he wanted to bang his head on the control panel and cry. Zane scowled at the screen, as did Ulrich. Teddy wasn't looking at anything in particular, he just massaged his forehead as if he had a headache, Emilio slumped back in his chair with a sigh, but Cruz remained calm.

"What do the symbols represent again?" Cruz asked, sparking Asher's interest.

Asher whirled around to face his brother with wide-eyed astonishment.

"Yes!!" he exclaimed. "Of course." Asher turned to me. "They represent the elements, don't they? Earth, wind, fire, and water. But what do the other two mean? I can't remember."

"The other two symbols represent the universe and life," I told him.

The corners of Asher's eyes twitched as he thought. "Life is the most precious gift anyone can give. Your mother loved you, Bexley. She would want you to embrace your life and live it to the fullest."

Dominic typed the word "life" into the keyboard and hit "enter".

The room illuminated with a bright green hue as billions of symbols fluttered across the screen. File boxes popped up one by one. We had done it. We unlocked the protected files, and now all that classified information was at our fingertips, we could finally identify the traitors and clear our names. The download was complete and Dad and Zane spent the next hour clicking through each file; their faces twisted with rage at what they found. Our uncles and my husbands peered at the screen, shaking their heads with disdain. Whatever it was, it was bad. We were all in agreement that the truth had to come out. Susan wasn't just a turncoat agent; she stole information from countries across the world and sold them to the highest bidder. She had an elite network of spies working for her, influencing world leaders like they were all puppets on strings. Those protestors outside the Houses of Parliament were right. Our elections were being rigged. Her people were feasting around the table at number 10 Downing Street, blackmailing MPs like Malcolm into doing their bidding. The world had to know. We had to stop Susan once and for all.

Dad removed the pendant key and gave it back to

me. "The charm contains the evidence, Bexley. It's all on there — everything we need to expose Susan and put a stop to her reign of terror once and for all. Your mother entrusted it to you to keep it safe."

I secured the chain around my neck just as the monitors began to glitch.

We all glanced at the combined screens on the wall as a woman's face appeared. Her blonde hair was pulled back from off her face in a military-style twist, and her blue eyes stared ahead like ice chasms. Whoever she was, her cold, unyielding gaze held no emotion as she commanded the attention of the room. Her face was unfamiliar to me, but Zane, Dad, Ulrich, and Teddy blanched as if they had just seen a ghost. Dominic frantically typed away on the keyboard, but nothing he did made the slightest bit of difference. We had been hacked, and this mystery woman was now in control.

"It's her," Braxton uttered. "She's a lot older than she is in the photo Dad showed to us, but I would recognise her anywhere," he remarked, gritting his teeth with contempt.

"Chameleon," Uncle Zane addressed her coolly. "Or do you still go by Susan?"

My eyes rounded on the woman who murdered my mother, sickened by her false smile.

"I believe you have something of mine?" she stated, looking directly at me. "I have something belonging to you too," she announced, turning the camera lens to show another angle of the room she was in

I recoiled with horror as the struggling figure came into focus. She had Caz gagged and bound to a chair. Tear tracks glistened on her cheeks; her eyes were bloodshot and raw. Susan angled the camera away from my helpless friend and glared at me as if she meant business.

"I was thinking . . . perhaps you would be willing to trade?" she purred as if she held the upper hand.

CHAPTER

Thirty-Nine

Bexley

"And you expect us to fall for that?" Asher roared, unleashing his anger. "We know you have an accomplice. What a coincidence that you're there with Bexley's friend, Caroline. How do we know that she's not the mysterious "C" that's been working alongside you, tipping you off, and passing information back to your spies?"

Susan returned him a tight-lipped smile. "Clever

boy," she replied in a condescending tone. "But you're only half right. She only told me that Bexley went to Sandbanks to be with you. I hated that house. It was too open plan. That was more to Safi's taste, not mine. But the artillery room was my idea. We had so much fun down there, didn't we, guys?" She chuckled, wiping away a fake tear.

"I always knew you were a callous bitch, Susan," Zane insulted her, "but this time, you've gone too far. We will find you, and we will kill you. Don't expect any mercy from me for old time's sake." He cast a scathing look at Teddy, who bowed his head with shame

"I keep telling you, I didn't help her to fake her death, but I may have given her the idea," Teddy admitted for what I felt was for the umpteenth time by the exasperated tone of his voice. "I thought her questions were all hypothetical. How was I supposed to know she was going to betray us?"

He really did sound remorseful. I didn't blame him for trusting who he thought was a friend, and I don't think my dad did either. Zane was just lashing out.

"None of that matters now. We can't erase the mistakes of the past," Dad growled. "But if anyone is going to kill her, it will be me. She murdered my wife. She has to pay."

Zane grunted in agreement. Ulrich's expression hardened. Teddy nodded sadly.

Susan made a mock sad face and shrugged. "Aww, old grudges die hard. For what it's worth, she had it coming."

"You will burn in hell when we're through with you," Asher vowed. "You've hurt too many people and caused too many problems."

"I'm still your mother," Susan remarked. "You're still a part of me despite all of Zane's brainwashing. It's not too late to join me. The world can be ours for the taking. I'm so proud of the strong men you've become. We could be so powerful."

Asher snorted, cutting her off, "You can't take any credit for that. That was all our dad's doing. Aunt Safi was more of a mother to us than you could ever be. Keep your pride while you still have a shred of it left." He said it better than his brothers would have done. Even when Asher was mad, he remained level-headed. His brothers were red in the face like they were about to lose their shit.

As the Wolfe brothers banded around Asher in a display of solidarity, Susan's calm façade crumbled, and a flicker of anguish flashed through her eyes.

They were her sons. The soldiers she planned for. They were her flesh and blood. And it was killing her to see how much they despised her.

"I think what my twin was trying to say was, go fuck yourself," Braxton seethed.

I swallowed down the lump in my throat and spared a panicked glance at my husband. "Brax, what are you doing? Don't piss her off. She's going to kill Caz. We have to do something."

Dominic put his arm around me, trying to comfort me, but that only made me feel claustrophobic. I shrugged him off, needing the space to breathe.

"What if it's a trap, Bexley," Dominic reinforced what Asher said. "Caz could be the accomplice. We could be playing right into their hands. What if she's Susan's daughter? She could have been playing you all along."

"But if that was true, then that would make her your sister," I pointed out the obvious. "I know Caz. We live together. Don't you think I would know if my best friend was a terrorist? I've met her parents. They showed me their family photo albums. There's no way that any of it was fake."

Asher and Dom winced doubtfully. I knew what

they were thinking — what they were all thinking; that I had been played. What they didn't know was that I had known Caz since we were kids. There's no way she could have been playing me for all that time. They were wrong about her. Teddy glared at the screen with tears burning in his eyes. The disappointment clouded Ulrich's expression too. Dad was hankering for Susan's blood, and Zane was just as livid

"Oh, so you know about my secret," Susan cut in. "It's true. I do have another child." She stroked Caz's cheek and Caz recoiled from her touch. Susan narrowed her eyes and glared down at her with disgust. "And what a fucking disappointment she is too"

"I fucking knew it," Asher growled.

I almost threw up at the revelation.

Caz was Susan's illegitimate child?! What the fuck?!

Dad and his friends looked murderous, like this news had delivered them all a sickening blow. Me too . . . because I thought I knew everything about Caz. Uncle Zane flashed a pleading look at his sons, searching for answers. Dad, Ulrich, and Teddy were floored by the news too. It wasn't like we were keeping it from them on purpose. We were going to divulge that crucial piece of information right after we decrypt the files. Now the cat was out of the bag, and it left the older guys reeling.

If Caz was an illegitimate child, then who was the father if not Uncle Zane?

"Caz is your daughter?" I murmured, feeling nauseated by that.

Susan rolled her eyes as if she was growing bored with us.

I just couldn't believe it. The revelation stunned me

I looked at Caz. "You were lying to me. You used me. I don't believe this." I held my face in my hands as I struggled to breathe.

Caz sobbed apologetically into the camera, trying to mumble something through the gag in her mouth. It sounded like "I'm sorry, I didn't know . . ." She tried to communicate something, but Susan grabbed a handful of her hair and yanked her head back.

Could it be that she genuinely did not know, or was I being suckered yet again?

"Let me tell you what really happened," Susan said mockingly for our benefit as well as for Caz's. She was talking to her, but this was meant for everyone to hear. "I know it states you were a foundling on your birth certificate, but that isn't true. It's fake. I never registered your birth. You've been walking around using a fake ID all your adult life. If you were to disappear right now, no one would care because you don't exist. You were just a pawn in my master plan. But think what you will about me; I'm not all bad. You weren't left on a church doorstep as you thought; I gave you to a respectable family. They were so desperate for a child, they agreed to lie about your age. You're two years older than you think you are. Who wouldn't like to knock a few years off their age? I know I would." Susan's voice was devoid of emotion as she spoke to Caz. "I checked in on you from time to time, wanting to see how my investment was coming along. How do you think your adoptive parents could afford to send you to the same prestigious school as Safi's brat and keep you in the lap of luxury? I funded your lifestyle, and in return they work for me."

I could hear the supercilious tone oozing from Susan's voice as she continued, "Do you remember how the teachers made you sit together on the first day? It wasn't a coincidence that they paired you off as friends. I orchestrated everything and used it to my advantage. Your success was down to me. I had to keep you on par with Miss Perfect over there. The good grades. The fancy clothes. It all paid off because you remained best friends." Susan chuckled.

"Oh, and the bastard boyfriend who broke your heart . . . he was my idea. You were getting too complacent. I needed to do something to knock you off your high horse. So, I made sure you lost everything because I knew Bexley, being the good Samaritan she is, would take you under her wing. You were so easy to convince. Just like your father, whichever one of them it is, you are so stupid, gullible, and easy to manipulate. You were so thrilled that I came back to find you, that you didn't stop to question why I gave you up in the first place. It wasn't because I was a secret agent. I didn't do it to protect you. I'm not here to help Bexley. She has something of mine and I want it back. You've served your purpose; you're no longer useful to me. But you mean something to her, and so I know she'll make the right choice. She's her mother's daughter . . . she's so fucking righteous; it makes me sick. You can hate me all you want. All my children do." Susan let go of Caz's hair and rolled her eyes as if she thought Caz was pathetic. Then she swaggered towards the camera. "Don't blame her, Bexley. It's not her fault. I can be very persuasive when I want to be. She was quick to trust me . . . so desperate to be accepted. I told her that I was here to help, and she believed me just like that," Susan mentioned, clicking her fingers. "So, yeah . . . she is my daughter, but she's not my accomplice." A wry smirk curled the corner of Susan's lips as she turned to look at someone off-camera. "I think it's time for the grand reveal, wouldn't you agree?" she said to whomever was loitering back there.

CHAPTER
Forty

Bexley

The atmosphere all around us shifted as a hulk of a guy walked into view. He was huge; his vest tee clung to his muscular chest and tattoos decorated all the visible skin aside from his face. I didn't recognise him, and from the frowns on everybody's faces, neither did they. It was Emilio who stood from his chair and approached the monitors disbelievingly

"Carlos?" he choked the name as if he couldn't believe what he was seeing. "Tell me this is some kind of sick joke."

The Hispanic guy grinned. "You wish, lover," he replied with a wink. "Baby, our play toy is here," he gruffed, and from somewhere off-camera, a female giggled

Braxton caught Emilio as he sagged with shock and held him in a bear hug to steady him. Caz was innocent. Susan had used her in the cruellest way. I couldn't believe this was happening. This vile creature had hurt everyone I loved. I hated her, and I hated him for hurting Emilio.

"You bastard," I swore through gritted teeth.

The so-called married couple who lured Emilio into a trio had been playing him all along. But why? Was it because we would never suspect them? As the old saying goes "Keep your friends close and keep your enemies closer". Susan had played us all. She really was the master of manipulation, and poor Emilio had been crushed by her cruelty.

Another figure emerged from the edge of the screen, but this time it was a beautiful Spanish woman. She pulled a hunting knife from its sheath on her utility belt and held it against Caz's throat. My friend's muffled cries were like a dagger through my heart. I wanted to reach out and save her but there was nothing I could do from here.

"Now, now, Bexley," Susan warned me. "Name-calling isn't nice. Tania gets a little protective of her fake husband." She turned to Tania and nodded once in a private command.

Tania pressed the blade against Caz's throat, making her shriek with terror. Blood dripped down her throat and soaked into the collar of her blue and white striped T-shirt. Tania was going to make Caz suffer just to punish me. I knew I had to fix the mistake I made.

"I'm sorry!" I bleated, desperate to stop them from hurting Caz. "Let her go and I'll give you whatever you want. Just don't hurt her."

All eyes landed on me, and the air in the room thinned. What did they expect me to say? I couldn't just stand and watch them kill her. We had to buy Caz more time so we could think of a plan to save her. The tension in the room was suffocating me.

Susan nodded at Tania, and she lowered the knife, then wiped it on her cargo pants. Then Susan gripped Caz's chin and forced Caz to look at her, turning her face from side to side. I could see the hatred blazing through Caz's eyes as she glared at her captor. But there was pain there too. And defeat. I could only imagine the horror that Susan had put her through. The anguish of learning that she was her mother, and that she never loved her . . . never cared for her as a mother should.

"You have twenty-four hours to return to your Cheshire home, Bexley. If you contact the authorities, your friend dies. You wouldn't want that, would you, boys? To have your sister's death on your hands," Susan spoke into the camera before cutting the transmission.

It left us all feeling dazed and sickly.

"She had a child," Zane muttered, letting the information hang in the air around us. "She had a child and she kept her from us. How did you know about this? Why didn't you tell us?"

Why did they keep repeating "us"? What did they all have to do with this?

The Wolfe brothers and I exchanged anxious glances.

Oh, God . . . please, no.

"Never mind that. What do you mean by *'kept her from all of you'*?" I asked, bouncing my gaze around at Dad, Teddy, Ulrich, and back at Uncle Zane. I produced the haematology report and held it up as evidence. "We only found out about the pregnancy because of this. Before that, it was just speculation because of the clues. It turns out that Mum knew, and she hid the proof with a flash drive. What I want to know is, how come you're all looking as sheepish as fuck?"

I saw the colour drain from my father's face and he clasped the back of a chair for support.

"Dad," I pushed myself to continue. "Please tell me it's not what I'm thinking. I don't think I can take anymore bombshells tonight."

My husbands gathered around me, swaddling me in a protective bubble, ready to comfort me if I crumbled

"It was before your time, Bexley." Dad eyed me beseechingly. "Zane, Ulrich, Teddy, and I were in a polygamous relationship with your mother and Susan."

My jaw flopped open, and I stammered to speak. "What?! All of you . . . my mum . . . Susan . . . all of you?" I had no right to judge, and I didn't — I couldn't. Not when I was in the same sort of relationship with the Wolfe brothers. It still shocked me to learn that my mum had slept with my dad's friends, maybe even Susan, and that Susan had sex with my father.

Oh, God, this confirms it . . . Susan had sex with my father! It's true. He admitted it.

It was like all the air got sucked out of the room, and I struggled to breathe.

Ulrich nodded. "We had an arrangement that was like your own. We were all part of the same team and we got close — just with the women though. We're all straight men. We just shared Safi and Susan between us, and we found a dynamic that worked."

I palmed my forehead and groaned. "Oh, God . . . spare me the details."

My husbands grimaced at this information, as if the news of their arrangement shocked them too. I was glad to see I wasn't the only one perturbed by our parents having an orgy. It didn't matter how old we got; none of us wanted to have that imagery implanted into our minds.

"I married Susan so that she could legally obtain my frozen sperm samples in the event of my death. We loved both women equally. They were our world. But when we thought Susan had been killed, we stopped the arrangement," Uncle Zane cut in. "We went our separate ways. Your parents chose to remain together and got married, and your mother got pregnant with you straight away."

I exhaled a relieved sigh, pleased that my dad was my biological father.

Uncle Zane continued, "Teddy fucked everything with a pulse and that's how he got Emilio."

Teddy jerked his head back, having taken offence.

"He's not wrong, Dad," Emilio agreed.

Zane kept going. "Ulrich followed his own path, fucking nuns until he kicked the habit." His attempt at a joke didn't seem natural to a gruff guy like Zane. Ulrich just chuckled silently. Zane hadn't finished; he continued regardless, "And I went ahead with our original plan — creating the perfect soldiers that Susan and I always talked about. It was the best decision I ever made, and I don't regret it for a second." He gathered his sons in a group hug. "Whatever happens next, just remember that we're a family. That young woman is still your blood. She's innocent. We have to get her back no matter what."

"Yeah, but who's her father?" Emilio asked, raising an excellent question.

My father and his friends exchanged furtive glances, and I knew as well as they did, it could be either one of them.

"It doesn't matter." I surprised myself as I said that. "She's my best friend. My husbands' sister . . . and potentially mine." I caught sight of my dad's sorrowful expression and my heart squeezed with emotion. "I'm going home to face Susan. I don't expect you to come with me."

I turned to leave and felt hands gripping me at all angles.

"Not without us you're not," Cruz enforced, holding onto me the tightest. "We're in this together."

I turned around and found my men were all there, unwilling to let me go without them.

Emilio swallowed thickly and took a step forward. "Like hell are you going without me. Count me in."

Teddy, Ulrich, Zane, and Dad exchanged determined glances. Then Dad locked eyes with me, admiring me proudly.

"Let's end this," he spoke directly to me, and I nodded

"For Mum." I brought the pendant to my lips, and kissed it.

CHAPTER Forty-One

Bexley

If Susan Wolfe thought I was going to walk into an ambush without a plan of action, then she was gravely mistaken. My husbands helped me to stash a few tricks up my sleeve. It would buy us more time to grab Caz, then get us the hell out of there. We just had to get back to the UK without being captured by the British military. It would take days for Dad's ship, the Triumph, to get there. And even then, agents would catch us before we crossed over into British waters. The only option we had was to take Ulrich's jet and land it onto a private airstrip because the Civil Aviation Authority would never grant us the permission to land. Even then, we would risk the Airforce shooting us out of the sky, or tailing us to our destination. Ulrich could only scramble the signals for so long, and then we would appear on their radar. We had twenty-four hours, and time was running out. I hardly said a word as we flew across Saudi Arabia, then Italy, and France. The guys went over all the things that could happen when the landing gear touched down on the tarmac.

"We go home," Asher suggested, stunning everyone in the cabin.

"Home?" Braxton repeated. He paused as if he was expecting Asher to tell him he was joking. "As in home — home? What about one of the disused airfields closest to Bexley's house?"

Dominic side-eyed Cruz, seeking his twin's reassurance. I was waiting for Dad or Zane to jump all over his suggestion, but they seemed keen to listen to whatever he had to say.

"Yes . . . home," Asher confirmed. "There's no way we can risk landing anywhere else. The agency will corner us with no means of escape. I know

Sandbanks is a long way from Cheshire, but we can buy Bexley some time."

"How?" Braxton asked, unconvinced. "They'll expect that, and they'll be waiting for us to trip the alarm."

"That's what we want," Asher replied confidently.

"It is?" Braxton stammered, still not convinced.

"I know what you're thinking, Ash," Cruz spoke out. "And it's exactly what we want. We can create a diversion and that will give Bexley the chance to get to Cheshire before the deadline"

Dominic scrunched his face with disapproval. "And how are we supposed to go with her if we're carted off to jail in handcuffs?"

"We're giving her a head start," Asher explained. "We have the evidence that will vindicate us all. If they capture Bexley, we can kiss goodbye to everything. Susan will get her hands on the files, and it would have all been for nothing."

"How are we going to get the Ministry to listen to us? We're wanted fugitives. They will shoot us where we stand," Braxton muttered exasperatedly.

Dominic pulled out his laptop and fired it up, the light illuminating the cabin. "I know how we can get their attention," he uttered, tapping away on his keyboard. "I've just contacted Interpol, our contact at Buckingham Palace, and our old team at MI6, telling them I have concrete proof that the Chameleon is behind this. I've sent the recording I made of Susan's transmission, and a list of all the people who are affiliated with her. If they want the proof, we have it. They will have to listen to us now and discard everything that Malcolm said'

"But that won't stop them from getting heavy with us when we touch down at Sandbanks," Braxton commented. "How will Bexley get away?"

"We'll improvise," Asher reinforced. "I checked the CCTV on my phone app, and the chopper is still there on the helipad." He pulled out a T-shaped tool from his jacket pocket and dangled it in front of him. "They can't gain access to the chopper unless they force entry, but I do suspect they will have bugged it, but that's a good thing. It'll mean they can track it to Cheshire. Then they will find the Chameleon, and her accomplices."

It snapped Emilio out of his misery and his eyes flared wide. "I already told you; I'll get Bexley there. You deal with the authorities, and send the coroner over to Bexley's place."

Teddy gripped Emilio's arm. "Don't go in there, all guns blazing, or you'll get yourself killed."

Emilio sneered. "Don't worry. It won't be me leaving in a body bag."

"It won't be our wife, either," Cruz said, throwing me a reassuring wink.

I flashed Cruz a soft smile. "Don't worry about me. I'll be fine."

"We'll get there as soon as we can," Cruz assured me, squeezing my hand. "It will take more than an army to stop us."

Asher and Dominic checked the surveillance cameras in and around their beachside home and found that no one was there. We knew it was a trap to make us think it was safe. They could be there within moments. The plan was not to throw them off the scent, we had to lead them to Susan.

"Bexley," Dominic said my name, grabbing my attention. "Do you have that thing I gave to you?" He didn't say what it was; he just flared his eyes in a silent signal.

I nodded, tapping my jacket pocket. "It's right here"

I put on the earrings that Dominic designed, and shoved some other items into my pockets. One was a vital necessity so we could pull off this plan. The items were small enough for me to conceal, and could be passed off as everyday essentials. It meant that if

Susan forced me to surrender my gun, I still had the means to protect myself

Ulrich's jet made a slow descent over Northern France. The lights twinkled on the ground like the sky had been turned upside-down. We flew over Normandy Beach, then across the onyx waters of the English Channel.

"Here she is . . . home sweet home," Dad muttered ominously.

We braced ourselves ready for a sudden attack. The beach, the land, and the sky seemed deserted. It was too quiet. We all agreed this seemed too good to be true. Ulrich deployed the landing gear, and we came to a skidding halt on the floodlit tarmac beside the house

Asher thrust the T-shaped key into Emilio's hand. "I take it, you know how to fly a helicopter?" he asked

Emilio snatched the metal tool with a confused frown on his face. "No, but I can fly a plane. I didn't think you needed a key to start the engine," he muttered sarcastically.

"You don't," Asher replied straight-faced. "You need it to secure the doors. If the key isn't inserted and turned to the 'on' position, the turbine igniters won't fire up, and the engines won't start."

Emilio nodded, looking confident that he could do this. My men took turns to kiss me goodbye. And then Dad hugged me. Zane, Teddy, and Cruz got out of the cabin and checked around for any sign of a threat. Dominic, Ulrich, Braxton, and Asher covered us as we ran towards the 'copter.

Lights appeared across the waterfront, and the heavy thrum of 'copter blades sliced through the air like a giant wasp. The agency was coming, and we didn't have much time. Emilio climbed into the cockpit, and Dad practically flung me in after him, then slid the door shut. My hands were violently shaking as I buckled my harness and pulled on my headset. Emilio shoved the key into the slot, securing the doors, then started the turbines. The propellers began to whirl, gathering speed. I couldn't hear gunshots, but I could see the guys walking towards the agents, surrendering with their hands in the air. No one was shooting. That had to be a good thing, right? As Emilio lifted us off the ground, it gave us a better view. Jet skis littered the edge of the beachfront, and agents scurried across the sand like ants. The rival helicopter turned its spotlight onto us, dazzling us in the eyes. Emilio swung us around and headed north. They followed us, mimicking our movements as we meandered through the sky.

"What if they shoot us down?" I asked, craning my head around to see.

"They won't," Emilio replied, sounding sure about that. "You're precious cargo. They need those files you're carrying, and don't forget you're the key to unlocking them."

"I hope everyone will be all right," I expressed, worried about what lay in store for them.

Emilio didn't answer. He glared dead-ahead with a frown as fierce as thunder.

"I'm sorry about Carlos and Tania," I mentioned

Emilio released a heavy sigh. "Yeah . . . me too." A long moment passed between us before he spoke again. "I just can't believe I let them play me like that. Fuck love. I'm done."

I placed my hand over his. "Don't say that," I spoke affectionately. "You will find someone worthy of your heart. If polygamy has taught me anything, it's that love knows no limits. You'll meet someone else, and you'll fall just as hard. That's life. Don't let them take that away from you too."

He hummed in agreement but didn't say much else. I spared another glance behind us and saw we were still being followed.

"The agent's helicopter is still there," I told him.

"It's weird. I don't think they're chasing us. They're too far behind."

Emilio flashed me a reassuring smile. "Take that as a good sign," he replied. "It means your men have persuaded them to trust us."

I exhaled a sigh of relief and pulled my phone from my pocket. There was a message from Dominic, telling me that everything was going to be all right, and to stick to the original plan. As I clicked off the text, something weird happened. My phone reset, and my old home screen popped up, along with all my old contacts. The message from Dominic had disappeared, erasing all the evidence. I knew what I had to do. It was all part of the plan. I scrolled through the list of names and pressed to dial Caz's number.

"Hello, Bexley," Susan answered in a honeyed tone, just like I suspected she would. "What a coincidence, we were just talking about you."

"Oh yeah?" My tone came out clipped. "Why don't you just cut the bullshit and enlighten me?"

Susan cleared her throat. "I was just explaining the asphyxiation process to Caroline," she answered in a threatening promise. "I told her for every minute that you run late, it will be a further minute I'll deprive her of oxygen." She chuckled, much to my outrage. "We have a special breathing tank, just for the occasion. It'll last for twenty-four hours, but after that, well . . . you're an intelligent girl. You can do the math."

"I'm almost there," I forced out the words, choking down the bile in my throat. "If she dies, I will finish what my mother started. I'll destroy you. Your life's work will be for nothing."

"Thanks to you, it already is," she snapped.

Emilio flashed his eyes to me, and I saw the panic within them. "Ten minutes and we'll be there," he assured me.

"I want a fair trade," I reminded Susan. "Caz . . . in exchange for the files."

"Just be here on time," she seethed, then the line went dead

From up here, the aerial view of the landscape came into focus. I could make out exactly where we were, recognising the M6 motorway as we flew past Stoke-On-Trent, then circled over Nantwich. I could see the oil refinery all lit up at Stanlow; it was near the estuary at Ellesmere Port It meant my stately home was just a stone's throw away.

We're coming, Caz. Just sit tight until we get there.

CHAPTER Forty-Two

Bexley

W e landed in a field not far from my house. It wasn't a big enough area for the agents to land alongside us, which was just as well. It meant that Emilio and I could sprint across the grass and cut through a gap in the hedge without being accosted.

"Who do you think the father is?" Emilio asked as we hurried down the country road.

Only the crossroad junction was lit by lamp posts,

the rest of the lane was cloaked in darkness. Few cars came down this way, preferring to use the bypass several miles back the other way. Moonlight was our only light source, so it was just as well I knew my way around

"It could be either one of them," I answered, not wanting to think too much into it.

"But you know her best," he pressed. "Who do you think she looks like?"

This was going to make me sound like a jealous bitch, but it was how I felt, and I didn't know how to explain it without sounding awful.

"I don't know. It's hard to say. I just know that I don't want my dad to be her father," I replied, the words leaving a bitter aftertaste in my mouth.

We arrived at the front gates to my property and we stopped to catch our breath.

"I don't mean that in a nasty way," I mentioned. "I just don't want it to be *my* dad. Anyone else but him."

"I know what you're saying," Emilio added, understanding it from my point of view. "You don't want to have a sister by your mother's killer. That's completely understandable."

I swallowed hard as he uttered the words, having not thought about it that way before. Emilio had raised an excellent point. Susan was Caz's mum, and she murdered my mum. Meaning, my half-sister would share the same DNA as my mother's killer, and my dad. That was just too much to process. The actual reason I didn't want Caz to be my half-sister wasn't because of that. It should have been because of that, but it wasn't. The real reason was because I wanted my dad all to myself. It was a jealous reason, and I was ashamed of myself for feeling that way. He was *my* dad. It had always been him, Mum, and me. I wasn't prepared to share him with anyone. The thought of him and Susan together made me feel physically sick. I didn't even like the thought of him banging the housekeeper in the Maldives. Emilio clapped me on the shoulder and asked if I was all okay, but I was far from okay.

"No," I told him truthfully. "That wasn't the reason at all. It should have been the first thing to pop into my mind, but all I could think about is keeping my dad all to myself. The guys have learned to work through their issues and share me between them, but what does it say about me? I'm clinging to my father like a spoiled, jealous child who is afraid he will love me a little less if Caz turns out to be his daughter. I haven't learned how to deal with my jealousy issues at all. If anything, this just proves just how jealous I am.

I can't stand the thought of him getting intimate with another woman other than my mum, which is totally unreasonable. Dad is allowed to have a life. He shouldn't have to live like a monk. I'm just having a hard time letting him go."

Emilio huffed a smile. "You're talking about it, and that's a start."

"But it's not right though, is it?" I swallowed down a lump of remorse. "I know how badly Caz has been let down throughout her life, and I know my dad would make her feel like a priority. He would never pick a favourite. He isn't like that. He would love us both equally. I have loved her like a sister since we bonded through our school days. It's my stupid jealousy that's the issue. I'm a terrible friend, and I'll be an even shittier sister."

"Yet here you are, prepared to die to save her," he pointed out. "I don't think you're terrible at all. In fact, you'll be the most loyal, bravest, best friend, and sister that Caz could ever ask for. She could be my sister yet. She'll need to take a DNA test, then we'll find out who her father is when we get her back in one piece."

I cleared away the overgrown shrub from blocking the keypad, then typed in a code to unlock the gates.

"I'll go on ahead," I told Emilio. "If you creep around to the back of the building, climb the trellis to the balcony bedroom, you'll be able to let yourself in"

The code I typed into the keypad activated a warning signal. It meant that the doors and windows were now unlocked. I designed the system myself. It allowed my dad to see everything that was going on via an app on his phone. He could instruct the agents on what to do when they get here.

We reached the end of the drive and saw that my front door had been left ajar. Crumpled cigarette butts littered my doorstep. Topiary trees stood at either side of my door in tall pots, and someone had shoved an empty cig packet into one of the spherical shrubs. Emilio darted around the landscaped garden, keeping out of sight of the windows. Susan would think I came here alone, just as we planned.

I reached for the gun that I stashed in my waistband, keeping a firm hold on the grip. Carlos and Tania's voices could be heard muttering in Spanish. The sounds were coming from the kitchen and it seemed like they were disagreeing about what they should do next. I just hoped that Emilio remained unseen, using the cover of night to cloak his movements. As they had probably noticed, the security lights were no longer working as they should. Only I had access to the security system because this was my domain, my houseful of tricks to trap them inside. I used the app on my phone to trigger the locking mechanism in the kitchen, sealing the doors and windows shut, and isolating the electricity supply. They had access to running water, but that was about it. I heard them panicking, rattling the door handle, and wondering what was going on. Then three gunshots echoed around the house. One of them had tried to shoot at the locks, but it was no use, that wouldn't be enough to open the seven-point locking system I had installed. Aside from the glass windows, this house was like Fort Knox.

"Bexley," Susan chimed in a sing-song voice meant to intimidate me. "I know you're in here. Come out, come out, wherever you are."

I heard footsteps coming from inside the living room, then saw movement from the upstairs hall. Emilio made a "Psst" sound and waved to me as I backed against the wall, my gun pressed lengthways against my chest. He jabbed his finger at the doorway, informing me that Susan was there. I sidestepped around to the dining room doorway, where I could enter the living room from another access point. The false bookcase served as a secret passage, allowing me to take Susan by surprise and gain me a better vantage point. The floor-to-ceiling windows would provide the perfect view from the gardens. If the agents wanted a clear shot at the Chameleon, they would get one from there. Emilio watched from the balcony hall as I slipped through the false door, then Susan's footsteps came to a sudden halt as she discovered an empty entrance hall. I found Caz tied to a chair in the same position I saw her in the night before. Those bastards had beaten her and then strapped an oxygen mask to her face. Her left eye was swollen shut and she had dark purple bruising all over her face. Any jealousy I felt about Dad being her father vanished in that instant. Sure, she was my best friend, but a strong protective urge swept over me, making me want to open fire at Susan and empty a cartridge of bullets into her chest. What if she was my sister? My flesh and blood. That same fierce protectiveness Dad and I shared had me seeing red

Caz lifted her beaten gaze and noticed me standing there. She shook her head, spilling a fresh tear from her eye. I raised my hand to my lips, silencing her. Then I edged through the open doorway, just in time to see Susan coming back. She raised her weapon at the sight of me standing there with a gun pointed at her head, the sheer look of bewilderment painted on her face as to how I managed to slip past her unnoticed.

"Don't move or I'll shoot you," I cautioned her, seeing her hands slowly rising at either side of her head

"There's no need for hostilities, Bexley," Susan spoke calmly.

She seemed way too composed for a woman who was staring death in the face. Asher taught me all about the art of bluffing, and Susan Wolfe was calling my bluff

CHAPTER Forty-Three

Bexley

S usan's lips pulled into a tight smirk, making her look smug as fuck. Only she had the audacity to act like she was the cat, and I was the cornered mouse, and not the other way around.

"I think I've passed the point of caring," I returned in a flat tone. "Hostility is all you deserve."

The two of us locked eyes with each other in a silent stare-off, one daring the other to make the first move. I saw the sag in her elbows and knew I had to act fast.

"Caroline, in exchange for the files," I reminded her.

A window smashed from inside another room, barely making Susan flinch.

"That will be Carlos," she muttered calmly. "He always makes such an awful mess in the kitchen."

The sound of gunfire rattled my nerves. I hoped Emilio was okay. Then Susan walked to the side of me, forcing me to walk in a cautious circle. Caz made a startled noise which alerted Susan's attention. I knew it could only be Emilio, having watched me go through the secret door in the hallway.

"Who's here with you?" Susan demanded to know. "I told you to come alone."

"Paranoid, are we?" I chuckled, loving the slip in her demeanour.

I kept my gun poised and ready as I dug inside my jacket pocket to retrieve the fake flash drive that Dominic had given to me. I held it between my forefinger and thumb to tempt her.

"This is what you want, isn't it?" I held it out as a bargaining chip. "Take it and go"

Bullets pitted the living room windows like opaque stars as Carlos and Tania shot at them, trying to get them to shatter. The lapse in my attention cost me dearly as Susan seized the opportunity to reach for her weapon.

"Do I look stupid?" Susan hissed, pointing her gun at me. "Safi Barker would have chosen something more symbolic to hide the files. Not a cheap piece of plastic"

"How would you know what my mum would or wouldn't do?" I defended my dead mother's name. "Maybe you don't know her as well as you think you did. She hid this right under your nose the whole time. She even sent us all on a wild goose chase to go looking for it. That was Mum," I added proudly. "She always did have a great sense of humour."

Susan's face twisted with anger. A barrage of gunshots reverberated around the grounds as the Wolfe brothers, and the rest of our crew, gunned Carlos and Tania down in a surprise attack. Susan's horror-filled eyes trembled as she witnessed the grotesque scene; the way their arms flayed with every impact, their blood splattering against the glass.

"Hand over the files," Susan demanded, her voice rushed with desperation.

I tossed the fake flash drive at her, and she caught it single handed. Then Susan fired a shot against my chest, sending me reeling backwards. I landed onto the coffee table, firing a shot that hit a weak point on the window, exploding it and sending tiny shards of glass skittering this way and that. Susan scampered away, leaving me panting for air, winded from the impact. My gun had fallen out of my grasp and was somewhere among the splintered wood. I took the earrings from my ears and flung one at Susan. It missed and stuck into the doorframe like a knife cutting through butter. The other landed somewhere in the hall, clinking against the marble floor tiles, and I swore with frustration at having missed.

I rolled onto my side and sucked in a lungful of air. My bulletproof vest had saved me from taking a critical hit, but the fall had knocked the wind out of me. Susan could appear at any moment. The house was surrounded. There was nowhere left to hide. I clambered to my feet, staggering into the dining room.

"What happened?" I shrieked, finding Emilio giving mouth to mouth to an unconscious Caz.

He flashed his eyes up at me and they were wide with panic. "I took off the oxygen mask and she started gasping for air," he explained. "I think she had a panic attack, and then she passed out. I tried sitting her up to open her airways, and that's when I noticed she had stopped breathing"

"She's an asthmatic," I told him. "Keep doing what you're doing. There's an inhaler in the cabinet."

I rummaged through the entertainment unit, looking for the spare blue inhaler that I fucking knew was in there somewhere. After swiping everything onto the floor, I found it and tossed it to Emilio.

My eyes flicked to the huge glass windows and saw the carnage outside. Agents stormed the grounds, armed with large guns. Red laser lights scored through the darkness and crossed over one another, seeking out their target. Emilio pushed the mouthpiece between Caz's lips and pressed the inhaler to administer the Salbutamol.

"Caroline, breathe . . . please breathe," Emilio encouraged, holding her upright against his chest. "I don't know what the fuck I'm doing, so don't you die on me, okay?"

Caz sucked in a laboured gasp, her eyes bulging wide. Emilio sagged with relief as she wheezed and spluttered, the deep lines of concern creasing his forehead

"Are you okay?" he asked, his voice shaky and unsure

Caz focused on him, then pulled him down for a kiss. Emilio blanched, then began peeling her arms away like he was fighting off an octopus.

"You saved my life," Caz uttered breathlessly. "You're my hero."

"I might also be your brother, so please don't kiss me like that until we know for sure," he muttered awkwardly

Dad's voice boomed from a megaphone, ordering Susan to come out and give herself up. They couldn't risk wading in; they were treating it as a hostage situation. We just had to lure her out, so we could get her.

"You need to get Caz out of here," I urged. "Susan is still around here somewhere. Her gun is loaded; she has nothing left to lose."

The click of a gun made me freeze on the spot.

"That's right," Susan spoke from behind me. She must have snuck in through the secret door after Emilio had forgotten to close it. "If I'm going down, I'm taking you down with me," she vowed.

Emilio reached for his gun and Susan admonished him tauntingly. "Ah, ah, ah . . . toss your weapons over here, or I'll blow Bexley's head off"

Emilio complied grudgingly, and I slithered my fingers inside my jacket pocket to retrieve a tube of lipstick. I could hear Braxton and Dominic going crazy outside, and Asher and Cruz telling them to stand down. Uncle Zane intervened; his order of, "Hold your fire," boomed around the grounds.

"And you, Bexley," Susan commanded. "Throw down your weapon."

I slowly turned to face her, holding the lipstick in my hand. "I'm unarmed. I dropped my gun when you shot me," I told her, jerking my head to the heap of wood that was once my Laura Ashley coffee table. "It's right over there."

Susan's eyes darted back and forth as if she didn't quite trust me. "What's that in your hand?"

I exhaled a heavy sigh. "Just my lipstick," I admitted, holding it up as evidence. "If I'm going to die, I want to die looking my best."

Susan chuckled evilly. "Vanity is such an ugly trait," she replied, eyeing me like a cockroach.

I applied the lipstick, being careful not to smear any of it onto my teeth. Red dots danced all around the room, looking to get a clear shot of the Chameleon. She noticed them too, and I knew as soon as they started shooting, that she would fire a single shot that would end my life. One way or another, this was my day to die, and I wasn't going down without finishing the job.

"Do you want to know what else is ugly?" I said, fuelled by adrenaline.

I dropped the lipstick, and it rolled across the floor. Emilio stopped it with his foot, noticing what it was. He swallowed thickly. The silent, "What have you done?" blazed in his eyes.

"What?" Susan scoffed

I took a step towards her, then another. Everything that Asher had taught me about bluffing played at the forefront of my thoughts, and this was the daddy of all bluffs. Dominic would be proud of how I used the security system to my advantage. He never did get to teach me how to surf, and that saddened me. But I couldn't let my feelings hamper my mission. I remained as composed as Cruz during a time of crisis. And now, I was about to give her a taste of what Braxton would do. In a lightning move, I grabbed her gun, angled it up at the ceiling, and kneed her hard in the crotch. The shot went off, raining plaster dust down on us.

"Betraying your own family," I replied, then pressed my lips to hers in a kiss of death.

"No!" my husbands' roared from outside, then broke into a run

My knees sagged and my body swayed. I pulled away just in time to see the veins bulging around Susan's eyes, turning the whites blood red. She dropped to her knees and clawed at her throat, her nails scoring deep welts on her skin. A white mist formed before my eyes, then my muscles went into a violent spasm. I couldn't breathe. My lungs had stopped working. The poison was killing me.

"Bexley!" A frantic cry filled my ears, and then someone rolled me onto my back.

I couldn't see, but I could hear everything. My body convulsed as the poison entered my bloodstream. My veins were on fire. My insides were burning. I couldn't breathe, talk, or scream. It all hurt so much

"What should we do?" another familiar voice echoed through my ears.

"I have something that'll help," another said, and I recognised him as Dom because of what he said next. "I knew I'd need an antidote to the Kiss of Death."

A sharp pin prick pierced the side of my neck, lessening the pain. I was weightless like I was floating on a cloud. Someone lifted me off the ground and carried me outside.

"The air ambulance will take the women to the hospital," Uncle Zane spoke.

It was easier to determine who was who without focusing on the pain. I wanted to know whether

Susan was dead, but I was barely cognizant. I couldn't muster the strength to speak.

"We've recovered three bodies from the scene," someone who I didn't recognise informed Zane. "Two females and a male," he confirmed.

"Ughh," I murmured, trying my best to talk.

My human stretcher placed me onto a flat surface and climbed into the air ambulance with me. I could hear my husbands arguing about wanting to travel with me, but the paramedic insisted that only one other person could accompany Caroline and me in the helicopter.

"We'll be there as soon as we can, baby," Asher called out to me.

"Is she . . ." I croaked, my words struggling to leave my parched throat.

"Take it easy, Bexley," I recognised my father's voice. He must have been the one who carried me. "You got her. She's gone."

CHAPTER Forty-Four

Bexley

I heard footsteps echoing down a long corridor, the soft rattle of doors, and caught the fragmented pieces of a conversation as I opened my eyes.

"She'll make a full recovery," I heard a woman say.

Blinking my eyes brought the room into focus, and I saw all my loved ones standing around the bed, gazing down at me.

Where the hell am I?

"Bexley!" Asher spoke, darting forth to take my hand. "You're going to be okay. You're in the hospital."

My throat was sore and my muscles ached. Images from that night came back to me in flashbacks. The last thing I remembered was my dad telling me that Susan was among the dead. The relief flooded through me and I felt so overwhelmed, I grimaced with the urge to cry. My heart monitor started beeping like crazy, and the nurse elbowed her way through to my bedside.

"It's all right, Bexley. Everything is going to be fine. You're safe now," she spoke soothingly, placing her palm against my forehead. "I did say she could only have two visitors at a time," she admonished them all.

As far as I could make out, everyone was here. Dad, my uncles, Emilio, and the Wolfe brothers.

"Where's Caz?" My voice sounded squeaky and strained

"Right here," Caroline answered

My husbands moved aside to allow her through. Her face was badly bruised and she had butterfly stitches across her right eyebrow.

"Are you all right?" I asked, my eyes swelling with pity

Caz managed a painful smile. "Never mind me. What about you?" She diverted the question at me

"Apart from feeling as if I've been run over by a steamroller, I'll live," I replied jokingly.

"You're all over the news!" Caroline rushed her words excitedly. "Everyone is calling you a hero."

My family beamed down at me, confirming what she said was true.

"You did it, Bexley. You brought down the Chameleon and put a stop to her schemes," Cruz mentioned

"The agency arrested Malcolm last night," Asher told me. "And thanks to him, we have a list of names that they are working through as we speak."

"It's over," Braxton uttered. "We can all go home"

Dominic shrugged. "Bexley can't," he announced, confusing me. "There's something she has to do first."

They all grinned, and that only raised my paranoia

"Oh yeah," Caz murmured knowingly. "You lucky cow; you're going to Buckingham Palace to meet with the Queen." She sounded envious of that.

The doctor kept me in for another night under

close observation. I heard the nurses muttering about news crews camping outside, waiting to snap pictures of me leaving. The agency moved them along, then escorted me out through another exit. My husbands arrived to take me to London with an S.A.S escort. I wore a brand-new navy suit that Caz had picked out for me, my mother's necklace, and a pair of new shoes. Dad refused to let them take the pendant from me, telling them to wait until I was well enough to hand it over. And now that the time had come, I was ready. It was time to lay my mother's ghost to rest.

We arrived at the palace and were escorted to the ballroom. The Queen's bodyguard, the Yeomen of the Guard, was there. Two Gurkha officers escorted Her Majesty soon after. It was all so exciting. I wasn't sure what to expect. My husbands failed to mention the real reason why we were there, keeping it a secret. The military band began to play our national anthem as the ceremonial investiture took place. Queen Elizabeth thanked us for our service, then presented us with the St. George's Cross. I didn't know what to say. I was speechless, My father wept proud tears of joy as she presented one to me. I bobbed in a curtsy, then reached out to accept our monarch's handshake. She looked me in the eyes as she thanked me, and it was the proudest moment of my life. I could feel my mother's presence alongside me, sharing my emotions. After all, she helped us every step of the way. This was just as much her victory as it was ours.

A little while later, after we enjoyed lunch at the palace, we stopped at the MI6 headquarters where we received a hero's applause. Dad showed me where Mum used to work, and it brought me to tears as I saw they had dedicated the cryptography department to her. Her name was etched into a golden plaque, right alongside the one dedicated to Alan Turing, the mathematician who cracked the Enigma code.

"There's a job here if you want it," Dad announced, shoving his hands in his pockets. "It's only right that you follow in your mother's footsteps."

"I think I already did, didn't I?" I muttered with amusement, hinting at forming a harem.

Dad rolled his eyes and his lips quirked into a smile. "If you want to settle down, that's okay too. I just want you to know, you have options."

"I know," I replied gratefully. "Thanks Dad. I'll give it some thought."

Dad hugged me, and from the corner of my eye, I saw my husbands talking to the agents they knew. They were telling them about Caz, and how thrilled they were to have a sister. I realised things would be different from now on. The world had changed; the rumours of government corruption had been proven to be true. Politicians were up in arms over what had happened. The political point-scoring had begun. Character assassinations were taking place across every news channel worldwide. It would take a lot to restore the people's faith in democracy. People wanted to make sure their voices were being heard, and we had given that back to them. It was up to the world to decide what happened next.

"You'll be needing this," I mentioned, unclasping the necklace from around my neck. "I want it back when you've removed the files." I placed it into the palm of my father's hand.

"Of course," Dad replied, curling his fingers around it.

"What happens next?" I asked. "When are you going to take the paternity test to find out which one of you is Caz's father?"

Dad sucked in a long breath, then released it slowly. "We've all provided a blood sample," he mentioned. "The results are in, but we thought it was best to wait until we're all together."

I nodded. "How has Caroline been handling things?"

"She seems fine. The boys have been great with her," he answered fondly. "Especially Emilio, although I think he will take it the hardest if they turn out to be siblings."

My stomach dropped a little. "Oh goodness me," I muttered, dragging a hand down my face. "I hope for his sake, they're not."

"And hers," Dad mentioned. "She seems quite taken with him."

"We ought to get it over with . . . before they end up getting hurt," I suggested, much to Dad's agreement.

Dad thought it would be best if we all met up that night at the beach house. Agents had already begun the clean-up process, putting everything back to how it should be. Emilio and Caz were already there, lapping up the sun. My new shoes were pinching at my heels, so I took them off and padded across the tiled floor in my stockinged feet. Asher flashed his eyes to me as he was talking. Dominic, Braxton, and Cruz wore the hint of a smile as they listened to what he was saying.

"As I was telling you . . . it's great to be back, but we have an announcement to make." He paused, sharing a knowing look with his brothers. The agents who weren't part of their conversation all stopped to listen to the announcement. "We're forming a subbranch of our own; it's called the Alpha Elite," he revealed

"Are you taking applicants?" one guy inquired.

"There won't be an application process," Cruz answered. "Only the best will be handpicked to join our team."

I hung back without saying a word. This was their dream. It was something they always talked about during our mission. I had spent my childhood wanting to be a part of their group, despising them for excluding me. Now I wasn't so sure if being part of their team was something I wanted. Dad had given me options. I could stay here and work for MI6 like my mother always wanted, or I could choose to do neither. This was my decision. If I choose to stay at home and raise a family, it would be my call to make. So, what *did* I want? I couldn't answer that yet. This wasn't a choice I could make on a whim, I had to give it some thought.

"Bexley . . . where are you going?" Asher asked, noticing I had turned to leave

I paused before I reached the lift doors, and glanced over my shoulder.

"Home," I replied. "I'll see you at dinner."

And I left it at that.

I found Ulrich outside eating fish and chips on a

park bench. He had more pigeons flocking around him than the crazy bird lady at Trafalgar square.

"Can I catch a ride with you?" I asked, still carrying my shoes.

He crumpled the vinegar-stained chip wrapper into a ball and tossed it into a nearby rubbish bin.

"Don't you want to wait for the guys?" he asked, sounding wary as to why I wanted to leave so suddenly.

There was no particular reason other than to clear my head. I wasn't having second thoughts or anything. I just needed to take a step back and figure out what was best for me. Not for selfish reasons. We just didn't have to live in each other's pockets. No matter what I choose to do, I would still be part of the Wolfe pack, and that was enough for me.

"Nah," I replied, scrunching my nose. "They'll catch up with us later."

"How does it feel to be a heroine?" Ulrich asked.

"I don't know," I replied, thinking about it.

The sun-baked pavement was warm and hard against my feet, making me feel grounded. I sucked in a lungful of air, but regretted it. The air quality in London was bad, but at least the scent of fish and chips masked the engine fumes. That counted for something. The world had changed, but the scenery remained the same. The sweltering heat forced me to remove my jacket and drape it over my arm. It was so hot. The only time a breeze occurred was when a car or a bus drove by.

"I don't really feel any different," I decided.

Ulrich broadened his smile and jerked his head for me to follow.

"I don't know about you but I could sure use a drink," he mentioned as we walked. "Jaxx wants to open the DNA results tonight. I'm so nervous," he admitted, and it must have been hard for a man like him to say that out loud. "I could have a daughter. There's every chance she could be mine. This might be the last chance I get to be a father."

He was rooting for it to be him. My heart squeezed that little bit tighter, wishing for a good result. Not for jealous reasons. Those feelings had changed. I hoped for both Caz's and Emilio's sake, that it wasn't Uncle Teddy. I guess we would all find out the truth by tonight.

"There's a bottle of red with our name on it," I remembered the wine that Father Fournier gave to me in France.

Ulrich huffed a smirk. "What are we waiting for? Let's go home."

CHAPTER

Forty-Five

Bexley

T he first thing I did when I got home was change into shorts and a vest tee. I ambled through the house with flip flops on my feet, welcoming the simplicity of foam-padded flats. Ulrich and I joined Emilio and Caz on the veranda, basking in the evening sun and watching the sky transition from blue to a hazy orange. There was just enough of Father Fournier's wine to fill four glasses to the top.

Luckily, we had a cellar full of Malbec at our disposal. Lord knows we needed it. Caz begged me to tell her all about the palace, meeting the Queen, getting an award for outstanding bravery, and not letting me leave out any details.

"Do they wipe their backsides on 24 carat gold leaf toilet paper?" Caz inquired jokingly.

I spluttered as I took a sip of wine. "No . . . and if they did, I would've swiped one"

"Royalty," Ulrich scoffed. "They all shit, fart, and belch the same as we do," he commented dryly. "Strip away everything else and we're all the same."

When all was said and done, he was right. Take away the money and the status, and we were all the same. I leaned back on my deckchair, my gaze drifting across the beach and far out to sea. I thought about everything, deciding what I wanted to take from my experience. For once in my life, I was focused. I had found a purpose. My confidence had flourished, strengthening me from within. For once, I didn't have to be the best. I just had to be myself, and that was enough.

"They'll all be back soon," Caz mentioned with a nervous edge to her voice. "I'll find out who my dad is."

Her comment snatched my attention, and I

flashed her a small reassuring smile. "It will be fine," I told her, meaning it. "They are all good men. Any one of them is a step up from Susan."

Ulrich coughed as he swallowed, turning to me with an offended scowl on his face. "Thanks a lot, Bexley. We're nothing like her, thank you very much."

It lightened the mood and we laughed about that. Another hour rolled by, then another. Ulrich snoozed on a sun lounger beneath a parasol, Emilio went for a swim, and Caz and I changed into bikinis and fired up the hot tub. The sun had started to sink into the ocean and peeked out over the horizon. It was a beautiful evening, and no matter the outcome of the results, it would all be fine. I told Caz all about my adventures, about Braxton getting hit on by a granny, Dom pretending to be a female wedding planner, Cruz being mistaken for a Fairy King, and when Asher and I endured a high-speed car chase through Madrid. I relived every detail, including the Versailles Ball, my vineyard wedding, jumping out of an aeroplane, and abseiling down a waterfall in search of the final clue. It was an incredible experience, and Caz couldn't believe I was ready to trade it all for a desk job. If she thought I was mad, then how would my husbands take the news?

"As fun as it was, I don't think I could do it every

day," I confided. "I'm not saying never again, but not just yet."

"What about the adventure? The adrenaline rush? The thrill of the chase? Won't you miss it?" she asked, unable to fathom why I wouldn't want that.

"You should let them train you," I suggested. "You're one of them now. This is where you belong. If you want to dodge bullets, then be my guest. I'll stay here with all the Malbec, and hold the fort."

Caz leaned back on the edge of the hot tub and closed her eyes. The frothy water splashed droplets onto our face and the water jets hit my muscles in all the right places like a deep tissue massage. Nope. I wasn't ready to face another mission just yet. I craved a peaceful life. One with sun, sea, sand . . . my gorgeous husbands around me, and plenty of wine.

"I've been thinking about that," Caz admitted. "And you're right, I do feel as if I belong in their world. It's like a missing part of me has been found, and I can finally get to be me." As she sighed contentedly, I felt the urge to ruin her moment in a sisterly/best friend kind of way.

"The first time we did it was here in this hot tub, you know?" I told her, witnessing her crack one eye open. "I bet there's still spunk floating around in the water." Of course, there wasn't. The boys had changed the water the following morning, but Caz didn't know that.

She leapt up, revolted. "Oh, you filthy cow. That's disgusting"

"I told you about it." I reminded her, chuckling.

The panicked look on her face told me she's forgotten. "Yeah, but that was before I knew they were my brothers. I don't want to sit in their cum-infested jizz pit. I'm getting out."

I laughed harder as she scrambled out and dried herself with a towel.

"That could be the very same towel that I wiped myself on after we did the deed," I mentioned.

"Ugh!" Caz grimaced with horror and dropped the towel as if it was contagious.

Emilio emerged from the water and jogged over to us.

"The guys are back," he announced. "I just saw their helicopter land."

We could hear it, but paid no attention to what it was because the agents came and went as they pleased. The clean-up team hadn't quite finished their job; they had yet to replace the broken windows, plaster the walls, and replace the bullet pitted furniture. That wouldn't happen overnight. The glass had to be brought over from Sweden.

Caz wrapped a fresh towel around her bikini clad body, and I climbed out to do the same. Dad and Teddy emerged through the patio doors, both carrying cold beers in their hands. Dad nudged Ulrich, and as he stirred from his slumber. Dad handed him a beer, and he took it exhaustedly. Teddy gave one to Emilio and he chugged it as if he was dying of thirst. I didn't ask where the hell mine was because I hated beer and my taste buds craved wine. Braxton stepped through the door first, followed by Asher, Dominic, and Cruz. I leaned up to kiss them all one by one, and Cruz placed his hands against my waist.

"Is everything all right, love?" he asked, sounding worried. "Why didn't you wait for us?"

"I needed some space to think," I replied, tapping his nose with my finger. "That's why."

"About what?" Asher interrupted, scrunching his brows with concern.

"That sounds ominous," Braxton gruffed, looking equally unnerved.

Dominic was the only one who seemed chilled with what I might have to say. "Have you given it some thought?" he asked me. "Do you know what you want?"

His brothers glared suspiciously, wondering if he

knew something they didn't. I hadn't discussed any of this with Dom. He was either very perceptive, or he observed how excited I was to be shown around my mother's old place of work.

"I have," I replied. "And I have decided I want Mum's old job. I hope you don't mind."

Dad's lips pulled into a proud smile. "I had a feeling you would," he said.

I was met with mixed responses from my husbands. Dom seemed genuinely pleased for me. Asher, being the understanding man he was, was respectful of my decision. It was Cruz and Braxton who took it the hardest.

"Why though?" Cruz asked. "I thought we were great together."

"We're a team," Braxton voiced, his tone laced with disappointment. "It only works if we all stick together."

"We don't have to be stuck to each other's arses like glue to be part of a team," I told him, pulling out of Cruz's arms to hug him next. Braxton looked cute when he pouted. He was still a moody kid at heart. "You once said to me that I should do what I feel is right, and passing on my mother's skills feels like my calling. I feel closest to her when I'm solving puzzles. It's what she and I loved to do"

Their moods lifted that instant, respecting my choice. We all had our own dreams to fulfil. They didn't have to be the same, as long as they all lead us back to this spot, we would never be apart.

Cruz prepared the barbecue, Caz and I chopped the salad, and Asher and Dad seasoned the tomahawk steaks that they brought back from London. Zane peeled the potatoes, and Emilio and Braxton retrieved more beers from the cellar. We all pitched in; even Ulrich and Teddy busied themselves, laying the table, and gathering the plates and cutlery from the kitchen. This was a special occasion. A day to be remembered. During our victory feast, we would find out the identity of Caroline's father. It was such a huge deal for all of us, coming together as a family

We ate, we drank a little more, and we shared stories to pass the time. All the while, I couldn't help noticing the stolen glances between Caz and Emilio. I felt for them, I really did. It was me who told him not to give up on finding love. He was the perfect match for my quirky best friend.

If anything, please don't let Teddy be her father. We all deserve a little happiness.

Zane went back inside the house, only to return with four white envelopes. The time had come for us to find out the results of the paternity test, and Caz and Emilio were dreading it.

"Bring back Jeremy Kyle," Dominic muttered comically

Admonishing scowls landed upon him from all angles, but nobody said anything. We were too anxious to find out the truth. Zane handed them out to each of his friends, and Caroline held her head in her hands as she took deep breaths to steady her nerves. Emilio instinctively leaned forward to rub her back, gently whispering to her that it would all be okay

Zane was the first to peel open his envelope, pulling the paper from inside. My stomach was in knots as he read the results.

"I'm not the father," he announced, sighing disappointedly

If I felt sick, I hated to think how Caz was feeling. My gaze flicked to her, and my eyes overflowed with empathy, noticing she was close to tears.

"Dad," Emilio urged. "Please . . . we need to know." He prompted him to open his envelope.

Caz laced her fingers through Emilio's as they waited for Uncle Teddy to read out the test results.

"It's not me," Teddy revealed

Both Emilio and Caz crumpled with relief, then

they kissed each other tenderly as if they were soulmates who had been reunited at last.

It didn't matter what the result was going to be. Whatever the outcome, I would be happy for her. I found myself walking down the stairs to the beach, feeling the heated soft grains beneath my feet. My stress diminished as I glanced out to sea, finally at peace with my life. A comforting hand came to rest on my shoulder, and I turned to find Dad standing there beside me.

"I'm not her father, Bexley," Dad said gently.

I stared ahead and bobbed my head in a nod. "It's fine"

She wasn't my half-sister, but at least Ulrich had a daughter. I turned around to see them embracing and it brought a lump to my throat. Ulrich swiped away the tears from her eyes, and held her close to his chest as if she was a little girl again.

"You'll always be the most precious person in my life, no matter what happens. Nothing will ever change that," Dad spoke with sincerity.

I knew that. It was something I had always known. The only thing standing in the way of my dad moving on wasn't the memory of Mum. He would always love her, and miss her terribly, but that wasn't what was stopping him from living his life to the fullest. It was me. He needed to know that I would be okay. This was my chance to show him just how capable I was at deciding my own future. He didn't need to hold my hand any longer. I would be just fine on my own.

"I love you, Dad," I murmured, my words sounding raw with emotion. "Just promise me . . . whatever you do . . . just be happy, okay?"

My father's soft chuckles vibrated through me as I hugged him tightly. He knew exactly what I meant. And as I peered over his shoulder, glancing up at the veranda, I saw the definition of happiness smiling back at me. Our unique little family. We were all connected. Bound by love and our devotion to one another. Never to be torn apart by hatred again.

Epilogue

Bexley

Two years passed since I followed in my mother's footsteps, both personally — with four amazing husbands who treated me like a goddess, and professionally — at the heart of the MI6 brain network. The cryptology department was like a baby to me, as was Alpha Elite for my husbands. I received a text from Caz and Emilio announcing their engagement. Emilio posted a selfie of them both on the beach with a huge diamond ring on Caz's finger, and tagged it with "#shesaidyes". They were planning to marry next year at our parents' retirement base in the Maldives, and Ulrich was going to walk her down the aisle. Speaking of fathers, Dad and the guys were happy. Their new reverse harem was working out nicely. At long last, things had fallen into place.

The agency restored the beach house. It was like living at Tracy Island, not knowing which buttons and switches activated what. The guys didn't leave me the instruction manual, so I had a few mishaps within the first six months. One actually made the news when a local resident thought he saw a UFO flying along the Jurassic coast. The offending contraption looked like an ordinary T.V remote to me. How was I supposed to know that it activated Dominic's drone? I spent ages pressing the buttons, wondering why the television wasn't working. It was only when I took the back off, intending to change the batteries, that I saw the computer wizardry inside. That night, it was all over the news that the Navy shot down the drone and it landed somewhere in the English Channel. To this day, Dominic still thinks it malfunctioned. I didn't have the guts to tell him otherwise.

It was his own fault for leaving the controller lying around.

We had more important things to focus our attention on. I was ready . . . according to the home fertility kit I purchased from the internet. My husbands were on their way back faster than Ulrich's jet to get me pregnant on our anniversary night. Dinner was ready, the candles all lit, and the champagne was chilling on ice. I planned everything down to the massage oils on the nightstand, not that I had time to prepare everything myself as well as get ready. I had a team of highly skilled agents on hand to assist with all my culinary requirements. Cooking was never my forte, and nor would it ever be. I wanted tonight to be perfect. The guys had been gone for three weeks, although it felt like much longer.

The rustling of material alerted me to someone creeping through the kitchen door. My agents had been gone a while, so I seized my gun and spun around

"Don't even think about touching dinner until your brothers get here," I warned, seeing a startled Braxton drop a roast potato back onto the dish.

He held his hands up in surrender, his eyes flitting from my pistol and the sexy black dress I was wearing. "You look stunning," he returned, his brain stuck between the desire to eat and the urge to have sex.

I lowered my weapon, my lips spreading into a wide smile. "You look like shit," I remarked, noticing the dirt on his hands, face, and clothing. His lopsided smirk made him seem more handsome.

The dirt didn't stop me from hugging him and pulling him down for a kiss.

"Happy anniversary, babe," he murmured, his eyes filled with love.

He smelled of sweat and determination, no doubt wanting to be the first to get back to me. Cruz appeared at the door a moment later, stopping on the decking to pluck at his bootlaces. He had a little more decorum than his brother, removing his sandy shoes on the veranda. In the short time it took for Braxton and Cruz to strip, Asher returned armed with a huge bouquet of flowers that I put into a vase and filled with water. Dominic arrived sporting an outgrown beard, and he'd tied his hair up in a bun. They joined their brothers and stripped on the veranda, then used the outdoor showers we had installed to scrub up for dinner. Dom pulled his hairband free and shook out his shoulder length hair. He was reverting to his surfer look, and I had to admit, it suited him well.

"I've missed this sight," I mentioned, sipping the remainder of my glass of Malbec as I leaned against the doorframe to watch them showering.

The water rinsed the soap from their bodies, sluicing it away down the drain. One by one, they grabbed a towel and stepped back onto the decking. The sun was setting, the frayed edges blending with the hazy sky. It was magical. I couldn't have asked for a more perfect evening. They ate dinner in nothing but the towels around their waists. The need for clothes was redundant considering I was their dessert. We went to the bedroom, and I climbed onto the middle of the bed

"Why don't we add a little mystery to the evening?" Asher suggested, taking one of his silk ties from the wardrobe.

"I'm ready," I tell them. "According to the fertility test, it's the perfect day to try."

They dropped their towels and stalked closer to the bed, already hard and ready to take me. Asher blindfolded me using the tie. The loss of sight heightening my other senses, making me more attuned to their scent, their touch, and leaving me guessing who was who.

"We're gonna switch things up a little," Asher said; the mattress dipped and creaked as they surrounded me

"We want you to feel everything we give to you,"

Dominic murmured as they took off my dress, my shoes, and my underwear.

They were going to impregnate me, but we were never going to find out who. That was the deal. They underlined that in the contract.

Hands were sliding over my naked skin, slathering massage oils all over me to work out the knots in my back and neck. Despite the blindfold, I closed my eyes to enjoy the feeling. A murmur of approval reached my ears, letting me know that they liked what they saw. Warm hands encompassed my breasts, gently squeezing, teasing my nipples between their fingers. I felt around blindly, finding bare skin over muscle, and long, thick cocks aimed in my direction. I was so hot between my legs, my swollen clit throbbed for the slightest contact.

"Move over so I can lick her," Braxton rasped, his voice gruffer than ever.

I imagined my pussy looked flushed and inviting because he groaned hungrily. He muscled between my legs and then gave me his hot, wet tongue.

"It's been a while, princess," Cruz murmured against my lips. "We've got to prep you before we stretch you."

"Are you not planning to take it in turns?" I asked as Braxton ate me like a brute.

A dark chuckle told me otherwise. "You're getting doubled P'd twice over," Dominic answered, revealing their intentions.

The imagery thrilled me to the core. Lips found mine and suddenly I was swept away on an orgasmic current, forced to feel everything, and getting dragged to the depths. Braxton's tongue coaxed me through it, his brothers held me down as my muscles convulsed, my limbs seizing with ecstasy before I drowned in bliss. Fingers pressed into my hips, holding me tight against Braxton's face. I wanted to wriggle, but I couldn't. It was too sensitive. My body quaked in their arms.

"There she blows," Cruz murmured as I moaned loudly. "That's it . . . take it all from him."

A silent exchange took place when they decided who should team with who. One of them rolled me on top of him, and I straddled his hips, leaning up to take the cock as he thrust into me. They give no indication which one of them it was, and this all added to the mystery. My knees trembled as they angled me forward, pushing between my shoulder blades to position me where they needed me to be. Then hands appeared at my hips; the blunt presentation of a second cock poised ready at my stuffed entrance, slippery with lubricant.

"Go slowly." I heard Asher say.

His voice came from the right side of me, so I knew he wasn't responsible for the incredible stretch I was receiving. Who needed sight when I could recognize their voices?

"Uh, baby, you feel so good," Cruz groaned from behind me, pushing his length deep inside me.

"Christ!" Dominic grunted from beneath me. The tremulous, "Fuck," skittered from his lips as Cruz matched his depth

It meant that Braxton was suckling my left nipple, teasing it with his teeth. Cruz worked his hips into a slow, sensual rhythm, sliding his cock against his twin as he rocked into me. The sinful degradation of being fucked by two brothers at once, their dicks gliding through my drenched pussy, with another brother kissing me, and one sucking my tits was too much. I didn't think I could come again so quickly, but my body knew what it wanted, letting them use me however they pleased. With trembling legs, my clit grazed against the thatch of hair covering Dom's groin. Their cocks slurped through my pussy's wetness, pushing us all to the brink of no return. I knew they were close. I could feel the urgency in Cruz's thrusts, the increase in his momentum, Dominic's strangled groans as his cock swelled inside me, his fingertips clinging to my hips for anchorage. Asher and Braxton moved back, no doubt watching and waiting their turn. The scent of sex clung heavily to the air, our combined musk floating through my airways, scrambling my senses. I felt the pressure rising, the tremendous stretch, then bliss. Cruz's harsh breath blasted against my ear with a loud groan, his hips jerking as he pumped his seed inside me. Dominic roared as he came, his fingers digging into my flesh. Heat warmed me from within, my skewered pussy drinking greedily. They never gave me much time to recover, passing me between them like a shared toy. Those were my boys. They always loved to share. My empty cavern was filled once again, stuffed to the brim by more Wolfe cock.

Asher's soft groaning let me know that he was the one I was saddled upon, so I leaned down to kiss him. Braxton must have liked the view because he slapped my arse and fucked me like a stallion, his long thick cock hitting the same magic spot inside me that made my eyes roll into my skull.

"Is this what you want? You wanna be fucked and filled like a bitch in heat," Braxton gruffed, delivering another rough slap that made my pussy clench.

"Yes!" The word flew past my lips, my mind tumbling into ecstasy.

Mine and Asher's chests were pressed flat together, our hearts pounding in sync. His breathy grunting was an indication that he was close to cumming. I was almost there, and Braxton was too, his heavy balls slapped noisily against my labia in wet swats.

"Give it to me!" I begged for it.

My greedy pussy sucked hungrily, slurping everything she could get. Braxton pulled my hair to arch my back. I was so used to his dominance, loving how he took control during sex that I came in a second, my pussy snaring their cocks like a bear trap. Heat flooded through me, filling me up with their combined cum. Four husbands. Quadruple the chances of getting me pregnant. Although, the paternity of our children would never be revealed.

We slumped on the bed in a tangle of limbs, still joined at the groin like a conjoined creature until their dicks softened and slipped free from my smashed pussy. I didn't get up for almost half an hour, turning to rest my feet on top of the headboard to keep their seed inside me. Some of it had merged with my juices and trickled down my butt crack, cooling as the air swirled around us. We wanted to start a family so badly, I would go to any lengths to make it happen.

A little over a month later, our wishes came true as two pink lines appeared on the test stick. Then nine months after that, we welcomed our daughter, Sofia Wolfe, into the world. She was perfect. I wondered who she would look like. It was too early to tell. She had her fathers wrapped around her tiny finger and were willing to fall on swords for her. They would die to protect her. . . and me . . . which made us targets. And in our line of work, there was always a twisted opportunist just waiting for us to let our guard down. We were happy. Caz and Emilio were happy. Our fathers were enjoying retirement. We didn't see it coming. A lone Wolfe with an axe to grind had been waiting in the wings, watching us, studying our movements, and determining our weakness.

A Wolfe brother . . . another of Susan's test tube soldiers, who was hellbent on retribution.

ALSO BY
Kelly Lord

Captured by the Beasts

Ravished by the Beasts

Rescued by the Beast

Loved by the Beast

One Night with Pops